# THE RA

# CAME DUWN

## JULIAN SHAW

Red,

I hope you have an amazing time reading this. Thank you for taking a chance on me!

Don't lose your marbles!
(you'll see...)

Julian

Book Cover by Julian Shaw with the assistance of DALL E 2

Paperback First edition 2023

ISBN 978-1-7394397-0-5

https://julianshaw.uk/

*For all those who love the world*

*The foolish man built his house upon the sand,*
*And the rains came tumbling down.*
*The rains came down and the floods came up,*
*The rains came down and the floods came up,*
*The rains came down and the floods came up,*
*And the house on the sand fell flat!*
*The wise woman built her house upon the rock…*

# Chapter One

❦

# The Train Journey

Peering desperately into the gloom, a young man stumbles down a stone staircase. Two hooded men in black robes flank him, holding tight to the hessian shawl covering his exhausted body. They are deep underground now and far from the train station. Today was supposed to have kicked off the holidays – long and relaxed lie-ins, plenty of unhealthy food, and countless nights gaming online, not much different from the young man's latest semester as a philosophy student. Instead, he crashes through an unfamiliar darkness, his breathing rapid, his bottom lip trembling, and nothing makes sense.

*He remembers a train. The sound of smashing glass, creaking steel, thumping bodies, and horrific screams. It all echoes through his mind.*

The musty smell of his captors' black robes gives way to the stench of something industrial ahead. An expansive workhouse floor and the machinery of production. The warmth from hundreds of iron kilns pulses past them. All around, thousands, if not tens of thousands, of workers, are slaving away. Their bodies are grotesquely emaciated, burnt, torn, and scarred.

*He remembers holding someone's hand on the train as the catastrophic derailment unfolded. His sister's hand.*

No one looks up as the three men pass through the workhouse. Their collective gaze is fixated on the dance of clanging hammers silhouetted in the molten glow and the crackling snap of the fires. The hooded figures leading the young man don't linger. They march him to a doorway marked "Arrivals".

A papal silence suffocates the Arrivals chamber. Crucifixes, crescent moons, and hexagrams hang devoutly on the damp stone walls, illuminated by flickering lanterns. In the far corner, where a wooden confession booth waits, the young man is forced into an upright chair facing the wall. His wrists are strapped to the armrests, and a deep glass bowl of steaming translucent and viscous liquid is balanced on his lap. Vapour snakes up around his face.

"Don't spill," instructs one of the hooded figures, placing a gloved hand under the young man's chin and raising his face towards his own. The fear in his captive's bloodshot eyes is sufficient reassurance that his instruction will be obeyed.

The captors make their exit, leaving the young man hunched and alone. He sniffs, and a sharp jolt of pain erupts through his bruised ribs. He hangs his head and lets his eyes droop into the dizzying mist. As his face falls, a hatch slides open in front of him. A robed individual – a minister of sorts – reclines on a throne, shrouded in the dark.

The minister inspects the young man with his small sharp eyes, running bejewelled fingers through his slicked black hair. "Where shall we begin?" he asks.

The young man lifts his head hesitantly. His body writhes uncomfortably. "Am I dead?" he asks, unnerving himself with the familiarity of his voice.

"Something like that," says the minister. "What is the last thing you remember?"

The minister's question ignites the young man's consciousness. He glances down at his hands, familiar and clammy. He bites his lip in contemplation. Only now does he wonder about the reality around him. How on earth did he get here? Where is he? Who is this man?

"Tell me what you remember of the train journey," says the minister. "Tell me everything."

The young man looks back at the minister, nervously holding his gaze. The memory of the train crash is becoming a tumbling chaos of images all around him. He shivers but doesn't say a word.

"I'm not asking you; I'm telling you," says the minister. His voice seems far away, far outside the urgent distraction of the man's memories. The minister leans forward on his throne, pressing his face to the hatch. Vapours surround them both. "Tell

me, Gareth Edwards. Tell me what you remember from your
fateful train journey to London."

\* \* \*

A wet, miserable morning welcomes the first London-bound train
into Shrewsbury station. In the dark, the heavy carriages screech
their urgent presence into the pattering of the rain and come to rest
alongside the platform. A young man steps forward to board with
his mum and his sister. Gareth Edwards, in the twilight of his
teenage years, is awkward in posture and full of trepidation. Before
he steps over the threshold, he strains his eyes through the blustery
darkness to catch a final glimpse of Mynydd Aaru looming in the
distance. The mountain's imposing form is an alluring backdrop to
Shropshire's cosy, undulating hills. It will be the last familiar
landmark for a while.

In a few minutes, the train is rocking and rattling through
the countryside, and Gareth finds himself tumbling around
unarticulated daydreams. His mum clicks her fingers. "Gareth,"
she snaps. "Go and get me and your sister a coffee." She shakes a
few coins out of a leather wallet.

Gareth looks nervously into the aisle. "Can't Cerys get
them?"

"Oh, be a man," his mum exhales, frowning. "It's getting
coffee. You can't hide behind that phone screen all the time."

Gareth locks his phone and frowns towards his mum. She
was always using his gaming habits to criticise his social failings.
But the very idea of going to the buffet car and ordering a drink
made his stomach clench. So much between his seat and returning
with two coffees could go wrong. The swaying train might throw
him into the lap of another passenger, the buffet car might have a
queue, or they could run out of coffee; then what would he do?

Cerys nudges Gareth. "Ask if they have almond milk when
you're there," she says with a grin. Gareth grimaces. Ordering
unusual things makes it even worse.

Wandering through the sparsely populated carriages of the train, Gareth notices the individual travellers sitting alone, some sleeping, some reading, but most scrolling through the endlessness of their smartphones. The bright phone screens illuminate them as though they are exhibits in a museum, hunched statues of contemporary society. He catches the eye of a skinny old lady sitting alone. Gareth smiles awkwardly, and she smiles back, her green eyes appearing younger than her frail body. There is a peaceful quietness that has settled throughout the train. The exception to this inactivity is the buffet car.

While a coffee percolator bubbles away, Gareth ambles up patiently behind a man in a high-visibility jacket. The tall man, light brown in complexion with wiry black facial hair, has placed an obscenely large can of energy drink on the counter and is digging deep into the pockets of his paint-stained jogging bottoms, searching for coins. Without luck, he turns and drops his damp sports bag onto the floor to rummage in there. He glances up and catches Gareth's prying eyes.

"Don't sweat, brother," he says with a flat and sarcastic Midlands accent. "It isn't a bomb."

"I…no…I didn't," Gareth stutters, his cheeks glowing, trying to avert his eyes from the contents of the man's bag.

The man laughs confidently. "Just kidding, bruv. You don't look like the type to think like that!"

Gareth smiles politely back at the man, but his brow is already glistening, and he can feel an anxious sweat clinging to the back of his T-shirt.

"What can I get you, pal?" the man behind the counter asks Gareth, not content to wait for the man in the high-visibility jacket.

"Er, two coffees, please," says Gareth.

"Milk?"

Gareth nods and raises a finger hesitantly. "One with almond milk, if you've got it, please?" He knows immediately that he has said this too quietly. His chest tightens with the expectation of having to repeat himself.

"You're going to have to speak up, kid."

"He said one with almond milk," says the man in the high-visibility jacket, standing up and scattering a handful of coins on the counter. He gives Gareth a grin.

Gareth smiles back but clenches his fist in frustration with himself, digging his fingers into his palm. It doesn't hurt because his fingernails are bitten so low.

"Two coffees coming up. One regular. One with almond milk," says the man behind the counter, scooping up the coins and starting on Gareth's order.

Gareth avoids the gaze of the man in the high-visibility jacket as he leaves, staring instead at the newspaper stand, jampacked with the day's papers. The front pages are an eclectic mix of mostly non-newsworthy stories in the run-up to Christmas. One paper, however, catches his eye. Below a large and ominous photograph of a mountain face shrouded in swirling grey and white mist is the headline, "*Welsh Mountain Tragedy: Scores missing on Mynydd Aaru*".

"Are you wanting to buy a paper, too?" says the shop assistant, placing two steaming cups of coffee on the counter. Without looking up, Gareth slides the newspaper onto the counter and pays for the items.

Wobbling, trying not to spill boiling coffee on unsuspecting passengers, Gareth returns through the snaking train. He finds himself trailing the man in the high-visibility jacket who ambles lethargically in front of him, distracted by his phone. Imminent arrival at Telford means a handful of people are on their feet reaching for bags, flinging on damp coats, and dawdling down the aisles. Gareth is grateful to the man in front, who clears the way. He nods appreciatively at each passenger who has to cower over an empty seat to let them pass.

By the time they reach the connection with the rear carriage, the train has stopped, and the vestibule doors are open. Aside from the few exiting passengers, a raft of newcomers are now bundling into the warmth of the train. Tears of coffee soak into the cardboard sleeves of Gareth's cups. A few reach his clammy hands.

The first commuters, middle-aged white men dressed in black and grey suits, shake the drips off their limp umbrellas and barge past Gareth and the man in the high-visibility jacket. Next, the train conductor squeezes past. She has long, silky white-blonde hair and an enchanting beauty contrasting her bland and ill-fitting uniform. The man in the high-visibility jacket shamelessly ogles her as she passes, not noticing the dad and his young son, who tumble into the carriage behind her. The precocious little boy dances around in front of his dad, cheerfully singing a nursery rhyme, complete with actions.

*"…the rains came down, and the floods came up. The rains came down, and the floods came up. And the house on the sand fell flat!"*

The man in the high-visibility jacket, still peering at the conductor, collides with the young boy, knocking him to the ground.

"Oi, watch it, fella!" shouts the dad. He doesn't even check on his son. He instinctively steps over the little boy and squares up to the man.

"Easy, brother. I'm sorry. I didn't see you," says the man. He raises his hand to keep a distance from the baying dad.

The dad slaps the man's hand away and pushes out his chest. Despite his paunch, his bullish nature transforms him. He steps up to his opponent's face, and the two men lock eyes.

The little boy gets back to his feet and grasps his father's leg. "I'm OK, Daddy," the boy says, pleading innocently to the looming figure above him. A hiss from the hydraulic air brake of the train makes both men blink.

"Your lot are always the same," says the dad. "You think you own our country now."

"What's that supposed to mean, brother?"

"You know exactly what I mean."

The man in the high-visibility jacket clenches his fist. His sharp nails sink into his palm, drawing blood, but he doesn't throw a punch. He glances down at the young boy clinging to his dad's jeans. "Sorry, kid," he says, and without looking back at the dad, pushes his way down the carriage.

Oblivious to the tension, the little boy releases his dad's leg and hurtles off.

"Noah!" shouts his dad, but too late. The boy collides with Gareth this time. Hot coffee spills down Gareth's wrists and onto his trousers, scalding him, but nothing splashes onto the boy. Unaware, the boy carries on running down the carriage.

"Kids!" says the dad to Gareth, without a hint of apology, striding away after his son.

Gareth feels the eyes of everyone on him. He is standing there with the coffee dripping down his hands and a wet stain spreading down the front of his trousers. His heart rate rockets. Through no fault of his own, he has become the centre of attention, and that is the last place he ever wants to be. He has to get out.

He paces to the end of the carriage as quickly as he can without running, keeping his eyes fixed on the floor. His stomach clenches painfully, and he stoops to lessen the agony. In the vestibule, he places the sodden half-empty coffees into the bin and stumbles into a tiny toilet cubicle where his eyes meet his reflection.

Now, and only because he is out of sight, he feels a fury rising inside him. He is consumed with sweaty embarrassment and anger. Angry with himself for getting so embarrassed. Angry with the bigoted dad for causing the scene. Angry with the coffee cups for spilling. Even angry with Cerys for wanting almond milk. He stares at himself and clenches his jaw. He lifts his right hand and flicks his middle finger at his reflection. "You prick!" he says to himself and to all those people and things that brought on this situation.

\* \* \*

Fifteen minutes later, the train has stopped again. They are at Wolverhampton station now. Gareth has calmed down, his trousers are nearly dry, and he has two new coffees. He steps back into the vestibule of the rear carriage, thinking he will have earned a rest when he finally rejoins his mum and sister.

An old wooden case slides into the carriage from outside, blocking his path. Out on the blustery platform, an elderly gentleman struggles with the wind and rain. Instinctively, Gareth places the coffee down on the floor and leans out of the train, offering his hand. Planting his walking stick firmly onto the platform edge, the older man reaches up and grabs hold. His elongated and wrinkled face is wrought with determination, but the warmth of his hand is surprising.

"I hope the weather's nicer over there than here," says the man, noticing Gareth's eyes prying the Zürich baggage tag on his case. Gareth's face prickles pink. "Good for the grass in the meadows, though."

Smiling to concur, Gareth gathers his coffee and turns away to rejoin his mum and sister. The paper cups are again looking neglected. Brown streaky stains circle them like the spilt wax of an old church candle. Nonetheless, he places the cups on the table and shuffles back into his seat.

His mum doesn't look up. She is staring blankly out of the window. Scattered across the table in front of her are some handwritten notes, a few formal-looking letters embossed with the logo of the High Court in London, and a newspaper cutting from the *Derby Gazette*. On the cutting, a grainy black-and-white photo shows a crane pulling a car wreckage from a lake. Another photo is a thumbnail of a woman with a voluminous crop of short blonde hair. She has a ghostly stare. Cold and distant.

Gareth arranges the papers into a neat pile, ensuring the newspaper cutting is hidden away. The thumbnail of Rose Drinkwater has haunted him his whole life. He nudges the cup towards his mum. "Your coffee is here, Mum."

She glances down at the documents and places her hand resolutely on them. "Today's the day," she says. "Fifteen years fighting, and today we get the truth."

"I guess…" exhales Gareth, unfolding the newspaper he bought and looking at the front cover.

"For goodness' sake, Gareth," says his mum. "A bit of enthusiasm today is the least you can do for your father."

"Why?" asks Gareth stubbornly. "What did he ever do for me?"

"Don't you dare…" starts his mum furiously. "If he were still with us, he would have done anything and everything for you."

"No, he wouldn't," says Gareth. "He would have been in prison. And still would be."

"For a crime he didn't commit."

"You don't know that!"

"I will by the end of today's hearing."

Gareth feels a familiar fury rising inside him. He clenches his jaw and turns to the window. A dark cloud in the sky has burst, and rain lashes down against the glass. His reflection is sliced and distorted.

"Has this got almond milk?" asks Cerys, prizing the lid off her coffee and inhaling the dancing fumes.

"No. I forgot," says Gareth obstinately. He didn't have the energy to explain the whole drama of getting the drinks.

"Whatever," says Cerys sarcastically. "You're so pathetic at times, Gaz." Gareth doesn't respond.

Nearing the penultimate stop at Watford Junction, the London-bound train is now filled with commuters. Damp coats and dripping bags steam with a malodorous stench, filling the artificially warm cabin. Sitting a few rows in front of the Edwards family, the older man digs deep into his jacket pocket. Next to him, the white-blonde train conductor is on her feet, holding out her hand. She has just started a check of passengers' tickets before they get to Watford, after which any chance of moving through the packed train will be impossible.

Grasping the cloth pouch that houses his cards and tickets, the older man produces a faded rail card. The conductor squints her eyes to read its details and draws a sharp breath. It looks like she is about to start a rehearsed monologue about "failure to show a valid pass for travel" when she catches herself. She glances over her shoulder, lifts her bright hazel-coloured eyes towards him, and smiles. "Are you travelling far?" she asks.

"Far enough," he responds. "I'm headed right into the cold heart of Europe. I'm hoping to find my way back to someone I once knew. Someone very dear to me."

"How lovely," she says instinctively. "I hope you have a delightful journey."

This little interaction between the two strangers conforms to some social etiquette they both share. Despite this, Gareth feels he sees the conductor's eyes betray to the older man a sense of longing. A longing, maybe, to be regaled with his story of loss and hopeful reunion.

An automated announcement on the train informs the passengers of their imminent arrival at Watford Junction. Unlike previous stops, nobody moves on hearing this. Everyone is staying aboard until London. Gareth is distracted. Having seen the conductor's longings, he now indulges his own: revisiting fantasies of a happy childhood with his dad. He allows these to swirl around in his mind. The pain associated with them dropping, like black ink, into the crystal-clear pool of his past.

The train comes to a complete stop. Outside the window, a large billboard fills the view. On it, the advertised product purports to give the consumer twice the bottled spring water in the same-sized bottle. Across the billboard, the phrase "*Don't forget your return journey*" is plastered in a gigantic font. Gareth doesn't consciously register the advert. His attention has been captured instead by a feeling of absolute certainty that he is being watched.

His eyes scan the scene. There is not a soul in sight, but the feeling grows, and he senses that whoever is watching him is getting closer. He doesn't know how he knows it, but he knows that it is a lady watching him. Then he sees her.

Stepping from behind the billboard is a lady with the palest skin Gareth has ever seen. She is draped in a long blue dress, her hair is drenched, and she stares at the train. Her eyes are warm. Warm like an open log fire beckoning you close on a dark winter's evening. As she stares, Gareth feels his eyes, his soul, or some essence of his being, betray to her every moment from the tale of his life – his pain, his loss, and his unfaltering love for his mum and his sister. The lady looks back for a moment, betraying nothing but a feeling, and then as quickly as she appeared, she turns and strides away down the platform. Gareth's eyes and his thoughts chase the lady, but she is soon out of sight. Gareth's sense of her presence lingers a little longer but eventually fades.

Gareth wonders if the lady has boarded the train further down the platform, towards the front. But something tells him she is much further forward than that, but not so far that they won't be in her proximity again soon.

"No, no, no! Bloody hell!" a voice shouts out behind Gareth. The man in the high-visibility jacket has leapt to his feet and is charging through the carriage. "Wait a second, stop the stupid damn train!"

The man rushes to the front of the carriage. He is barging past everyone standing, and knocking the heads of those sitting with his sports bag. Passing the older man, a whirring crescendo indicates the train's motors kicking in. As the carriage lurches forward, the world falls away behind them. The man stares out and swears some more. He looks furious; with himself, the train, and everyone around him.

Like a tethered Rottweiler, the man chucks his bag on the floor and crashes into an empty seat beside the older man. He pulls out his phone, punches his blunt fingers into the screen, and slaps the device against his ear. Everyone in the carriage holds their breath, waiting for the next outburst. But it doesn't come. After waiting for five or six breaths, the man pulls the phone from his ear and stares at the screen. He nods at his phone, and a knowing smile appears on his bearded face. "No signal. Yeah, that figures."

The man breathes out loudly and rocks his head back, closing his eyes in defeat. The rest of the passengers in the carriage go back to their own thoughts and their own screens, glad and disappointed that the melodrama didn't explode. In the seat next to the angry man, the older man dares to look across at the passenger beside him.

Unexpectedly, and unseen to everyone except the older man, a tear trickles down the cheek of the man in the high-visibility jacket. This simple physical expression of vulnerability shatters the aggressively masculine mask. Sensing an intrusion, the angry man's eyes open. His head shoots right, but only to see the back of the older man's head, who has looked away. Believing his secret tear is safe, he wipes his cheek and starts typing a furious storm of messages on his phone.

\* \* \*

Within ten minutes, the train is at full speed, and they are nearing their destination, hurtling through the sprawling urban peripheries of the capital city. Out of the window, large gardens and picturesque homes give way to retail parks, complex road networks and exhausted residential enclaves. These, in turn, morph into run-down housing estates and pock-marked tower blocks, punctuated by a diverse religious residue of stubborn churches and fledgling mosques. Then, once again, the landscape changes. Houses get bigger, emerging as Georgian and Edwardian structures invigorated by wealthy inhabitants, and railway lines from every direction converge.

"Excuse me," a gentle, quiet voice interrupts the silence around Gareth. He looks up. An old lady, whom he had seen when he wandered through the train, is grasping hold of the seat rest behind him. "I noticed you had got yourself a coffee. Would you mind showing me where I can get one, please?"

"Of course, dear," Gareth's mum responds before he has time to think. "I'll show you where you need to go. I could do with stretching my legs." She hauls herself to her feet and offers her arm to the old lady for support.

"You are so kind," says the old lady. "Thank you." She stumbles as the carriage shakes and grasps Gareth's shoulder to stop herself from falling. She looks at him. "Sorry, my love," she says.

As the two ladies make their way down the carriage, Cerys leans towards Gareth and whispers mischievously in his ear. "I think that old lady hoped *you* would escort her to the buffet car." Gareth looks at his sister, who has a cheeky grin. "She doesn't know you're only into women with avatars and names that start with an @ sign."

"Shut up, Cerys," says Gareth, finally scratching the itch of his morning's frustrations. He has taken enough already today. "Look in the mirror. At least when my girlfriends hit me, it's just in a computer game." Gareth immediately hates himself for saying this. He has crossed a line. It is such an unkind and unfeeling thing to say, especially so soon after Cerys' break up. "I'm so sorry, Cerys. I didn't mean that," he says, trying desperately to take it back.

"You have no idea what you're talking about," says Cerys, turning her face away. "You've always been like this, Gareth. Sticking your nose in where it's not welcome."

Cerys leaves no invitation for Gareth to respond. He feels a nauseous self-loathing and doesn't even notice as the iconic landmark of the national football stadium whizzes by outside the window. The milestone triggers the regular commuters to vacate their seats and start a queue towards the front end of every carriage. Gareth glances down at the mesmeric image of the mountain on the cover of his newspaper. There is a haunting allure to its summit. Like a tremendous cresting wave, it gives a sense that it is ready to consume him. During this moment of reflection, Gareth feels her again – that feeling of being watched by the woman in the blue dress.

A violent jolt rocks the carriage. Gareth's feeling leaps away. He looks up. The standing passengers are no longer standing. People are scrabbling up from strangers' laps, looking worried. Gareth instinctively grasps hold of his sister's hand. A microsecond of calm tempts him to let out a breath of relief. Another jolt is accompanied by the scream of buckling steel. As Gareth squeezes Cerys' hand, the horizon out of the window plunges away. His body tenses, and he closes his eyes.

The two rearmost carriages of the early morning train from Shrewsbury to London clatter and crash, tumbling over and over. Smashing glass, creaking steel, thumping bags and bodies, crunching stones and horrific screams are all squashed into one awful sound. The violence of the derailment throws the bodies of passengers indiscriminately into, over, and around the carriage. As the passengers make their horrendous impact with different parts of the train, Gareth feels a stratospheric rumble erupting all around him, accompanied by the brightest white light. And then the world falls silent.

*On the morning of Tuesday 17th May 1938, the No.21 underground train from Ealing to Barking was crowded with commuters on their way to work. At around five minutes to ten the train received a signal to stop in the tunnel midway between Charing Cross and Temple stations. While the passengers waited in the dark, another train – the No.59 Circle line train – was given an incorrect signal to proceed into the same tunnel. Hurtling through the tunnel, the No.59 collided with the rear of the No.21. The rearmost carriage of the stationary No.21 was thrust into the preceding carriage, penetrating its body. It continued its destructive course upwards until it collided with the roof of the tunnel. Buckling metal, splintering timber, smashing glass, and arcing electrics filled the tunnel until all went dark and quiet. Six souls were lost in this tragedy.*

# Chapter Two

◆

# Penitence

"The train crash killed you," says the minister, tucking his robes under his legs. Gareth's mind hurtles back into the dark, cramped confession booth. His hessian shawl is damp and uncomfortable. His wrists are rubbed raw by the leather straps. "Your lifeless earthbound corpse is still there, crushed in the train's wreckage. But your soul has left the bounds of Earth forever."

Gareth looks down at his hands. There isn't a scratch on him. The first moment since the crash he has acknowledged his own physical presence. "Your soul projects the familiar in our world," says the minister. "What you see of your body now is what you knew before the crash."

"Where am I?" Gareth asks. "I thought I saw London after the crash."

Gareth recalls the haunting sight; a carriage full of shadows. The chill and the cold muffled silence that settled on everything. The strangeness of the appearance as though nothing had happened. No evidence of a crash, no broken glass, and no bodies on the floor. And he remembers glancing out of the window, recognising the urban fabric of London before dozens of hooded figures, congregated on the tracks, started smearing a thick black paint over the rain-soaked windows.

The minister leans back on his throne and sighs. "Mr Edwards, I wouldn't waste your energy worrying about where you are. More important is *why* you are here." He looks at Gareth with a powerful menace in his dark eyes. "Have you heard of penitence?"

"I think so?" says Gareth, the word conjuring oppressive religious images from his childhood.

"At the moment of death, your life must have been teetering on the fulcrum of good and evil. You've been lucky. You have arrived in the realm of penitence with a chance to tilt your fate towards good. But to do this, you...we...will need to find out what prevented this tilt before. This meeting today, probably one of many we will have, will allow us to understand exactly what you have done wrong. Because, until you know what you have done wrong, penitence will be hard to pay."

"Am I in Purgatory?" Gareth asks, not entirely sure he is well versed enough in religious ideas to ask this question, never mind understand its answer.

"Not exactly," says the minister. "But for now, that might be a helpful way to think of your situation."

"And who are you?" Gareth asks, wishing he could have asked this more politely.

The minister's eyes narrow, and the muscles in his jaw clench. Grasping the frame of the hatch, separating them with his long fingers, he pulls his face right up to the threshold. Gareth can smell his breath and see the bloodshot whites of his eyes. "I am your judge," he whispers. "The one appointed to uncover the dark blemishes in your soul."

Gareth feels the bruise above his left eye throb. The hooded figures had been brutal on the way to this meeting. He remembers the ranks and ranks of them at the station. They had swarmed around him and the other passengers and assaulted them. Were these men acting on behalf of some god? Some almighty deity? He had heard of wrath. Was he now feeling it?

The minister stares at Gareth for a moment, despite the young man awkwardly avoiding his gaze. "Exposing your shame and cleansing your soul will be traumatic for your mind and painful for your body. But these links between your body, mind and soul must be broken. The mind is the source of impurity on Earth. The body, a vessel into which these impurities drip. You have probably been lying to yourself your whole life. Lying to yourself that you are good, or good enough. Lying to yourself that there is nothing deep and dark dripping inside you. Well, I can tell you now, you don't end up here without darkness in your mind and a flood in your body. And it is my job to find this darkness and stop it from consuming your soul forever."

The notion of his own internal darkness frightens Gareth. While he had grown up believing he wasn't a 'bad' person, per se, he had always harboured a little niggling doubt. An image flickers in his mind. An idea he had invented far back in his childhood. A projection of a woman drowning in a man's strong, cruel hands. Gareth begins to sweat.

The minister looks at Gareth and says very simply, "Where do you want to start?"

Gareth looks back, not sure what this means. In his hesitancy, the minister chooses to interject for him, a smirk across his face. "Well, shall we start with lust? The sins of the flesh…"

The suggestion is like a sharp slap to Gareth's shame. Lust and sexuality are not topics that he speaks about with anybody. They aren't topics that he acknowledges to himself. His sweating becomes uncontrollable. The minister smiles and gets himself comfortable. A strange sensation comes over Gareth. A drip of sweat from his forehead falls into the glass bowl resting on his lap. The moment the drop hits the sticky, viscous liquid, it turns a vibrant red and swirls around.

"Very good," says the officer. "We've started."

The interrogation begins, picking over Gareth's relationship history, of which there is a lot. Ever since he was sixteen, he has had a habit of moving from one girlfriend to the next. Despite being exceptionally socially anxious and generally reclusive, he hates being alone, and he has had a string of relationships formed through interactions that started on online gaming platforms. The minister asks him for the intimate details of these relationships.

At first, Gareth just sits there, his eyes lowered, before he begins to talk about those things that embarrass him the most. He starts to tell of the handful of occasions where he has been intimate with women he met online, and not just via webcams. Yet, despite the anguish and torture he feels in telling of these moments, the minister is disappointed.

"Is this OK?" asks Gareth, ashamed of his retold juvenile intimacies.

"Well, you don't convince me," says the minister. "You see, there's nothing 'wrong' with these moments. It's more pitiful than wrong. You've barely been intimate by the sound of things. But I want to know something else..."

"I saw how you walked in here – the shy, unconfident, awkward shuffle. You're not the type where your 'sins of the flesh' are with other people. The sins of your flesh are probably self-inflicted. They're probably those moments you have spent alone with yourself, where you entertained your filthiest thoughts. Tell about those times."

Gareth feels the blood drain from his head and his heart pound. He feels sick. It is true. These are the things that he feels the most shame about. He has been made to feel self-loathing about this kind of thing ever since he was a twelve-year-old boy at Sunday School. And it has consumed him with shame and guilt throughout his teenage years.

"Remember. Penitence must be paid," says the minister, grinning at Gareth. "It looks like I've hit a chord. Maybe I can help you to hang out your dirty washing. What kind of things get you off?"

The next hour is the worst hour of Gareth's life. Or is it the worst hour of his death? He has never spoken to anyone about his sexuality, never mind a stranger. It is excruciating. His stomach churns, and involuntary gases build up in his bowels, making him writhe with discomfort. Made all the worse by the minister enjoying his pain. Indulging as he squirms. Laughing at him and denigrating him.

The shame Gareth feels is exhausting. And in everything that he says, more beads of sweat drop from his head into the glass bowl. Bright crimson swirling around. The drips fill the bowl until red swirls everywhere, all red save for one bead of sparkling yellow.

Gareth feels himself collapsing with exhaustion. Mercifully the minister stops the questioning and straightens himself on his throne. He looks at Gareth with a severe expression on his face. "So, it seems that you are a lustful creature. A shameful being whose soul fell short because his body and mind were consumed by darkness. Tell me now, reflecting on that person you were, that you have been, would you do it differently if you went back and tried again?"

Gareth looks up. Suddenly he feels some hope. This question offers an opportunity. "Could I go back?"

"No, of course not," the minister thunders. "You're dead." But Gareth's response confirms to the minister something he needs to hear. "You're a long way from paying your debt, young man. Now get out of here."

Suddenly Gareth becomes aware that it isn't just the two of them in the confession booth. This is mortifying. Other men had come in at some point and had heard his confessions. The two men, officers of some kind, standing behind his chair, have listened to it all. One comes forward now and removes the glass bowl from the room. "A good yield," he says.

"Good for a first attempt," says the minister. "Plenty of darkness to sap out of this one."

The other officer squeezes next to Gareth and unties the leather straps on his wrists. "Wait," says Gareth, summoning some energy. "What has happened to my sister?"

Cerys had been with him after the crash. They had still been together after the initial assault as well. Sometime after that, though, the details were unclear; he remembers the passengers had been separated into two groups: men and women.

The minister holds up his hand to pause the officer untying Gareth's wrists. "Women," he begins, "have their own process. Their own opportunity to pay penitence. You won't see any women here in the workhouse. And that, it seems, will be for your own good." He gives Gareth a slimy grin. "Focus on yourself, for that is all that matters now."

The minister doesn't allow Gareth to interrupt again. The officer is instructed to escort him away.

"Seems like I know you pretty well now," says the anonymous black-clad man somewhere down an unfamiliar dark corridor. "Costumes, eh? I bet you love women dressing up and telling you what to do… Well, I will be telling you what to do now, so you best not get off to me!"

Gareth looks back at the man, bemused. It is strange; he remembers talking about cosplay and the sexual fantasies he had trawled through on the internet, but the shame he had felt telling of these things only minutes ago seems to have evaporated entirely. Those memories, which had been so deeply imbued in guilt, now feel like cold, distant facts to Gareth. It is as though the vibrant drips of sweat swirling around that bowl have taken with them the emotions and sensations of his memories. The man grabs Gareth by the shoulder and throws him through a doorway. A doorway Gareth hasn't even seen is there. He stumbles as the door slams behind him.

The room he finds himself in is small and cold. Three metal framed beds are pushed up against damp walls. One is occupied.

"Hello?" Gareth says.

"What?" says the figure indignantly.

"Sorry. I don't know where I am. I've just been sent in here."

"Me too, brother," says the man on the bed. "You been here long?"

"No, I've just got here today," says Gareth.

"Same here. Stupid train crash." The man turns over in the bed. It is the man from the train who had been wearing the high-visibility jacket. "The name's Hassan."

"Hi," says Gareth. "I'm Gareth."

"Do you believe what they are saying, brother? Purgatory? I never believed in this place," says Hassan, and before Gareth can answer he asks, "How about that interrogation? Awful."

Gareth doesn't want to talk about his conversation with the minister. "Yeah. It was bad."

"Did they beat you up too?" Hassan asks, revealing a shiny purple eye and a large cut under his chin. "That's my problem. I never comply willingly. I always fight. I was brought up to fight. That's how you get by, isn't it, brother?"

"I guess," says Gareth, opting for the easier conversation, knowing he has avoided every conflict in his life. He had never even seen a fight up close.

"They just kept going on about my rage, making me tell all these things from my life. The times I've lost control – the times I laid into my dad, the controlling idiot. Anyway, I suppose they weren't the best things I did. It's probably why I'm here in this place, right?"

"Maybe," says Gareth, not sure if agreeing with Hassan is what he wants.

"I wonder what happened to the other passengers," Hassan continues. "There were those two women. You knew one of them, right? Your girlfriend, was it?"

Gareth's cheeks prickle, and his palms go clammy. "My sister," he says, looking down.

"Sorry, brother! No disrespect meant."

"No, it's OK," says Gareth, almost apologetic for Hassan's mistake.

"And those other passengers? The unconscious ones. They were creepy, right?"

"Yeah, really creepy," says Gareth, not hesitating to agree with Hassan this time.

Most passengers from the train had been in an unconscious trance when things had settled after the crash. At first glance, they had appeared normal. But they weren't. It was like they were asleep with their eyes open. They had an unsettling absence, utterly unaware of everything around them. Gareth remembers seeing a fly land on the cheek of one woman. She didn't twitch or flinch; she just left the fly to crawl right across her face before it flew off of its own accord.

"I doubt the interrogators got much sense out of them," says Hassan.

Before Gareth can respond, the door opens again. A third person stumbles in. The Zürich-bound older man from the train. He doesn't say anything as he wanders over to the spare bunk. Gareth catches his eye. His expression is surprising; he looks eager, if not excited. Not scared or confused. He acknowledges Hassan and Gareth with a gentle smile before slumping onto the bed and sighing.

Gareth feels it impolite to ask the older man about his interrogation experience. In the silence, the older man lays back on his mattress and closes his eyes. "Don't worry, boys," he says. "I'm sure we'll all get through this. I've met plenty of brutes in my time. They will try to bludgeon you with your shame and belittle your fears. But the truth is, they fear you. They fear that if you don't cower, your soul is fundamentally different from theirs, which scares them. It threatens their control, not just of you but of themselves…"

"Oh, and I'm Albert, by the way. Albert Newman. I should have started with that. I'll finish with it instead! Good night."

*On the evening of 3rd September 1878, the paddle steamer SS Princess Alice made a "Moonlight Trip" down the river Thames to the pleasure gardens at Rosherville. On her return to Swan Pier, near London Bridge, she was full to capacity with around seven hundred passengers. Coming downstream at the same time was a coal-carrying sailing vessel, the Bywell Castle, ultimately bound for Alexandria, Egypt. With neither boat noticing their collision course in time, the Bywell Castle struck the starboard side of the SS Princess Alice and split her hull in two. The Princess Alice sunk within four minutes of the impact. The tragedy was compounded by its location. For where the Princess Alice sank was at the point where London's sewage pumping stations were located. Raw, fermenting untreated sewage was washing around this point in the river and was fatally ingested by many of the passengers who didn't perish in the immediate sinking. In all, around seven hundred souls were lost in the tragedy.*

# Chapter Three

♦

# Fire and Marbles

Hard labour, it turns out, is the way that you pay your penitence. Below the workhouse, at the deepest part of the underground complex, a giant furnace is where every man starts. A deep pit, like the heart of a volcano, it is hundreds of feet wide and just as deep. All around the edges, countless condemned souls spend their weary hours shovelling coal. And as the coal splashes into the pit, orange sparks travel back up, singeing the hair or the skin on their arms. Their wrists and forearms become horribly scarred from this work, scars which the guards at the furnace call "Satan's Scalds".

"When you've paid your debt, Lucifer's talons won't be able to mark your skin anymore," they are told.

The months in the furnace are dull and repetitive. Hour upon hour is spent shovelling. Sweat and soot congeal on eyebrows and lips. Barely a word can be spoken, and there isn't a moment's rest. The men are told when they arrive that this is their first offering of penitence. Penitence for the darkest thoughts and deeds on Earth. Eventually, when the guards deem these blemishes clean – when their bodies are lean, and their Satan's Scalds have hardened – the men at the furnace can graduate to the main workhouse, where the labour will continue at a kinder pace.

The workhouse, full of kilns, is fuelled by the giant furnace below. At the kilns, the condemned men are made to shovel sand into an oven, melting it into liquid glass. In turn, this glass is rolled into a ball on wet newspaper before vials of sticky resin are injected into the molten globe – a resin made in part by the colourful drips of sweat produced in interrogation. Knowing where the vials came from is haunting, but the beauty it creates when swirled into the molten glass is other-worldly. Finally, the glass ball is dipped back into the kiln, making it into a perfect sphere. The vast industrial workhouse is a production line for the creation of marbles.

Groups of condemned men and boys occupy the rows and rows of marble-making kilns. The slogan *"Sweat is debt. Freedom is earned"* is etched around the door of each kiln. And each of the men working there is under no illusion. This is how they will pay the remainder of their penitence.

After three months of toil, Gareth, Albert, and Hassan graduate from the lower furnace. They are allocated an unmanned kiln near the far edge of the main hall. The embers inside it are still glowing from its previous occupants. In their first week, they are taught how to use the kiln to make marbles. And every night, they are taken back to their cold, bare dormitory, exhausted from a relentless day of labouring, and told to get some sleep.

"What a prick," says Hassan as the dormitory door slams shut. "He knew that last wrack of marbles was fine. He just wants to feel like the big man when he smashes our hard day's work. I could have him. No doubt."

"Please don't," starts Albert. Gareth feels the scorched skin on his back. It is still raw from the flaying that Hassan's last outburst had caused them.

"Sorry, fellas," says Hassan. "Just where I'm from, a brother needs to stand his ground."

"You're from Birmingham, right?" asks Gareth.

"Sparkhill, brother," says Hassan. "But, yeah, it's in Brum. You ent gunna be a big timer in Sparky unless you straighten a few jaws. Not that it matters any more, though. We're stuck in this place now, eh? How long do you think we're gunna be here? Those lads reckoned they've been here years."

Three devout religious young men work at an adjacent kiln to them. They claimed to have arrived at the workhouse decades ago, victims of some shipping disaster. Each man has a naval tattoo of an anchor underwritten with *SS Princess Alice* on his right bicep. Their Satan's Scalds look like they have been at the workhouse a while. The skin on their forearms is horrendously mutilated.

"They also say they've seen people leave," says Albert, upbeat. "Men who have paid their debt in interrogation. Men who can't produce any more colourful sweat."

The interrogations with the minister have continued throughout the months at the furnace. Once a fortnight, the men are taken away to the confessionals. Gareth's minister has focused on the same thing every time. The "sins of the flesh". The attention has got to the point where Gareth is now numb to questions about his sexuality. Nonetheless, colourful sweat still drips down his face and fills the bowl.

"Brother, the fucking colour pours from my forehead like monsoon rain. I'm gunna be here forever. They say it's linked to how fucked up you were on Earth, right? Like, the more colour, the bigger piece of shit you were?"

"That's what they say," says Gareth, feeling ashamed.

"I don't know how you're still here then, Gareth," says Hassan. "You're like a bloody saint. I can't imagine you had much colour in you to start with!"

Gareth forces an appreciative smile towards Hassan. He feels a pang of cold guilt inside. He knows how readily the crimson sweat falls down his face, and it doesn't look like abating any time soon.

"They started asking me about Tia's mum last time," says Hassan. "Fuck me, that got the colours pouring. They needed a second bowl!"

"How old was your little girl?" asks Albert.

"Tia was three years old, bother. An angel. What I'd give for one last look at her. You know, all these interrogations, they wring out all the other memories from my life, making them feel cold and distant. But Tia, she still feels so close and so real. I'm never letting her go, brother. Never."

"You shouldn't," says Albert.

Gareth looks at Hassan. Despite his aggressive exterior and evident vitriol towards some people, he has a beautiful integrity in his love for his daughter. This tenderness takes the edge off his inaccessible masculinity.

The dormitory door opens, and a guard leans in. He reaches across and extinguishes the room's lantern, plunging them into darkness. It is time to crawl into bed and get some sleep. Lights out mean no more talking and no leaving the dormitory. Hassan has learnt that the hard way. The guard goes without saying a word.

The door slams shut. "Good night to you too," shouts out Hassan sarcastically.

Usually, Gareth would be asleep in minutes. Long days at the kiln are exhausting. Instead, as Hassan starts to snore, he lies awake, staring absently at the crack of light under the door. He wonders what memories from Earth he couldn't let go of. He feels jealous towards Hassan and the purity of his love for his daughter. He doesn't have a connection like that. Whenever he thinks of his life, his mum, or of Cerys, he can't stop the looming feeling of intimidation billowing like storm clouds in his mind.

There is a creaking from Albert's bed. In the darkness, Gareth can see the shape of the older man sitting up in his bed. He opts to conceal his prying and watches as Albert clambers gingerly to his feet. Albert stands still momentarily as though checking if he has woken anyone. Content that he is in the clear, he wanders to the door and steps out into the candle-lit corridor, flooding the dormitory with light. He closes the door behind him.

Gareth is too intrigued to lie awake, wondering what Albert is doing. He rolls out of bed and tiptoes to the door, not waking Hassan. He pokes his head into the corridor and sees Albert's shadow disappearing towards the guard's quarters.

Gareth takes a deep breath. He is guaranteed a day back at the furnace if he is caught out of the dormitory. But he can't help himself. He was always bravest when sticking his nose into someone else's business. Maybe Cerys was right about him.

Gareth tucks himself against the damp wall of the corridor and shuffles along, just out of sight of Albert. The old man is being just as sneaky. He creeps around every corner, looking back over his shoulder repeatedly.

Rounding one corner, the chatter from the guards' quarters echoes into the gloom. It sounds lively. Gareth hasn't considered what the guards do when the kilns are closed. Evidently, they don't need an early night after a hard day's work. The volume pulses momentarily, and the lanterns hanging over the entrance to their quarters swing and flicker. Someone has just gone in.

Gareth squints. He can't see Albert's shadow anymore. The older man may have just entered the guard's quarters. Before he can consider the implications of this, a warm palm slaps over his mouth and pulls him back into a shadowy nook.

"What are you doing out here?" whispers Albert urgently, his face close to Gareth's. His eyes dart between the young man and the corridor.

Gareth stares back. "What are *you* doing here?" he responds.

Albert puts his finger to his lips and beckons Gareth to follow.

"I've been watching them," whispers Albert. "Our so-called divine 'judges'."

At the entranceway, Albert puts his ear against the door. The volume is steady and loud. As he wraps his fingers around the handle, Gareth slips nervously into his shadow.

Light and sound flood out of the little crack in the doorway. Albert pushes Gareth forward to peek in. Inside he sees a large lounge bathed in a swirling mist. There are men – guards and even ministers from the workhouse – leering and lurching around the floor, evidently intoxicated on something. Crashes and hisses from smashing marbles percuss an orchestra of orgasmic moaning and groaning.

Gareth notices that the men are passing an object around between them. A woman. A young woman, half-naked, with a vacant, glazed expression and an unfocused stare. Gareth is horrified. But this is also the first woman he has seen in months. He finds himself inadvertently gazing at her body. Her curves and extremities are writhing in the candlelight. He horrifies himself with his own impulses.

Albert nudges Gareth aside and closes the door. "Holy appointed judges, I think not. There's something else going on here; I just don't know what." He looks at Gareth, his eyes sparkling mischievously. "Come on, let's get back to the dormitory before we are caught. And it's probably best we don't say a word to Hassan. Confrontation with the guards won't help, and I don't think Hassan commands another way of dealing with this information."

* * *

Work resumes at the kilns the following day. Hassan is in a foul mood because a group of men from a nearby kiln taunted him on their way to their fortnightly interrogation, implying they knew they were about to be freed. This was a ridiculous taunt, given that no one knew when the colour sweating from their forehead would clear. Nonetheless, the dig got under Hassan's skin, and standing around the kiln, it doesn't feel to Gareth like a good time to raise the late-night discovery about the guards and ministers. Undermining Hassan's already fragile obedience in the workhouse would need to be carefully timed.

A man comes rushing across the workhouse floor. He is one of the men returning from interrogation. "They've been freed," he says, exasperated. "The other men from my kiln. They have. They've gone."

Hassan looks at the man, perplexed. "You're fucking kidding me!?" he says, angrily shovelling coal.

"They can't have been that bad, after all," offers the man.

"They definitely were!" exclaims Hassan. He angrily kicks loose bricks of coal across the workhouse floor. The coals go skidding off in all directions. "This place is nonsense! It really is! I'm going to be here forever!" He sits down stubbornly on the upturned coal scuttle and puts his head in his hands.

A guard wanders to their kilns, alerted by the flying pieces of coal. "I see we've had two workers leave?"

"I thought freedom was linked to how hard we worked?" exclaims Hassan, looking up. "And those two men did fuck all each and every day!"

"It is about paying off your debt," the guard responds bluntly.

Hassan stands up. He has a coal shovel in his hand and looks like he will let his frustration get the better of him. Indeed, the guard assumes this and backs away. But Hassan has changed since they first arrived at the workhouse. He turns to the kiln and shovels the loose coal back into the fire with more force than is necessary.

The men's own interrogations come a few days later. They are marched, as usual, through the dark corridor and into the confessionals. Gareth feels very different about the meeting now. The illusion of reverent authority has been shattered with the knowledge of how the guards and ministers behave after hours. The session feels just like a process now. A process where he hopes he'll see his sweat go clear and he'll be freed. Albert gives Gareth a reassuring shoulder squeeze before they go into their booths.

The interrogation happens as usual, but the discussion of Gareth's shameful past hardly affects him. He has told these memories so many times. It is almost as though the guilt has drained out of him. In fact, the colours that drip from his forehead now, as he talks about his sexuality, start to lose their colour altogether. This fills Gareth with hope. Unfortunately, seeing the change also prompts the minister to adjust his enquiry. He moves the conversation from lust to envy and jealousy. Much to Gareth's dismay, this change of topic reinvigorates the colour in his sweat. Instead of dark crimson, he fills the bowl with deep blues and sparkling greens.

After an hour or so, there is finally enough colour in the bowl, and the minister brings the interview to a close. As always, he sits back on his throne and asks Gareth about the connection to his life on Earth. "So, tell me, do you long for the life you had?"

Gareth looks down at his bowl, swirling with the colour of his memories. The memories feel so distant and alien already. Recalling them in these interrogations has rinsed their connection with his soul. His memories now seem, literally and metaphorically, a world away. He glances at his wrists, strapped to the armrests. His Satan's Scalds are raw from rubbing against the leather straps. This sensation is painful and immediate. All he wants now is a way out of the workhouse. "No," he says, "not really…" And he means it.

The minister pauses momentarily before glancing at the guards behind Gareth. "I think that will do for today. We are finally making progress."

\* \* \*

Gareth senses a change in the workhouse. After his latest interrogation, the guards treat him differently, as though they anticipate his time at the workhouse is ending. Hassan and Albert say the same. The pace and expectations of their work decrease significantly. And with potential freedom on the horizon, Gareth does not feel so concerned with uncovering the truth about the guards or ministers any more. Tragically, this is different for Albert.

One morning Gareth squints through sleepy eyes at the dormitory ceiling. Improved treatment from the guards has meant he has been left to wake up of his own accord. A very welcome change from a few weeks ago. He rolls onto his side. Like him, Hassan is waking too, writhing lethargically in his bunk. But Albert's bed is empty.

"Albert?" asks Gareth, sitting up and rubbing his eyes.

"Where's he gone?" says Hassan.

Gareth suspects he knows. The older man had mentioned another investigation into the guards' quarters sometime soon. Still unwilling to share this information with Hassan, though, he shrugs. He hopes Albert is back quickly or the guards will catch him.

Too late. The door swings open. "Down at the kilns in ten minutes, please, gentlemen," says the guard automatically. He stops just short of closing the door. "Wait a minute, where's the old man?"

Gareth and Hassan exchange a glance.

"Stay where you are!" he instructs them, alarm rising in his voice, and he rushes away.

"Oh, Albert's in the shit now," says Hassan. "What was he thinking? We're so nearly free."

Footsteps and shouting echo down the corridor. The dormitory door bursts open again. Five or six guards storm in. One strides up to Hassan while others aggressively turn over Albert's bunk.

"What do you know?" he splutters, breathing heavily. "Where's the old man?!"

"I've no fucking idea," says Hassan coolly. "Your guess is as good as mine."

"Is that true?" another guard spits at Gareth. He nods, hoping he looks convincing.

"He can't have got far," shouts one of the guards. "We must search every room and every corridor. *No one* goes missing from *our* workhouse!"

"Too right!" shouts another.

"Disobedience to the rules is disobedience to God himself!" shouts the guard beside Hassan, his face red with rage and his chest swelling. "You two…down to the kilns, now! I hope you can adjust quickly to making marbles without the old man. Otherwise, it's off to the furnace for you, too."

Rumours of Albert's disappearance flood the workhouse in the next few days. It doesn't take long for every man to hear some version of the story that a fellow captive might have escaped. These rumours are met with fierce rebuttals from the guards. Official claims are announced that Albert has been captured and is being interrogated while an appropriate sentence is delivered. Despite these claims, no one sees Albert and the rumours continue. Soon, every man at the kilns is being treated with suspicion, punishments are distributed for the slightest misstep, and the guards adopt a practice of reciting workhouse rules on megaphones all day long.

Gareth and Hassan are no wiser than any fellow captive about the circumstances and outcome of Albert's disappearance. Nonetheless, they are treated as though they know something. They are monitored around the clock. A guard is stationed permanently in their dormitory, and two guards are assigned to their kiln. Under this scrutiny, Gareth and Hassan dare not discuss the old man. Instead, they discover they can be quite an effective workhouse pairing. Neither man can bear the thought of returning to the furnace, and this fear drives them to produce a tremendous glut of marbles without Albert's help.

A few days later, as the fervour of suspicion starts to abate, Gareth and Hassan are called for their next interrogation. Gareth finds it surprisingly unsettling to head to the confessionals without Albert. While Albert never usually said much on the regular walk through the dark corridors, it was always comforting when he was there. Like having a treasured grandparent with you or a loyal pet. He felt exposed without him.

"What did the old man tell you?" the minister asks Gareth in the booth, unable to stifle his eagerness to hear. They haven't even touched on Gareth's shame. His bowl is still clear and shimmering on his lap. "Did he show you anything?"

"Not that I know of," says Gareth, bemused. "Albert never really said much at all. He told me he'd been a teacher once, on Earth, or something like that. And he seemed like a kind, gentle person. Not a troublemaker. He never showed me anything or told me anything unusual." Gareth feels his heart rate rise. Concealing his late-night wandering seems necessary for his own good. "Is there something I should know?"

The minister inspects Gareth. It seems he is trying to suss him out, weighing up the gamble of telling him more about Albert or trusting that Gareth honestly doesn't know anything.

"He never mentioned a husband? Or a boat? Or an expedition?"

Gareth doesn't have to conceal anything now. These are three completely unrelated things to him. He has no idea how they might relate to the older man. He shakes his head, his eyes wide and confused. "He never said anything about any of those things."

Again, the minister stares at Gareth. He waits and, this time, weighs up that Gareth must be telling the truth. He genuinely knows nothing more about the old man.

"Well, I am sad to have to break this news to you," says the minister with cold, emotionless eyes. "But the old man died this morning. He died in interrogation. His soul has gone to the Beyond. May God forgive his shortcomings."

The minister shuffles on his throne, relaxing his posture and adopting the usual tone of his interrogation. Gareth stares at the floor. He had only known Albert briefly, but this was devastatingly sad.

"How did he die?" he asks the minister cautiously.

"That does not concern you," the minister responds, narrowing his eyes. "Nor does it concern me. We are here to discuss you. So let's get on with it…Do *you* still harbour any longing for your old life?" he asks Gareth.

Gareth ponders for a moment. In the chaos of the last few days, and now with the news of Albert's death, he can't think of his life back on Earth. "No," he says. "My old life seems far too distant now. I can remember it, but it feels cold and unfamiliar."

Gareth expects to be interrogated further. But he isn't. For the first time, the minister himself comes around to his side of the booth. He picks up the bowl of clear liquid from Gareth's lap and carelessly pours it over the stone floor. The liquid splashes and hisses into a delicate mist. Placing the empty bowl on the floor, the minister unstraps Gareth's wrists from the chair. Gareth looks at him, trying not to betray the nerves sloshing inside his stomach.

The minister pulls open a drawer concealed in the wall. A tray of marbles sparkle with a full spectrum of fantastic colours. He runs his fingers over the tray, looking for a specific marble. He finds it – a bright red marble with a single yellow spot in the middle.

"Do you remember this marble?" he asks Gareth, his face only inches away. "It was created from our first session together. This marble is for you now. It is known as your Interrogation Stone. It can be a reminder to you of how far you have come. Keep it safe. One day you might need it."

Gareth takes hold of the cold spherical stone and grasps his palm around its smooth surface. It is heavier than he anticipates. After another pause staring at Gareth, the minister begins again. "OK, Mr Edwards. You have now graduated from the workhouse. You have paid your core penitence. You have exposed the darkness of your past life, but now I am satisfied that you have entered a new phase. One where you don't look back.

Where you look forward. One where you can contribute well to your new life, here in the Meadow."

*A shortage of tram drivers following the First World War meant that the driver of the No.20 Dover Corporation Tram on Crabble Hill on 24th August 1917 only had five weeks' driving experience. Around mid-afternoon his tram was seriously overloaded, carrying around seventy passengers (more than the allotted forty-eight) as they climbed up Crabble Hill. When he went to apply the brakes near the summit, they were unable to hold the tram's weight. Before the driver could do anything about it, the tram plummeted down the hill, quickly getting out of control before it reached a sharp bend in the track. On this bend, the tram toppled off the rails and collided violently with a brick wall. Eleven unfortunate souls were lost in the tragedy.*

# Chapter Four

♦

# The Meadow

After months of the same routines in the same place, Gareth is uneasy as he leaves the interrogation. Hassan greets him as he opens the dormitory door, beaming at him. "We're free!" he exclaims.

Hassan has lost his workhouse shawl and is in the clothes he was wearing when Gareth first saw him on the train. The man in the high-visibility jacket. On Gareth's bed, in a rough heap, are his clothes as well. His magenta hoodie and coffee-stained blue jeans. He hastily pulls them on and places his Interrogation Stone into his pocket.

"Apparently, we are leaving this place together," says Hassan. "I can't believe it, brother!"

Gareth glances across at Albert's bunk. It has been left in an untidy mess since the old man disappeared. "No, me neither," he says, absently, haunted by the thought of the old man's death.

A moment later, a squad of guards arrive. "OK, you two. Let's get going."

Gareth and Hassan are led up a flight of stone stairs and through a labyrinth of small corridors that open into a distantly familiar railway platform. Standing at the platform is an old London Underground train carriage. There is a number 21 plate above the doorway. Memories from the train crash flash through Gareth's mind.

"It's just a short journey from here to the Meadow," a guard announces.

At the front of the carriage, there is no engine. Instead, the carriage is being pulled by half a dozen horses. A rider sits at the front, holding the reins. Gareth and Hassan step into the carriage, followed by one of the guards. The two men sit tentatively, and the train trundles into a dark tunnel.

Emerging out of the Underground tunnel five minutes later, the horse-drawn train arrives at a dilapidated, run-down station. Piles of horse manure and damp hay litter the platforms. Concrete booths on the platforms are occupied by bored-looking guards dressed in the same uniforms as the guards from the workhouse. On the concourse, dozens of people are milling around. Some are talking in open clearings, many are making emotional farewells, but most are being tightly shepherded by uniformed station staff down pathways towards their outbound trains.

A multi-storey building looms outside the station, a stone's throw from the concourse. It is a magnificently gothic structure, though the roof appears to have sprung a leak. A steady flow of water spews down its face, establishing the building as a de facto water feature. Luscious creeper plants have embraced this and wrapped themselves tightly around the building, reaching the upper floors. Around the base of the building, drains are overwhelmed and water pools in dark, deep and dirty puddles.

Two police officers stand waiting for the men on the platform. The officers' uniforms and berets are a deep purple, and their combat belts are loaded with what look like small spray canisters. As Gareth and Hassan step out from the train, there is a commotion on the concourse. A man wearing dirty black overalls is shouting at the top of his voice, pursued by another couple of police officers. "The mines! The mines!" The man hollers, trying to wriggle free from an officer who has caught hold of his arm. "The departed are slaves. There is no dignified end! Stand up and fight!"

A second officer catches hold of the man. He twists his arm, turning the man's torso around and under his own, an expertly rehearsed manoeuvre. As he tightens his grip, the first officer brandishes a spray canister from his belt and plunges it into the captured man's mouth. As the canister is discharged, a hiss erupts, engulfing the man's head in a dense wet mist. Both enforcement officers immediately release their grip and turn their faces away.

The man in overalls, wide fear visible in his eyes, straightens up and arches his back in a futile attempt to free himself from the mist and take in a gulp of air. Instead, he draws the fog surrounding his face into his mouth and swallows it.

For a moment, the man in overalls looks around, shocked. Then, outside of his control, he transforms in front of them. The tension in his body dissolves away; his arms and belly drop from their rigid defensive stance and hang soft and limp. His eyes roll up into his head, returning in an unfocused stare. He has become just like one of the 'unconscious' passengers the men had seen exiting their train all those months ago.

"What the hell just happened to that man?" asks Hassan.

"Never you mind," says one of the officers greeting them, adjusting his belt of spray canisters. "Save your questions for the Professor."

"Who?" says Hassan.

"You'll see," responds the officer, striding off. The officer with him nods at the men, indicating they should follow in front. Gareth and Hassan comply hesitantly, walking through the station and outside towards the gothic building.

The vast building looms menacingly. Its sheer magnitude gives it a cathedral-like quality. Above the entrance, a sign indicates they are entering a research facility belonging to 'Virgil College'. A facility for 'Water Science and the Knowledge of Openings'.

"This is where you will receive your official welcoming to the Meadow," says the leading officer.

* * *

The 'Waterfall Room' is at the top of the building – a large room with heavy oak furniture and floor-to-ceiling bookshelves. Whoever usually occupies the space has a thirst for reading. The books are tightly squeezed into over-burdened shelves. They might have originally been in some order, but this order is long gone. The books cover a great range of subject areas. There is a section dedicated to philosophy and theology with great old leather-bound books and heavily worn paperbacks with pages falling out. There are geography books and maps alongside travel diaries and journals, and there is a large section of heavy-going science texts with peculiar titles like *The Science of Openings*, *The Potency of Water*, and a collection of a dozen or so volumes entitled *Psycho-active Marble Creation*.

The fourth wall gives the Waterfall Room its name. It is made entirely of glass and is permanently shimmering as water cascades outside. The rooftop leak is no accident. Barely discernible through the water, Gareth can make out the entrance to the station below. They must be near the top of the building. From inside, the shimmering light gives the room an unusual sense of activity and impatience, in contrast to the restful space of academic reflection. The officer invites the men to take seats around a large oval table. "Wait here," he instructs them. "I'm going to get Professor Pelling."

Leaving the room, the officer pulls out a small velvet pouch from his pocket, removes what looks like a marble with a florescent yellow and blue fleck in the middle, and pops it into his mouth, sucking intensely as he leaves the room.

"Did he just eat a marble?!" exclaims Hassan.

"That's what it looked like!" says Gareth, an air of bemusement in his voice. He feels in his pocket for the small red marble with the yellow spot and nervously rolls it between his fingers.

The door opens again. A tall and skinny man enters. He wears a pair of oak brown corduroy trousers, a loose flannel shirt and a crumpled deep blue blazer. His hair is unkempt and shoulder length, with stray greys dancing in a thick covering of dark brown. His face is worn, but his tiny spherical eyes are bright and friendly. His hands fidget restlessly, scratching his bristly chin and revealing a deep scar across the back of his left hand and a wedding-ring finger that has recently been de-jewelled (the tan line is evident).

"Good Risen," says the man in a cultivated home-counties accent. "My name is Metford. Professor Metford Pelling. I am a professor of Openings here at the London School of Meadow Science. I hope you like my Waterfall study suite? I have been asked to come and meet you both and to say, Welcome. Welcome to London, and welcome to the Meadow".

He looks around at the two men. "I'm sure arriving here has been a bit of a surprise. Most arrivals from the workhouse will need time to adjust. But rest assured, you will find the Meadow the most accommodating place. After all, this is your home now. Though, I'm sure; it doesn't feel that way right now."

The Professor wanders to the waterfall wall, pauses momentarily, and then turns back to the two men. "People have been arriving here in the Meadow for all of human history. The Meadow exists in parallel but entirely separate from Earth. The land, and the oceans, are all geologically reminiscent of Earth, as you will see. The shapes, forms, rivers and mountains are all familiar and may even look the same to the untrained eye. Yet they are unique and unconnected."

"We believe the Meadow is a realm that exists in-between life on Earth and death. We refer to life in the Meadow as our second life, our re-life. We don't know how long each of us will find ourselves here. Indeed, many have very fleeting stays here."

"You recall that most of your fellow passengers from the train were in a trance-like state on arrival? We call those arrivals Drifters – they were already making their way out of the Meadow. They were 'going on', as we say here. They were continuing their journey straight through to death. However, people like you and I have washed up here in the Meadow. We have had an incomplete separation between our mind, body and soul. Our lives on Earth were cut short too soon. And our souls, deep in our consciousness, are unable to travel into death, yet."

"So, is that it?" asks Hassan. "Our penitence is paid? Our guilt and shame from Earth forgotten?"

The Professor looks back at him and gives an evasive answer. "Your time at the workhouse is over. Your life is your own again. You can live as you see fit…" He leaves a lingering silence. It is a pleasant change for Gareth not to hear references to shame and penitence. "Well, your life will be your own pretty soon," the Professor begins again. "First, we need to get you registered. We will accommodate you in one of our delightful colleges here in the

Meadow while this is done, helping you learn and adjust to Meadow life. At the same time, we will enrol you on a study course, where you will work through the Meadow Assimilation Programme, the MAP, teaching you about the services, laws and governance of the Meadow. After that, and only when you feel ready, you will graduate as a free Meadow citizen."

Gareth unsuccessfully tries to stifle a yawn. It has been a long time since they had woken up in the workhouse dormitory that morning. "Excuse me, Professor," he says. "It was warm sunshine when we arrived here today. Would I be right in thinking we are in summer?"

"Hmm, would you call it summer?" the Professor asks rhetorically, looking at his bookshelf. "The seasons here in the Meadow are slightly less structured than on Earth. It is more, erm, I think we'd say, more creative. This is one of the areas where the Meadow deviates from Earth. We don't see predictable cycles of weather or seasons. There are no patterns to the length of our winter or any warning of an impending storm. A heatwave can last ages or no time at all. It can be winter when you wake up and summer when you go to bed."

"I don't understand," Hassan interrupts. "How can the seasons change in a day?"

"It is tough to answer how. Or why," the Professor responds. "It seems that arrivals bring certain artefacts, certain debris, from Earth into the Meadow with them. A populous arrival, like yours, can bring vast things – like trains – but also weather and seasons. If I have been informed correctly, you brought a cold grey morning with you."

"But," Gareth starts, trying to think as he speaks. What the Professor says is like a riddle, and he always feels more engaged when his intellect is tickled. "Surely this is chaotic? How can you function?"

"It is amazing how life adapts," the Professor responds, smiling at Gareth's intuition. "Come, look out the window with me for a moment."

The Professor steps to the glass wall and cranks a handle on the wall, immediately diverting the cascading water off the window. The men have a clear view of the street and station entrance below, with the water gone. Only now does Gareth realise how much greenery there is in this new London. Trees and shrubs more than line the streets; they *are* the streets. "Now watch the wildlife on the floor and watch how the plants react to the changing weather," the Professor instructs.

The men look down into the great shadow cast by the building. Nothing happens. People continue to mill around at the base of the feature, stepping in and out of the shadow. The plants that occupy vast areas of the floor stay as they are. "Am I missing something?" says Hassan impatiently.

"Give it a moment."

Suddenly, the sunlight dims dramatically, and a ferocious snowstorm swirls around the building. Amazingly, the plants around the building curl up or droop while the snow dances around them. It is like they are animate creatures. Some leaves turn orange or brown instantly, and some plants even drop their leaves. "Life adapts," the Professor says again, enjoying the astonishment on the men's faces.

"This must be very confusing," says Gareth. "Surely people need some certainty about the weather and the seasons?"

"It is essential," responds the Professor, "not to confuse the essence of time with the measure of time. On Earth, you will have been encouraged to think of time measured and divisible by a single universal quantity – the second – a fragment of time derived from packaging every moment. This fragmentation led you to count down the days to Christmas…to see what time the rain would come…to divide your lives into four predictable segments: spring, summer, autumn and winter. Your sense of time was much like your understanding of value. You viewed the value of all things on Earth through a single unit, the cost. Yet, like the value of things, the real essence of time comes not from its measure or duration but from the quality it holds for the lives occupying it. As you know, spending quality time with someone you love cannot be measured. Likewise, taking a break from work depends on your ability to switch off, not the quantity of time you have."

The men nod in agreement with the logic but still try to get their heads around it. Gareth enjoys the challenge of understanding. "How long does it take to fall in love? How long does it take to mourn a death?" the Professor asks rhetorically. "It is pointless to keep and measure time without a care for its meaning. Here, in the Meadow, where our seasons and our weather are entirely unpredictable, changeable, and inconsistent, it is much easier to free ourselves from an obsession with organising and structuring the elements of life around an arbitrary constant. You know the saying '*make hay while the sun shines*'? We apply this religiously here in the Meadow. If it is daylight and warm, most people will take advantage; get outside, see friends and family, and join in with sports and games. But if it is dark, stormy, or generally miserable, people will catch up on sleep, read or study, and generally go about life at a slower pace."

The cogs whirr in the minds of the men. What the Professor says almost makes sense, but it is hard to envisage. Looking at the people milling around on the station concourse below, no one is specially dressed for cold or hot weather, nor is anybody in a rush. There is a serenity to the street below that could never happen in a city where the men have come from.

"Now let me practise what I preach," the Professor starts. "The sun has re-emerged and is warming the ground with an evening glow. I'd like to secure a tram for you before it gets dark. Please, follow me."

"Where are we going, Professor?" asks Gareth.

"I am taking you to our university campus. You will get rested there for a while, and then we can formally enrol each of you tomorrow. It won't be a long journey to the campus, but I insist we take the scenic route. I think it is only fair that you get to see your new home."

Back in the depressing concrete station, the Professor directs the men onto a shadowy damp platform where dripping ivy clings to everything. Stood silently on the tracks is an antique double-decker tram car with *Dover Corporation Tramway* engraved on its side, a number 20 on the rear, and a *Leney's Ale and Stout* advert posted around its upper deck. The old tram car has room for two dozen people on the upper deck via a spiral staircase, but there is no space on the lower deck. The lower deck is crammed full of hay. As they walk around to the front of the tram car, rather than an electric motor, the vehicle is tethered to two immense Shire horses, quietly chomping on some damp hay.

"Why the horses, Professor?" asks Gareth, "Are the engines broken?"

"No, not to my knowledge," says the Professor. "Our problem is technology and expertise. Many arrivals into the Meadow bring damaged vehicles – crashes seem to be one of the most common reasons for a life to be cut short on Earth – but we don't have the skills or parts to fix them here. Still, we don't want to waste the free resource, and the vehicles are often perfect as makeshift carriages. Plus, with the natural world thriving, we have an abundance of horsepower to pull them."

A tall man in a long black robe emerges from behind the tram. He carries with him a long leather whip. Barely acknowledging anyone, he pats the horses and clambers onto the tram car. He grasps the horse's reins in his hands and tucks the hem of his robe under his feet, before turning to look at the men.

"New arrivals just out of the workhouse?" he asks. The men nod. "Then hop on, Squires," he instructs them. "Meadow Campus, I'm assuming Mr Professor, sir?" he stumbles over the correct address for Professor Pelling.

"That's right," confirms the Professor. "The scenic route, if you please?"

"Right, you are, sir."

The three men clamber up the rickety spiral stairway and spread across the damp iron seats on the upper deck. A crack of the whip starts a creaking of iron casters on the tram track. The two powerful horses let out some heavy breaths as another whip crack flashes across their flanks, and the tram picks up speed before entering a dark tunnel at the end of the platform.

Within a short time, the tram emerges into a steep-sided concrete tramway which slowly ascends to street level. The steep walls on either side of the tram are covered with green ivy. Above the walls, Gareth can just see the upper floors of London townhouses, looking much like on Earth. One difference, however, is that these houses are covered in plants. Creepers have made their way up all the walls, and balconies are blossoming with explosions of flowers and shrubs. And there are definitely more trees. Gareth can't see street level yet, but it appears that a canopy of trees is reaching up to the second or third floors of all the townhouses, almost as though the tops of the townhouses are emerging out of the roof of a dense forest.

The enclosed tramway ends and Gareth realises that the trees he can see are indeed part of a forest. Trees not only line the street but populate the actual roads of this new London. The density of their canopy casts darkness across the streets, with only occasional shafts of light penetrating to the ground. The road Gareth expected to see is a dense reddish-brown floor, a mix of dry plant matter – leaves, sticks and twigs. It is literally as though the tarmac, paving stones, and concrete that makes up the streets of London have given way to the emergence of an ancient forest. It is both bizarre and beautiful.

The trees converge on the tram, and soon they run along a track within the forest. Gareth examines the lower floors of townhouses and shops as they pass by. Most are dark with their curtains closed. A few have lights on, illuminating the forest floor. He can't make out if any people are inside, but empty bottles on doorsteps and newspapers stuffed into letter boxes indicate they are inhabited.

The tram comes to a stop.

"Little delay, folks," calls up the driver. "We'll be on the move again shortly."

Gareth takes in the scene for a peaceful moment without the clunking of the carriage, appreciating just how much nature thrives in this new London. There is even a family of red deer in a nearby street, who scratch the forest floor looking for bugs, and a badger who sticks its nose out of a decaying log, perturbed by the large vehicle that has stopped near its house.

It isn't long before he sees local people too. A young family wander past, all dressed in loose brown tunics with trousers that come in at the knee. They are on their way to sell some handmade goods in another part of town. They briefly acknowledge the tram but with apparent indifference. Then a tall lady rushes past, apparently late for some appointment. She looks anxious, gripping what looks like a canvas gas-mask container. The Professor notices Gareth eye's following her curvaceous figure and chuckles. Gareth flushes red. He is mortified to be caught.

A moment later, the view of the street is blocked as another train trundles past them, heading away from London. The passing train contains a series of old brown and cream wooden carriages marked with the letters L.N.E.R and a faded "Newcastle" destination plate. Like their tram, the train is drawn by a team of horses. Over their strong backs, dark purple coats are draped, each with the same symbol embroidered on them – it depicts a water droplet with an arrowhead inside it – and the title "Department for Onward Transport" written in embossed gold letters. The powerful animals struggle and strain, their hooves digging into the stones around the track. A rider wearing a black uniform sits atop the front carriage, holding a knot of reins. He nods towards their tram in acknowledgement while brushing away the lowest branches of the trees he passes.

Looking into the adjacent train, Gareth sees packed carriages. Young women mostly occupy the front carriages. None of them acknowledges the tram car but face forward in a trance-like absence as though drugged. Gareth is determined not to be caught by the Professor staring at the women this time. Following these carriages, many more people are packed into half a dozen dark, windowless carriages. Only a grate on the carriage door gives a glimpse at the passengers inside. They don't sit but stand, squashed beside each other, without room to move. These passengers have entirely vacant expressions, and they look dirty and emaciated. Many have missing teeth and patchy lice-ridden hair. They seem to have been herded into the carriage. The sight is depressing.

"You remember what I told you…" starts the Professor, twisting to look back at the men from his seat, "…that your fellow passengers from the Earth train, those who were in a trance-like state on arrival, were making their way out of the Meadow. This is how the 'unconscious' arrivals – people we call Drifters – make their way."

"Where are they going, Professor?" Hassan asks.

"They are going to a place we call the Source, a few days' train ride northwest, to a place high in the Welsh mountains. A place where we have traced the emergence of the highest water source in the Meadow."

"Why are they being taken there?" Gareth asks.

"If they weren't taken there, they would go of their own accord. You see, people don't 'die' as such in the Meadow. Our end in this realm is less brutal. Instead, we meet our demise by going 'unconscious' and drifting to the Source. As you've seen, some people are already unconscious when they arrive here. So, when people go unconscious in the Meadow, they immediately and silently embark on their own journey to the Source. Nobody knows why this happens, but it has always been this way. You will likely see some Drifters in your time here who have yet to be picked up by the Department. You will see them, gaunt and dusty, wandering alone through rain and shine, night and day, heading out of the city to the Source. The Department for Onward Transport's sole purpose is to help these people on their way."

"And what happens when they get to the Source?"

"I've never been there or seen it myself, but I am told that a great precipice of rock emerges out of the clouds at the summit of the tallest mountain. This precipice is called the Perihelion. The Drifters gravitate to this point on the mountain. The protrusion of rock hangs hundreds of feet over the swirling mist below. At its edge, the precipice is only wide enough for one person to stand. Here, on this ledge, an unexplainable torrent of water emerges; its droplets plummeting into the vast emptiness below. This is 'the Source'. Without coercion or explanation, the Drifters find their way to this edge, close their vacant eyes and step off, tumbling with the water droplets into the mist, never to be seen or found again."

"Where do their bodies go?"

"That's just it. We don't know. Hence, we call it 'going on'. Many in the Meadow assume that the jump starts a journey out of this land and into death. A journey that our spirits were supposed to take from Earth, but a journey that was interrupted by washing up on the shores of the Meadow. If the Meadow can be seen as a second life, the leap from the Source signifies our second death."

Gareth looks at the faces of the Drifters in the passing carriages again. He can imagine them standing alone on a precipice, ignorant to the wind and rain that assaults their expressionless faces, closing their eyes and stepping off into the horrendous unknown below.

A few moments later, the L.N.E.R carriages have passed, and their tram can get on its way again. The horses retake the strain, walking at first, then trotting. Soon they are trundling through the trees of the urban forest again, low branches occasionally whipping their faces. They take a sharp left turn, and their tramline enters a vast boulevard.

Great oak trees form a high cavernous canopy. A diverse range of shopfronts line the street, and a frantic hubbub of people overwhelms the forest floor. Looking at the shops, Gareth can see they cater to many tastes. There is Ernest Halfpenny's Dance Hall, Atherton's Picture House, Funky Keith's Disco, and Daisy Marie's Yoga Retreat in their immediate vicinity. A great diversity of people mill in and around the shops. At one extreme, people wear roughly cut animal hides strapped with woven twine. Then there are women in elaborate corseted dresses, fanning themselves, and men in ill-fitting wool suit jackets and wide flappy trousers playing street games. And there are people in sports tracksuits, bell-bottom trousers, and skinny jeans. It doesn't look as though people are dressing up, either. It is as though every era of human history mingles in the street. It is as though people from all periods of history are here together.

The tram reaches the end of the street, and a great river comes into view. The river is a beautiful sapphire blue, and the banks are awash with perfect white sand. In the evening sunlight, bathers are strewn across the sands, soaking up the rays.

"Is that the river Thames?" asks Hassan. "I don't remember it looking so inviting back on Earth!"

"Here, we call this river the Lethe," responds Professor Pelling. "Yes, it does look very inviting, doesn't it? But it is perilous.

All groundwater here in the Meadow is dangerous – potentially fatal if consumed. The river channel is fed by tributaries all around the Meadow, filling the river with water that has travelled through or across the ground on its way to the Lethe. Consuming such water dissolves your memories of your past life and ultimately dissolves your memory of yourself. With no memory of yourself, a soul will always 'go on' to the Source. Rainwater – water that hasn't travelled on or through the ground – is safer but still best to avoid. The water in the river Lethe is particularly potent. One pint of water drunk straight from the river will incapacitate you. Any more, and your soul will relinquish its hold on this place, and you will 'go on'."

Gareth notices several young people splashing in the shallows. Some even venture deeper to swim. Seeing his confusion, the Professor adds, "So long as you don't consume the river water, you will be OK. But most here are wise enough to stay clear altogether."

The tram reaches a junction and stops while a crowd of commuters cross the tracks. Beside an office complex, Gareth sees a dark alley occupied by a group of young people huddled around a fire pit. The young people, all dressed like Victorian street urchins, have a bag of vibrantly coloured marbles. They pass the bag around, each taking a marble and sucking it. They appear to experience some kind of high, sometimes convulsing or writhing as they do so. As soon as the high is over, they spit the marble into the fire, where it glows for a short while before dissolving into the flames and leaving a momentary mist.

"Professor, I've noticed a few people sucking marbles now," says Gareth. "The police officer took one back at the station too."

"The marble," says the Professor. "This is what we call a 'memory bead'. Forged in the workhouses, as I'm sure you know, and infused with the liquid sensations and memories extracted from new arrivals into the Meadow. When people suck on one of these marbles, they experience a sensation that takes them momentarily outside themselves. A high, if you will. These sensations can range from euphoria to thrill, but even fear or loathing. The sensations are generally indicated by the colours swirling inside the marbles. But it's a lottery, really, which specific sensation you get."

Gareth rolls his interrogation marble around his pocket. "I must warn you, though, marbles are extremely addictive. Inhabiting the highs of a marble can offer momentary escapism, but too many too often and the mind will lose the ability to feel any sensation outside of the high…"

The Professor is interrupted when one of the young people in the alley shouts, "Oh my God, oh my God!" A young man is on the floor, eyes closed, with a marble's vibrant colour dribbling from his mouth. His friends are in a frenzy of panic. Amidst their commotion, the young man gets up and, with an eerie calmness, walks away past the tram, colour still dribbling down his chin. He has a vacant and distant look.

A young woman in the alley cries out while the others gather their things and pour the remaining marbles onto the fire. They fizz and hiss as they dissolve in the flames.

"This," says the Professor mournfully, "is the clearest example of the danger of marbles. A marble can only be sucked so many times before the bead bursts. On exposure to air, the centre of the marble fizzes into a mist which, if it is in your mouth, has the same effect as a spray of the most potent groundwater."

"So, has that lad just become a Drifter? Is he 'going on'?" Gareth asks.

"Sadly, yes."

Gareth looks at the man's distraught friends, crying as they try to stop him from walking away. They grasp at his shirt and spin him around. But, no matter what they try, he turns and walks away again.

"Let me reassure you; most marbles pose no risk of bursting. The key is that the older the marble, the greater chance that it will burst. Unfortunately, these old marbles are the most potent, which is why some people take them, for the heightened sensation. But they are brimming with sensation to the point that they may burst at any time."

"How can you tell a marble is old?" Hassan asks.

"As a marble is sucked, its colourful core draws on energy from the person sucking it. This pulls more and more colour into the marble until it is eventually dull and black. This process takes years. The duller and blacker the marble, the older it is. An entirely black marble is the oldest (some can last hundreds of years) and will have been sucked by many different people. You cannot tell what sensation such a marble will give you; its original colour is so dark you cannot tell. But you know that the sensation will be incredibly intense. Nonetheless, every marble has a lifetime, and there comes a time when it can be sucked no more and bursts."

Gareth is reminded of the police officer sucking a marble at the station. "Why do the police use marbles if they contain such a risk?" he asks.

"An excellent question," says the Professor, smiling again at Gareth's intuition. "You see, there is a final element to the marble – the third string of the Web of Marble Time. I have told you about the string of Marble Present – the sensation it gives you in the present moment. I have told you about the string of Marble Future – the possibility of a marble bursting and sending someone 'on'. There is a third-string: the string of Marble Past – the reason marbles are called 'memory beads'."

"Every time the marble is sucked, an imprint of the sucker's memory is etched into the marble. Either a memory of that present moment or a memory from their past, whichever is the focus of their mind when they suck. This memory is perfectly accurate to the memory of the sucker. If such a marble were to be dissected, then the last memory of the marble, its imprint, can be witnessed – this imprint can be used in a court of law as evidence. The police have hundreds of marbles on their person, sucking a single marble after every incident. This way, they have evidence for court should they need it. The sensation the police get when they suck on a police marble is one of self-righteousness."

Gareth feels the marble in his pocket again. He dreads anyone ever dissecting this marble and hearing the recollection of his first interrogation.

The tram reaches the university campus – a unique teaching and accommodation complex spanning the river Lethe, doubling as a bridge connecting the north and south banks. According to the Professor, it houses hundreds of arrivals at any time, all at different stages of enrolment in the Meadow Assimilation Programme.

The Professor facilitates check-in for the two men and collects their room keys. "Go and find your rooms," he tells them. "Have a moment to settle and rest. Try and process some of what you've been through today. If you've got the energy later, there's the Jacuzzi Bar under the central arch. It would be great to see you there."

\* \* \*

Gareth's room has a fantastic view overlooking the river. Like many campus rooms, it is built into one of the bridge arches. The contrast to the dormitory in the workhouse is stark. Fully furnished, the room is comfortable, warm, and delicately lit with flickering lanterns. Standing there, he feels himself relaxing for the first time in ages.

He wanders over to the window. Out on the river, boats are trundling up and downstream – great old galleons, industrial paddle steamers, nifty fibre-glass sailing dinghies and plastic kayaks. The evening sun is just setting on the beaches where people lie, taking in its warmth. Gareth gazes in fascination as, without warning, the weather suddenly changes. A flash of white light on the horizon is followed by a snowstorm washing down the river, sending people scurrying under umbrellas.

The evening turns to night, and after a necessary short nap in their rooms, Gareth and Hassan make their way down to the campus Jacuzzi Bar. Gareth hadn't dared go to the bar alone, so he had waited patiently outside Hassan's room for half an hour while Hassan attempted to neaten his beard with a pair of nail scissors.

The Jacuzzi Bar has an incredible view over the river. The sun has gone down completely, and bright lights from the riverbanks illuminate the sparkling water. The bar is lively, with people sitting around booths and tables, talking fervently. Live music is playing upbeat jazz. The two men stand and take in the scene.

"Glad to see you could make it," says Professor Pelling, arriving unannounced behind them. "I've found us a window-side booth."

In the booth's centre, overlooking the dark river, is a bubbling fountain filled with hundreds of marbles. Long twisted silver spoons are scattered around the fountain. "Sit down and help yourself to a marble," says the Professor.

The men look at him, "I thought you warned us they were dangerous," says Gareth.

"Yes, they have their risks," he responds. "But they are also a great social lubricant. Anything in moderation."

The Professor dips his spoon into the fountain and gathers a small pink marble which he ladles into his mouth and closes his eyes. He smiles. "Mmm, blissful relaxation," he says. "My favourite." After a few seconds, he spits the marble into his hand before dropping it into a chute at the end of the table. A delicate mist emanates from the pipe.

"It will help you relax," the Professor says, sensing Gareth's nerves.

Hassan picks up a silver spoon and glances into the bowl. "Any recommendations, Professor?"

"You can never really be sure what sensation you'll get. At least in a popular bar like this, you can be sure that the marbles will be safe and the sensations pleasant. I've found the pink marbles to best guarantee a gentle, relaxing vibe."

Hassan swirls his spoon around. Instead of taking the Professor's suggestion, he picks a sharp red marble. He puts it in his mouth and closes his eyes. A grin forms on his face. His eyes open and dart around. "These are great!" he says.

Gareth hesitantly swirls his spoon around amongst the remaining marbles in the fountain. He looks in at the bright colours of the marbles, glinting like Koi Carp in the bowl. A glittering purple one catches his eye. He ladles it onto his spoon and nervously extracts it from the fountain. It rattles precariously. He glances at the Professor for a final signal of reassurance, then drops the cold glass ball into his mouth.

The moment the marble rolls against the moist surface of his mouth Gareth is filled with a fizzing sensation through his entire body. This feeling settles quickly into a sense of intrigue. He looks around the Jacuzzi Bar. The marble acts like a pair of glasses, cloaking the perceptions of his entire mind. Everywhere he looks, he sees mystery and is filled with fascination. There is a man he notices at the bar. A man in a hooded cloak who is keeping himself to himself. He looks like he is doing all he can to avoid the attention of those around him. He spots a woman sitting in a booth, nodding absent-mindedly at a friend across from her. She is secretly communicating with another woman across the bar through subtle hand gestures. While the sensation of the marble fills Gareth's mind, everyone seems to be up to something.

The sensation evaporates when Gareth drops the marble from his mouth and into the chute. He blinks rapidly, regaining his composure. Looking around the bar, the sense of mystery is gone. It feels just like any raucous university bar on Earth. He spots a group of young men standing around a fountain throwing marbles up and catching them in their mouths. They are laughing a lot. Certainly not mysterious.

"You get used to it," says the Professor, smiling at Gareth. "And you'll soon be able to regulate the flow of the sensations."

Gareth smiles. He is in no rush to have another marble yet. He leans back to take in the atmosphere. All around them, he notices couples sitting together, sharing marbles. It looks like a very intimate experience, passing marbles mouth to mouth. "What's the benefit of sharing marbles?" Gareth asks the Professor.

"Every time you suck a marble, an infinitesimal part of you is imprinted into the marble – the string of Marble Past." The Professor fishes another pink marble from the fountain and places it in his mouth. "When friends or couples share a marble, they share these parts of themselves. At least, that's the theory. In reality, it is likely such a popular social practice because people are sharing an identical sensation."

Gareth notices a couple of women sitting at a table near theirs. Hassan sees them as well. The two young women, probably in their early twenties, have their hands on each other's thighs. They share a bright red marble between their mouths, rolling it around with their tongues.

Hassan stares at the two women, indulging the trappings of his arousal. Gareth feels a primal urge too, but he is ashamed of this. He looks away quickly, and his eyes guiltily glance at the Professor. He is devastated to see the Professor looking back at him and knows the prickling of his cheeks is a giveaway of his shame.

Trying to pretend he hasn't noticed the two women or the inspecting eyes of the Professor, Gareth throws his gaze in the opposite direction. His eyes fall on a young couple sitting around a small table in impenetrable silence. Their marble fountain is bubbling away, but they aren't sharing any marbles. The woman looks sad, desperately sad. She reminds him of Cerys.

"Professor," he begins, "it wasn't just me and Hassan when we arrived at the workhouse. There were quite a number of us, and we weren't only men. My sister was with us too. She was conscious when we arrived, and yet she was taken away. Do you know what will have happened to her? Will I ever find her again?"

The Professor looks at Gareth and holds his gaze for a moment. His eyes shift left and right, checking for eavesdroppers. Hassan is busily fishing around the fountain, looking for another bright red marble, and isn't interested in their conversation. The professor leans in close to Gareth. "I assume you were greeted by hooded figures in black robes when you arrived?" he whispers. Gareth nods. "These are officers from the Distillery. A corporation that owns the workhouses – the same body that runs and governs the Meadow." The Professor checks nervously over his shoulder again.

"The Distillery holds power and makes the rules here. The Distillery first decreed that the Meadow exists as a realm for penitence – penitence for the failures of our Earthly lives. They are the arbiters of this penitence and claim divine sanction for these activities. They deem that hard labour is the correct method for penitence for men: the fiery furnace and the arduous kilns. But not for *women*." The Professor looks uneasy.

"I must be careful speaking of these things. But you have a right to know. You see, the Distillery believes that women who arrive in the Meadow have not served God's 'perfect' design correctly. A design that, they claim, incorporates subservience to men. Newly arrived women are taken to the Palace of the Distillery. A place, in the Distillery's words, where women are 'schooled' in obedience. Schooled in providing for the men of the Distillery." The Professor drops his gaze. "I think you might be able to join up the dots. I'm sorry."

Gareth feels his subconscious wobble. He feels guilty that he hasn't thought of Cerys much in the last few months. A jab of revulsion sears through him as he imagines what Cerys might have been experiencing in the Palace while he shovelled coal into the kilns. He rubs the scars on his wrists anxiously. "Does no one challenge the Distillery?" he asks.

The Professor responds in hushed tones. "Here in the city? No, not really. It would be perilous to challenge them. They rule the city with an iron fist. Outside of the city, though, maybe. Some of us try and challenge them in our own ways, but it is very dangerous to do so. The Distillery police, and their vigilantes, carry with them canisters of something called Thermocline Mist."

"Yes, I've seen those," says Gareth. "The officers in the station carried them on their belts."

"Well, one spray of this Mist will send someone 'on'. It is deep ocean water – water collected from the thermocline depths under the ocean's surface. Up against men armed with this Mist, most who talk against the Distillery in the city don't last long. So, you will understand why I am cautious. Nonetheless, it fills me with rage the way female arrivals are treated. There are so many women we see who leave The Palace, wandering the streets here in the Meadow, traumatised by their experience and unable to embed in Meadow society. We call these women the 'Flickers'. Like flickering candles, their souls are just about to burn out."

Gareth looks again at the women around the bar. He sees a very different picture now. None of the women have scars from the molten glass on their wrists and arms, but he senses much deeper scars. He feels a pang of scratching guilt for the way he lustfully noticed the two women sharing the marble before. He turns the heavy cold Interrogation Stone over in his pocket.

"What was all that about women?" asks Hassan, emerging out of a marble high. He spits the red marble into the disposal chute and grins at them. He hasn't been listening to a word the Professor has been saying. "Something about a palace?"

The Professor frowns at Hassan, but the young man's attention is already gone. He has caught the eye of a woman sitting alone by a nearby marble fountain. She smiles at Hassan, and that is all the invitation he needs.

"Sorry, fellas," says Hassan, stroking his beard. "A brother's got to do what a brother's got to do."

As Hassan gets up, the Professor gently grabs his wrist. "You're a free man," he says. "But be careful with how many marbles you share. Every marble is a risk. Try not to lose your mind."

Hassan grins. "It's OK, Professor. I can handle my marbles," and he winks at them.

*On the afternoon of Sunday, 26th October 1623, three hundred people were assembled in an upper floor room at a town house in Blackfriars, London, participating in a Jesuit religious service. Midway through the service, under the immense weight of the crowd, the main floor beam snapped and the whole floor plummeted into the room below. A concertina effect followed, and the mass of worshippers collapsed through the beams of the lower floor as well. In all the congregation crashed through over twenty feet together. Ninety-five poor souls were lost.*

# Chapter Five

◆

# The Distillery

Gareth struggles to get to sleep. Images of his sister in the palace, his mum in a train wreck, and flashbacks from the furnace are hard to shake. Exhaustion wins in the end, and he sleeps deeply until he is woken early by seagulls squawking outside his window.

This morning, a series of administrative requirements need to be worked through with the Professor and some Distillery bureaucrats. Names, age, skills, arrival details (i.e., 'train crash'), and biometric data – height, weight, skin colour, eye colour – all need to be collected.

Hassan is extremely hungover. He didn't heed the Professor's warning to limit his marble consumption last night. As a result, he is not in the mood for any conversation and sits with a permanent frown on his face while his details are collated. In contrast, Gareth is refreshed and eager to get the administrative requirements out of the way.

Once their formal registration is complete, the Professor takes the men across the campus bridge to a stone amphitheatre on the banks of the river. It is a bright sunny day, at least for the time being, and they join a hundred or so other provisional citizens for an introductory lecture on citizenship and the Distillery.

The stage at the centre of the theatre backs onto the river – a grand setting for a lecture. Flanking the stage, great purple banners hang, embroidered with a symbol. The Speared Drop is the emblem of the Distillery. It depicts a water droplet pierced by an arrowhead. The same sign they had seen on the horses pulling carriages out of the city.

A man stands behind the lectern on stage. He eyes the gathering audience with indifference. His robes, flapping in the breeze, are the same dark purple as those worn by the ministers at the workhouse. Gareth feels an instant revulsion towards him. He reminds him of a stuffy old vicar, like the ones he experienced in his childhood.

"Every one of you here today died an untimely death on Earth," the man starts without warning or introduction. His voice, austere and pious, echoes around the amphitheatre. "You died without the normal separation between your mind, body, and soul. The failings of your past life somehow clinging to your soul like a cancer. And so, you ended up here, in this realm. With our help, you have each paid penitence to loosen the grip of your dark past. Now you have entered your second life, here in the Meadow. A time to feed your soul and end, once and for all, that poisonous connection you still have to your Earthly bodies and minds."

"Wow," whispers Hassan in Gareth's ear. "This brother's a bit full-on!" Gareth smirks in agreement.

The man on the stage reaches behind the lectern and then holds aloft a vast golden sand timer the size of an ornamental clay pot. "Time was your mortal enemy on Earth," he announces, inverting the sand timer and placing it on the stage. "Your bodies started decaying from the moment you were born. Here in the Meadow, your *mind* is your mortal enemy. It has been decaying from the minute you arrived. And when it eventually gives up, your soul will abandon it and depart this realm. Your opportunity in the Meadow is to dwell *better* in your body and your mind. To live in such a way that when your soul is finally freed, it will go to a better place. For the depths of Hell await you otherwise."

The lecturer's gloomy posturing continues in this way for almost an hour. Like a sermon, it feels like he is aiming his lecture at a vulgar congregation of sinners. Gareth zones out for most of it. He feels a disdain towards men of the Distillery that will take a lot to shift. He might have felt an obligation to listen reverently to the man had he not already heard about the Distillery's palaces from Professor Pelling, or seen the behaviour of the guards and ministers after hours in the workhouse.

Gareth's attention is recaptured, however, when the lecturer moves on to Meadow citizenship and the governing infrastructure of the Distillery. He hears that the Distillery are responsible for trade, law and order, and education like any other government. But more interestingly, they have some rather unfamiliar responsibilities as well. There is an Office for Arrivals – a department that manages all arrivals from Earth (and operates the marble workhouses and Distillery Palaces). There is the Department for Onward Transport, which facilitates the shepherding of Drifters to the Source. There is an Office for Water – responsible for the safe consumption of water-based products (including marbles), the use of all waterways, and the licensing of Thermocline Mist. And there is a department called the Council of the Almighty. Nothing much is said about this department, but there is a mystical suggestion that the Council of the Almighty hold some form of a divine link to God.

The lecture concludes with an unusual ritual. Bags of royal blue marbles are passed around the audience, and students are asked to take one while a monk from the Council of the Almighty recites a Latin supplication. Placing a marble in his mouth, Gareth gets an immediate sensation that engulfs his whole body – a mixture of calmness and fear, simultaneously comforting and uncomfortable. The feeling lasts maybe a minute, and as it fades, the prayer concludes. The students are instructed to smash their marbles onto the floor. Little bursts of blue mist erupt around the amphitheatre as the obedient audience hurls their marbles at the stone steps.

After the lecture, Professor Pelling takes Gareth and Hassan for their official sketching back at the campus. Rather than a photograph, a sketch is drawn of each new arrival for a page in the 'Provisional Citizenship Database', one of the hundreds, if not thousands, of logbooks stored by the Distillery bureaucrats at the campus, keeping track of arrivals.

While Gareth and Hassan sit for their official sketching, the Professor talks to them about the colleges in the Meadow. "The Distillery influence most things here in the Meadow," he says regretfully. "But not everything. The Meadow colleges, like where I work, keep themselves distinct and free of external intervention. We work best when left alone, and the Distillery, despite being very interested in our work, generally respects this."

"I work for Virgil College – one of the most prestigious institutions in the Meadow. We have been established for over two hundred years now. At Virgil, we research the unusual phenomena of the Meadow – the properties of water, Unconscious Bias (understanding the lives and needs of Drifters), and the nature of Openings from Earth. We drive our own research agenda inspired by our own intellectual curiosity. We pride ourselves in our distance from the Distillery. My research specialism is Openings."

"What kinds of things can you research about Openings?" asks Gareth, intrigued but trying to stay still for his portrait.

"Oh, there is so much to explore," says the Professor, his eyes lighting up. "We have recently developed tentative abilities to predict the locations and moments that Openings will appear. It is helping us to build an understanding of the connection between Earth and the Meadow. Indeed, there aren't just people coming through Openings. As you've seen, vehicles, objects, and weather travel through too. Such items are useful to Meadow society, but we are most intrigued by their impact on the fundamental laws of nature – laws like the conservation of energy and the laws of motion. Our research is tentative and theoretical at present. But it is rather intriguing."

The Professor inspects the interest of the two men. Gareth leans in, eager and attentive, much to the frustration of his sketch artist. But Hassan has switched off. The Professor chuckles to himself, then reaches into his bag. "Here," he says, laying a handful of books before the men. "It will be worthwhile looking at these in the coming days. They are the core texts for your citizenship course. Most of the questions you might have about life in the Meadow can probably be found in them."

Gareth glances at the titles. *The Distillery and Law & Order* looks very tedious. *The History of the Meadow* looks much more enjoyable. And there's a fascinating little book of prayer seeming to incorporate all religions from Earth. "I wonder how they've managed to amalgamate those ideas", he thinks to himself.

"Sadly, the tentacles of the Distillery are starting to wind their way into the colleges as well," says the Professor. "Not all colleges value their independence anymore. And even those of us that do, many of our large programmes – the citizenship course as a prime example – are directly commissioned by the Distillery."

"The other main college in the Meadow is Dante College. It is more than a little influenced by the Distillery. Dante is a selective college based south of the Lethe, who handpick their citizenship students from the new arrivals. Much of their research is theological and feeds directly into the work of the various departments of the Distillery. The men who run the Distillery departments – and yes, they are all men – are mainly graduates from Dante College."

"We'll be doing our citizenship programme with Virgil College, though, will we?" asks Gareth.

"Not necessarily," says the Professor. "Dante runs their own programme as well. You'll get a flavour of both colleges in the coming days. And I believe college allocations are happening by the end of the week."

The Professor clicks his fingers and rummages in his bag again. "That reminds me," he says, pulling out a paper invitation. "You are due to get your first flavour of Dante College this evening… you, and your fellow arrivals, are expected to attend a formal Welcome Dinner hosted by the college. You will take a barge downstream from the college pier just before sunset. That'll be an experience!"

The sketch artist clears his throat. He looks rather put out that he hasn't had the men's full and undivided attention during their sketching. As though their conversation somehow disrespected his craft. "Alright, Mr Dar and Mr Edwards," he says. "Your official portraits are complete. Good risen." He smiles sarcastically at the men, revealing a unique dental implant. He has a bright blue sapphire incisor in his mouth. It sparkles in the sunlight.

* * *

All the new citizenship students, the same people from the amphitheatre, gather on the barge. It is a warm, clear evening with a ruby sun setting upstream. There are people of all ages and backgrounds, and a few people Gareth thinks he recognises from the workhouse. The barge is crewed by a handful of priestly looking men wearing black cassocks emblazoned with *IHS*. It is to be the first time Gareth and Hassan have travelled in the Meadow without the Professor.

The barge journey takes them a short way down the river Lethe. Marbles are on offer, and most students consume them abundantly, exhibiting the joyful mirth of a people who have embraced their new home. In contrast to their joy, Dante's College is an austere and looming white stone building on the south bank of the Lethe, accompanied by a stern, cold welcoming party.

Inside the college, the students are led into a vast dining hall, packed with regimented tables and complete with seating plan. On the walls hang huge paintings of serious-looking scholars. All men in robes with religious artefacts clutched against their chests; Bibles, Torahs, Qurans, Apocrypha, and crucifixes.

A great noise fills the hall as the citizenship students find their places. Gareth and Hassan are seated together, but with them are three absentees. Gareth notices empty seats at all the other tables too. At the centre of every table, marbles are piled generously in fountains. Soon, the fizz and mist of discarded marbles fill the hall as the students help themselves, and the energy settles to a gentle hum of conversation.

The doors to the hall open. "Please be upstanding for Dante College's latest graduates," a voice calls out.

A group of exquisitely dressed students stand in the doorway. The female students wear dark green dresses, and the men wear green blazers. Everyone stands up, encouraged by the announcer, who then initiates applause, which they obediently join. The graduates stride into the hall and filter amongst the tables. Three graduates, two men and a woman, join Gareth and Hassan.

"Good risen," says a young skinny man with short black hair and piercing black eyes. "Nice to see some new arrivals, ready to learn." Gareth smiles back politely and reads the man's name tag. James Chadwick.

"How was the workhouse?" grins the other man. His name is Henry Price. Thick necked and muscular, his chest heaves up and down under his tight green blazer.

"It was awful, brother," says Hassan, straightening himself in his chair and eyeballing Henry.

"Well, you're out now," says James Chadwick, upbeat. "Things only get better from here."

The young woman who has joined their table sits quietly, listening. She has a bright, kind face. Her eyes sparkle welcomingly towards Gareth and Hassan. She doesn't have a name tag. James and Henry don't acknowledge her at all.

"So, you're recent graduates?" says Gareth, looking directly at the girl, trying to draw her into the conversation.

"That's right," says James, assuming command of the response. "We are the *top* recent graduates from Dante's College. We've been selected to join the Distillery's graduate scheme. Brightest futures, apparently."

"Congratulations," says Gareth. "You must have studied hard?"

"Studied hard, but also, I think we are just the naturally gifted," says James. Henry sniggers like a teenager.

"How long does it take to graduate?" asks Hassan.

"Well, it depends," says James. "We did ours in about six months. I think the normal time is about two years. But I've heard some people are so bad that they don't even graduate. They get sent back to the workhouse…"

"No, they don't!" says the girl, getting her first words in. She catches Gareth's eye and smiles at him.

"They do," says James, looking at her with a menace in his eyes. "Trust me, they do."

"So, is Dante's College a good college?" asks Gareth, sensing the girl feeling uneasy and changing the focus.

"The best college," says James arrogantly. "The best college for the best people. You have to be selected to go here, you know. Otherwise, you probably end up at Virgil." He sneers at his own mention of Virgil College.

"My sister went to Virgil," says the girl bravely. Again, she glances towards Gareth, hoping to catch his eye, but he is absent-mindedly straightening the marble cutlery before him.

"Do you still talk to her?" says James with another smirk.

"I do when I can," she responds. "But my sister doesn't get many passes for the Paddock these days."

"What's the Paddock?" asks Gareth.

"Everywhere in the city south of the river Lethe. We're in the Paddock now," says Henry.

"You need a pass to come here?" asks Hassan.

"The Paddock is a special place. You can't have anybody and everybody coming here," responds James. "You need to keep the *right* type of people here."

Gareth glances up at James Chadwick. He is leaning back; his arms spread eagle on the backs of other people's chairs. He has an air of unshakeable self-importance. Gareth can't stand him. As for Dante's College, he isn't sure that would suit him either.

Their conversation is mercifully interrupted by a loud gong from the front of the dining hall. An older man steps up to a lectern. "We will start proceedings this evening with a short meditation," he says, raising a bright royal blue marble between his forefinger and thumb. Another Latin supplication is chanted while all the students, new and old, place a royal blue marble in their mouths.

A minute later, the prayer is over, and another man approaches the lectern. The man appears important because James, Henry, and the girl all sit up as soon as they see him. He is tall and rotund. A big mop of floppy, messy, black hair lies over the top of his head. He has little beady eyes and a broad cheerful grin. "Welcome, young and old," he says, his voice booming across the hall. "Welcome, new students. Welcome to the Meadow." James whoops, as do a few others in the crowd.

"I'm very excited to welcome you to Dante's College, the greatest college in the Meadow, if I may," he chuckles. "A college with great history, great reputation, and great pedigree." He smiles again, looking around at the paintings of the men all over the walls. "There will be much for you to learn during your citizenship study.

I hope some great minds will join Dante's College and, hopefully, one day find yourselves emblazoned in green sitting at another one of these formal dinners." James and Henry look around the hall smugly.

"I digress. This isn't about collegiate rivalry or point-winning skulduggery. Tonight is about you; a lavish welcome to you all. Because it is time for you to thrive. A time for your lives to shake off your old shameful ways and blossom here in this great place that we call the Meadow!" The green students whoop and holler again.

"While you are here studying, you will learn about all the great things you can be and do. You will learn of our great history. You will learn of the service you can bring. And you will learn how to invite the Creator to dwell in your lives. But let me offer you all words of caution. As with the fallen realm from whence you came, there are those in the Meadow beset to ruin the great gift God has given us. I speak of the wreckers of this realm. The marble addicts. The envious poor. The gluttonous wastrels. And, I fear, there are even darker forces here in the Meadow. So, I say to you, *trust* in God, and *act* in a way befitting of this, your second life!"

More rapturous applause crackles from the graduates. "But that's probably enough of my mumbo jumbo," chuckles the man. "I think it's time to get absolutely sloshed with marbles!"

Cheers reverberate all around with this announcement. At the same time, in filter dozens of female servers. Women with a distant look in their eyes, drifting around the tables silently, gormlessly, laying more large pots of colourful marbles onto the tables. There seems to be no limit to the marbles they are allowed to consume. Gareth feels uncomfortable. Professor Pelling certainly warned them about over-indulgence in marbles.

"Before we guzzle marbles, we will say a grace," the man at the lectern booms out. "For what we are about to receive, may the Lord make us truly thankful. Amen."

"Amen!" shout the graduated students, as do a few new students, evidently remembering an etiquette from Earth.

"So, it's a Christian God, is it?" mutters Hassan, looking slightly dejected.

"Not necessarily," says James. "Alexander Oxbow-Fawcett was a devout Christian on Earth and has kept it going."

"He's the man who was speaking," interjects Henry helpfully.

"But look at the paintings of our revered scholars," continues James, gesturing to the walls. "Dante's College is a multi-faith institution. We believe that all faiths are correct in some way or another. The one thing we are not is atheist." Henry laughs in agreement.

Gareth inspects the vast looming portraits hung around the banquet hall again. There is a sickening familiarity with the types of people being honoured. They are all pompous, privileged, and self-righteous-looking men. "Not atheist," Gareth starts, feeling mischievous and sick of James' arrogance. "But possibly sexist?"

This suggestion immediately affronts James. "What's your problem?" he reacts, inspecting Gareth with his beady eyes.

"Nothing," responds Gareth defensively. He feels a shot of anxiety pulse through his stomach. "Just an observation." The girl shuffles in her seat awkwardly next to him and stares at her marble cutlery.

"Well, I'll let you know that women are treated very well here in the Paddock. Aren't they Lucy?"

James hauls the girl, against her will, into the discussion. She nods and smiles at them, but the joyous energy in her smile has been neutralised. "Everyone knows their place here," says James. "And our women are always treated with the greatest respect."

"I'm sure they are grateful for such empowering chivalry," mumbles Gareth sarcastically. The cramping of his stomach takes hold, and he leans forward onto the table to ease the pain.

James misses the subtlety of Gareth's sarcasm and moves the conversation onto marbles. Lucy catches Gareth's eye again and smiles. Embarrassed by her attention, Gareth averts his gaze.

The conversation and marbles occupy the diners in the hall most of the evening. But as the fountains empty, the energy in the room starts to dissolve away. The doors to the hall open once more. A stern, angular and uniformed woman enters. She strides purposefully up to the lectern.

"The Professors of Dante's College would like to invite all men here, new students and old, to retire to the smoking room." The woman's shrill voice echoes through the room. "The women will stay here with me. We will dutifully clear this dining hall and maintain its splendour and beauty for another day. Thank you."

The lady gets down from the lectern. A little door near the front has been opened, and a greying old gentleman in deep green robes is beckoning men to follow him. Some of the men are already on their feet.

Gareth glances at Lucy across the table. She looks back at him, her eyes sparkling out of dutiful habit. He feels guilty for selfishly absorbing her kind smiles before without reciprocation. He offers a consolatory smile to her as she stands up and starts piling the used marble spoons into the empty fountain.

Much like the dining hall, the smoking room is expensively furnished. Bottle-green leather chairs surround a dozen log-burning stoves unusually placed right through the room. Much to Gareth's disappointment, James and Henry stay with them. Cutting himself a cigar, Henry offers them around to the other men. They each decline. Small crystal egg cups (that's what they look like to Gareth) are on the table, each with a bronze-coloured marble, resembling whiskey, placed inside.

The mystery of why so many log-burning stoves is soon cleared. James swills a marble around in his mouth, then spits it into the furnace. The marble hisses, and a mist drifts out, dissipating around the men. He opens a globe next to them. It is full of whiskey marbles. He drops another marble into his egg cup. "Great being a man, isn't it?" he says, reclining in his chair.

"It seems very backward to me," says Gareth. "Women expected to tidy while the men sit and enjoy a whiskey."

"It's not backwards," says James defensively. "It's how it was always meant to be. God ordains a certain relationship between man and woman. Here in Dante's College, we respect that."

Gareth shuffles in his chair, staring inquisitively at James. He doesn't respond immediately but looks James right in the eye.

The ounce of respect he generously gave James when they first met has evaporated rapidly. "What makes men and women so different to you?" Gareth asks.

"Ha!" James recoils, surprised. "What do you mean, what makes us different?! It's obvious."

"Is it? The surface differences might be. But even we – me and you – we look very different. Yet you deem us the same," says Gareth.

"That's just ridiculous," scoffs James. "Everybody knows that men and women are different."

"I'm not so sure," muses Gareth. "I'm not so sure."

James is irritated. He looks wounded like he is going to do or say something stupid. He doesn't like it when someone happily disagrees with him.

"Well," Hassan weighs in, trying to lighten the mood. "Either way, it works pretty well for us guys." He throws a marble into his mouth and grins.

"I like this guy," says James, jabbing a finger towards Hassan but looking pointedly at Gareth. Gareth clenches his stomach anxiously once more. He hates disagreements but has always found his tongue braver than his body and his heart stronger than his mind.

Changing the topic, Hassan recalls something talked about in the opening speech at dinner. "When that man, Alexander Oxbow-what's-his-face, was speaking, he said something about 'dark forces' operating in the Meadow. What are these dark forces, brother?"

It is James' turn to look uncomfortable. He shifts in his chair and looks over his shoulder. He looks like he isn't going to say anything, but then his need to show off takes over. He leans in covertly. "It is said that there are souls consumed by the Devil's hunger who have managed to sneak into the Meadow. Evil souls under the spell of Satan."

"Satanists here in the Meadow?"

"That's right. As Earth has become over-run with darkness –"

"Which it has," interjects Henry, trying to show that he's in the know too.

"– the devil thirsts for more. Evil souls have been sent on a journey into the Meadow to try and dwell in the undergrowth here and undermine the Distillery's divine right to rule. We call it the Evil Thirst. They are not talked of much because their mention is forbidden outside of the colleges. But I've heard a bit about it."

James looks around nervously again. "I would warn you, though," he continues. "Don't tell anyone that you have heard of the Evil Thirst. You certainly do not want to be accused of belonging to or sympathising with them. The Distillery has legions of undercover officers seeking to kill off the Satanists wherever they lie. And they will leave no stone unturned in their quest to stamp out any trace of Satan in this realm." James sits back and draws a deep drag from his cigar.

Gareth crosses his legs and leans back as well. He looks at James. "I'm rather cautious of fearing something I cannot see when it is being peddled by an authority I have not chosen."

James stares at Gareth, daggers in his eyes. "The Distillery is the authority of God. Take a tip from me, chap, and heed my warnings." James is trying desperately to appear menacing. "You'll only find yourself going 'on' before you're ready otherwise."

The awkward silence returns around James' threat. James looks at Gareth with suspicion in his eyes. Once more, Hassan interrupts the silence. "I bet I could spit my marble into the stove from further back than any of you."

"Ha!" laughs James, immediately moving on from the moment. "That's the marbles talking. I'm a pro-Bead Hurler. You'll never beat me." James swills a marble around in his mouth, rocks back in his chair and spits the marble straight into the stove with a smash and a hiss.

"Oh yeah?" says Hassan, a big grin on his face, loading another marble into his mouth. He rocks back and spits his marble into the stove from maybe an inch or two further back than James. The contest is on.

The more marbles Hassan and James have, trying to out-spit one another, the more confident they get. Henry joins in as well, leaving Gareth to sit alone, excluded. He observes the chest-beating masculine competition, perplexed. He never feels the urge to compete like this.

By the end of the evening, marbles are smashed all over the floor. A constant hissing and mist surrounds the table. James, Henry, and Hassan laugh heartily with one another, and the topic of the Evil Thirst is not uttered again.

\* \* \*

Gareth is exhausted as he and Hassan finally return to the campus late in the evening. Hassan has now sucked his body weight in marbles and is suffering the consequences. He is unsteady and unusually emotional. He gave an overly warm embrace to James Chadwick as they left Dante's College and even tried to hug one of the officers guarding the barge. The officer was having none of it. Now that they have disembarked, Hassan is leaning on Gareth, unsteady, sobbing about missing his daughter Tia.

The dark streets on the route back to the campus are empty. Turning a corner, they face a huddle of homeless beggars congregated in an alley. The beggars stare at them. Gareth notices an older woman with a mouthful of dirty black marbles and more handfuls stuffed into her long coat pockets. All the beggars in the alley are sucking on dirty black marbles.

"Have you got any marbles, my dears?" the old woman rasps, grinning through the glass in her mouth and holding out her hand. Gareth tries to ignore her and walk on.

Another beggar crawls up. She holds out her hand but doesn't say anything. She can't, not with the sheer number of marbles in her mouth. She blinks rapidly like she is struggling to stay awake. Gareth feels sorry for her. She is in a pitiful state, looking like she has given up on life. Just then, a sharp hiss erupts from her mouth. One of her marbles has burst. From her stooped crawl, she stands up, her eyes glazing over completely, and without hesitation, she walks away. No one with her seems to care. This fact upsets Gareth immensely. The lady has just 'died', and no one around her cares. He watches helplessly as the woman rounds the corner of the street, drifting and alone.

Hassan moans against Gareth's shoulder, then convulses awkwardly. A bright red marble spews from his mouth and bounces on the ground, somehow not smashing. Instantly one of the beggars scuttles over and thrusts the marble greedily into her mouth. The beggar lets out a relieved and eager moan as the sensation of the marble fizzes into her body.

"I really don't think these marbles are good for you," says Gareth to Hassan.

"I know, brother," says Hassan, looking ill and ashamed.

"We're nearly at the campus," says Gareth, hoisting Hassan to a more comfortable position on his shoulder. "Let's get out of here."

\* \* \*

With Hassan safely in bed, Gareth sits alone in his room. It is dark, and only a gentle starlight from the cold clear night peeks through his curtains. He pulls out his Interrogation Stone. The blueish light illuminates the bright red sphere with the single yellow speck in his hands. How powerful, dangerous, and intimate this little marble seems. Gareth inspects it carefully, rolling it around between his fingers. The perfect sphere is cold and smooth. It reflects the starlight but distorts the reflection of his face. He places it back into his pocket and lies down.

Within minutes Gareth is asleep. But his dreams are filled with a chaos of sights and sounds. Images of beggars, the hiss of smashing marbles, the looming faces of pious scholars, and the sloshing colours of sweat dripping from his forehead. He fidgets and turns but doesn't wake.

There is a rapping at the door. Gareth's eyes shoot open. He doesn't know how long he's been asleep. He clambers out of bed and wanders over to the door. "Hello?" he calls out tentatively.

"Gareth, it's Professor Pelling," says a voice urgently. "You need to come with me, now!"

Gareth squeezes open a crack in the door and looks out. Standing with Professor Pelling is Hassan. "What's happening?" he asks.

"I haven't got time to explain. Put on some warm clothes. We've got to go."

*The Horse Shoe Brewery stood at the corner of Great Russell Street and Tottenham Court Road, London. In the vicinity was St. Giles Rookery, a densely populated slum housing the poor and destitute of the city. Inside the brewery a vat of brown porter ale, equivalent to three and a half thousand barrels, was fermenting away. Unbeknownst to the people who lived around the brewery, one of these vats was faulty. On the afternoon of Monday 17th October 1814, the tank ruptured. The force alone collapsed the back wall of the Horse Shoe brewery. A huge wave of hot fermenting ale hurtled into the streets destroying the cheap and poorly built tenements in its wake. The tragedy claimed the lives of eight souls.*

# Chapter Six

•

# The Tide And Time Tavern

The Professor hurriedly leads Gareth and Hassan down to the riverside. It is a cold, quiet night, and the stars light up the river. Their breath whispers into small clouds. Underneath a bridge arch, the Professor lifts a tarpaulin, revealing an old wooden canoe big enough for the three of them.

"Someone has reported you two to the Distillery Police," says Professor Pelling. "They allege you are Satanists who have evaded capture at the workhouse. Supposedly, within you resides the Evil Thirst of the devil attempting to take root in the Meadow."

"I bet it was James Chadwick," says Gareth. "He was the one that told us about the Evil Thirst."

"No matter how it has happened, you are both in very great danger," says the Professor, carefully sliding the canoe towards the water's edge. "The Distillery Police are looking for you."

"Do they know we are here on campus?"

"They will find out soon," says the Professor. "That's why we have to get you away tonight. I know a place north of the river. A place unsympathetic to the Distillery. I know they will keep your whereabouts hidden."

"Why can't we just explain ourselves?" asks Hassan. "They can't have any concrete evidence against us. We haven't done anything."

"That won't matter to the Distillery Police," says the Professor. "This is a grave allegation. No one I have known ever leaves Police questioning conscious."

The Professor pushes the canoe into the cold dark water. It looks barely seaworthy. "This could be a perilous trip," he says.

"If the weather changes, we must get to shore as quickly as possible, no matter where we are. We must not get swept away by the river." The Professor looks at both men seriously, then hands them paddles. Despite their concerns about the vessel, they have no choice and carefully step into the wobbly canoe.

The riverbanks are quiet as they paddle upstream. Street lanterns on the shore illuminate their faces. On the river's south bank, they see grand townhouses and fantastic old willows lining the streets. On the north bank, they see a tightly packed shanty town with roughly constructed tin roofs, all cobbled together with no pattern or order. A dense canopy of conifers lines the streets on the north bank.

Further up the river, the Professor points out two warehouses, one on each side of the main river stream. Red lamps illuminate the terracotta rooftops of both buildings. "Those are the Meadow's printing presses," he says. "Both publishers are responsible for the most popular newspapers in the Meadow: *The Daily Rain* and *The Shipping Forecast*. They are also the distributors of Distillery-produced marbles – the marbles made in the workhouses. Every edition of the paper comes with a pouch of new marbles."

The canoe reaches a point on the north bank where the riverside is particularly overgrown. The Professor indicates a small opening in amongst the coniferous forest. They approach carefully until the canoe settles on the mud of the riverbed. The men amble out tentatively.

"Looks like we got here just in time," says Professor Pelling glancing up. Above them, the stars are veiled by cloud and the first whistles of wind rustles through the trees. They scamper up into the dense conifers and along a cobbled pathway. Gareth recognises the cobbles as belonging to an old street. A moment later, warm lanterns glow outside a pub in front of them: the *Tide and Time Tavern.*

The downstairs windows of the tavern are shuttered up. Upstairs a lamp illuminates one small window. As they approach, Gareth sees a shadow move in the upstairs room. Despite the late hour, the Professor strides up to the front door and raps gently on the knocker. A moment later, an eyehole opens, and a quiet woman's voice comes from inside. "Is that you, Professor?"

"It is."

"Can you be sure you weren't followed?"

"Absolutely sure," says the Professor. "We travelled by canoe and came straight up from the riverbank."

"Good. Good," says the voice, and the eyehole slides shut. There is the sound of multiple iron bolts being undone, and then the tavern door opens. An elderly lady, barely five feet tall, with small warm brown eyes and long grey hair, stands before them. "Come on in," she ushers urgently, quickly closing the door behind them and bolting it again.

A lamp light is flickering at the bar. Bar stools stand upside down on top of tables. The lamps cast eerie shadows around them. "Take a seat," the old lady says, gingerly pulling stools from one of the tables. She is wearing a silver necklace with half a dozen lockets, which rattle like coins in a purse as she slides the stools towards the men. She lights another lantern, and soon the room feels warm and welcoming.

"It is great to see you Kim-Joy," says Professor Pelling. "Thank you for agreeing to take in these two at such short notice." The men smile politely.

"No problem at all," says the old lady, tucking her necklace back under her blouse. "I'm just glad you got them here before anyone found you."

The old lady passes the men some warm coffee marbles, which roll around inside porcelain mugs. "It's a privilege to meet you both," she says. "I am the landlady here at the Tide and Time Tavern and have been as long as I can remember. We welcome anybody here. Anybody. We are a refuge as well as a tavern. A safe place for those in need."

Gareth and Hassan thank Kim-Joy and introduce themselves. Kim-Joy exudes a warmth that they both feel and appreciate.

"You both look tired. I suggest trying those marbles," says Kim-Joy, nodding to the mugs in their hands. "They will help," she adds, noticing Hassan's face as he contemplates more marbles.

The coffee marbles warm right through. They are less potent than the marbles they had on the campus. If anything, these marbles make them sleepy.

"I shall take my leave," says the Professor to Kim-Joy.

"Are you not staying with us, Professor?" asks Gareth.

"I'm afraid not. Suspicions will be raised when you two aren't at the campus in the morning. I'll become a de-facto suspect in your disappearance if I'm not there either."

"Will we see you again, Professor?" asks Hassan.

"I hope so," he says without much conviction. "I try and visit here whenever I can." He smiles at Kim-Joy.

"You're always welcome, Professor," says Kim-Joy. "You take care on your journey back. The weather is on the turn. Stay close to the banks."

"I will," says the Professor, and he pulls over his dark black shawl. "Good luck," he says to the two men before leaving through the front door into the storm.

With the Professor gone, Kim-Joy leads the two men to their room in the loft. The little room is illuminated by a lamp sitting in the window. There is a single bed for each man, with prickly grey sheets and a lumpy pillow. It isn't the luxury of the campus, but at least it is safe. The two men are exhausted, and Kim-Joy doesn't linger long. "Get some rest," she says. "We can properly introduce ourselves in the morning."

Gareth and Hassan don't talk after Kim-Joy leaves but simply clamber into their beds and close their eyes. As he falls asleep, Gareth feels his Interrogation Stone in his pocket pushing into his hip. He is too tired to get more comfortable. Outside he can hear the harsh whistling of the wind and the rain battering against the window. He pictures the Professor paddling frantically in the old wooden canoe back to the campus. He hopes he makes it back safely.

\* \* \*

Bright sun filters in through the window of the loft room at the Tide and Time Tavern the following day. Gareth and Hassan wake up to find the curtains open and a fresh summer breeze blowing in. A door is open downstairs, leading to the beer garden. Exploring further, they find large coniferous trees surrounding a bright grassy clearing. It is as though the beer garden is in the middle of a forest.

A delicate morning dew clings to the ground, but the warmth from the blossoming sun washes through the coniferous canopy. Sat on a white metal chair, reading in the sunshine, is Kim-Joy. "Good risen," she calls cheerfully. "Help yourselves to some pick-me-up marbles at the bar. They're the yellow ones that look like they are filled with sunshine. Then do come and join me out here when you're ready."

The men take the invitation before joining the old lady outside. "What a beautiful day," Gareth says, looking at the bright blue sky. "I hope the Professor got home OK last night. The storm sounded horrendous."

"Oh, he's a very competent boatman," says Kim-Joy. "I'm sure he'll be OK."

"It's a nice place you have here," says Hassan, admiring the garden. "How long have you been the landlady?"

"Ooh, a long time," she says. "Around five hundred years now."

Hassan grins. "No, really," she says, looking at him sincerely. Hassan raises his eyebrows, then senses Kim-Joy isn't joking.

"One of the beautiful mysteries of the Meadow," says Kim-Joy. "Nobody here ages. Everybody stays the same age as when they arrived. I don't look or feel a day older than sixty-eight. Of course, mentally, I've matured, and I'd like to think I'm wiser. I think I am in the minority of those who have been here for over two centuries, however. But there are plenty of centurions around in the Meadow."

"That's incredible," says Hassan.

"Professor Pelling is one of the old ones too. I think he's a double centurion. He's always been part of Virgil College. One of the founding members of the Institute of Openings, I think. A very good and wise man. You did well to come across him so early in your time here."

Gareth has a thousand questions for Kim-Joy and struggles to know where to start. Anticipating the questions, Kim-Joy turns to the book she was reading. An old scrapbook of memories. It is a collection of thoughts and cuttings from the centuries she has lived in the Meadow.

"Arriving in the Meadow centuries ago, it was very different," she starts, flicking through the book. "We didn't go to a workhouse or Palace of the Distillery. No such places existed. There was no real authority in the Meadow then. In fact, many arrivals didn't come across anyone else for years after they first appeared. Most wandered alone and, I suspect, wandered until they went 'on'."

Kim-Joy holds up the first page of her scrapbook. On it is a short diary entry in a rough spidery scrawl. In the top corner is a simple little sketch. It looks a bit like the Distillery's symbol. "I wrote this in the first month I was here," she says. A date is legible in the top left corner: 22nd December 1665.

"I arrived from a fire at a pub. A pub owned by my son, where we lived with lodgers from a nearby brothel. It was a year before the Great Fire, not that I knew that then, while Bubonic Plague swept through the city. At that time, the government in England ordered giant bonfires to be burned every night in the streets to ward off transmission of the plague. On windy nights, some of these fires burned out of control."

"One night, when a strong winter breeze blew through London, embers from one of these bonfires caught the thatch of our pub." Kim-Joy points to a section of the Tide and Time Tavern roof where the thatch is fixed with corrugated iron. "Within minutes of the blaze starting, the whole pub was alight."

"Is the Tide and Time Tavern your home from Earth?" asks Gareth, incredulous that he might be looking at a five-hundred-year-old building and its landlady.

Kim-Joy nods. "Amidst the blaze, my son and I tried to free some female lodgers trapped inside. We managed to save some of them, but a handful of the young women and I became trapped in the fire and falling debris."

"I perished that night and found myself here in the Meadow with the young women and my pub. Mercifully, there were already handfuls of other people in the London area at that time, so we were able to establish some sense of community. Sadly, I am the only one still around from that time."

Kim-Joy shows the two men a beautiful pencil sketch on the next page of her scrapbook. The old lady is unmistakable in the picture, smiling with her arms around two young women and a young man. Her son, presumably. She is wearing the same silver locket necklace that she wears today. "It is so important to remember who you are and where you came from," she says. "If I hadn't written my memories, I think by now I would have completely forgotten any of my life on Earth and would, in all likelihood, have 'gone on'."

Kim-Joy flicks through her scrapbook to the first blank page near the back. Pulling a pencil from her pocket, she looks up at the men and smiles with a mother's warmth. "If it's not too personal to ask, would you mind telling me about the circumstances that led to the two of you arriving in the Meadow?"

Gareth and Hassan are more than happy to oblige. Recalling the train crash is quite a cathartic relief, and it feels good to air the persisting connections they feel to their lives on Earth. While they talk, Kim-Joy scribbles notes in her scrapbook and sucks on a handful of navy blue marbles.

"And what about your Interrogation Stones?" she asks, closing her scrapbook. "Have you kept hold of those?"

Both men reach into their trouser pockets and produce their marbles. Gareth inspects Hassan's as he holds it out in his palm. It is an angry red marble with a smudge of pink floating in the centre.

"Excellent," says Kim-Joy. "Always keep those safe. They hold your freshest memories of Earth, even if they might be rather painful and embarrassing ones."

\* \* \*

It transpires that the Tide and Time Tavern is the go-to place for sailors on the river Lethe. On the high tide, which it will be tonight, returning crews from dangerous trips out into the ocean will congregate at the tavern for downtime, meeting loved ones and being merry. It will also become a place for recruitment. The dangers of being a sailor in the Meadow, where too much water or going overboard are regular occurrences, means there is a steady stream of demand for new sailors. And there isn't likely to be a shortage of volunteers. Sailing is a lucrative job, so long as you stay dry.

Gareth and Hassan are set to work by Kim-Joy restocking the bar for the evening. There are dozens of heavy wooden crates full of marbles that need shifting from the cellar. Gareth struggles to carry one marble crate at a time. In contrast, Hassan engorges his ego by taking three, sometimes four, at a time. He doesn't say anything directly to Gareth, but the smirk he gives him when Gareth struggles to lift his single crate onto the bar is belittling enough.

It turns out marbles are not only created through the slave labour of the workhouses. Artisan marble crafters ply their trade all around the Meadow, crafting unique and unusual sensations (one crate claims to give the customer the feeling of *'anarchic bravery with a hint of irony'*). And it isn't just the British Isles that has its reciprocal geography in the Meadow. A whole range of European marbles are there in vast wooden containers. They must have been cargo on risky journeys across the ocean at some point.

Gareth is teetering with a crate full of *Horse Shoe Brewery* marbles when there is an aggressive hammering at the tavern's front door. "Quick," shouts Kim-Joy urgently. "Get back down to the cellar now!" The concern in the old lady's voice is unmistakable. Quickly as they can, Gareth and Hassan disappear into the cellar.

Peeking through the slats in the cellar hatch, Gareth watches Kim-Joy open the front door. Three tall men invite themselves into the tavern. They wear flat caps, zipped-up black jackets, and faded blue jeans. Without a word, they wander around the pub's ground floor, looking for something.

"Excuse me," says Kim-Joy. "Can I ask you who you are? And what right you have to come into my tavern when we are closed?"

"We're with the Distillery," says one man.

"Have you got your ID?" she asks confidently.

"We don't carry ID," says another man. "But maybe this will suffice." He pulls out a canister of Thermocline Mist, which he waves brazenly in Kim-Joy's face.

"Look, I don't want any trouble," Kim-Joy says nervously. "I just want to know why you are here."

"There has been word," begins the third man, returning from the kitchen, "that someone is harbouring fugitives north of the river. We have good reason to suspect some new arrivals are not who they say they are. Souls consumed by the Evil Thirst, under the spell of Satan." He spits on the floor.

"There's nothing of that sort around here," says Kim-Joy, appalled by the man's actions. "We're just a small pub. We cater for the sea-faring community and some local poets. We haven't seen any new arrivals except those looking for work. But if I see anyone, I'll be sure to let the Distillery know."

The men look at Kim-Joy with suspicion. "Just you remember, little lady," says one of the men, encroaching on Kim-Joy, "protecting Satanists is tantamount to thirsting for the Devil yourself."

"Good day, gentlemen," says Kim-Joy, defiantly going to the front door. "Good luck with your search."

Still looking around as they walk out, the three men leave without another word. Kim-Joy shuts the door and bolts it. She stands momentarily, watching as the men disappear into the coniferous street. She doesn't look back towards the cellar.

"OK," she says quietly and nervously. She beckons Gareth and Hassan out of the cellar. "Well, you two have certainly made a quick impression in the Meadow…Under the eye of the Ferrymen already!"

"Who are the Ferrymen?" asked Gareth.

"Vigilantes. They roam the city, doing the Distillery's dirty work," she replies. "They don't have identification and are not formally recognised, but nobody carries Thermocline Mist other than them. They frequently come snooping around this tavern because of the company we keep," she says with an air of pride.

"We might have to start thinking about finding you a safe place to live outside the city, though. The Ferrymen don't tend to give up hunting fugitives in the city very quickly. Do you know anything about the northern lands of the Meadow? Or the north-south divide?"

Both men shake their heads.

"Well, the southern Meadow is where support for the Distillery is strongest," says Kim-Joy. "People in the south support the Distillery's claim to rule and their understanding that the Meadow exists as a realm created by God for individual souls to pay penitence and seek reward."

"In the northern lands, however, support for the Distillery is weak. Despite hosting Distillery workhouses and palaces, northern settlements are governed by the Water Boards – elected councils whose primary function is the redistribution of wealth amongst their constituents. They might work with the Distillery on some things, but the Water Boards value their devolved powers and won't cooperate with vigilantes like the Ferrymen."

"Like the Distillery, The Water Boards believe the Meadow exists to pay penitence for deficiencies on Earth. But in contrast, they don't see penitence as a personal reckoning but rather a collective debt of humanity. A debt to be paid through collective suffering and collective toil."

Kim-Joy pulls from her pocket a folded map of London. Gareth can see that it is an old road map of the city as it was on Earth. It has been scribbled on and annotated heavily by Kim-Joy.

"The divide between north and south is replicated in London," she says, running her finger along the line representing the river Thames. "The divide runs along the Lethe. This half, to the south, is known as the Paddock. It is the Distillery's clearest stronghold in the Meadow. Here is where you will find the greatest accumulation of wealth and privilege."

"Yeah, we've come across the Paddock before," says Gareth, frowning.

"Well, we'll have to find you somewhere in the northern lands soon. Get you out of the gaze of the Ferrymen. For now, you'll just have to keep a low profile," she pauses. "I know it will be hard but try to relax. The crowd coming to the pub tonight will help." She smiles warmly at them.

\* \* \*

The evening sun descends behind the conifers, casting long shadows across the pub garden. It won't be long before revellers arrive. Kim-Joy excuses herself to go and ready the bar. She suggests that Gareth and Hassan go to the riverbank to watch the spectacle as the trawlers arrive. It is the monthly arrival of the North Sea trawlers which guarantees a full and busy tavern. She reassures them that with the arrival of the boats, there will be so many new people around that they won't need to hide from the Distillery this evening.

At the riverbank, half a kilometre walk through the conifers at the end of the pub garden, the men are greeted by the splendour of the Lethe. Swarming across the channel are dozens of small vessels, canoes, sailing dinghies and rowing boats. People cheerfully sing, chant, and even dance on the larger crafts. Several ships have drums and musical instruments being played merrily. No doubt many marbles are being sucked as well. Gentle mists surround many of the boats.

On the distant south bank of the river, at the edge of the Paddock, it is still and quiet. Austere buildings stand obstinate and lifeless on the riverbank. Gareth can just make out the silhouettes of police officers mobilised to guard the bank.

A short while after Gareth and Hassan get comfortable, the river spectacle turns to a fleet of trawler boats making their way upstream. The trawlers are in tight formation, dozens of them, flags hoisted high, and all the crews on deck. Bright-coloured flares: reds, greens, and blues send billowing clouds of colour across the river. The carnival atmosphere heightens the closer the trawlers get, and the number of small vessels increases to a point where the river can barely be seen. The music reverberates across the north bank. Gareth and Hassan can't help but smile and tap their feet in time to the song and dance. It is the most joyous thing they have seen since they arrived in the Meadow.

When the trawlers are closest, they see the faces of the sailors standing on deck. The bands of men and women crewing the boats are muscular and weathered. The energy of the welcoming parties is washing over them, and most are dancing or swaying arm in arm as they make their way up the river. There is also a sombre note. Gareth can see each trawler is towing a life raft sporting an ensign at half-mast. Many of the revellers on the river are throwing flowers over these rafts. These must be memorials to lives lost at sea.

As the last trawler passes their vantage point, Gareth and Hassan wander back up through the forest of the pub garden, a lightness to their mood. Already several people have arrived at the tavern. Groups of people sit on tree stumps, smoking pipes and sucking locally brewed marbles in the garden. It is fascinating for Gareth to see the variety of people in the tavern. It isn't the usual single demographics he finds in pubs on Earth. Families and couples from so many eras of British history are there. People who came during the Blitz in the Second World War, some from industries of Victorian England, and even artisans from the Tudor period in their elaborate frocks and smocks. Everyone at the tavern talks excitedly, laughing heartily, and generally provides social warmth to the already warm evening.

A folk band are tuning their instruments by the fireplace as the men step inside. Kim-Joy is hard at work serving behind the bar. She decants marbles into ramekins, sometimes small buckets, for groups of people cheerfully propped up at the bar. She is on very familiar terms with most of the clientele. "It's quite a spectacle, isn't it?" she says, noticing the two men. "It makes the river really come to life." She almost has to shout to be heard over the hubbub of the bar.

"It really does," agrees Hassan.

"Well, you know where the marble stores are," prompts Kim-Joy, a cheeky and devious sparkle in her eye. "I'm sure you spotted some you fancied earlier. Help yourselves. And if you are willing, you can help me behind the bar. There's a lot of custom here tonight!"

As the night wears on and the misty haze of marbles takes over his mind, Gareth finds himself propping up the bar, leaning lethargically on his elbow, his eyes drooping. Entertaining the crowds in front of him is a fantastic folk band, the *General Electrics*. The group of young girls play stringed instruments with impossible energy and timing. Such is the infectiousness of their vibe that they don't need drums to keep a beat; revellers in the pub provide the percussion, thumping bar stools and tables all night. A permanent mist surrounds the band as marbles are continually smashed on the floor around them.

Most of the *General Electrics'* songs tell stories of the sea, souls lost, and adventures navigated. And many songs tell of early days in the Meadow, of fond times before the Distillery. One song, in particular, captures Gareth's imagination. It is a song that everyone seems to know. It goes like this:

Out of circadian, She heard us play,
Our tune brought life to Her breath.
Her true winds stoked our fires,
While our music reached her depths.
*Her loving rain is falling free,*
*The soil thirsts, the raindrops sink into the sea.*
New arrivals filled the ground,
Gathered in uncertain plights.
Where all was still, now filled with sound,
The men of strength announced their rights.
*Her loving rain is falling free,*
*The soil thirsts, the raindrops sink into the sea.*
Over time, we built our towns,
To shelter from Her clouds and tears.
Violating with our nouns,
The very thing we shouldn't fear.
*Her loving rain is falling free,*
*The soil thirsts, the raindrops sink into the sea.*

Gareth doesn't know what time it is as the night draws to a close. At some point in the early morning, the music eventually stops, and most of the revellers leave the Tide and Time Tavern. Exhausted, Gareth and Hassan help Kim-Joy to clear the tables and encourage the last stragglers out of the bar. Kim-Joy bolts the pub door and asks Gareth and Hassan if they mind clearing the final tables and turning off the lights while she goes to bed herself.

Placing a bar stool on a table, Hassan stops and looks at Gareth. Once again, as has become the norm for Hassan, he is in quite an emotional mood from too many marbles. Something is on his mind. "Are you OK?" Gareth asks.

Hassan pauses. He is struggling to get it out. "You remember that night at the campus, the first night we had with the Professor?" Hassan asks rhetorically. "You remember that I didn't stay with you and the Professor? I spent the night with a lady I met in the bar."

Gareth avoids Hassan's gaze. He isn't too comfortable talking about this. "Well, something happened," he continues. "I'd had a lot of marbles by then, and I wasn't really in my right mind. And well, you see, she had returned to my room and sat on my bed. I thought I was reading the signs she was giving off. But then, when I tried to make a move, she didn't play ball. So, I, you know…" and he looks to Gareth guiltily. Gareth stares at Hassan.

"What did you do?" Gareth asks him fearfully.

"As I said, I'd had many marbles," Hassan pitifully offers his excuse again. "I might have come on a bit…strong." He looks to the ground.

"Did you do something? Did you hurt her?" Gareth asks plainly. He is concerned by what he is hearing. Hassan is leaving many gaps.

"No, brother," responds Hassan quickly. "No, I promise, no. I would never hit a woman. It's just that when she refused my advances, well, I got a bit shouty. I think I said something about her wasting my evening, that women on Earth were more my type, and that she was lucky I didn't force her to stay."

"Then she started crying and shouting back at me. It turned out she worked for the Distillery, and she said she was going to report me. At the time, I was just pissed off for being rejected and thought it an immature threat to 'report me' for wanting to have sex. But now I remember exactly what she said. She said, 'You're a deviant, a sexual temptress. You only met me today, and you're trying to have sex with me. I'm going to report you to the highest authorities I know. The Evil Thirst consumes you!"

Gareth looks at Hassan. "I think," says Hassan, "I think it was me that has got us into all this trouble with the Distillery. I'm so sorry…"

"You weren't to know," Gareth reasons. But Hassan's story troubles him. First, it bothers him that Hassan isn't aware of how his temper and sexual advances, not just the physical force of his hands, can be deemed a way of hurting someone. And second, he is troubled that a rigid conservatism exists in the Meadow, where a sexual advance is considered an 'Evil Thirst'. The guilt around his own sexuality, the guilt that he dredged up repeatedly in the workhouse interrogations, begins to surface again. He feels the smooth red marble with the yellow spot in his pocket. His Interrogation Stone feels heavy again.

*The great Sanger's circus, with its clowns, performers, musicians, and animals, had set up their show in Taunton, Somerset. The year was 1920, and the circus had arrived in the small town amid great fanfare. On the afternoon of 15th July 1920, around one-and-a-half thousand local people had made their way to fill the big top for the day's performance. One of the highlights was the boxing bout between Pimpo the clown and an 'army' sergeant. As the audience revelled in the japes of Pimpo's act, the scream of 'Fire!' that sliced through the circus tent took a moment to be taken seriously. But, once the crowd realised the danger they were in, seeing smoke and flames, panic erupted. A stampede rushed to the two small exits of the tent. In the chaos children, adults and the elderly were crushed, trampled, and burned. In all, five souls were lost in the tragedy.*

# Chapter Seven

◆

# Trouping North

A cold splash of water wakes Gareth. His bedsheets are sodden and cold. The window! In his marble-filled slumber, he must have left it open. Three nights of the trawler people occupying the Tide and Time Tavern has been full-on, and simple things like personal hygiene and shutting bedroom windows have been overlooked.

Outside, a winter storm rages. Coniferous foliage is scattered over the dark bedroom floor, and the sash window rattles in the wind. Another wash of rain showers Gareth's face, sparking him into action. He throws off his wet bedding and rushes to the window, sliding it shut. Immediately the room feels calmer. The gentle rumble of Hassan's snoring was the only sound. *"He can sleep through anything,"* thinks Gareth. To be fair to Hassan, his bed is out of the splash zone, so he is still dry and warm.

Gareth looks out at the cobbled street being buffeted by the weather. He is surprised to see a horse tethered to the front gate, bowing its head into the rain. The skirt of the horse's saddle is emblazoned with a coat of arms. Not the Distillery emblem, though – for that is Gareth's first worried thought – but the badge of something called 'Colney Hatch: Sisterhood of the Flickers'. He has never heard of them. Either way, someone visiting the tavern at this time, in this weather, is rather curious. He was sure all the revellers had departed before he went to bed. He has no idea what the time is, but it is undoubtedly the sleepy side of midnight.

Careful not to wake Hassan, Gareth chooses to investigate. He carefully lifts the latch on the door and sneaks out onto the landing. The candles are nearly burnt out in their dishes. Another thing he had forgotten to do before turning in for the night. Downstairs he can hear hushed voices. They sound urgent and secretive.

Gareth shuffles to the banister, intrigued, and peers into the dark hallway below. Strong winds are pounding the front door, making it thud against its frame. A gentle flickering light comes from the bar and a low hum of voices. One of the voices is Kim-Joy. The other is female but unknown to Gareth. He just catches the end of their conversation.

"Where do the rumours come from?" Kim-Joy asks.

"Freelancers from Crofter's Hope," says the woman.

"Here in the city?"

"That's right. The artists and archivists. All part of the guild."

"And you've heard it first hand?"

"Second hand. I was speaking to Nailah Hussain-Drake, of the City Circus. She deals with the guilds a lot."

"Yes, I'd trust Nailah with my life," says Kim-Joy. "And they say he's back?"

"Not exactly… A fresh bounty has been put on his head, a minister is in the dock, and the Distillery is interrogating the archives again."

"That's hardly conclusive."

"I know. But it's something…"

"True."

Chairs creak and scrape against the stone floor. Gareth backs away into the shadows of the landing.

"It's good to see you," says Kim-Joy, entering the hallway with the woman.

"The pleasure is mine," responds the woman. She is tall and wears a long riding coat. Gareth catches a glimpse of her long auburn hair before she lifts her hood.

Kim-Joy unbolts the heavy front door and allows the gale to blow in, rattling the ornaments hanging in the hall. The lady steps out into the darkness. The two women mutter something that Gareth can't quite decipher, cover their faces with their right hand, and bow to one another. A ritual Gareth hasn't seen before. Then the hooded lady wanders away.

Before Kim-Joy shuts the door, Gareth is already back in his room. He peers out of the window at the hooded lady clambering onto her horse, trying to catch a glimpse of her face. Too late. She rides off into the night and doesn't look back.

* * *

"Wake up, lazy bones," says Kim-Joy, entering the attic room and striding over to the curtains, her necklace rattling as she opens them. She notices the pile of damp sheets on the floor but ignores them. "I know you enjoy your marbles, but work must be done!"

Gareth and Hassan sit up in their beds and rub their eyes. Bright light is shooting into the room from the opened curtains.

"Sorry," says Gareth. "I didn't realise I had lain in so long."

"Oh, it's not a problem," says Kim-Joy, a warm smile across her face. "It's just there's a lot of tidying to be done downstairs, and I figure the help of two young men such as yourselves wouldn't go amiss." Gareth smiles guiltily. "I'll get some breakfast ready; then we'll get you started on the jobs."

"Kim-Joy," says Gareth, halting the old lady's departure.

"Yes…" she says, half out of the doorway.

"Who was that lady who visited in the middle of the night?"

"Come again?" says Kim-Joy, buying herself a moment.

"Sorry. I wasn't prying or anything," Gareth fibs. "The bad weather woke me, and I just happened to notice a lady leaving the pub."

"One of the joys of being a place of refuge for all and sunder," she says, inching out of the room. "We get visitors at every ungodly hour. Not that long ago it was the arrival of you two, don't forget! Come down for morning marbles, and you'll meet more of our unexpected guests."

Gareth smiles. It is true; they did arrive unannounced in the middle of the night.

Before heading downstairs, Gareth wanders over to the bedroom window. Outside, a blanket of snow covers everything. The weather has shifted to one of its extremes again. The conifers are sagging under the weight of fresh snow, and deer prints meander across the cobbled street. There's no trace of the late-night visitor. "It looks cold out today," he says to Hassan.

Kim-Joy has already made plans for the cold weather. By the bedroom door are warm fur coats and fleece-lined rubber boots. In a few minutes, Gareth and Hassan are dressed and wrapped up, ready for breakfast and some cold work.

"I thought you'd like some warm winter marbles," says Kim-Joy as the men appear downstairs. She holds up a deep ladle she has been using to stir a steel pot over the kitchen stove. The smell of cinnamon and spice wafts around the room.

"Smells amazing," says Hassan.

"Ooh arr, they're the best," says a weathered figure hunched over at the far end of the bar. Steam from warm marbles dances up from the ramekin in front of him.

"I'm glad you like them," smiles Kim-Joy, ladling marbles into a couple more ramekins. "Gareth, Hassan, may I introduce you to Cyril Speight? Skipper of the *Guiding Star*. North Sea trawlerman for more than one hundred years. Regular at the Tide and Time!"

"G'risen," says the man, doffing the rim of his cloth hat.

"Hello," says Gareth politely. Hassan offers a stiff nod towards the man.

"Been 'ere long?" asks Cyril.

"Nearly a week now," says Gareth, turning to Kim-Joy for verification. She nods, smiling.

"I wo'n ask what you done to end up 'ere," says Cyril with a wink. "Less I know, less I say."

"Oh, they're good boys," says Kim-Joy. "But someone's got it in for them. They're only a week out of the workhouse, and the Ferrymen are after them."

Cyril spits onto the floor at the mention of the Ferrymen. "Scum o'the Meadow them lot," he says. "Well, an enemy's enemy is a friend." He smiles at Hassan and Gareth, then pulls from his pocket two greeny-blue marbles. "*Sailor's Mist*," he says. "Best marbles in the Meadow. I know the Mersysider who makes them. Have a slurp…"

Neither Gareth nor Hassan feels they can refuse. Gareth drops a marble from Cyril's grubby leathery hand into his mouth. The sensation is immediate. The ground around him feels unerringly steady, and he is awash with a serenity he has never felt before.

Cyril winks at him, his bushy eyebrows creasing as he does so. "You'll never feel more grounded than when you're a-slurping on *Sailor's Mist*– absolute God-send for a trawlerman. Don't discard it. Use it next time you're feelin' outa sorts." He leans over to Kim-Joy. "Have you got a marble pouch spare for the lads?"

Kim-Joy reaches behind the bar and pulls out two small silk bags. "You can keep your Interrogation Stones in these, too," she says.

Cyril pats Gareth on the back. It's more familiar than Gareth feels he's comfortable with. "She's a gem, our Kim-Joy. A precious treasure buried in the dark depths of the city."

"Oh, give over," says Kim-Joy, blushing bashfully. "That's the marbles talking, Cyril." The trawlerman grins at her and drops another steaming marble into his mouth.

"OK, you two," says Kim-Joy. "We've got a lot of jobs to do today. I've got my work cut out in here. But there are empty marble-stained ramekins to collect up and fire pits to clear out in the garden. Do you mind sorting that?"

"No problem," says Gareth without hesitation. Kim-Joy smiles appreciatively.

Still feeling serene from the *Sailor's Mist* a short while later, Gareth and Hassan trudge into the snow with sacks and wicker baskets. Their warm breath meets the cold air and forms billowing, short-lived clouds. Their job is to fill their sacks with ash and baskets with discarded marble-stained ramekins. The discarded mess from last night is all around the garden and into the trees.

Within an hour, their sacks and baskets are almost full. Without warning, a lump of snow smashes Gareth across his face. Then another dull thud crashes into the tree beside Hassan, followed by a cheeky girlish laugh. "I can't resist!" Kim-Joy calls out, emerging from behind the bins with a snowball in her hand. Gareth looks to Hassan. He has a great big grin on his face.

"That makes you fair game," Hassan shouts as he piles snow into his hands and launches it towards Kim-Joy. She ducks behind the bins just in time. Hassan starts to gather more snow, so

Gareth takes his opportunity. He scoops snow from the tree branches beside him and dumps it over Hassan's exposed back. Kim-Joy roars with laughter, and Gareth flees towards the pub. This time Hassan catches the old lady straight in the face. She splutters and grins wildly.

A joyous half hour later, Gareth, Hassan, and Kim-Joy re-enter the tavern, soaking wet, rosy-cheeked and steaming. They pull off their wet coats, kick off their boots and wander into the bar, laughing with one another. Kim-Joy has snow in her hair. Hassan has snow in his beard.

It is lovely and warm in the tavern. Cyril Speight has a fire going and sits in an old leather armchair with his feet up. He has laid some coffee marbles out, ready for them all. They gratefully pop one into their mouths and huddle around the fire to thaw out. Gareth lets out a sigh of contentment. What a wonderful morning!

"So, what disaster brought you two into the Meadow then?" asks Cyril, stoking the fire with a sharp iron poker. "Was it another automobile accident? Seeing a lot of those these days."

"No, brother," says Hassan. "Train crash, just outside London."

"Arr, that was you lot was it? Made a hell of a commotion when you all arrived. Don't think I've seen the Distillery mobilise that many police since that flying machine crashed a few years ago. You remember that one Kim-Joy?"

"Of course," she says. "We had the pilot here for a few weeks. Arrogant chap but with a kind heart. Mike Meadowcroft." She picks up her scrapbook, which is sitting open on a cabinet, and flicks through. "Here we go," she says, holding up a signed pencil drawing of a passenger aeroplane. "He told such a tragic story of the crash. Completely avoidable disaster if he and the co-pilot hadn't been too proud to listen to each other."

"What's that little mark at the top of the page?" says Gareth, noticing a sketched symbol resembling a water droplet encircled by an arrow. It was very reminiscent of the logo of the Distillery. He had seen it in the scrapbook when Kim-Joy last showed them the entries.

"Oh, that," says Kim-Joy, closing the book. " Just a little mark I've adopted to pick out some of the more memorable entries from my centuries here." She flicks a glance at Cyril, who nods his head nervously.

"This train crash you two boys were in," says Cyril, "did you know the Distillery has impounded the carriages for some investigations?"

"What's that?" says Kim-Joy.

"Yeah. Strangest thing," continues Cyril. "I was doing some work on the *Guiding Star* over at the east docks this week when I saw a couple of train carriages being taken apart in the covered shipyard."

"A train in the shipyard? That's unheard of. And the Distillery was working on it?"

"No doubt. And they were pretty keen that no one saw them. I just happened on it when I was looking for some spare anchor chain. Some officers spotted me and interrogated me for like an hour. They wanted to see if I knew something about the train. Pricks, the lot of them."

"How unusual," says Kim-Joy.

"I know," says Cyril. "Something strange is going on down there. Everything from the carriages was laid out like evidence from a crime scene. Can't figure out what they would be looking for in an arrival vehicle. Was there anything peculiar about your crash?" he says, somewhat ambiguously to Gareth and Hassan.

"Anything peculiar?!" says Hassan with a smirk. "Of course there was. Trains don't derail every day!"

"Obviously," says Cyril with a cynical grimace. "I mean, was there anything peculiar in the moments before the crash?"

"What like?" asks Hassan.

"I don't know," says Cyril. "Any unusual commotion? Or special cargo?"

"Or notable passengers?" adds Kim-Joy.

"I don't think so," says Hassan. Gareth shakes his head too. He is trying to wrack his brain about the crash, but it feels so distant and long ago. He doesn't think there was anything unusual going on before they derailed.

* * *

In no time at all, the Tide and Time Tavern feels like home. Contributing to the day-to-day running of the pub and getting to know regulars like Cyril Speight, Gareth and Hassan feel like part of the furniture. If it wasn't for the regular updates on the strange goings-on at the covered dock, or the Distillery investigation into their derailed train carriages, the two men might have completely forgotten there was a time and a world before the Meadow.

"They're offerin' rewards now," says Cyril, arriving at the tavern one morning with fresh boxes of *Sailor's Mist* for the cellar. "Rewards for anyone with information about your derailment or knowledge of your whereabouts. A handsome sum too."

Gareth struggles under the weight of the box of marbles passed to him. "What's the reward?" he asks nervously.

"Don't worry, kid," chuckles Cyril, patting him on the backside. "I'd never take so much as a marble from the Distillery. I'd rather take a spray of Thermocline!"

Gareth smiles. Cyril is loud and overly familiar, but he is also honest.

"How do you get hold of Thermocline spray?" asks Hassan. "I feel like we're at a disadvantage with the Ferrymen carrying it."

"Slippery slope, that," says Cyril, frowning. "But I must say, you'll need to be ready to defend yourselves somehow. It's one thing having the Ferrymen after you. Now there's a reward on your heads, too; you'll have almost every soul in the city after you."

"About that," says Kim-Joy. "I don't think the Tide and Time Tavern is going to be safe enough soon. It's only a matter of time before someone says or does something stupid. We need to find you somewhere outside of the city."

"But where can we go?" Gareth asks. "We don't know anywhere but here."

"I know people," says Kim-Joy. "Word is out that I am looking for some onward transport to the north. There is a travelling Circus in the Meadow. The Sanger Family Circus. They have been in the Meadow for over one hundred years, entertaining huge crowds and bringing joy to the Meadow. I have put a call out to them."

"Are we going to have to pretend to be circus folk?" asks Hassan grinning.

"Sanger's circus prides itself on giving opportunities to hidden talents and the unwanted and lost souls of the Meadow. Don't knock it until you've tried it! They have 'talent scouts' here in the city. Really, they are a cover for the charitable wing of the Sanger family, protecting the hunted here in the city – the souls the Distillery have marked. This includes the women abused at the Palaces of the Distillery: the Flickers. It also includes the likes of you, the fugitives and those on the run. Sanger's circus provides covert travel to their circus school in the north, where they house people with accommodating communities up there."

"One of the circus folk was here at the tavern a few nights ago. I told her we might need a few spaces for the journey north. She informed me the scouts would be coming by the tavern in the next couple of days, so the two of you should ensure you are ready to leave."

* * *

It is good to know that Kim-Joy had made plans to avoid the Distillery, but Gareth is sad to know their time at the Tide and Time Tavern is ending just as it has started. He feels a real connection to Kim-Joy and the tavern. Setting off into the unknown again is daunting. He has never really embraced change. He usually opts for routine and predictability. Now he feels a familiar pit of nerves opening up in his stomach.

The final few days in the Tide and Time Tavern are bittersweet. Kim-Joy helps the two men to pack, gathering a range of clothes from a stockpile in the cellar – clothes to suit them for all kinds of weather – and a clutch of marbles to enjoy on the journey. She also gives them each half a dozen special marbles – marbles she had sucked whenever they had told her about their life and memories of Earth. Imprinted, therefore, on each marble is the recollection of their memories. She tells them to keep these marbles safe. They can dissect these marbles and rekindle that memory if they ever find themselves unable to remember where they come from or who they are.

"Never," she tells them, "be tempted to suck on these marbles. Sucking will erase the memory forever."

Gareth opens his marble pouch and places the six beautifully sparkling marbles next to his Interrogation Stone and the *Sailor's Mist* from Cyril.

"I take it neither of you has heard of Inseparable Stones?" Kim-Joy asks them. Gareth and Hassan shake their heads.

Kim-Joy reaches for one of the silver lockets dangling from her necklace. Holding the locket carefully in her palm, she prizes it open. A warm light pours out, and into Kim-Joy's hand rolls a small glowing sphere. It is a marble of sorts. Its glow feels as though it is warming and brightening the room around them.

"All the marbles you have seen until now have been created from the sensations extracted from a single creator. But it is also possible to create marbles from shared sensations." She hands the marble to them to inspect.

"Shared sensations are incredibly potent. Too potent to suck – hence the marbles glow. So there isn't much interest in these marbles from a consumption point-of-view. But they are incredibly precious for other reasons. They bind the memories of multiple souls and provide multiple perspectives when they are dissected. Close friends, couples, and soul mates often create an Inseparable Stone to cement their commitment to one another."

Gareth turns over the glowing marble in his hand. It looks molten and is warm to the touch. It seems to draw him towards it a little. He wonders whose sensations are shared to have created it.

"Beautiful, isn't it?" says Kim-Joy.

"It's incredible," says Gareth, smiling.

"If you're willing," says Kim-Joy. "I'd like to create an Inseparable Stone with the two of you now… The future is uncertain, and it would be comforting to know you have a marble that always connects us."

"Have you got a marble kiln here?" asks Gareth.

"No, but the log burner can get hot enough with a good stoking. I've done it before, don't worry," she says, smiling, noticing Hassan's scepticism. "Are you up for it?"

Gareth looks at Hassan, who winks at him. "It can't hurt, can it?"

"Oh, thank you," beams Kim-Joy. "I'll go and get the bowl to collect the resin… I hope you don't mind, but the best memory for us to use will be your recollections of the train crash that bought you here."

"Really?" says Hassan, confused.

"Absolutely," says Kim-Joy, wandering off behind the bar. "I love a good Arrival story. Even if I have heard it before."

"Kim-Joy," says Gareth as she rejoins them, holding a steaming bowl of clear resin. "Why do you look after us so kindly? I mean, I'm so grateful that you do. But aren't you concerned about the Distillery and the risks of being associated with us?"

"Oh, Gareth," the old lady responds, her eyes twinkling. "I have seen the Meadow long before the Distillery took control. I saw a time when their idea of penitence was just one of many interpretations of life in the Meadow. It was a happy time."

"When the dictum came from the Distillery, about a century ago, saying that the purpose of life in the Meadow was to feed the soul and break the connections between our mind and body, it was a sad day. It meant that the people of the Meadow were made to feel guilt for their fondness for Earth. And with this guilt, many became full of despair. This can't be right. It's not how I understand things."

"I believe our connections to our lives and bodies on Earth must remain for a reason. Even if this reason is just to give us hope. So, I have dedicated my life to keeping my little part of the Meadow vibrant and healthy. In a way that it was before the Distillery. I can't understand why, other than power and control, you would want to stop people from remembering their life on Earth."

Kim-Joy inspects Gareth and Hassan. "When I look at the two of you, I see a spark and energy in your souls. A spark that exists because of an ongoing connection to your lives on Earth. You both still love people on Earth. Your mum, Gareth. Or your little girl, Hassan. To me, that love is what gives your soul energy and purpose. I see it as my opportunity to preserve such sparks. Just because an authority tells you to stop loving," she says, looking at the men, "doesn't mean you do."

Kim-Joy smiles kindly at Gareth and Hassan. "Now let's make that Inseparable Stone."

\* \* \*

With their bags fully packed and their marbles hidden away safely in their pouches, it is now a case of waiting for the circus to come. The single glowing Inseparable Stone they made has been encased in a silver locket necklace and given to Gareth at Kim-Joy's request. "So long as this marble exists, our souls are connected," she had said, ethereally, when she gave it to him.

They don't have to wait too long for the circus to arrive. One dark evening, when the tavern is quiet, there is a knock at the front door. As is usual, the two men step inside the kitchen, where they can't be seen. Just in case it is an unwelcome visitor.

Opening the door, Kim-Joy is met by the surly face of a tall man in his mid-fifties. He has deep creases across his face and a scar cutting his top lip. The man is dressed in a circus showman's uniform, including a bright red top hat and long black cane, yet it would take a courageous person to snigger at his look. Such is the man's presence and the intensity of his stare.

"Mr Drake!" beams Kim-Joy. "What an honour!" She ushers the men out of the kitchen.

The tall man at the door bows his head and introduces himself. "My name is Milton Drake," he tells them. "I am the head showman from Sanger's circus, where we delight in bringing great entertainment to the people of the Meadow. I have travelled with this circus for many years. This circus is my life. The circus family, my family. And, it is out of duty to the charity of the Sanger family that I accept the two of you to join my travelling troupe to the north." He thrusts his hand out towards Gareth and Hassan, looking to confirm their accord.

Hassan steps forward and shakes the man's hand. Both men nod at one another silently and deliberately, as so many men do. Milton reaches his hand out towards Gareth. Nervously Gareth wipes his hand on his trouser leg, a lingering habit, before shaking hands. Milton's palm is dry and firm. His grip vice-like. Gareth flicks his eyes up at Milton but can't hold his gaze.

"Wow, you're clammy," Milton remarks, releasing his grip. "Don't be nervous, kid; I don't bite." Embarrassed, Gareth offers a weak smile, but Milton has already turned back to Kim-Joy.

Glancing out past Milton Drake and beyond the tavern doorway, Gareth can see two wonderfully decorated gypsy caravans harnessed to an immense Indian elephant. It's not the sight he expected. Atop the elephant is a young athletic figure who waves a hand towards them. Kim-Joy waves enthusiastically back.

"Is that you, Ashley?!" she calls out from the tavern.

The rider slides off the elephant's back and runs to the tavern doorway. She throws her arms around Kim-Joy. "Kim-Joy! I haven't seen you in such a long time. I had forgotten that this was your place." Kim-Joy's eyes sparkle as she embraces the young woman.

After an exchange of niceties, Ashley steps back from Kim-Joy, giving the men a clear look at her. The young woman, maybe twenty years old, is slight, with square shoulders. She has bright green eyes and short brown hair shaved close to her scalp on one side. She wears loose denim dungarees with a baggy long-sleeved cotton shirt pushed up to her elbows underneath. She smiles at the men and reaches out her hand energetically.

"Are you an elephant tamer?" asks Hassan as he shakes her hand.

"Pimlico doesn't need taming," says Ashley. "I'm more of a friend and colleague to the old boy. We work together, and I help him navigate. I'm more his carer than his tamer, I suppose."

When Ashley shakes Gareth's hand, he is relieved to feel her hands are as clammy as his, although she doesn't seem embarrassed by it. He also notices her wrist and lower arm are scarred, much like his, as though she has spent time in the workhouse making marbles. Noticing Gareth's gaze, Ashley shuffles her sleeve down her arm to hide the scars. "It's lovely to meet you all," she says, smiling. "I'm so glad to bump into you again Kim-Joy. Please do come up and see the circus sometime."

"Don't worry, I will," says Kim-Joy. "There are two new performers I will be longing to see." She looks at Gareth and Hassan and winks.

"I assume there's some baggage we're going to need to load into the carriage?" says Milton Drake, abruptly ending the introductions.

"Of course, of course," says Kim-Joy. "Lads, will you go and get your cases from the loft?"

"I'll help," says Ashley.

"My daughter can help, too," says Milton. He turns his head towards the carriages and shouts out. "Kasiya! Come and help with the bags!"

Another circus hand, a young woman with curly black hair and olive skin, emerges from the rear caravan. The tall, gangly woman is closed and cold. She barely mumbles a greeting to anyone as she wanders upstairs to collect the bags.

"She still struggling?" Kim-Joy asks Milton as Kasiya disappears upstairs. Milton nods regretfully.

With their bags all loaded, Gareth and Hassan warmly embrace Kim-Joy and thank her for their stay at the Tide and Time. Then Milton invites them to leave the pub and enter the front gypsy caravan.

The caravan is filled with cushioned chairs, rickety bunks, and a scattering of blankets amongst a collection of useful crockery and camping essentials. It is all lit by a few hanging lanterns. Cosy, but probably not comfortable for any length of time. Taking them by surprise, one of the beds is already occupied. A sleeping lady's long white-blonde hair falls out from under a wool blanket.

"Who's that?" Hassan whispers to Milton.

"Another guest we collected from the Paddock this morning. She's had a rough time since arrival," says Milton, not worrying about whispering. "She's heavily medicated and won't wake up until the morning, so don't worry about your hushed tones. We'll introduce her properly when she comes around."

As the men get themselves comfortable, Ashley clambers back up onto the elephant. The caravan pulls away slowly. Gareth looks fondly out of the window. The Tide and Time Tavern is like a beacon of warmth, standing there with the old lady on its threshold at the end of the cobbled street amongst the conifer trees.

The pub disappears, swallowed by the city as they round a corner into an unknown street. In the dark, the unfamiliar city is not a welcoming place at all. Gareth feels an uncomfortable tightening in his stomach, and he wonders how long it will be before he experiences a warmth like the tavern again.

Milton Drake lights another hanging lantern inside the carriage. "I hear from Kim-Joy that the Distillery has targeted you," he says. "Kim-Joy told me that you have been accused of being consumed by the Evil Thirst, and you've only been here in the Meadow a few weeks. That's no mean feat!" A grimace that is trying hard to be a smile comes across his face. The men can see the scar stretch out on his upper lip and sense his blue eyes, probing them, "Don't worry, we're no fans of the Distillery in Sanger's circus." He leans back and takes a deep lungful of herbal smoke from his pipe.

* * *

The journey is long and bumpy through the night as the caravan rattles down endless winding cobbled streets through the city's vast expanse. Milton makes them keep the curtains closed so no unsavoury characters can spot the passengers inside. They are wanted men, after all. This doesn't help with the motion sickness they all start to feel. To make matters worse, Milton acknowledges that people rarely notice the caravan's passengers anyway because they have an Indian elephant pulling at the front. It isn't every day you see an elephant, even in the Meadow.

Milton, it turns out, had not been a circus performer before he arrived in the Meadow a century ago. He had been a British army sergeant on Earth. He had been to India on detachment with the army and had only been back in England for a few years before he died. His link to the circus was via a tragic experience he had before his death. He was watching a circus performance in his local town when tragedy struck. The circus tent had caught fire mid-performance. Milton saved three children from the fire, but the flames severely burned him. He hadn't died in the circus fire, but he spent a traumatic year on Earth suffering from his injuries. Then tragedy struck again. His family home suffered a devastating fire. This time he couldn't save anyone – his wife, daughter, or even himself. Milton shows the men his back and his chest. Harsh burns, similar to those on Gareth's arms and wrists, scar his body. On arriving in the Meadow with his wife and daughter, Milton tells them they had happened upon the same travelling circus that had come to his town on Earth a year earlier. Recognising the circus leader, a lady called Kathleen Montague, a victim in the fire, he had quickly acquainted himself with the troupe, and the family had joined their work.

The men talk late into the night and early morning. They have so many questions about the journey ahead. But eventually, Gareth and Hassan fall asleep on the blanket-covered benches in the caravan. As the last person awake, Milton checks that the men aren't likely to fall out of bed before clambering outside to join his daughter in the rear caravan.

\* \* \*

Gareth lies with his eyes open in the warm and gently rocking gypsy caravan. Shafts of morning light stream in through the net curtains. Across from him, asleep still, is Hassan. Lying asleep at the back of the caravan is the anonymous female figure. Her white-blonde hair drapes over the edge of her bed.

The front hatch of the caravan opens, and Ashley wriggles in. Her dungarees slide in first before she lands with a gentle thump. "Good risen," she says, smiling at Gareth. "Sleep well?"

"Yes, thank you," he replies quietly, feeling awkward because he is the only one awake. "Did you not sleep?"

"I got a bit. Milton and I share the riding. I'm used to these long nights, though. I'll get plenty of rest when we get to the circus.

We'll probably stop soon. Pimlico needs a drink, and I could do with a chance to freshen up. How do you like the Meadow, now we're out of the city?" she says, pulling back the net curtains.

Gareth peers out of the window. Wild animals graze in a vast open countryside, and flocks of birds fly through a bright blue sky overhead. There are no buildings, houses, or roads. No suggestion of human life at all. It looks like the picture postcard from a rural idyll. The Meadow outside looks like it's living up to its name for once.

"It's beautiful," says Gareth, unable to think of anything more interesting to say.

Ashley smiles at him and lets him watch as a vast reservoir comes into view. The caravans slow down. "This is Pimlico's favourite place for a drink," she says. "If you want to step out a moment and stretch your legs, I'll coax our other passengers awake." Ashley nods towards Hassan and the sleeping lady at the back.

The bright sunlight is dazzling, and the fresh air is invigorating. The reservoir is vast and blue. It feels like early summer. The flowers are out. All around, butterflies flap, and bees buzz.

"Good risen, young sir," says Milton in his natural growl. He is untying Pimlico from the front of the caravan. "Fine day, isn't it?"

Pimlico wanders down to the reservoir by himself. The great beast is content to suck up some water and gently dabble it down his head and back. "I never met such a loyal animal," says Milton. "In all my time in India, a relationship between man and beast was never as reliable as in the Meadow."

Gareth looks out into the distance and notices, beyond the reservoir and down into the valley, what looks like a cluster of train lines all heading in one direction. Long trains travel along them, pulled by large packs of horses, their lights still on from journeying through the night.

"Those are the Distillery's Onward Transport," says Milton. "All the train lines here head northwest to the Source. There are hundreds of passengers filling the trains every day from the cities. The Drifters and the Founderers on their final journey to the Source."

"Founderers?" asks Gareth.

"Foundering souls. Those in the Meadow who aren't Drifters, not quite. But their consciousness hangs by a thread, leaving them semi-conscious. They are aware of the present but completely disconnected from their pasts."

"How far away is the Source?" Gareth asks.

"It is many weeks' ride from here, but just a day by train," says Milton.

"Have you ever been?"

"I got near the Mountain of the Source many years ago. It's an intimidating sight, especially for someone not ready to 'go on'. The Drifters outnumber you. Those unconscious souls are all around you and head automatically in one direction, up towards the great misty mountains. I never got near enough to see the mountain or the Perihelion Cliffs. But I saw the trains unloading at Pont Fawr, the last station before the Source. That's a sight I can never forget."

There is a pause while Gareth wonders if Milton will volunteer the details. When he doesn't, Gareth asks instead, "Why can't you forget? If you don't mind me asking."

Milton exhales and rubs the stubble on his chin. "There are three groups of passengers who travel on the trains," he says. "Those who arrived in the Meadow unconscious. Those who have become Drifters during their time in The Meadow. And the Founderers."

"The Founderers, with no memory of their pasts, have always been deemed by the Pond life as partially human, similar to slaves."

"Pond life?" asks Gareth.

"My affectionate term for the Distillery and the Water Boards," explains Milton. "Anyway, like slaves, the Founderers are treated as commodities. Most of them are traded before they even reach Pont Fawr. Traded as labourers to the Water Boards who are always looking for hands to work in the cities. But some don't get traded. I don't know why they don't, but they remain on the trains all the way to Pont Fawr. From what I saw of this group emerging from the trains, they seemed to be victims of brutal and violent treatment on their journey. And it was clear that once they reached Pont Fawr, the Distillery had no further use for them. Canisters of Thermocline Mist were emptied all over the struggling and bruised Founderers the moment they stepped onto the platform. Their screams carried for miles around."

A memory flickers through Gareth's mind. Black-clad men swarming him and his sister as they exit their train from Earth. It is the first and last moment he can remember immediately after the crash.

"Even more distressing though," Milton continues, "were the Drifters disembarking at Pont Fawr. The Drifters aren't even treated as partially human by the Distillery. They are treated like cattle. Their minds have already gone, and the Distillery barely attend to the needs of their bodies. They are crammed into the carriages, and with no space to move, their bodies shut down. They are barely alive when they get to Pont Fawr. Any wounds they had when they boarded the trains – which are many – are left to fester and rot. But the soul will always try to move towards the Source, even if the body has basically died. And so, at the station, I also saw the hordes of these crawling and shuffling cadavers exiting the trains, heading over the bridge at Pont Fawr, and drifting into the mist."

Gareth watches as the last long train trundles off into the distance. He thinks of Cerys. He knows she had been taken to one of the Distillery Palaces. A sickening image washes through his mind as he visualises her, bruised, confused, and afraid, exiting one of those unfriendly trains on a dark misty platform. Gareth desperately hopes that Cerys isn't on one of those trains. He feels so helpless and disconnected from her right now and from himself.

Just then, Milton's daughter, Kasiya, steps out from the rear caravan. Gareth hadn't seen her since they left the city and almost forgot she was with them. She is dressed in tight-fitting jeans and a scarlet cashmere jumper, and has perfectly applied make-up and excellent posture. Kasiya wanders past them without a word, down to the water's edge next to Pimlico. She cups some water in her hands and dabs her face delicately. As she walks back towards them, Milton grabs her arm and pulls her gangly body into an awkward embrace in front of his. In her early twenties, the woman looks uncomfortable in her father's arms. "My daughter, Kasiya," says Milton proudly, drawing unwanted attention onto the young woman. "She is fabulous at picking out perfect marbles for any occasion."

Kasiya peers out, her dark curly hair covering most of her face, though Gareth catches her eye. Despite her reluctant demeanour, she is undoubtedly beautiful. Gareth gazes into her deep black eyes and across her smooth olive skin. He explores the shadows hiding part of her face and follows the straight ridge of her nose down to the crevice above her mouth. Following the curve of her mouth, he inadvertently moistens his bottom lip. He sees a beautiful young woman peeking out from the shadow of her father, a man of high-standing, protective but stifling. He is thrilled by the idea of shining a light into the shadows. In something of a distraction, he smiles at Kasiya, and her mouth offers a reluctant twitch in return.

"Go and warm us some of your mum's famous honey marbles," Milton says, cajoling Kasiya like a child. "I'm going to go and stretch my legs alone for a minute."

Taking Milton's cue for privacy, Gareth wanders back to the front caravan with Kasiya. Inside, Hassan is sat up with a coffee marble already rattling around his teeth. Opposite him, Ashley is wafting herbal smoke over the occupant in the bed. The blonde lady has started to stir.

"Will she be OK?" Gareth asks.

Ashley looks back solemnly. "She will be OK. I just hope her pain subsides, and she finds herself."

"What do you mean?" asks Hassan.

"You may have heard of the women known as 'Flickers'," says Ashley. "Women who were taken into the Palace on their arrival, and who experienced brutal trauma at the hands of the men who work there. Many of the women who emerge lose something vital in their souls during that time. Their spark for life is almost extinguished. They are not unconscious when they leave, but they are not fully conscious either. They are Founderers, as we say. These poor women are often found in the Paddock wandering lost and alone. When the circus finds these women, we take them in and nurse them. We want to allow them to experience beauty and love in the Meadow. But we know they are very fragile, and it is often not long before they become Drifters."

Another waft of the herbal smoke, and the figure in the bed stirs. Ashley draws the long white-blonde hair away from the woman's face, and her eyelids flutter open. Gareth looks at the young woman, glimpsing her bright hazel-coloured eyes. He recognises her. Barely there, but just about. There is a connection already established somewhere else from another time. He has met her before. Their eyes have met before. Their souls have imprinted on each other before. And he knows where. The lady was the conductor of the train that crashed on Earth.

The lady betrays to Gareth a tiny ounce of familiarity herself – just a flicker of recognition. "Hello," she says, confused. "Do I know you?"

Before Gareth responds, Ashley puts her hand on the young lady's shoulder. "Don't worry, Rosalyn," she says. "It's me, Ashley. We found you in the Paddock a few days ago. You're with the circus, remember? We're here to look after you."

Rosalyn looks at Ashley, a vacancy returning to her face. She puts on a polite smile. One of compliance and confusion. "Who are these men?" she says, looking fearfully back to Gareth and Hassan.

"They are friends," says Ashley. "Don't worry; they won't hurt you."

Rosalyn looks back at Gareth and says it again. "Do I know you?"

Gareth looks at Hassan and then back to Ashley. "I think we may have met her before."

"You have?" says Ashley, surprised.

"Yes," says Gareth. "I think Rosalyn was on the train that crashed and led us to the Meadow."

Rosalyn pauses. Then, almost as though a memory flutters past her mind, she goes blank. "I don't remember," she says. She looks lost. Gareth feels sorry for her, knowing what may have happened.

"Hi," a clear voice next to Gareth interrupts his thought. "The name's Hassan." Hassan reaches out his hand to the fragile young woman. She compliantly puts her hand out, and Hassan grasps hold and plants a chivalrous kiss. "We're friends," he says and gives an eager smile to the young woman.

Gareth looks at Rosalyn. The last time he had seen her, he had seen Cerys. The Distillery had taken away both women. Gareth longs to know what Rosalyn might remember of Cerys if anything. But he can tell that the fragile woman before him does not need reminding of her time in the Palace. Not now. Gareth hopes this doesn't mean there will never be a chance to ask her.

*Balham Underground station was one of many tube stations adopted as a civilian air raid shelter during the Second World War. Around eight o'clock on 14th October 1940, a red No.88 double-decker London bus was trundling through the dark street above the station, on its way through Balham. From inside the bus, a Barratts Shoes advert plastered on the shop's brick wall was in clear sight in front of them; "Walk the Barratt Way". All of a sudden, an armour-piercing fragmentation bomb, dropped from a Luftwaffe plane high above, exploded in the street. The impact collapsed the tube station roof below, breaking water and sewage mains in the process, and created a great crater in the road in front of the No.88 bus. The ensuing scene was one of horror and panic. The bus plunged into the crater, while the station filled with earth, water, and sewage. Four hundred people managed to escape the destruction, but tragically more than sixty souls were lost, most of them drowning.*

♦

# Chapter Eight

# The Evil Thirst

Full of Kasiya's caravan-boiled honey marbles, the troupe ready themselves for the day's travel. Gareth and Hassan join Milton at the water's edge to freshen up. Milton reassures them they don't have to worry about consuming the reservoir water. It is pure rainwater and poses little risk of making them unconscious. Gareth carefully cups the water in his hands and splashes it on his face while Hassan and Milton strip off their tops in the warm sunlight and shovel the cool water over their bare torsos. On Milton's right shoulder blade, Gareth notices a tiny tattoo. No bigger than a postage stamp. It is a small black mark that resembles the symbol he had seen in Kim-Joy's scrapbook – a water droplet with an encircling arrow.

After the quick freshen-up, Ashley harnesses Pimlico to the front caravan again, the other passengers check that the luggage is secure, and Milton takes the reins. With the curtains open, there is plenty for the passengers to see as they set off in the daylight. Meandering rivers and floodplains dominate much of the scenery, their sweeping curves sprawling in broad open valleys. Then they pass through a magnificent ancient oak forest with gnarled old trees as far as the eye can see, casting flickering shadows into the caravan. Pimlico enjoys the forest. He stomps through the leaf litter, trumpeting joyously, blowing golden leaves like confetti over the caravan.

They pass a few travellers on the tracks. Only a handful of people, primarily lone riders on horseback travelling between the scattered towns and villages. They are interesting-looking folk, like weatherproof Bedouins, wearing full-body robes expertly fashioned from animal hide. Both men and women, the travellers stop briefly to share a smoke on their pipes and swap stories from the trails ahead. In these moments, Gareth and Hassan are kept out of sight. They are wanted men with a bounty on their heads. Any travellers from the city will know this.

While Milton steers the caravans, the passengers have plenty of time to chat. Kasiya and Rosalyn aren't particularly active participants in the conversations, but they seem to get some strength from being in the company. Hassan, Gareth notices, has an entirely different demeanour with Rosalyn around. He is almost embarrassingly chivalrous, checking on her comfort, warmth, and energy with forced regularity. A core element of Hassan's soul is evidently awoken with Roslyn being in their presence.

Similarly, although he is unable, or unwilling, to recognise it in himself, a core energy in Gareth's nature is also triggered by the more visible presence of Kasiya. Indulgent daydreams about the young woman occupy his mind, and he finds himself seeking eye contact with her deep black eyes whenever possible. He thinks he is being subtle – and that is how he subdues his deeply embedded sense of guilt for this behaviour – but Kasiya will have noticed that on the few occasions she glances up towards him, he always needs to avert his eyes – a false modesty.

Both men's primal interests would be palpable to any keen observer, but Ashley is too animated in her discussions about the final destination of their journey to notice or care.

"Lin is only a two-day ride away now," she says, beaming. "It's the most wonderful little town, right on the coast. The countryside is stunning. The people are so lovely. And with the circus, the whole place brims with energy and life."

"And it's such a unique settlement for the Meadow," she continues enthusiastically, not requiring anyone else's input. "Usually, built-up areas here have grown slowly over time. Amassing community members over centuries as individual disasters on Earth occur sporadically. This normally gives the Distillery or Water Boards time to install their authority. But it was different in Lin. Some devastating flood in the 1950s brought through hundreds of inhabitants, buildings, and vehicles all at once. This rapid influx of people meant the new arrivals could establish their community before the Distillery even knew of their arrival. As a result, Lin has formed its own self-governance, much to the frustration of the Pond Life. The town hasn't even adopted a stance on why the Meadow exists. They pride themselves as the home of free thinking and an alternative way of life in the Meadow."

"It sounds great," says Gareth. "But Sanger's circus is older than that, right? How did they end up in Lin?"

"I think the circus is over a hundred years old now," agrees Ashley. "As far as I know, the Sanger family discovered Lin when they were scouting venues almost half a century ago. The story goes that the anti-authoritarian vibe drew them in. They approached the community to consider basing their operations there, and a close reciprocal relationship has flourished since. The town is a safe place for the circus to bring in and house new arrivals and provides space to develop their shows. In return, the circus brings wealth and skills to the community, helping them sustain an existence independent of the Distillery and Water Boards."

"At the heart of Lin is a hotel, the Princess Victoria. It has been the home of Sanger's circus for decades now. It is a fabulous and grand Edwardian building named after an old ship lost in the original flood of Lin. It houses the circus family and provides space to prepare new shows."

"How many people are in the circus family?" asks Hassan.

"Oh, hundreds," says Ashley. "Most of them are spread around the Meadow, touring. But dozens live in and run the hotel. The queen of the circus, the troupe's originator, Kathleen Montague, lives permanently at the Princess Victoria. She orchestrates the whole operation from there."

"And are we going to have to become part of the circus?" says Hassan, looking uncertain.

"Only if it suits you," says Ashley, grinning. "There are roles for everyone somewhere."

Ashley turns and rifles through a pile of items next to her. She pulls out a newspaper and holds up the back page to the men. It contains a full-page advert for *Sanger's circus' Latest Show: Evapotrapezium.* "You see," she says, "We've got gymnasts, magicians, dancers, animal handlers, trapeze artists. You name it;

we'll perform it! There's bound to be something that takes your fancy!"

The advert is bright and colourful. It exudes life and thrill. The circus certainly looks intriguing. As Ashley places the newspaper back down on the bench, Gareth notices the name of the publication: *The Shipping Forecast.*

"Is that paper from the publishing house on the Lethe?" he asks, remembering the late-night boat trip with the Professor.

"Unfortunately, yes," says Ashley, turning over the paper to reveal the front page and its bright red title. "Advertising in *The Forecast* is certainly no endorsement of its content," she says sternly. "We collect them whenever we find them lying around so that we know what nonsense the handmaidens of the Distillery are spouting out now."

Gareth looks at the headline on the paper. "*Wave of Satanists Flood the Meadow*". Underneath, next to a drawing of Distillery police officers wrestling an assailant, he reads the opening few paragraphs of a sensationalist story. It states that Satanists have been captured in large numbers amongst new arrivals in the Meadow. It argues that there is a need to clamp down more harshly on those accused of having the Evil Thirst and that stronger powers need to be given to the Distillery police. It also calls for formally recognising the "great work" done by the Ferrymen. Gareth frowns but can't help flicking through the rest of the paper.

Halfway through, Gareth's heart skips a beat. A "WANTED" poster fills the page. "*Three Satanists Spotted Heading North,*" it says. There is a call for information on three "extremely dangerous" men. Below this are large formal sketches of the three men. Gareth stares, stunned, at the accurate drawing of his own face. The official sketch done of him while he sat with Professor Pelling less than a fortnight ago.

"Hey, that's us!" exclaims Hassan, peering over Gareth's shoulder. "Amazing. We're wanted men! Badass, brother!" he grins and turns to see if Rosalyn is impressed. The young woman, however, has nodded off on the rear bench, not for the first time. The physical legacy of her time at the Palace will take time to wear off.

"Who's the third fella?" says Hassan, nudging Gareth.

Gareth stares at the picture. It's a rough sketch depicting a skinny, decrepit older man. A filthy beard obscures his face, and his grey hair is ruffled with debris. It is like someone has tried to draw the stereotype of a homeless beggar.

"No idea," says Gareth.

"It sounds like they are still obsessed with our train," says Hassan, pointing to what's written below the pictures.

*"These three fugitives arrived in the Meadow aboard a London-bound train carrying almost four dozen others in the weeks leading up to year-end. It is understood that five–ten passengers arrived as either conscious souls or as Founderers. If you have any information about the train or these passengers, you must report this to the Distillery police immediately. Any information will be richly rewarded."*

"Was there something unusual about your arrival?" asks Ashley, leaning in, interested.

"Not that we know of," responds Gareth. "But the more our train is mentioned, the more I wonder if we missed something." He muses on the image of the elderly beggar.

"They don't seem to know that Rosalyn was on our train, though," says Hassan, upbeat. "Otherwise, her picture would be there, too, right?"

Ashley turns to look at Rosalyn, asleep on the bench. "Possibly," she says, frowning. "Though the Distillery tends not to get official sketches done of women who leave their Palaces as Flickers. They don't see the point in keeping records of them."

Gareth looks at Ashley. There is sadness pooling in her eyes as she looks at Rosalyn. "If you don't mind me asking," he says, "when and how did you arrive in the Meadow?"

"Oh, sorry," says Ashley, a little taken aback. "I forgot I had never told you. I arrived in the Meadow about seventy years ago. It was a time of great activity in the Meadow. A time when the cities proliferated because of the Second World War." Gareth stares at Ashley. She doesn't look a day older than twenty. It is almost unimaginable to think she is from the 1940s.

"I was a young bus driver at the time, covering a shortage of men in these roles. One grey evening during a bombing raid over London, I was driving my bus through the chaotic streets of Balham when a bomb fell from the sky and exploded on the road in front of me." Ashley speaks quickly and nervously, barely taking a breath.

"Arriving in the Meadow, I was met with absolute chaos. There were so many of us arrivals, all at once. The Distillery at the time was struggling to manage the influx of people. We were brutally herded into great sorting hangers in the city, and with the minimal introduction, we were put to work in their rapidly expanding marble workhouses." She glances around, seeking approval with her eyes.

"I noticed you had the scars, the 'Satan's scalds'," says Gareth, clutching his wrists. "How come you weren't sent to the Palaces like other women?"

Ashley looks away again, a memory flickering through her mind. She catches Kasiya's eye, who smiles reassuringly back at her. She turns back to the men. "There was such chaos when people arrived then. I think my short hair and my… my boyish physique," she says, looking embarrassed, "must have been enough for those brutes to assume I was a boy." She pauses again, evidently feeling some internal trauma in the memory. "I think I may actually have been fortunate." She looks sadly towards Rosalyn, asleep still on the bench.

"I'm sorry," says Gareth.

"Oh, it's nothing," she dismisses. "We've all been through it, haven't we? It's the one thing I guess we all want to forget and the one memory we can't." Gareth and Hassan nod in agreement.

Still asleep, Rosalyn lets out a pained moan from her bench. "Get off me!" she shrieks unconsciously, wriggling and writhing uncomfortably. Ashley jumps up and leans over Rolsayn.

"Shhh," she whispers gently into Rosalyn's ear, "It's OK." She rubs Rosalyn's back comfortingly and looks back at the others sadly. "At least the scars from the workhouse heal," she says to Gareth and Hassan.

While Ashley is talking, the caravan comes to a stop. The front hatch swings open, waking Rosalyn from her nightmare, and a soaking-wet Milton stumbles in from the blustery rain outside, shivering. "I forgot my coat," he grumbles. "A novice mistake."

Seeing her father's needs, Kasiya jumps up and passes across the warm blanket she had been sitting on. He grunts a thanks of sorts, though he doesn't actually look at his daughter.

"I hadn't even noticed the weather," says Ashley. "I think it's probably time we swapped over anyway." Selflessly she flings on some extra layers and a long fleece-lined trench coat, ready to take over at the reins. With the hood up, she looks comically wizard-like.

"Thank you, Ashley," says Milton, gaining some colour in his cheeks and fingers.

The young woman braces herself for the rain and exits the caravan. As the door closes behind her, Milton looks at Rosalyn and Kasiya, huddled under a patchwork blanket. "I need to dry off, ladies," he says, breaking some kindling to put on the stove. "Maybe you would rather move to the rear caravan before I remove my wet clothes?"

It was an instruction, not a question. Gareth catches Kasiya's eye as she ushers Rosalyn out. The presence of her father makes her appear younger again, her agency gone. Nonetheless, he still feels the impulse to grab one more glimpse into her eyes before she leaves. He smiles at her. She looks away.

In a moment, the troupe is on the move again. Thanks to the roaring stove Milton stokes impatiently, the front caravan becomes a cauldron of warmth. He sits crossed-legged facing the fire, his boots, trousers, and soaking shirt steam on a rail. His damp bare back faces the men. Gareth glimpses his tattoo again.

"Mr Drake," Gareth begins tentatively. "I am interested in the tattoo on your shoulder. Kim-Joy at the Tide and Time Tavern had a few drawings just like it. If you don't mind me asking, what does it mean?"

Milton stops stoking the fire. He slowly reaches his left hand onto his shoulder and massages the skin. "I suppose there is no harm in telling either of you," he growls.

He turns fully to face the men and lowers his voice, the burning embers from the stove illuminating him like a shadow.

"You both have heard of the Evil Thirst here in the Meadow, haven't you?" He leaves a long pause while he inspects the agreement of the two men.

"This is the symbol of those so-called Satanists. It is called The Encircled Drop." Gareth and Hassan stare at Milton. "Yes," he says. "I am a member of that group. As is Kim-Joy. I'm sure you can forgive her for not telling you. But hear this; we do not refer to ourselves as Satanists. We are not consumed by some 'Evil Thirst'. Nothing could be further from the truth. We are, what *we* call, Well Wishers. If we thirst for anything, we thirst for the water of love."

"This symbol," Milton leans his shoulder towards the men. "It represents a core belief of Well Wishing – the belief of passage in any direction between the realms – returning to Earth from the Meadow being one of these passages. This is why there is an encircling arrow. We believe our souls, like droplets of water in a natural cycle of evaporation and condensation, are always in motion and can return to a previous state or go on to a new one." Milton looks at the two men in front of him. They are alert and transfixed.

"You believe there's a way of going back to Earth?" Hassan blurts out.

"Yes," he responds matter-of-factly. "We fundamentally don't believe that our existence here in the Meadow is just to pay off debts for our wrongdoing – neither individual nor collective debt. We believe the Meadow is an invitation to discover and pursue love. Here, on Earth, or in the next realm."

Milton absorbs the confusion etched on Hassan and Gareth's faces. "My apologies," he starts again. "It might be useful for me to give a bit of context first. Who the Well Wishers are, and where we come from."

"Let me tell you how our movement emerged, or at least tell you the legend of our beginnings that has passed between us for generations." Milton grabs a blanket that he drapes over his shoulders and shuffles into a comfortable position.

"The story begins many millennia ago, at a moment when the first settlers found themselves in the Meadow. One small group of these early settlers lived in a primitive society around the northern border of England and Wales. They existed as a nomadic people, moving with the changing weather, not understanding how or why they had arrived in the Meadow, but being compelled to survive, nonetheless. They knew their bodies didn't want food or drink, but their minds craved something. A sensation of being alive. And from their early experiments with consumption in the Meadow, they knew that water did something to satiate this craving."

"One hot and dry evening, the community were gathered around a deep well they had just finished digging high on a hillside. They plunged bucket after bucket into the well, drawing up water for their parched minds. They weren't to know that the groundwater they drank was harming them. Then, as their minds teetered on the edge of consciousness, a lady appeared. A lady who wore a dark blue dress which flowed all around her, and whose dark skin contrasted her sparkling blue eyes."

"Before the settlers could work out who she was, the woman commanded them to stop drinking and listen to her message. A message, she told them, of truth. The truth of love's transcendence and its eternal entanglement with water. A truth that spanned all realms of existence, from Earth, through the Meadow, to the Beyond. A truth that all physical and spiritual things revolved around a constant intertwining of love and water."

"Love and water, she told them, were the only tangible entities that co-existed in all spaces and at all times. But she told them love and water were distinct. Love was pure and impermeable. Whereas, while water could be pure, it was vulnerable to contamination."

"As the lady spoke, according to the legend, the heavens opened, and the rains came down. The lady dipped one of the settler's buckets back into the well and left another to collect the rainwater. She passed both buckets around, encouraging them to look and taste. Both waters looked identical, but one was light and dulled their senses, filling them with fear, while the other was heavy and sharpened their minds, filling them with joy. Dirty water, she told them, repelled the pools of love in their souls. In contrast, pure water –the heaviest, densest substance in the Meadow – embraced their souls and magnified their existing stores of love. The lady instructed the settlers that in all things that they do, they should do them with love. All else, *including* penitence for sin, was futile and would ultimately wash away with dirty water. The Meadow, she told them, existed for love. As did the Earth."

"The lady then told the settlers there was a journey open to them. A journey 'back' to Earth they could only take if they loved the Earth and their minds were clear. A journey that she was about to take but would return one day to take them with her. Then, as suddenly as she had appeared amongst the settlers, the lady exited their presence. The settlers realised their well had collapsed in the heavy rain, but they were no longer afraid of their thirst. They cupped their hands to catch the falling rain, and their hearts became light with the hope of rekindling their lost lives on Earth."

"The legend then takes a darker turn. Another group of settlers happened upon the lady wandering along a riverbank shortly after this first encounter. This group, all men who had arrived together in the Meadow, never gave the woman a chance to speak. They attacked and assaulted her, then forced her into the river, where they tried to drown her. The lady went unconscious, and the men watched as her limp body drifted to the riverbank. Incredibly, they witnessed her stand up and wander towards the hills. As she did so, a mist descended around them, and the woman disappeared. The men heard a voice from the skies: '*My beautiful daughter, you have been brave. Go and be with your brothers.*' There was a flash of white light in the mist, and the woman was never seen again."

"For years, the first settlers to encounter the lady wandered the Meadow, waiting for her return. At that time, inspired by her message of love, they devoted their energy to recollecting and memorialising her words. They carved her message on stone tablets, celebrated the falling rain, and retold her words wherever they met other communities in the Meadow. But, as with all things believed, some people didn't accept the message, and these deniers started to rebuke it, claiming the belief itself was harmful; there was no return; it was a trick, a dangerous illusion that blinded people from the truth. The longer time that passed from the initial encounter, the easier it became for settlers in the Meadow to dismiss its truth, and even the early settlers themselves started to doubt."

Milton shakes off the blanket he has wrapped around his shoulders. The caravan got very warm while he was telling his tale. He turns to the stove and closes the vents to stop the embers from burning so brightly. His tattoo shines clearly on his shoulder blade. Milton turns back to the men and continues. "In place of the lady's message of transient love and its entanglement with water, a warped notion grew. A notion that believed the Meadow existed not as a *consequence* of love but as a *punishment* for its deficiency on Earth. That the Meadow was a realm for penitence. A realm where people were required to earn their way back into the love of the Creator. It was a belief that said love on Earth ended on Earth, and the Meadow was simply a staging post for an onward journey to the final realm, the 'Beyond'."

"In this belief, water lost its connection to love altogether. Water became an implement to be brandished by those with power– a resource to control and contaminate souls in the Meadow. The dangers of dirty water were clear for all to see, but the benefits of pure water were overlooked. The Meadow became a dry realm. Thirst became a disavowed state of mind, and people stopped drinking water altogether."

"The Pond Life has perpetuated the lies about love and water. In the century or so they have governed, they have elaborated the lie, each in their own way, and have attempted to stamp out Well Wishing. Great leaders of the Well Wishers, women like Kim-Joy, have had to hide their true identities. They call us Satanists, consumed by the Evil Thirst, and they have forced us into the shadows. They have forced the believers to disappear and for the true message to be lost."

"Do the Distillery know about Kim-Joy?" Hassan asks, amazed that the old lady could hide something so huge and so dangerous amid the Distillery stronghold.

"We, the so-called Thirsty Evil, the Well Wishers, are a persecuted people," responds Milton. "Kim-Joy is only the name that she adopted after the banning of our beliefs. If we had met her before this, I doubt we would have recognised her. We, members of the Well-Wishing community, have had to be very adept at hiding who we really are."

"I hear that, brother," says Hassan.

"And so," Milton continues, "with the banishment of Well Wishing, the memories of the first encounter with the lady faded from consciousness in the Meadow. Yet her message was never lost entirely. An oral tradition continued in the shadows of Distillery control. Passed between believers. And this tradition kept alight the flame she had ignited in the people. So long as this flame existed, even as a flicker in a vast sea of darkness, there remained hope. A hope for her return, a belief in transcendental love, and a belief in the value of pure water."

Milton takes a breath and prods the stove. "Adding occasional splashes of fuel to this belief have been the rumours since. Emerging at many moments throughout history, there have been rumours of believers finding a way to take the lady's journey without her, the journey in love and water from the Meadow back to Earth."

Milton pauses and allows silence to settle in the caravan. The wind and the rain outside have stopped, and there is just a gentle rattling of the items hanging around the caravan's walls. It is now dusk outside, and the only source of light inside is the fading embers in the stove. Gareth and Hassan are deep in thought. There is a lot to process. What Milton has told them changes everything. Gareth feels the silver locket hanging around his neck absent-mindedly.

Looking at Gareth, Milton comments on how pale he looks. "I think you could do with some fresh air, Gareth," he says. "Why don't you join Ashley on Pimlico for a while? See if the air and the evening sky can give your mind some peace."

It seems like a reasonable idea. There is a little boyish part of Gareth that is teased into life at the thought of getting to ride an Indian elephant. He pulls over a thick trench coat. Hassan tells

Milton that he needs an early night to process these new ideas and rest his head. Milton agrees and hands Hassan a blanket and cushions to get himself comfortable.

Gareth opens the hatch and clambers out onto the caravan's axle. It is a cold, clear evening, and bright stars fill the sky. It takes a while for Gareth's eyes to adjust to the light before he can make out the whole form of the elephant before him. Ashley calls out from on top, "Is that you, Milton?"

"No, it's me, Gareth. Milton suggested I might benefit from riding on Pimlico with you."

"That sounds wonderful," says Ashley cheerfully. "I'd love some company. Have you ever ridden an elephant before?"

"No. Never anything like it. I've never even rode a horse," says Gareth.

"There's nothing to it, really," says Ashley. "Just try not to look down at the ground. Keep your eye on the horizon. I'll throw you down a rope. Let me know when you've got it."

A thick, knotted rope tumbles over Gareth's shoulder. "Got it," he calls back, grasping it tightly with both hands.

"Now put both of your feet firmly against Pimlico's behind, then take your weight in your arms and walk your hands up the rope as you walk your feet up Pimlico's back."

Gareth looks at the grey mass in front of him. Really? Was it that simple? He takes the tension in the rope and puts a foot on the elephant's hide. It is firm and steady. He takes his weight on the rope and places his other foot. And just like that, Gareth finds himself clambering over the back of the Indian elephant.

On top of Pimlico, Ashley sits on a wide wooden platform harnessed around the elephant's body. Gareth's eyes adjust to the starlight, and he can see Ashley's friendly face emerging out of her hood as she beckons him to sit beside her. Gareth smiles. The confusion he feels from Milton's revelations becomes less urgent as the beauty of the moment engulfs him. It is incredible that he is sitting on an elephant in the middle of a fantastic open plain in the starlight of an unknown realm.

"Quite a sight, isn't it?" says Ashley. Her green eyes sparkle in the starlight.

"It's amazing," he says, looking at the countryside around them.

Gareth and Ashley sit in silence for a short while, taking in the world. Remembering he has a pouch of marbles in his coat pocket, Gareth pops a warming one into his mouth and offers them to Ashley. "No thanks," she declines. "I prefer a clear head when I'm riding."

The marble clinks quietly against Gareth's teeth. The only other sounds are Pimlico's occasional sighs and the odd hoot of an owl.

"So why did Milton think you needed some time up here? I had assumed you were all getting an early night," says Ashley.

"We were busy talking with Milton. He told us about Well Wishing."

At the mention of Well Wishing, Ashley instinctively checks over her shoulder and leans in. "Spit it out," she demands quietly but urgently, holding her hand in front of Gareth's face. Confused, Gareth complies, dribbling the wet marble out of his mouth. Ashley flings the marble to the ground, and it shatters and hisses, leaving a mist in the caravan's wake. "There must never be a marble record if you ever talk about Well Wishing," she explains apologetically. "Sorry if you were enjoying it."

"No, it's OK," says Gareth. "I hadn't even thought about that."

"So, wow. Milton spoke to you about Well Wishing? He must have seen something in you that he trusts. We don't usually tell people about our links to this movement. Not until new arrivals have settled into the circus, at least."

"Are you a Well Wisher too?"

Ashley looks back at Gareth. "Yes," she says proudly. "All of us at Sanger's circus are Well Wishers."

Ashley's pride doesn't land with Gareth in quite the positive way she intends. A nervous reluctance catches him in his chest. Ashley picks up on his body language and reads his mind. "Don't worry," she says. "No one will be trying to convert you to Well Wishing. Maybe Milton will, but that's more down to how he is than Well Wishing. It's not some cult, I promise you." She looks rather desperately at Gareth in the starlight.

"No, it's OK," says Gareth, responding out of kindness. "I'm just trying to process it all."

"Of course. Of course," says Ashley nervously. "Sorry, I know I always talk too much."

"No, honestly, it's OK," says Gareth, relating to Ashley's nerves more than her words.

In the awkward silence that follows, Gareth leans back and takes in the vast night sky above them. Thousands of stars dance around. Only they aren't like the stars on Earth. He can't pick out any familiar constellations. "The stars are different," he says to Ashley.

"Different to Earth?" she asks.

"Yes. They are all moving," he observes.

"True," says Ashley. "They are heading north, past the Source. You see, it is not believed that they are stars at all. Here in the Meadow, it is believed that they are the burning lights of souls who have perished on Earth but haven't been deposited in this realm. Instead, they are moving on a different journey, straight through to the Beyond. The next realm."

"Is that for real?" asks Gareth.

"Yes," says Ashley. "You see, around the Mountain of the Source, it is said you can see sparks floating up at night from the mist, going into the sky and joining these stars on their journey away to the north horizon. We believe these new sparks are the flickers of light from the souls of Drifters who have plummeted off the Perihelion Cliffs, going on their next journey. Another direction for our souls, from the Meadow to the Beyond."

Gareth stares at the lights above him. Thinking of each light as a soul recently extinguished is beautiful and haunting. He wonders about his Mum. Is she still on Earth, or is she one of these stars washing through the night sky? He thinks of Cerys. Is she in the Meadow still? Does she remember where she comes from? Does she remember him? Will he find her before she drifts to the Cliffs?

"Do you believe that there is a way back to Earth?" Gareth asks bluntly.

"I desperately want to believe it," Ashley says before pondering for a moment in the silence. "I have no doubts about the Well-Wishing belief in love entangled with water. A glue holding together all existence in all realms that makes sense to me. To live for, and in, love draws in my soul with much greater persuasion than the fearful mantra of penitence. But I have been in the Meadow for decades now and have never seen, or even really heard, any suggestion that someone has found a way back to Earth. I'm not saying I can't believe it, but, well, it's just that it feels that holding onto such a hope could be quite self-defeating." She looks at Gareth strangely, almost seeking his permission for her opinion.

"And maybe it is just to protect me from pain," she continues, almost disavowing her own opinion. "But in contrast to believers like Milton, I'm less inclined to believe in a *literal* way back and forth between the Meadow and Earth. I'm more of the opinion that maybe just a part of our soul, the part that loves and is loved, can make the journey. The memory of love on Earth, for example, and the warmth you can get from these memories feel like they are more than merely projections of love. And when I think fondly of the people I knew, who died before I left Earth, and who I know loved me, I sense their love for me more clearly than just something in my imagination. These feelings are my proof that love traverses the realms. To me, the most important things we can do are to dwell in the acts and memories of love. Love given, and love received." She shuffles on the platform and sighs.

"So, I guess, no, I don't really believe there's a way back," she says, summarising her thoughts. "Sorry," she adds, nervous she might have shattered Gareth's hopes.

"No, it's OK," he responds. "I haven't decided if I'd even want to return if I could anyway."

"Really?!" says Ashley. She looks across at him incredulously. "Why not?"

Gareth shrugs. The truth is, he isn't entirely sure why. It isn't a conscious decision. When asked if he missed his old life at his final interrogation in the workhouse, he felt so cold and distant from it that he didn't care. He just wanted the torture of the workhouse to stop. Now though, in kinder company and with an intriguing new world to explore, the question itself feels different. He now cares about his old life, and his memories feel keener and closer. But his body and mind have found a new raft of stimulations in the Meadow, and his soul yearns to move forward, not back.

Ashley waits a moment to see if Gareth will elaborate. She says when he doesn't, "I would go back if I could."

*The tiny village of Burwell, Cambridgeshire, was hosting a popular travelling puppet show on the afternoon of the 8th September 1727. Due to the huge popularity of the show, the doors to the barn where it was being shown, were nailed shut, stopping non-paying customers from getting in. A stable hand, who usually tended the horses in the barn, found he was unable to gain access to the show and so he clambered over a partition to watch. His candle lantern set fire to some of the hay in the partition and quickly spread around the barn. With no escape, eighty of the one hundred and forty people viewing the puppet show perished in the blaze.*

♦

# Chapter Nine

# A Monastic Moment

The two gypsy caravans, illuminated by the bright rising sun, trundle along the banks of a wide meandering river where flocks of wading birds welcome the morning with hectic chatter. Not a single soul has passed them all night. Ashley had swapped the reins with Milton sometime early in the morning, but Gareth is still on top of Pimlico. His mind is restless.

Talking, inevitably, about Well Wishing, Milton asks Gareth if he had been 'religious' on Earth. Gareth hesitates a little. "No," he tells Milton. "I was raised going to church every Sunday and had been christened. But I never really believed in God or Heaven and Hell. They were just ideas like Father Christmas or the Tooth Fairy."

"So, what did you think of Well Wishing?" Milton asks. "Would you consider belonging to a religion now?"

Gareth hesitates again, feeling pressured by Milton's direct questioning and his dark, intense eyes. "Maybe," he says, lying to try and appease Milton. "Considering the alternatives, Well Wishing is one of the kinder perspectives I have heard."

Milton ponders Gareth's answer before continuing his pointed inquiry. What had been a sedate ride with Ashley through the night is now like an interrogation. Milton doesn't do 'relaxed'. "I presume you like the idea of returning to Earth, though?" Milton asks him, clearly indicating what he saw as the 'correct' response.

"Um, I think so," Gareth replies, trying to sound more confident than he is.

"You 'think so'?!" exclaims Milton. "How could you not want to go back? Did you want to die when you did?"

"No. Of course not," says Gareth defensively. "There's just so much for me to discover here, and Earth feels so distant and disconnected now."

Milton looks disappointed, almost anxious. "But you can remember your old life, right?"

"Yes," says Gareth confidently, which seems to encourage Milton.

"So, it's the draw of the Meadow, not the absence of a past, that drives you?"

"I guess…"

"And is it your body or your mind that's driving?"

"What do you mean?"

"Well, both can deceive the soul in this realm. Both can be indulged in the Meadow to the extent that all connections to the soul are lost. And if the connection to the soul is lost, it Founders, like a sinking ship. The neglected soul has only one path; 'on' to the Source."

Milton stares so intensely at Gareth that it feels like he is trying to perform keyhole surgery on his mind. "A *mind* deceiving the soul in the Meadow is a mind that denies any reflection on the past, denies bodily sensation in the present, and dwells entirely in contemplation of the future. A *body* deceiving the soul denies reflection of the past, but obsesses about bodily sensations in the present – impulses and urges – and neglects to think about the future."

"The Distillery, with their obsession for living in perpetual penitence, are prone to the former. Young people, such as yourselves, are prone to the latter. To the deception of the body in the Meadow." The scar on Milton's upper lip twitches. "I see the way you look at Rosalyn. And I can't blame you. She is a beautiful young woman. But you must be careful. Eyes are not the gateway to the soul, as people say. They are moths of temptation. Blinded by the impulses of the body, they can neglect their bond with the soul."

Gareth stares at Milton, bewildered. How simultaneously wrong and right the imposing man is. Gareth knows his body and mind aren't distracted by Rosalyn. But they are distracted by Kasiya, Milton's daughter. It's a relief to know Milton hasn't picked up on this, and is a worry at the same time.

"That's the problem with my daughter, Kasiya," Milton starts again. "She had something of a distraction for a man when we first arrived here. It took her a long while to let go of him. And she hated me for it. But I knew she had to let go, and I could not look on without helping her do this."

Milton looks out towards the horizon wistfully. "Anyway, now she is over him, and thank God, she has a chance of returning to Earth without losing connection with her soul." He turns and looks directly at Gareth. "Kasiya knows just how dangerous it would be to get into any new relationship here in the Meadow. Alas, she will always be a young woman. Sometimes she needs her father, with her best interests at heart, to stop her from making any stupid mistake." He holds Gareth's gaze. Gareth's relief at Milton's misinterpretation feels like he fell for a trap. Has Milton noticed how he looks at Kasiya? Gareth doesn't respond.

"You look exhausted, kid," says Milton, misreading Gareth's silence. "Go and take a kip in the caravan. And send Kasiya up, will you? It'll be lonely sitting up here on my own. I could do with a bit of time with my daughter before we arrive at the monastery."

Milton has planned for them to stop at a monastery just off the river Ouse, hidden in a forest beyond the gaze of Burwell, the nearest village. It is a monastery he already knows of and only half a day's ride from their final destination at Lin. When Milton announced this plan yesterday, it was the first time Kasiya spoke out against her father in the company of the others. She didn't want to stop at the monastery and had argued that she preferred to push through to Lin with another night ride. But Milton had been adamant and dismissed his daughter's request off-hand. He had some business he wished to attend to at the monastery, and that was more important to him. Priests of the Well Wishers inhabited the place, and he sought their counsel. With Milton's dismissal of her protestations, Kasiya had retreated back into her shell.

\* \* \*

A warm evening sun drops low in the sky, and the narrow river Ouse winds tightly amongst the tall fir trees. Pimlico and the caravans clatter over damp mossy stones and carpets of rotting brown needles. They hear the monastery before they see it. A low repetitive hum of the monks drifts through the forest, and the harsh clang of a bell echoes off the rocks around the riverbank.

The old monastery is built of roughly cut stones dredged from the river. It comprises a cloister of small buildings sheltered in the shadows of the trees, with a tall and crooked tower that creeps out from the roof of the forest canopy. The cloister opens onto the riverbank, where the channel has been diverted to gather bathing pools for physical and religious cleansing. When they arrive, the group don't see any of the monks, but eerie chants surround them.

"Good risen," Milton calls out into the emptiness. "We are godly people seeking refuge for the night. Can you provide it?"

There is no response. The chants continue uninterrupted. Hassan steps forward and tries to speak, but Milton raises his hand to silence him. Two loud gongs sound from the bell in the crooked tower. Milton turns to the others. "Follow me."

Milton reaches out and knocks on the door at the tower's base. A moment later, an extraordinarily tall, pale gentleman with a shaved head and long unkempt beard opens the door. He wears loose black robes.

"Good risen," the monk says quietly, looking out at the group as though he hasn't seen new people in years.

"Good risen, brother," says Milton. "Please tell the priests that High Councillor Milton Drake seeks an audience. And that he comes with five weary travellers, seeking refuge for the night."

At the mention of Milton's title, the tall man bows his head reverently. "Right away, High Councillor," he says.

"Thank you, brother," says Milton before reciting the first part of a mantra and covering his face with his right hand while bowing. It must be a Well Wisher's greeting. Gareth recalls seeing Kim-Joy perform this ritual in the middle of the night at the Tide and Time Tavern.

*"May the seas warm, and the clouds form…"* says Milton.

To which the tall monk responds, *"…and may the rain fall, filling the rivers of Love."*

As the monk exits into the tower, Milton looks back at the group. "It is worth knowing that creed," he says. "It has been passed on for centuries by the Well Wishers. The monastery here is one of the few sanctuaries for Well Wishers outside of Lin. Without our entry ritual here, the monks would have presented this place to us as they do to all other travellers, as grounds for the deepest religious isolation and solitary penitence. That is why they are left alone by the Pond Life. Only those of us from the Council of Well Wishing know of the true identity of this space. You are very privileged to be here."

\* \* \*

The monastery's inhabitants welcome High Councillor Milton Drake and his guests, and accommodation for the night is confirmed. A sociable evening of marbles and relaxation is promised, but first, they are requested to attend the chapel for a service of remembrance. Remembrance for Well Wishers lost at the hands of the Distillery and, rather curiously, lost to misadventure in the name of the belief.

Bright evening sunlight drifts into the stone chapel, coaxing warmth into the sombre space. Adorning the walls are depictions of stories carved into tessellating wooden slates. Below them, the cramped chapel floor is filled with pews. The monastery's monks are all present, kneeling with their hoods raised and their heads bowed. Their Gregorian chanting is low and undulating. At regular intervals, each monk hurls a marble into the nave. The marbles burst and whisper in a mist around the chapel floor.

Milton, wearing a borrowed robe, strides through the nave and joins the senior monks in the chancel. Gareth and the others sidle into an unoccupied pew at the back. Gareth is transported to his memories as an altar boy on Earth. These are not fond recollections.

While the chants echo soporifically, the senior monks mill around the altar, offering greetings – the now familiar, face-covered bow of the Well Wishers – and whisper to one another fervently. Occasionally a monk peers up through their hood and inspects the guests who sat politely at the chapel's rear.

Gareth studies the carvings on the walls. Many depict the origin myth that Milton recalled in the caravan. Slates show a woman, appearing to nomadic settlers, pointing to the clouds, and sharing water from two chalices. There are others where the same woman appears again, being beaten and abused by angry men or retreating towards a mountain.

"What's happening in *those* pictures?" whispers Hassan.

He points to a carved slate elevated on the altar. There are three sequential images on it. The first shows a figure running towards a place where three lightning bolts converge. The second shows the figure writhing in pain, ripping away the skin from his body. And the final image shows the figure wandering with an unfocused stare towards a mountain, his skeleton and internal organs exposed.

"The gruesome misadventures of Well Wishing," whispers Ashley, looking solemn. "For those Well Wishers who believe in a literal return to Earth, failure has been brutal. At the threshold of an Opening – the kind we each arrived in the Meadow through – many Well Wishers have tried to step back to Earth. But each time, they have failed. Their minds and their bodies have torn one another apart, literally. Leaving only the soul intact. It's another reason I'm inclined to doubt the literal belief."

"You're not serious?" says Hassan, a little too loud. A few nearby monks turn towards them.

Ashley nods her head. "Fuck," whispers Hassan.

A priest at the altar steps forwards and removes his hood. Dark creased lines carve out his weathered face. Gareth perceives a tension tightening in Kasiya next to him. The priest looks stern and powerful, and his voice commands their attention when he talks.

"Welcome, young and old," he begins. "We are gathered here today to remember the believers lost. Lost on the journey set out by the Daughter of God, the saviour of the Meadow."

"*Peace be upon Her*," mutter the monks around the chapel in devout unison, placing their hands over their faces.

The ritual of the religious recital is all too familiar from Earth and somewhat uncomfortable to Gareth. He looks for friendly reassurance along the pew. Ashley leans over to him. "Most Well Wishers aren't like this, I promise," she whispers, looking coy. "The priesthood and their monks have made their version of Well Wishing starchy and pious. But while we're guests here, we might just have to grin and bear it." She smiles at him.

"And Milton?" whispers Gareth.

"Oh, I'm afraid he likes this kind of thing," she whispers back, raising her eyebrows and nodding towards the chancel. Milton is kneeling devoutly behind the priest; his head bowed under his hood.

The rest of the service carries on in the same vein. The stern priest recites a monologue about the three realms – Earth, the Meadow, and the Beyond – and their connection through love. He then tells of the origins of love in the universe, which he calls the Mother's love, explaining that it originated with Creation.

The Mother's love, the priest goes on, is what compels spirituality on Earth and what draws arrivals in the Meadow to head to the Source; the desire to be with the Mother. In contrast, he tells them that the love revealed by the Sons of God on Earth is a love of the Earth and fellow humans, the love of the Creation. The priest concludes in his three-pronged thesis that the Daughter of God is the final aspect of love, its necessary flow between the Mother and her children. Between the Creator and the Creation.

"It is in the honourable quest to unite the love of the Creator and Creation that Well Wishers through the centuries have given their lives," says the priest, in summary. "Their deaths must be remembered and celebrated. They must not have died in vain. One day the paths between our realms will re-join. The cycle of love will be restored."

After the service, Gareth feels completely overwhelmed by its intensity. This isn't helped by the lingering fuzziness in his brain from the marble mist and his general exhaustion from the last few days. He is very grateful to step out into the monastery's cool cloisters and have a chance to chill out.

The monastery's inhabitants join them. Most are highly awkward hosts, sitting in silence and avoiding eye contact. But there is one monk who breaks the mould. Ibrahim is a young man with a heavily pock-marked face, dark brown skin and a toothy smile. He loves to talk. It is as though he has spent the last few years desperately waiting for guests to arrive.

While they enjoy sucking marbles from a deep and abundant bowl provided by the monastery (all the marbles are natural colours – browns, greens, and greys) – Ibrahim speaks to them passionately about Well Wishing and the monastery, his home. In contrast to Ashley's restrained interpretation of Well Wishing, Ibrahim has a childlike and enthusiastic naivety, believing all aspects of Well Wishing literally. He believes in the literal idea that all people's physical bodies, minds, and souls can traverse between Earth and the Meadow.

"What about those brothers who have tried to return and ended up ripping their skin off, though?" says Hassan, without subtlety, rattling a hazel-brown marble around his mouth.

Ibrahim looks at Hassan and flicks him a sarcastic smile. One that confirms he doesn't consider Hassan's question to have genuine merit.

"'*All things are possible to him who believes*'," says Ibrahim. "That was even written in the Earthly Bible. So, I don't think I need to worry myself with the failures of others."

Hassan frowns at Ibrahim. The young man's blind faith isn't a convincing argument. "So, have you ever tried to return?" he asks.

A flash of guilt flickers in Ibrahim's eyes. "It's not that easy to try," he says, attempting to quell any sparks of hypocrisy. "You can't just step through an opening back to Earth, you see. Though, tragically, many have tried."

Gareth looks across to Ashley. She is listening intently to Ibrahim's every word. "We don't know for certain how the Daughter of God – Peace be upon Her – intends for us to traverse the realms," Ibrahim continues. "But it seems logical that we must step back through an Opening. They are the only gateways to Earth we know of, after all. And before we step through, it seems we need to shore up the bonds between our mind, body, and soul. Otherwise, as you say," he looks pointedly at Hassan, "we might find ourselves 'ripping our skin off'."

"Why do you assume these bonds need shoring up?" asks Ashley.

"As you know, the story of the Daughter of God – Peace be upon Her – teaches us of the entanglement of love and water," he says. "Pure water reinvigorates the bonds between mind, body, and soul. I believe a successful return to Earth depends on the invigoration of the person stepping through an Opening. In other words, how connected their mind, body and soul are at the threshold of the two realms."

"That's an interesting idea," says Ashley, leaning in. "But to me, an obsession with the process of stepping between the Meadow and Earth seems unhealthily distracting. Fatally distracting even. Well Wishing is surely founded on the idea of love? Love for life and love for living. Love is the link across all time and space. Not the physical realms. Obsessing with returning loses sight of love."

"Maybe for you," says Ibrahim sorrowfully. "But for some of us, a literal return provides hope." He rolls up his sleeves to reveal his Satan's Scalds. They are deep and gruesome. Much worse than Gareth's forearms. Then he lifts the hem of his robe to reveal his lower legs. The skin all over them is blistered and weeping. His fibula is visible on both legs, and a lesion on his calf reveals the tight sinews of his tendons. "Visible or hidden, so many of us are deeply scarred by our time here in the Meadow. Our bodies are damaged beyond repair. Our minds are hazy. And our souls are tired." He looks around the group. Rosalyn looks queasy. Hassan drops the marble from his mouth and bows his head. Gareth rubs his forearms.

"Life here, particularly for those who spent years in the Distillery workhouses or Palaces, is beset with suffering. We have survived, but the bonds between our minds, bodies, and souls are extremely fragile. The Beyond is beckoning us, but it is an unknown realm. In contrast, I know Earth. I know that it had less pain than this. And so, the idea of returning home keeps me alive."

"I'm so sorry," says Ashley. A tear flees down her cheek, and tumbles to the ground.

"It's OK," says Ibrahim graciously.

"I never went to a Palace or workhouse," says Kasiya.

"No?" asks Ibrahim, absently searching through the bowl of marbles.

Gareth turns to face Kasiya. She looks nervous and embarrassed. "When me and my family arrived in the Meadow, the first people we met were performers from Sanger's circus. We joined them before we ever even came across the Distillery."

"That was lucky," says Hassan.

"So, you were never interrogated? You never went to the Palace?" asks Rosalyn.

"I never went to any Palace," says Kasiya. "But I have been interrogated. My father learned how important having a formal identity in the Meadow is. And for that, you need an Interrogation Stone. So, he convinced some elders from the circus Well Wishers to cross-examine me and form my stone. I don't like thinking of it, but I am sure my suffering is nothing compared to yours." Kasiya smiles politely at the rest of them and nervously tucks her hair behind her ear.

Gareth gazes at Kasiya. Shamefully, his mind swims through a chauvinistic fantasy of her. A nervous and beautiful woman, untainted by the Palaces but somehow pained and mysterious. Again, he seeks a forbidden glance into her deep black eyes. Maybe he is less subtle this time. Perhaps she is more amenable. But he senses that she looks back into his eyes with lukewarm longing.

"There is no interrogation without suffering," says Ibrahim. "I know many men who spent decades in the workhouse with me. Men who were wounded so deeply that they were Drifters when they left that place. If I never find a way back to Earth, I will at least find a way to make the Distillery pay for their cruelty."

"Cheers to that," says Hassan. He raises a cobalt-coloured marble and pops it into his mouth. Ibrahim nods and follows suit.

As the darkness draws in and the bowl of marbles empties, socialising ends early. The debris of smashed marbles litters the floor, and marble-stained ramekins are discarded around the cloisters. Even though they didn't engage in the conversations, the other monks indulged in plenty of marbles tonight.

Kasiya gets up and starts to gather up the stained ramekins. "You don't have to do that, Miss Kasiya," says Ibrahim. "You're a guest here."

"It's the least I can do," she says, looking kindly at him.

"I'll help as well," says Gareth standing up.

"Thanks," says Kasiya, smiling at Gareth. This smile is the best she has given him yet.

"Well, if you don't mind," says Hassan. "I'm getting an early night."

"Me too," says Ashley, yawning. Rosalyn follows suit.

So, as the others go off to the dormitories, Gareth and Kasiya head to the wash-up with Ibrahim. It's a small building on the far edge of the cloisters, overhanging the riverbank. Here they can clean the marble-stained ramekins and dispose of the marble debris.

In fading daylight, Ibrahim fills a large metal basin with river water, then shows Gareth and Kasiya the cupboards full of clean ramekins, ready for another day. He thanks them over-generously again for offering to clean up and bids them goodnight.

Gareth starts to pile the marble-stained ramekins onto the bench while Kasiya cleans. The conversation is awkward and fleeting, but Gareth has a phobia of silence and tries every topic he can think of to keep the conversation going. The problem is that his mind is scattered while he is alone with Kasiya. Where he had the confidence to look into her eyes when they were in the company of others, he is too shy in this private company.

Instead, he allows himself to glance at her arms and gentle, smooth hands as she rubs back and forth against the edges of the stained ramekins in the basin. Marble-staining, it transpires, is a stubborn stain that takes time and energy to clear from each ramekin. He watches Kasiya's hands dipping slowly into the warm water, plunging them deep down to her elbows and pulling them out again slowly. He watches as the water scurries up her forearm and drips off the point of her elbow. Kasiya doesn't notice him watching and isn't bothered by the awkward silence. She answers all of Gareth's questions and agrees with his opinions but never adds much to keep the conversation going.

Once the cloisters are clear, Gareth joins Kasiya, scrubbing the ramekins clean in the deep, warm basin. There are hundreds to clean, and it makes sense to work together. But as they get close to finishing, a simple but thrillingly unspoken game starts between them. A game of encroachment into each other's personal space. First, they grasp the same ramekin. Then their hands brush against one another as they enter the warm water.

The game takes over. Gareth forgets all about cleaning the plates. He starts to leave his hands lingering in the water longer than necessary, hoping to brush into Kasiya's. He even allows his hands to drift to her side of the basin. Then an impulse he doesn't consciously intend or control makes him grasp Kasiya's hand as it sinks into the water. He lets go instantly, embarrassed.

"Sorry," he says. She doesn't say anything.

Gareth reaches for another bowl. Kasiya puts her hand into the water again, and this time she grasps his hand. She holds it for a brief second and then lets go. She doesn't say sorry. Gareth looks up at her. The first time he has looked straight at her this close. She doesn't turn to look at him, though, so he turns away.

Gareth reaches in to grab the last bowl that has sunk to the bottom of the basin. Kasiya's hand reaches into the water again and finds his hand. As her warm, soft hand holds onto him, Gareth turns back to look at her. She is looking straight at him this time. Her deep black eyes shine into his. Her mouth is slightly ajar, and she holds his stare. Gareth blinks and moistens his lip. Kasiya stands motionless. Then she leans in and kisses him.

*A savage storm raged throughout the night on Saturday 31st January 1953. All across the east coast of England, the North Sea crashed against the land. A fatal combination of a high spring tide, a vast low-pressure system and a strong northerly wind created a sea surge which shot up the land. Sea defences all along the coast were breached and destroyed, as the millions of gallons of sea water swept inland. Tens of thousands of homes were damaged through the night and next day, leaving many thousands homeless. But the tragedies at sea were much worse. In all three hundred and seven lives were lost around the British Isles that night, including the sinking of a ferry, the Princess Victoria, with more than one hundred and thirty souls on board.*

# Chapter Ten

♦

# Circus Memories

Gareth's mind is a riot of excitement and nerves. He lies on his bed, staring at the ceiling. The impulsive and frenzied kisses with Kasiya have left a tingling in his body that won't settle down. All she said after their final kiss was, "See you later." Gareth can't unpick what that meant. Should he go and find her in her chamber? Or should he rein in his impulses and just see her tomorrow? Maybe Milton was right to warn about the pull of bodily desires in the Meadow.

A sound of shuffling feet echoes down the corridor outside. Gareth holds his breath and peeks at the slot of light washing in under the door. The shadow of two feet appears. They stand very still as though deciding whether to knock. Gareth wishes them to knock. Wishes *her* to knock.

Tap! Tap! Tap! The sound of soft knuckles patters on the door.

Gareth rushes up from his creaking bed. His body and its impulses are in the driving seat. In his haste, he skids into the door, rattling it loudly.

Standing in the candlelight as Gareth opens the door is Ibrahim, the young monk. Behind him, looking tired, is Hassan. His heart drops.

"High Councillor Drake has requested your attendance at the Council of Well Wishers," says Ibrahim. His chalk-white teeth gleam in his wide mouth.

Gareth, crestfallen, glances at Hassan. He shrugs back.

"It's a bit late, isn't it?" asks Gareth.

"Darkness is a necessary cover for such meetings," says Ibrahim curiously, offering Gareth a blanket.

"What does he want us for?" says Gareth, accepting the blanket and throwing it over his shoulders.

"No idea," says Ibrahim. "But it must be important. The priests never usually accept guests to join a midnight council."

"OK," says Gareth, intrigued enough.

The two men follow Ibrahim outside, across the dark, silent cloisters, and approach the crooked tower. It is a cold, crisp night, and the building is bathed in starlight. Gareth glances up to the girl's chambers opposite, wondering if Kasiya is awake. There's no sign of her.

"Follow me," whispers Ibrahim, holding his finger to his lips and stepping into the tower's base. He heads to the spiral staircase, where a faint orange light flickers. "The meeting has already started," he says, encouraging Gareth and Hassan to tuck in close behind him on the steep, spinning steps.

The stone is cold under Gareth's bare feet. The damp wall rough and uneven against his hands. His fingers trace the disorientating spiral leading them up into the gloom. The distant candlelight gradually fades, and Gareth's consciousness becomes consumed by the heaviness of his breathing, his eyes losing themselves in the suffocating darkness of Hassan and Ibrahim's shadows.

Somewhere up above, there is a familiar smash and a hiss. The discarding of marbles. Not one, but many. Gareth stifles his breath. Sneaking up another dozen steps with Ibrahim and Hassan, the voices become audible, and a heavy oak door halts their progress.

Ibrahim knocks firmly twice. The voices cease. A voice calls out from the other side of the threshold, *"May the seas warm, and the clouds form…"*

Ibrahim responds, *"…and may the rain fall, filling the rivers of Love."*

The door swings open, and the three men are ushered in.

"Welcome, Gareth and Hassan," Milton's commanding voice echoes around the candle-lit circular chamber. He stands in a heavy floor-length robe, surrounded by similarly dressed priests and monks seated around a table, their faces shrouded by the shadows of their cloaks. "Take a seat," he instructs, pointing to space at the far end.

The monks and priests are silent as the three men take their places, inspecting them suspiciously through their hoods.

"You can vouch for these men?" asks a shadowy figure, cutting through the silence. Gareth recognises the stern crackle of the priest's voice from the remembrance service.

"I can," confirms Milton.

"OK," says the priest, with authority. "Continue…"

"Thank you, Your Wellness," says Milton, bowing his head. "As I was saying before, we, the ardent and faithful followers of Well Wishing, have always believed there is a way back to Earth," he says, addressing the room. "Despite this steadfast belief, we have struggled to find the secrets of navigating the realms. Not for want of trying." Milton bows his head reverently again. "But now, I believe there is evidence of a successful journey taking place!" Milton looks around, the scar on his top lip twitching eagerly.

"This is why you convened the council?" asks the priest.

"Yes, your grace," Milton confirms, pausing. The priest nods and gestures for Milton to continue again.

"A few months ago, a passenger train crashed into the Meadow, right in the heart of London. You will no doubt have heard the commotion of its arrival even here? I believe *The Shipping Forecast* has only just stopped its daily coverage of the clean-up operation."

There are murmurs of agreement from the monks.

"Well, the Distillery has been attending to this arrival with peculiar scrutiny in the last few weeks. Despite converting the carriages into much-needed transport to the Source, they have since decommissioned them and started a complex salvage operation. Dismantling the carriages, out of public sight, in a covered dock on the Lethe."

"Very odd," says the priest. "And you have seen this?"

"Trusted friends and traders have," says Milton. "And from their accounts, we know the Distillery is compiling a catalogue of unusual finds."

"Unusual finds?"

"Curious things," responds Milton. "Scattered throughout the train. A rough depiction of the 'Encircled Drop' scribed into a headrest. Notes, left in seat pockets, quoting the Well-Wishing creed. And, most significantly, a luggage case containing a forbidden book of Dwr Folklore and a map of Mynydd Aaru."

"Are you serious?!" exclaims one of the monks. Gareth looks across at Hassan, bewildered.

"Absolutely," says Milton. "The Distillery are so concerned about this discovery that they guard the covered dock around the clock and have issued arrest warrants for any passenger who arrived on the train. There are huge rewards for information."

"But, if they've found that book and a map of the Mountain, that surely can only mean one thing…"

"The Cwtch Missions were a success!" exclaims Milton.

A few of the monks thump the table enthusiastically. The priest stands and claps Milton on the back.

"The Cwtch Missions?" asks one of the monks, sounding confused. Gareth and Hassan lean in, echoing his sentiment.

"My apologies. I forget some of you are not as long in the Meadow as me," says Milton, catching Gareth's eye. "Let me get you up to speed..."

"As you know, folk stories about Well Wishing have been told in the Meadow since ancient times – forbidden tales, known collectively as the *Dwr Folklore*. We have passed these stories by word of mouth amongst our community. Stories about the Daughter of God – Peace be upon Her – and stories about the early days of our belief." Ibrahim and a few others nod.

"There is one story, however, which is rarely told. A story contained in the rarest and most forbidden book of Dwr Folklore – the *Gweirglodd Mabinogion*. You may have heard of this book?"

There are excited whispers amongst the monks. "Only a few dozen copies were ever made. One copy is held by each of the High Councillors of Well Wishing." Milton reaches into his robe, then holds a small red leather book aloft. "In the Gweirglodd Mabinogion, there is the story of 'Beatrice's Hut'."

The interest amongst the monks reaches its peak. Barely a breath breaks the intensity of their concentration.

"The story of Beatrice's Hut tells of two Welsh shepherds arriving in the Meadow centuries ago, looking for their lost sheep. The shepherds encountered a woman living in a shepherd's hut – a *Ty Cwtch* in Welsh – on a mountain. The woman, Beatrice, tells the shepherds that if they follow her instructions, they will find their lost sheep. She tells them to traverse the cliffs around the mountain and collect a cup of pure water tumbling off them. Then she tells them to wait for a light that fills the sky before drinking the water and stepping into the light. Should they do this, they will find their sheep."

"One shepherd does as she says, and steps through an Opening, never to be seen again. The other shepherd is too proud and chooses to follow his instincts instead. But after months of searching without success, his pride falters, and he decides to embark on a journey to find the cliffs Beatrice spoke of. However, a thick mist surrounds the mountain, and he never finds them. Neither can he find the lady's hut. He perishes on the Mountain, lost in his quest and never seen again."

"Now the Cwtch Missions were a series of secret expeditions launched half a century ago, seeking to test whether the myth of Beatrice's Hut was real and might hold the secret to returning to Earth. The assumption was that the mountain containing the Source – Mynydd Aaru as it is called on Earth – housed Beatrice's hut, and the water that needed drinking was the pure water spewing off the Perihelion Cliffs at the Source."

"The Cwtch Missions were sanctioned by this Well-Wishing Council and attempted in secret. A dozen were launched, but each appeared to fail. A great number of brave souls were lost. With the failure of the thirteenth mission – a mission I led – the programme was disbanded."

Milton leans forwards, resting his palms on the table. "But some of us always hoped that one of those missions could have succeeded." He nods towards the priest. "Many failed before they got to the Mountain or were captured at Pont Fawr station. But a handful made it into the mist surrounding the peak. The fate of those that got that far is unknown. After all, with the Distillery police guarding the Source and the summit itself shrouded in eternal mist, we would never know if the believers had perished, been captured, or succeeded. The only way we would ever know for sure was if they found a way to communicate back from Earth. This communication is what I believe we have now found."

"Why do you think the finds from the train are from the Cwtch Missions?" a monk asks.

"We can't be certain," says Milton. "But it makes sense. A map of Mynydd Aaru and a book of Dwr Folklore were found together. Only an explorer from the Cwtch Missions would carry this, surely? But who? Was it left on the train as a signal? Or did it belong to one of the passengers?" Milton looks around the table and stops on the two guests.

"Maybe Gareth and Hassan can help us… they arrived on that very train after all…" Milton raises an arm towards the two men. The hooded figures all turn at once to scrutinise them. Gareth feels the tingling of embarrassment crawl across his body, and he lowers his gaze.

"You arrived on the train?" asks the priest urgently. Gareth and Hassan nod in unison. "Do you know anything about the artefacts High Councillor Drake talks of?"

Both men shake their heads. "Nothing? What about the passengers… did anyone say anything to you? Did you see anyone leaving the notes?"

Gareth looks at Hassan, hoping he remembers something because his mind is blank. The train crash is so distant and forgotten now. But Hassan just stares at the table blankly.

"Sorry," says Gareth. "We've been asked about this before. From the fragments of memory I have, there was nothing strange or unusual – except, of course, the crash."

"And do you remember the other passengers?"

Hassan looks up. "Some of them," he says. "I mean, obviously, there's Rosalyn…"

"She's the Flicker travelling with us," prompts Milton, noticing the priest's confused frown. "But a Flicker's memory can't help us."

"No," agrees the priest.

"And there was my sister, Cerys," says Gareth. A sting of regret tightens in his chest as he thinks of her.

"I assume she went to the Palace too?" the priest asks.

"I think so," says Gareth.

The priest gives a resigned nod. "Were there any others?" he asks, hopefully.

"There was an old man who was with us at the workhouse. Albert something," says Hassan. "He didn't seem the type to hold big secrets, though," he adds confidently.

"Albert Newman was his name," adds Gareth, trying to be helpful.

This announcement freezes the activity around the table. A collective intake of breath from the monks rasps like an icy wind.

"You are sure of this name?" asks the priest.

The intense and silent focus chokes Gareth momentarily. "Yes," he says. And when no one elaborates, he continues, "It's quite a common name."

"Yes…" says the priest, stroking his chin in thought. "But the chances of a Cwtch expedition leader's name being uttered in the same breath as these artefacts being found would be rather some coincidence." He pauses again. "What do you know of Albert's situation? When did you last see him?"

Gareth bows his head. "We knew him in the Distillery workhouse for a few months. He died in interrogation the day we left."

* * *

The sun shines brightly the next morning. The monastic chanting won't start until midday. In its place, the river's splashing, the birds' calls, and the woodland creatures' rustling are nature's melodic contributions to the day. The conversation around the cloisters bubbles with energy. Evidence of a potentially triumphant return to Earth, and discussion of Gareth and Hassan's memory of their train crash, are the topics of greatest interest. There is a palpable sense of optimism amongst the monks. On top of this, with only half a day's ride to Lin, the monastery's guests are excited about their imminent arrival at the circus. All of this slides Kasiya and the secret kisses to the back of Gareth's mind. He even ignores that she hasn't joined them this morning, at least until Rosalyn asks Milton where she is.

"Kasiya is having a period of spiritual reflection," says Milton cryptically.

"Oh," says Rosalyn. "She didn't mention anything last night."

"Don't worry. She won't be long," he responds. "The priest is leading her in a focused meditation this morning. It's always a good idea to rebalance your soul when your boat is rocking. And there's been a lot going on lately." He glances at Gareth, who avoids his gaze. Milton's eyes seem to penetrate his guilt.

As the conversation shifts back to the journey to the circus, Gareth peers nervously at Milton, trying to read his body language. Did Milton know about what happened with Kasiya? Had she told him? Or had he seen them? Gareth couldn't imagine that Kasiya would have volunteered the information nor offered to attend the meditation. The old stern priest was hardly a warm and welcoming person to spend the morning with. Milton must have instructed his daughter. In this case, he must have known something.

"So," Milton starts, addressing the travelling group and catching Gareth mid-thought. "I have agreed with the priest that I will try and make the journey to the Source again. A new Cwtch Mission. The priest has given his blessing." He scans them all. "And it might be worth your consideration that, if I am going to take this journey…" his eyes dart to Gareth. "…I might be looking for company."

Gareth looks around, trying to understand why Milton has focused on him. Hassan clears his throat. "I'll join you, Milton," he announces without hesitation. "I fancy my chances of finding the Source. I can help you to make it this time, brother." He pushes out his chest and looks towards Rosalyn, proud of himself.

Milton grimaces at Hassan. "I don't need any of you to commit to joining the journey now. Not yet. I'll get you to the Princess Victoria in Lin first. Settle you in, give you a chance to meet the circus folk, and get you enrolled in circus training. Only then, when you're in the right mind, will I see if you *really* fancy joining me on a journey to the Source." He pauses, thinking for a second. "It is a perilous journey. If any of you did volunteer, I'd need you to get some extensive survival skills first. I won't be as tolerant of burdens on that kind of journey." This last line verges on the scathing.

"I'm just saying," says Hassan. "I'd be up for it."

"Milton," starts Gareth, feeling pensive. "What makes the journey to the Source so dangerous?"

Milton sits up and looks at the group before leaning in. "All around the Source, down as far as Pont Fawr station, is a Distillery stronghold. Access in and out of the area is heavily policed. Any individuals caught in the vicinity are sprayed with Thermocline Mist. There are no questions asked. No chance to defend yourself or flee. There is a 'spray first' policy in operation."

"And if you manage to make it past the Distillery police at Pont Fawr, well, then there's the mist surrounding the Mountain. Breathing in the mist is equivalent to consuming litres of groundwater. Inhaling the damp atmosphere will slowly rid you of your consciousness and ultimately send you 'on'. With such dangers, anyone who attempts the journey must have a clear and untroubled mind – even the clearest minds will be foggy by their return. Any distraction poses a great risk of the mist consuming you. Many expeditions I have heard of have been lost this way." Milton leans back against his seat and exhales loudly.

"Is that why your mission failed?" asks Hassan.

Milton closes his eyes. "Compassion is not your strength, is it, Mr Dar?" he says sarcastically. A pained silence follows. "If it is OK with you all, I'd rather not recall the trauma of my mission right now."

Gareth looks at Hassan. He sneers and leans back in his chair.

"Who wants to go for a swim in the monastery pools?" asks Ashley, changing the subject. The conversation has got too serious for her at this time of the morning.

"I thought we had to be careful of the water in rivers?" Gareth asks.

"Oh, you do have to be careful," she says. "Whatever you do, don't drink the water. But it's really not that hard to avoid. It's different with young kids, but I think you should be able to manage. Besides, bathing on a warm morning like today is the most beautiful experience."

Gareth looks around at the others for confirmation.

"Honestly, the river Ouse is famously clean, contaminated with very little groundwater flow. It's one of the safest rivers for a good swim and might be the last clear water we can bathe in for a while. The circus is great, but the facilities are old and the water grim. Never mind the North Sea, which is cold, unwelcoming, and dangerous! I'm going for a dip here while I can!"

The three women, Ashley, Kasiya, and Rosalyn, are already at the bathing pools by the time Hassan and Gareth wander out. Milton isn't joining them. He has opted for some alone time in contemplation. The girls are chatting enthusiastically. Rosalyn is giggling, and Kasiya looks bashful. As soon as Kasiya sees Gareth, she goes quiet, and her cheeks go pink. Ashley can't help but grin widely at Gareth. They must know about him and Kasiya.

The three women wear shorts and T-shirts in the pool, but their body shapes differ. Ashley's skinny body and flat chest are hidden under her loose-fitting T-shirt. Her narrow hips comfortably settle into her shorts. Kasiya also wears a loose-fitting T-shirt, but her tall figure exposes her midriff. Her taught blemish-less brown skin is radiant in the sunlight. Rosalyn, in contrast, with her flowing white-blonde hair, has a buoyant chest which pushes tightly against her T-shirt, and her wide hips stretch the elastic of her shorts. Next to the curvaceous figure of Rosalyn, Ashley and Kasiya look curveless. Hassan can barely take his eyes off Rosalyn as she dips her toes in the pool.

The water is warm enough, but certainly not warm as the men enter the pools. Gareth shivers and has to talk himself into going deeper than his thighs. Contrasting Gareth's cautiousness, Hassan is straight in and up to his shoulders. Then he spots a tree branch hanging over the river channel.

"Check this out," he calls, leaving the bathing pool and grasping the branch from the riverbank. He swings back and forth. "This is how a real man bathes," he shouts, launching into the river. His splash soaks the rest of the group.

Rosalyn squeals as Hassan emerges with a "woohoo". Her smile gives him the encouragement that he desires. "Come on, Gareth," he says. "Be a man; come join me in the river!"

Gareth frowns. He has always wished that being a 'man' didn't require such an abundance of confidence or surplus of adrenalin. He has never felt that he has much of either to use up. He looks with an embarrassed glance at Kasiya, but she is in a world of her own, staring up at the trees.

"You don't have to," says Ashley. But Gareth doesn't register her voice. Reluctantly and somewhat more cautiously than Hassan, he wanders across to the riverbank and the overhanging branch. He pauses, trying to ignore the visions of impending catastrophe and takes a long deep breath. In the breath, he hears, deep in his memory, the taunts he used to get from his mum and his sister; "*Stop being such a whimp*"; "*Get on with it, your dad wouldn't hesitate*", and so on. "Shut up", he says to these voices. "Leave me alone." And he closes his eyes and swings from the branch.

Plunging into the river water is delightful. It is warm, clear, and fresh. He feels amazing. Coming up to the surface, Gareth opens his eyes and breathes out. He feels like he could stay in the water all day. He paddles over to Hassan, a broad smile across his face.

"If that's all it takes to be a man," says Rosalyn flirtatiously, "I'm in!"

"Oh yeah," says Hassan, the biggest grin on his face. "You think you can make a bigger splash than me?"

"It's not about the splash," says Rosalyn.

The group watch in amazement as Rosalyn climbs hand over hand along the branch and, without thinking, tucks herself into a ball, rotates through a somersault and slices into the water, almost without a splash. When she surfaces, she is beaming.

"Wow, Rosalyn!" shouts Ashley. "That was amazing!"

"Where did you learn to do that?!" says Hassan, astonished.

"I don't know," says Rosalyn. "I just knew I could do it."

"I tell you what, Rosalyn," shouts Ashley from the riverbank. "I know what training we will get you on at the circus: Trapeze!"

Smiling, Rosalyn swims over to join Gareth and Hassan.

"Seriously," says Hassan, "you can't remember where you learnt to do that? That's so crazy. Do you not remember anything from Earth?"

Rosalyn shakes her head and smiles cutely. The kind of smile designed to disarm a virile young man. It works on Hassan, but Gareth sees a sadness flicker across her eyes.

"What is the earliest thing you *can* remember?" Gareth asks. He wants to ask if she remembers, or knows, anything about Cerys, but this doesn't seem the right time.

Rosalyn looks at him, and momentarily, he thinks she is about to tell him something important. Then she drops her gaze and lies her head back in the water. Her white-blonde hair slithers out around her face.

"I remember fragments from the Palace and the moment Ashley picked me up," she says, sculling on her back. "But I can only truly piece things together from the last week with you guys. It is the strangest feeling. I feel like my body remembers more than my mind. I can do things I don't know where or when I learnt them."

"Living in the moment," says Hassan, dropping in the water so only his head is exposed. "That's the best way to live anyway."

Gareth notices Hassan's gaze is fixated on the bobbing up and down of Rosalyn's chest, repeatedly breaking the water's surface as she lies on her back. He chastises himself for looking as well and quickly throws his gaze away. Looking towards the riverbank, he sees Ashley and Kasiya negotiating the tree roots to come and join them in the river.

In a few minutes, the five of them are all in the river channel together, chatting, laughing, and swimming. Thoughts of Cerys, the Palace, Well Wishing, and dangerous journeys to the Source all float away. It feels excellent to Gareth to be with friends, carelessly soaking up the beauty of the surroundings. The water, it seems, washes away any worries. It has such peculiar effects in the Meadow.

* * *

When the caravans and their inhabitants are ready to leave the monastery, the sky has turned grey, and the wind has whipped up into a frenzy. They offer brief thanks to the monks for their stay, but most niceties are cut short by the fury of the weather.

Milton takes Pimlico by the reins, braving the elements and steering them eastwards through the forest towards Lin. The rest of the travelling group shelter inside the caravans, chatting cheerfully. Gareth still hasn't spoken with Kasiya about what happened in the wash-up. She doesn't seem bothered by it, but it is niggling him. Nonetheless, the general eagerness to get to Lin is palpable and keeps other issues like this at bay.

Within a few hours, the caravans reach the top of a hill beyond the far edge of the forest. The wind still kicks up leaves and dust from the road, but no rain falls from the clouds above. Milton calls them out of the caravan to join him.

In front of them, the vista of the Lin delta presents itself. In the far distance, the North Sea stretches away to the horizon. Closer in the bay lies the town of Lin. A small settlement surrounded by vast open fields, with tributaries of the river delta wiggling their way to the sea. The town is scattered around four or five major roads. Towards the northern edge is a complex of buildings surrounded by mature chestnut trees. It is too far to make out the details of the buildings, but it is possible to see a curious plume of black smoke rising from within.

"What's all the smoke?" Gareth asks innocently.

"I don't know," Ashley responds, looking concerned.

"And are those buildings…"

"…The Princess Victoria," says Milton quietly. Something is wrong.

\* \* \*

The gypsy caravans trundle slowly into Lin. The breeze whistles through the streets, blowing discarded newspapers and bits of ash across the road. The streets are deserted. A little way off, the crackling of burning wood can be heard. Turning Pimlico onto a side road, the entrance to the Princess Victoria appears.

Tall chestnut trees surround the gatehouse. A gaudy sign advertises Sanger's circus. '*All are welcome*', it says, alongside a picture of a rainbow pride flag and faded paintings of trapeze artists, elephants, lion tamers, and magicians. The iron gates leading past the gatehouse are bent, buckled, and left open. The doors and the roof of the gatehouse are charred black. The windows are cracked and smashed.

Milton clambers onto the track as the caravans come to a stop and tells the rest of the group to stay on their guard. He tentatively walks up to the gatehouse, his feet crunching over the burnt debris.

"Hello?" he calls out. Nobody answers. He pushes open the front door, and a shower of ash falls on his head. There is no sign of life.

Milton cautiously clambers back onto the caravan. "Something is very wrong," he says. "Be ready to turn and flee if we need to." He signals Ashley to take the reins and steer the caravans through the gates.

Their hearts are thumping as the Princess Victoria comes into view. Burning embers scatter the grounds in front of the Edwardian hotel. The hotel is damaged; the windows on the lower floors are smashed, and the doors are bashed in. But the building doesn't look to have suffered directly from fire. In contrast, on a wide-open patch of grass are the burning embers of a great red and white circus tent. A mangled steel and wood framework penetrates through the debris, and black smoke drifts into the midday sky. Little orange glows flicker on the ground. The shadowy imprint of the tent is a haunting indication of recent devastation. The only thing that has escaped unscathed is a large stone well standing prominently in front of the hotel. Its wooden bucket swings defiantly in the breeze.

Around the hotel, a hundred or so people are gathered, clearing debris, smothering embers, and trying to make order in the chaos. Their faces are ashen and tired. One of the crowd notices the elephant and the gypsy caravans as they come up the driveway. "Miss Ashley!" the lady calls out.

"Glenda!" calls Ashley, clambering off Pimlico and running to embrace the exceedingly tall lady.

"What happened here?" asks Milton, stepping down.

"The Distillery," says Glenda, her voice deep and full-bodied, and her arms wrapped tightly and gratefully around Ashley. "It was terrible…"

"The Distillery?" asks Ashley, releasing her grip and looking up, shocked. "Here in Lin?"

Glenda nods. "Fifty years of peace. Fifty years of irrelevance to the Pond Life. Then two nights ago, dozens of Distillery thugs storm in and destroy whatever they can." Glenda wipes her eyes with her dirty jacket sleeve, smearing ash across her furrowed brow.

"But why?" asks Milton.

"They had word that some extremely dangerous fugitives were being harboured here," Glenda says. Ashley turns to stare at Gareth and Hassan standing beside Milton. A pit opens in Gareth's stomach. "And they weren't going to be told otherwise," continues Glenda. "It's ridiculous, really. Don't they realise we're all fugitives of one type or another here?"

"So true," grimaces Milton, giving Gareth and Hassan a fatherly pat on their shoulders.

"Well," says Glenda, stooping, "there was no way the people at the circus would let them destroy the place without a fight. This is Sanger's circus!" A fire of defiance flickers in her eyes.

"I'm not sure the order of things that happened exactly, but when no one came forward with information, they started threatening people. I think some kid got walloped or did the walloping. Either way, a major fight followed. It was brutal. Some folk were sprayed with Thermocline Mist and sent 'on'. But our sheer numbers eventually overwhelmed them, and we chased them out of Lin." Glenda looks away into the distance. "They'll be back, though."

"I'm sorry to hear this," says Milton. "I wish we could have been here to help."

"You may still be able to," says Glenda, gesturing with her long, lanky arms for them to follow her.

Glenda, head and shoulders taller than anyone, leads them through the debris, past the stone well (Milton, Kasiya, and Ashley each throw a marble into the well as they pass, uttering a wish), and up the grand steps into the hotel.

Stepping through the entrance, they are greeted by the hotel's grandeur, which has escaped substantial damage from the fire. Gareth looks in awe at the bright colours and elaborate paintings on the walls. They show tightrope walkers in red leotards, great lions and beasts tamed by strong men with oiled moustaches, and people of all shapes and sizes doing wonderfully elaborate stunts. Hanging from the high ceiling, a chandelier made from stalagmites shimmers, reflecting the hue of the walls.

Despite the solemnity of the atmosphere outside, Gareth can't help but feel the energy in this great cathedral of colour. Ashley looks at him, buoyed by being inside the hotel. "Beautiful, isn't it?" she says.

"It really is," Gareth agrees.

Through a set of doors, the group enters a vast lobby where chequered marble tiles span the floor, and the ceilings are high and ornate. Great white pillars punctuate the space, filled with people in a cacophony of discussions. As the group steps in, the hubbub fades, and everyone turns to look at them.

A lady adorned in a technicolour robe, standing near the centre of the marble floor, holds out her arms. She has a beaming smile, and her long, flowing grey hair drapes down over her shoulders to her waist. Her yellow eyes sparkle. "Councillor Drake!" she calls out. "Oh, Milton, I'm so glad you are all safe. We have been so worried about you and your journey."

"We are safe," announces Milton stoically, stepping forward to shake the lady's hand. "I am so sorry to hear of events here while we were gone."

"Oh, we knew it would happen one day," says the lady. "The Pond Life always wanted an excuse to try and intimidate the good people of Lin. We have a great community here. They might have done some damage, but we forced them out. We'll be better prepared when they come back."

The lady looks across at Milton's companions. She smiles at Ashley. "It is fabulous to see you again, my darling. I'm sure Pimlico has loved having his favourite rider with him these past few weeks."

Ashley smiles reverently back at the lady and bows her head.

"And Kasiya, you look vibrant and beautiful, my dear." Kasiya averts her gaze. "I hope the time away from the circus with your father has been just what you needed." The lady looks back to Milton, who grimaces uncertainly in return.

"And you," says the lady, smiling at Rosalyn. "I had heard you were coming. My, you are gorgeous. I hope you find my circus to be a place of warmth. There are many, many girls from the Palaces like you here. Girls who have found their feet. Found their family."

Finally, the lady turns to the two men. "And you two, you must be the fugitives the Distillery seeks." The lady's words hit an accusatory note. Gareth hangs his head guiltily. "Oh no, don't be ashamed, my dear," she says, grasping Gareth's palm. "I mean that as a badge of honour!" And she beams at the two of them.

"I'm Kathleen Montague," the lady continues. "An old familiar face for anyone who has been to Lin before. This is my circus. I wish to extend the warmest welcome possible to you all, especially our three new arrivals. I am delighted that you have made it here. I am so sorry that you arrive at such a testing time." She smiles kindly at the group. Gareth feels her warmth wash over him like a familiar odour.

Kathleen turns to address all the people in the lobby. "Friends. A beacon of light in a dark week. High Councillor Milton Drake and his guests – two of the fugitives the Distillery are hunting – have arrived. They are safe, they are well, and they are joining our ranks!" The people around the atrium clap, beaming at them. Gareth can't help but smile back. Next to him, he can feel a similar fizz of joy emanating from Ashley. She is home.

Milton turns to Gareth and Hassan. "Bit of a different welcome here than you got from the Distillery, eh? One thing you'll find in the circus is the more the Pond Life hate you, the more you're loved here!"

Kathleen turns back to them, her demeanour more serious suddenly. "I need to get you all up to speed on what has been happening. Come with me."

She leads them through to a small room filled with armchairs and a round stone table. They sit down as Milton closes the door.

"As you have seen," Kathleen begins, "the circus was attacked a few days ago. This was the first time the Distillery has dared to breach the boundaries of Lin. We lost some brave souls in the attack. Two gatekeepers: Tom O'Brien and Samantha Parsons. They valiantly refused to let the thugs into the circus complex. They paid with their lives protecting us." Gareth notices Ashley lean into Kasiya, grasping her hand. She looks faint.

"Tom and Samantha were beautiful souls. They gave everything for our circus. Even in their final conscious moments, both were brave and wise. They sucked on marbles and managed to deposit these into a safe place. The Distillery thugs never found the marbles. They ransacked the gatehouse and set fire to it. But they never managed to erase the memories left behind. Samantha and Tom heard a conversation that tells us a great deal about the motivation for this unprovoked raid. I have already dissected Samantha's marble and seen her memory. We still have Tom O'Brien's memory bead intact. For all of your benefit, it will be valuable to see first hand what Tom experienced at the gatehouse that night."

Kathleen lowers the blinds. Milton stands up to assist. "Dissecting a marble gives us one glimpse at the truth. A true recollection of what happened," says Kathleen, mainly for the benefit of Gareth, Hassan, and Rosalyn. "But I must warn you that the memory may be traumatic. Once you see such a memory, you cannot unsee it." Kathleen pauses: her face shadowed in the darkness of the room.

"Would you do the honours, High Councillor?" she says to Milton. He wanders over and takes from Kathleen's hand a small dark green marble, laying it into a silk handkerchief he pulls from his pocket. He holds the cloth aloft in his palm.

In a deep and serious ceremonial voice, Milton says, "This is the last memory of Tom O'Brien, gatehouse keeper of the Princess Victoria." Kathleen, Kasiya, and Ashley bow their heads. The rest follow suit. "I will shortly offer you the deepest privilege of witnessing this noble man's final moments. A moment from the mist of his last marble."

Milton lays the silk handkerchief down and reaches for a golden nutcracker resting in the centre of the stone table. He delicately picks up the green marble and cracks it in the teeth of the golden implement. There is an oozing hiss, and a subtly luminescent mist engulfs Milton's hands.

Milton starts a procession around the room, offering the mist to each of them in turn and asking them to bow their head into his palms. Gareth watches as Ashley is first. The young woman makes herself as comfortable as she can in the armchair. She looks determined and nervous. As Milton holds out the mist in front of her, she leans forward, breathing in as the fog surrounds her head.

Ashley slumps back into her chair, her eyes closed as though she is deep asleep, and she doesn't stir.

By the time Milton reaches Gareth, half of the room is deep asleep. Gareth leans into the mist and takes in a deep breath. Suddenly his whole world is spinning. He loses his balance and falls back in his chair but doesn't feel it.

Through the darkness, a light appears in the distance. His consciousness is drawn towards it, and he finds himself in the gatehouse of the Princess Victoria.

It is a warm summer evening. The sun is almost down, and orange sunlight casts shadows into the gatehouse living room, where a young lady sits opposite Gareth. She looks at Gareth, smiles and says, "Tom, there's someone at the gate. Do you want me to go?"

Gareth spins around and sees Tom O'Brien. He is a tall man confined to a rickety wheelchair. His face is clean-shaven, and his eyes a brilliant blue. His legs are covered in a blanket, but the loose ends of the bandages are still visible. He smiles at the young lady.

"I've got it, darling," he says in a lilting, delicate voice.

Tom wheels himself to the front door, uses a walking stick tucked into his chair to hook it open, and looks out. Gareth follows behind, invisible. The grand iron gates outside are in place and shut, as they should be. The cobbled driveway is clear of debris, and beautiful bright yellow daffodils grow in the front garden.

At the iron gates, an old lady in a shawl is stooped.

"Can I help you?" Tom calls out.

The hooded older woman looks over. "Thank you, dear," she says, smiling. Her skin is dirty and grey, her eyes are sallow, and she has a mouth full of cracked yellow teeth. She approaches clumsily. "I have been travelling for many weeks to find this place. I am looking for some friends I lost. Friends of many years, who I believe may have sought refuge here in Lin."

The poor old lady is very frail. She stumbles as she walks towards Tom. He offers her his walking stick. "I'm sure we can help you," he says. "Come in and have a sit-down. I'll see if we have any record of your friends."

Back in the living room, Tom addresses his fellow gatekeeper. "Samantha, darling, this lady has lost her friends. She thinks they may have sought refuge here at the circus. Could you get her something warm while I get the records? Sorry, I never caught your name?"

"Claribel," says the old woman. "But don't bother yourselves, dear; I'm just here briefly."

"Oh, it's no problem," says Samantha, pulling up a chair as Tom wheels out to find the records. "Would you like a warm coffee marble?"

The old lady's eyes light up at the mention of a marble. "Oh, well, if you're offering, dear…"

Samantha passes the old lady a coffee-coloured marble. She snatches it and greedily thrusts it into her mouth. "Mmm," she says. "Thank you."

Tom reenters the room with a big old dusty book on his lap. "So, who are these friends of yours?" he says.

"Ooh," Claribel says, sucking on the marble. "Well, there's my good friend Gareth Edwards." Gareth feels a jolt of awareness at hearing his own name. Tom flicks through the book. "No, I'm afraid Gareth is not here," he says.

"What about Hassan Dar?" she asks. Again, the familiar name unsettles Gareth. Tom flicks through and shakes his head. "Maybe, my other friend, Albert Newman?"

Tom stops and looks at the lady for a moment. He glances back over at Samantha. "I recognise that name," he says. He flicks through to the 'N' surnames. Yes, there had been an Albert Newman at Sanger's circus. "I'm afraid," Tom says, "we did have an Albert Newman here. But he has not been here for almost forty years."

"Ooh," says the old lady. "That's a shame."

"When did you lose your friends?" asks Samantha, trying to be helpful.

"Oh," the old lady looks surprised, and she fumbles her answer. "Um, I don't quite remember. But I'm sure they said they would come here if we got separated."

"Well, I'm sorry, darling," says Tom. "Have you got somewhere safe to go?"

"Oh, yes," says the lady. "Oh yes. I just wanted to come knocking. Do you mind if I have another marble for the road?" she says, stepping up from her chair and grinning her yellow teeth at the two gatekeepers.

"Of course," says Samantha. "Can we help you to get home?"

"No, no, dear. I'm fine."

Claribel ambles out of the gatehouse clutching the marble and closing the door hurriedly behind her.

Tom looks at Samantha. "I haven't heard Albert Newman's name in a long time."

"No, me neither," says Samantha, pulling the book of records over and staring at it absent-mindedly. Gareth drifts over her shoulder and looks at the open book. Albert's name and a formal sketch of the old man look back from the page. Except, it's not Albert as the older man that Gareth remembers from the workhouse. Instead, he sees the sketch of a much more youthful man. A man with the same wrought face and determined eyes. But this is Albert Newman, 'the explorer' – the leader of a Cwtch Mission to the Source.

"I think I'll hold on to this marble," says Tom, placing his hand in front of his mouth. Slowly the world dissolves into blackness all around Gareth.

Gareth waits in the darkness for a few seconds, wondering what happens next, when the same setting in the gatehouse materialises again, but it is much darker now. Tom must have dropped the marble from his mouth and then put it back in again later that night. Tom and Samantha are both in the living room again.

"There's a carriage coming," whispers Samantha. "They don't look friendly."

Tom peers out of the window. Up the driveway, in the darkness, a horse-drawn carriage is making its way towards the gatehouse. Pulling the carriage are two mighty shire horses draped with purple cloths bearing the emblem of the Distillery. The riders are holding aloft flaming torches.

"The Distillery!" says Tom, not masking his surprise. "What are they doing here?"

"I don't know," says Samantha. "Something isn't right."

Gareth stares out at the approaching vehicle. He is shocked to see the old lady, Claribel, reclining on a seat at the front of the carriage. She grins madly as a man next to her in faded blue jeans, and a bomber jacket feeds her dark black marble after dark black marble. The old lady is evidently an addict.

Suddenly, one of the marbles bursts into the old lady's mouth. Samantha and Tom draw back from the window in disbelief. The marble's mist engulfs the old lady's head, and she tumbles off the carriage. Without slowing or altering course, the carriage careens over her, knocking her limp body to the ground. It is a violent assault.

Before Tom or Samantha have time to do anything, there is an aggressive rapping at the door.

"Who is it?" shouts Samantha.

"It's the Distillery," an assertive voice comes back. "We have reason to believe that Sanger's circus harbours three dangerous fugitives."

"I'm sorry," says Samantha defiantly. "You must be mistaken. There are no fugitives here. We're just a circus troupe." She gestures for Tom to hide. He looks reluctant, but when Samantha places her hand on her chest and mouths a silent 'please', he nods and wheels himself into the larder, closing the door silently. He can still see the kitchen through the slats in the wood.

"I'm not asking you; I'm telling you!" the voice shouts back. "This circus is harbouring… three… dangerous… fugitives!"

"You're wrong," repeats Samantha. "There are no fugitives here."

The man barges open the door. "We all know that's not true," he says forcefully, his presence looming like a monster into the room. "This whole circus is a lie, a den of sin, a haven for the Evil Thirst. The Distillery have known this for years. We've turned a blind eye because most of the scum you allow here are weak and pathetic losers. Individuals who we wouldn't waste our time tracking down. But on this occasion, the fugitives are too dangerous for us to ignore."

"We sent an informant here earlier this evening. She asked about the whereabouts of these three fugitives. She told us that an individual named Albert Newman had resided here. Now tell me.

Did you lie to the old lady? Is someone who claims to be Albert Newman residing here *now*?"

Samantha looks incredulously back at the man. "No," she says unambiguously. "Albert Newman left Sanger's circus forty years ago. He *died* forty years ago!"

The man strides forward, spotting the old book of records on the table. "Forty years ago," he says, flicking through the pages, "Albert Newman was public enemy number one. A servant of the Evil Thirst. A Satanist who distracted many minds into believing they could return to Earth. A criminal who we suspected operated out of Sanger's circus. When he died forty years ago, we celebrated his evil soul perishing in the Meadow."

"Then, two months ago, a train crashed through an opening in London, and three men stepped out into our world, conscious. Someone got to these men before they were formally processed, and now one of them has been claiming to be Albert Newman, returned from the dead."

"Albert has returned?!" exclaims Samantha, failing to quash her thrill at this suggestion.

"No," says the man, aggravated by the woman's idea. "Someone is *masquerading* as Albert Newman, trying to spin the same yarn that the troublemaker spun all those years ago – trying to corrupt the souls of our people. This trouble-maker... *this criminal*... and his accomplices must be stopped. Their short time in the Meadow must come to an end!"

The man steps up to Samantha and grabs her by the throat. Another thug steps into the room behind him.

"She causin' you trouble, sir?" asks the second man, pulling a canister of Thermocline Mist from his belt.

"I don't know," replies the first man looking directly at Samantha and forcing her against the closed larder door. The door behind which Tom, and now Gareth as an invisible observer, hold their breath. "*Are* you causing trouble?" he hisses, his mouth inches from Samantha's.

"No," whispers Samantha, struggling to breathe and conceal the marble in her mouth. "I don't know about these men you are looking for. They are not here."

"Well, if *you* are not going to cooperate, then I shall have to take this up with someone higher," rasps the man. He drops his hold of Samantha but kicks her brutally in the shins, flooring her. Unseen to the thug, a marble falls from her mouth and rolls under the door. "We know the fugitives were heading here," the man shouts at Samantha, kicking her again. She writhes in pain on the ground. "We know this so-called Albert Newman is at large. We will get all three of them; mark my words!"

Tom and Gareth watch in horror as, without hesitation, the man pulls a canister of Thermocline Mist from his belt and stoops down over Samantha, discharging the contents into her face. Samantha struggles and tries to move her face away from the cloud of mist but can't. Eventually, she runs out of breath and inhales the vapour.

Immediately Samantha's back arches, and her eyes loll backwards before returning in an unfocused stare. Her body goes limp and lifeless momentarily. Then she gently clambers up from the floor and drifts away. She has been sent 'on'.

Tom's breathing becomes shallow in the larder, his eyes wide in shock. Before he can process what he has just witnessed, the second thug in the room speaks up.

"Do you think she knew anything?" he asks.

"Probably not," the first man responds with callous disinterest.

"They're definitely heading here, right?"

"Almost certainly."

"And it's really him? Albert Newman, back from the dead?"

The first man nods, pulling out a cigarette from his jacket pocket and lighting it.

"What does that mean?"

There is a pause before the man responds. "It means we have to kill him."

Inside the larder, Tom silently picks up Samantha's discarded marble. Tears are falling down his cheeks. He carefully prises open a drawer. His tears splash into the dry, dusty contents. Tom places the marble into the drawer and then glances back towards the shafts of light coming through the door. Gareth notices his jaw clench. He drops the marble from his mouth into the drawer as well and closes it quietly.

As the memory begins to fade, Gareth watches as Tom unhooks a rolling pin hanging from the larder wall and spins himself around awkwardly in his wheelchair to face the door before forcing it open abruptly.

"You bastards!" Gareth hears Tom shout as light floods into the larder. Then the memory fades into complete darkness.

*Colney Hatch Asylum was an institution housing over three thousand of the "pauper insane" in the city of London. The facility posed a significant fire risk as many of the inmates were housed in temporary timber wings, and the complex was famous for its long corridors. On the night of 27th January 1903, the inevitable happened. One of the timber wards caught fire and aided by local strong winds, rapidly spread, out of control through the complex. Many of the women who resided in the asylum were burned in their beds, and the charred remains of others were found huddled together in corridors. In all, fifty-two women lost their lives that night. It was the worst peacetime fire in London's history and remained so for over one hundred years after.*

# Chapter Eleven

◆

# An Expedition Awaits

The banqueting suite in the Princess Victoria is lit with hanging lanterns and tea lights. Most of the town of Lin has congregated. Inside, a local folk band play a familiar song. The chorus, *"Her loving rain is falling free. The soil thirsts, the rain drops sink into the sea,"* echoes around the hall as herbs are smoked, and marbles sucked in enormous quantities. At the front of the room is a line of top tables. Kathleen Montague sits at the front, adorned in her technicolour robes. She wears a bright red beret to top it off and beams at the crowd.

Next to Kathleen are members of the Circus Council. Milton is on her right, beside his wife and Kasiya's mother, Nailah Hussain-Drake. Nailah is the head of the City Circus. Her roots are North African, and her smile is broad and wholesome. Next to her is Veronica Lacewitt, Senior Matron of Colney Hatch Sisterhood, the Home of the Flickers. She is a stern-looking lady with tight pulled-back auburn hair and a snuggly fitting black suit. Gareth recognises her as the midnight visitor to the Tide and Time Tavern. Finally, there is Glenda Burgess, Ashley's friend they met when they arrived. Glenda is a tall, gangly lady who heads Circus Security. In front of Glenda lie two black cloths, memorials to the fallen gatekeepers.

Kathleen stands and holds her hands aloft, ushering quiet amongst the crowd. Herbal pipes bubble away, with the occasional hiss of a discarded marble, but the audience's attention is captured. "Thank you," says Kathleen, casting her voice to every corner of the room. "A great tragedy has brought us all together tonight – a great tragedy which each of you met with great solidarity. I thank you all for your decision to come here tonight. Many of you I have known for decades. Some of you even a century. I am so very pleased to see each one of you.

"Three nights ago, we tragically lost three beautiful souls from our circus. Samantha Parsons, treasured gatekeeper of twenty years. Tom O'Brien, veteran gatekeeper of fifty years. And, Rosie McGregor, stable girl of one year at Sanger's circus." A young man sobs loudly at the mention of the last victim. "May I encourage you all to discard a marble in memory of these heroes of Sanger's circus."

There is a clinking like glass rain as people, in unison, fling marbles to the floor around them. Hisses erupt like a great release of tension, and a mist temporarily blinds the room before it rapidly fizzles away. "The fallen!" calls out Milton Drake, raising his pipe in the air, and the crowd respond.

"Three nights ago," Kathleen Montague continues. "A band of thugs broke into our sanctuary here in Lin and ransacked our circus." She pauses before shouting at the top of her voice, "We drove them away!" There is an emphatic cheer around the hall.

Kathleen lets the energy ripple around the people momentarily before she raises her hands again. "Many of you will want to know why: why did they come? Why now? Well, I can give you an answer.

"The Distillery has long hated Sanger's circus. They hate what we stand for. They hate that we are welcoming to everyone. They hate that we celebrate the beautiful diversity of life and love. But they also hate that we, and the town of Lin, provide refuge for those they deem to be 'troublemakers' in the Meadow. And it is true – many of you, me included, have been, or still are, hiding from the edicts of the Distillery. Nonetheless, this has never given enough reason for the Distillery to breach the peace in our town. Until now.

"Memory beads recovered from the gatehouse have shown us that the Distillery attacked the Princess Victoria three nights ago because they had word that three of their highest-ever priority fugitives were being harboured here at Sanger's circus." A few heads turn and peer around the room, but most continue to hold their full attention on Kathleen.

"Their intelligence was wrong. The fugitives were not here. Admittedly, two of them were only a few days ride away with High Councillor Drake," she winks at Gareth and Hassan, sat just in front of her. "But we weren't going to tell them that. And as for the third... well, nobody knows where he is. But by God, I hope he does turn up here!" Kathleen's enthusiasm falls on a sea of silence.

"A train crash in London brought the three fugitives into the Meadow together – three strangers, brought together by a catastrophe – one old, two young. And on the surface, there was nothing unusual about these three men. Which is exactly what the Distillery thought when they processed them in the workhouse.

"But when the older man escaped the workhouse, and the young men disappeared from the campus, the Distillery quickly discovered something astonishing. Something so significant that, if it got out, their whole structure of power in the Meadow could be brought into doubt. No, more than that, their whole system of belief could collapse. And so, they decreed that the three men must be found...must be killed."

There is a thick air of anticipation around the room. No marbles are being sucked anymore, and many pipes have gone out.

"The Distillery discovered that this was not the first time that one of the fugitives had arrived in the Meadow!"

There is an intake of breath from some in the room. Others look around, confused. "Yes, what I am saying," says Kathleen, "is that the Distillery discovered an anomaly. Someone they thought had left the Meadow and gone 'on' years ago had actually returned to Earth and come back." Now the gasps and intakes of breath are audible.

"Forty years ago, a series of expeditions left Lin, bound for the Source, attempting to collect pure water from the Perihelion Cliffs – the Cwtch Missions. Many of you will recall the era when we sanctioned the launch of these dangerous missions. So many brave souls from our community gave their lives in pursuit of the dream. The dream that the Missions could realise the great hope of our rebellion. The successful navigation from the Meadow back to Earth.

"For decades, we assumed these Missions all failed. We mourned our losses and reassessed the foundations of our movement. But now we have discovered and verified that the leader of the first Cwtch Mission, Commander Albert Newman, successfully made it back to Earth and returned. Commander Newman is back in the Meadow after an absence of forty years!"

An excited chatter engulfs the hall. Kathleen and Milton start a standing ovation. "To Commander Newman!" shouts Milton, hurling a handful of marbles to the floor. The ovation spills over into cheers and tears of joy. In the excitement, the band spontaneously start up a tune. Everyone joins in the singing and dancing, led by Kathleen and the whole top table.

After countless chorus repeats, Kathleen ushers quiet in the crowd again. "Our rebellion is strong. Our rebellion is true," she begins. "May today's news invigorate us. May it embolden us to tell the truth. We may still be a tiny number in the Meadow, but the Pond Life should rightly fear us." Another cheer erupts, this time dominated by lower masculine tones. "Sadly, we know the Distillery will launch another assault on Sanger's circus and the people of Lin. They will come with numbers and strength, and they will likely destroy the buildings, the books, and the Circus artefacts. Such is their fear of the truth we know.

"Based on reports from travellers who have passed through Lin recently, we expect the Distillery's return within a fortnight, so we do not have long. As you know, yesterday I called an emergency session of the Circus Council. We have been in session throughout the night. It is our regretful conclusion that, for the protection of you and your families, we now advise you to make arrangements to flee Lin. We have spoken with the mayors of sympathetic towns in the north. The mayors of Boston, of York, and Nottingham. And they have guaranteed refuge for the people of Lin.

"I do not want you to feel alarmed. We have faced threats before. But what the Council recommends, I believe, is proportionate and sensible in light of the threat we face. The spirit of Lin, and the spirit of the Circus, is far mightier than the

Distillery's impotent strength. This is why they will never win, and we will prevail."

From his seat, Gareth scans the faces of the people. Their joy has quickly settled, and all around, people look worried. Concerned silence ripples across the hall.

"I have a few more requests," says Kathleen, her voice echoing into the silence. "Commander Newman is somewhere in the Meadow. He is old and alone. And he is hunted with a ferocious hatred never before seen in the Meadow. But we know he is *somewhere,* and we know he is alive. We owe it to Commander Newman to send a search party and bring him home.

"I am looking for a few volunteers to head to London, the Commander's last known location, and join up with our good friend Professor Pelling at Virgil College to begin a search for Albert…"

Without hesitation, two gentlemen in the centre of the hall stand up. Both men are exquisitely dressed. Their suits complement the beautiful silk cravats adorning their necks and their fabulous postures.

"Hector, Edmond, thank you so much. Commander Newman will be delighted to see you both again." Kathleen's delight radiates towards the two volunteers, and she ushers them to join her at the top table.

"And my second request is a rather enormous one," Kathleen continues. "Commander Newman's successful return to Earth and back has shown us that the passage between the realms is possible.

"I know many of you have been in the Meadow so long now, and you have no desire to return to Earth. I, likewise, have no desire to return to Earth. Nonetheless, opening the passages back to Earth to give new arrivals a chance and the belief that they can go back is vital to our movement. Opening the passages would clear the way for the flow of love between the realms and end the stranglehold of fear gripping the Meadow for so long.

"Therefore, I am calling for another attempt to be made." There are whispers around the hall as Kathleen lets the announcement sink in. "We, the Council of the Circus, ask for volunteers to make the expedition to the Source once more.

"I don't ask lightly. This expedition comes at great cost to all who join it, for no one on such an expedition can remain in the Meadow. There are only two outcomes; you go to the next realm or return to Earth. High Councillor Milton Drake and the head of the City Circus, Nailah Hussain-Drake, have already agreed to lead this expedition with their daughter, Kasiya. Thank you all," says Kathleen, turning and bowing her head to Milton and Nailah. "But we would like a handful more volunteers. I know this is a great ask, but if there are any amongst you who are willing, please do step forward."

No one around the hall moves at this request. It is an enormous decision to make. Quite literally a 'do or die' commitment. Hassan leans over to Gareth and whispers in his ear. "We're gunna be hunted like Albert as long as we stay here," he says. "It's got to be worth a shot." And he stands up confidently, pushing out his chest and looking around the room.

"Mr Dar. One of the Distillery's most wanted! Thank you," says Kathleen. "Your bravery is admirable."

Gareth feels the eyes of the room turn on Hassan right next to him. His heart starts thumping like a malfunctioning piston engine. He can't think straight. He can't tell if an expectation that he will stand up is real or imagined. He can't tell if he even wants to stand up. He can't tell if he wants to return to Earth. "*Fuck it!*" the impulsive voice in his head announces, and he stands up.

"Mr Edwards," announces Kathleen. "Thank you!" Gareth wobbles on his feet, feeling every eye turn on him, piercing his confidence. He inadvertently leans on Hassan for stability. Looking at the top table, he catches Milton's eye. Milton's scarred lip twitches into a grin, and he nods at Gareth.

Gareth and Hassan wander up to the top table to stand alongside Milton and Nailah, while behind them, Ashley stands up, followed by the young man who had sobbed loudly at the announcement of the departed souls from the assault on Lin. Finally, Glenda stands up from the top table and offers herself.

All the volunteers, and Milton, Nailah, and Kasiya, are invited by Kathleen to stand together in front of the top tables. "In two weeks, Lin will no longer be the home of Sanger's circus. In two weeks, most of us, God willing, will be safely settling into new homes and new communities. In two weeks, these brave souls will set off on their quests. The circus will continue, and we will re-establish our links and our work when the time is right. But the journey of these expeditions will be dangerous and tough. So let us hold this group of ten brave souls in our hearts. The future of our movement may depend on them."

"For now, though," Kathleen's tone changes, and a youthful energy twinkles in her eye. "Let's put aside our worries about the future. There will be plenty of time for that later. We should enjoy each other's company tonight. The evening is young, and these marbles won't suck themselves!"

On Kathleen's announcement, the folk band take their places and begin playing with infectious energy. Buckets of marbles are brought to the tables, and a joyous atmosphere engulfs the entire hall. In no time, it feels like the Princess Victoria is the host of a raucous family wedding.

The ten volunteers, particularly Gareth and Hassan, inadvertently become minor celebrities in the celebrations. As volunteers for the expedition, two of the most wanted fugitives in the Meadow, and the only people who have met Commander Newman since his return, everyone wants a word with them.

Hassan thrives on the attention. He struts from group to group, telling people everything they want to know and basking in the adulation. In contrast, Gareth is sick and out of sorts. Social occasions like this have always made him anxious, never mind when he is the centre of attention.

All Gareth can see are hundreds of unfamiliar faces and almost zero obvious common ground. He wants to hide away in some quiet spot with someone he knows, maybe Kasiya. They still haven't had the chance to discuss what happened at the monastery, and it would settle him immensely to find out she still felt the same. But Kasiya doesn't leave her mother's side all night, and Nailah is not the shy and retiring type. Gareth briefly introduces himself to

Nailah, but most of the time, mother and daughter are surrounded by men from the Well-Wishing hierarchies, and he doesn't feel comfortable in those conversations for long.

Eventually, as the furore of the evening calms down, Gareth settles himself at the far end of the marble bar, consuming marbles with Ashley – she doesn't thrive in the hubbub of social settings either.

Chatting into the night, Ashley tells him all about her family on Earth. How she had left two loving parents and a younger brother when she entered the Meadow. Her elderly parents were in their seventies when she died, and she assumes they are already in 'the Beyond' by now. But her brother Dennis had joined the British Army and was away, fighting in France, when she died. She has no idea what happened to him in the war but is desperate to find out. He would be in his eighties on Earth now.

The mention of a sibling brings Cerys to the front of Gareth's mind. He feels guilty that he hasn't thought of her in a while – especially now that he has committed to an expedition to leave the Meadow. But he tries to excuse himself: so much has been going on, and she might have already left the Meadow anyway.

"Me and Cerys used to be so close," Gareth says sadly. "Especially after our father passed away."

"I'm so sorry," says Ashley.

"No, it's OK," says Gareth. "We were kids when it happened." As he says this, a crystal-clear memory flashes through his mind. His mum crying in the kitchen. The pot boiling over unsupervised. And one negligent place laid at the dinner table.

"What is she like, Cerys?" asks Ashley, looking genuinely interested.

"Steady," says Gareth, surprised at how quickly the word pops into his head. "She left school at sixteen and went straight to work. She never looked back. She strolled through life like she had already walked that path before. Not like me," he says, hanging his head. "I just follow the path laid out before me: school, sixth form, university…"

"You stood up tonight…" offers Ashley, putting a friendly hand on his shoulder.

Gareth looks up. "Thanks," he says. "Cerys would have stood up without hesitation, though," he disparages himself again. "I'm sure there were times when Cerys wasn't so steady," says Ashley. Gareth thinks for a moment. "Yeah, I suppose." He runs his finger along the bar absent-mindedly. "Boys. Cerys couldn't pick a nice one for trying."

"I've been there," frowns Ashley.

"She just got out of a *horrible* relationship before the train crash…" says Gareth, staring into the middle distance. Ashley looks at him sympathetically. "Dominic was bad news. I think she'd have taken the crash a week earlier if she had the chance."

Gareth remembers when Cerys reluctantly told him that Dominic had hit her. It was in her flat. She had dark makeup streaking down her face, congealed with her tears, and she was so scared. The memory makes Gareth feel sick. Then the thought of Cerys suffering in the Distillery Palace tumbles into his mind. He clenches his teeth. He cannot attempt to return to Earth without finding Cerys first.

"Gareth?" says Ashley, carefully interrupting his thoughts.

"Yes?" he says.

"I wanted to ask you about… well, about Kasiya…"

This catches Gareth by surprise. "Kasiya?" he says, looking back at her, his face flushing red.

"She told me what happened at the monastery." Ashley avoids his eyes. "I just want to make sure you're not going to hurt her, you know…she's been my friend for years, and I know how vulnerable she is…"

"I'm not going to hurt her," says Gareth, slightly affronted. "I really like her. But we haven't even spoken since the monastery," he pauses. "I think she's avoiding me."

"She does like you, too," says Ashley, smiling reassuringly. "I just think she's worried."

"Worried? Of what?"

Ashley inspects Gareth's pleading face. "Sorry," she says, "But I think that's for Kasiya to say."

"Alright," says Gareth, looking across the hall to where Kasiya stands with her mother. Nailah converses confidently with two priestly-looking men while her daughter clings to her shadow, quiet and nervous. Gareth can't imagine Kasiya is going to talk to him anytime soon. He'll have to manufacture any such conversation himself.

"Just be careful, you know," says Ashley. "Relationships carry a heavy burden in the Meadow."

"You sound like Milton," Gareth cuts back.

Ashley lets his flippant remark deflect off her and grimaces. "I'm just saying if you want to go home, make sure your body doesn't want to stay here."

"Yeah, OK," says Gareth, not fully listening to Ashley's warning. Kasiya has just glanced towards him, and he feels his heart flutter as she flicks him a smile.

* * *

The expedition meet on the garden terrace of the Princess Victoria the next morning. It is a crisp spring day with a low mist hanging over the surrounding fields. First down are Gareth, Hassan, and Milton. They chat, as men often do, about practical things. Things that don't require any personal or emotional contribution.

"How are we getting to the Source then?" asks Hassan. "We won't be jumping on a Distillery train, I presume?"

"Ha! If only," says Milton, pushing a pinch of dried leaves into his pipe and lighting it. "No, we'll be travelling in something like the carriage I picked you up from the city in. But more discrete, obviously. We won't be travelling by elephant! I've got my eye on a few horse-drawn merchant carriages. They are light-weight, unobtrusive, and sturdy; designed to tackle the most unfavourable terrain."

It's not long before the rest of the expedition joins them on the terrace. The first down is the young man, Billy McGregor. He is similar in age to Gareth but is so skinny and pale that he looks years younger. Billy has only been in the Meadow for a couple of years. However, his whole time seems to have been plagued by misfortune. He had sobbed at the celebrations last night because he had lost his sister Rosie in the Distillery attack. Rosie was a stable hand for the circus.

"I arrived in the Meadow from a car crash," he tells them. "We were all in the car when a stray rockfall wiped us out. Mum and Dad were unconscious when we arrived. Rosie and I followed them for about a month, trying to wake them. Only when the Distillery intercepted us around Manchester did we discover there is no waking a Drifter."

"And did the Distillery take you to a workhouse when they found you, brother?" asks Hassan, looking at Billy's scarred forearms.

Billy nods and clenches his teeth. "They'll pay for how they've treated my family," he says. Although he is slight in stature, Gareth can tell Billy has a steely resolve.

Next down is Glenda Burgess from Circus Security. She turns up in combat fatigues. Not especially for the expedition, but because these are her choice of casual clothes. Her black leather boots are buffed into a perfect shine, and her fuzzy hair is tied tightly in a bun. She grabs a handful of blueberry marbles before sitting down and introducing herself.

"Looks like I'm going to be the mum of the expedition," she says, smiling.

"Why do you say that?" says Billy. "Nailah is older than you."

"She's older in Earth years, but I've been in the Meadow far longer. Next year I'll be a double centurion... well, I would be if I hadn't gone back to Earth already!"

"Cheers to that!" says Milton, blowing out a plume of smoke and raising his pipe to the sky.

"That is unless I come straight back," chuckles Glenda. "I've got some stormy seas to survive when I get to Earth…"

"Come again?" says Hassan.

"Well, I arrived here in the Meadow from a shipping disaster. Many of us did in those days. A drunken captain and rough seas were the fatal combination for me. We ran aground at Dutchman's Bank in the pitch black of night."

"So, when I return to Earth, I'm going to find myself back in the foundering hull of a paddle steamer... that'll be interesting!" She grins at the men and rubs her hands together eagerly. "I like a good challenge."

Following close behind Glenda is Nailah Hussain-Drake. She arrives with Ashley in tow. The two women are chatting energetically as they stroll onto the terrace.

"The dream team!" says Nailah, noticing the others and opening her arms wide, beaming at everyone. "What an honour..."

"The honour is ours," says Glenda. "If half the stories about you and the City Circus are true, you're a legend. I hear you once broke into the London Palace and single-handedly freed a hundred women!"

"Haha. Not quite!" says Nailah. "The women freed themselves. I just created the diversion." She winks at Glenda, struggling to stop her beaming smile from sparkling.

Nailah exudes an air of unshakable competence. Her eyes are bright, and when she talks, she is magnetic.

"Is our daughter not joining us?" asks Milton.

Nailah's gaze flicks across at her husband. "Not quite yet," she says. "She's feeling a bit... under the weather...She'll be down later." Nailah offers an apologetic smile to her husband, who returns one likewise.

"Is Kasiya OK?" asks Ashley.

"Oh, yes, dear," says Nailah reassuringly. "She'll be fine."

Finally, the remaining volunteers arrive as a couple: Hector and Edmond – the two men tasked with finding Commander Newman. Like last night, Hector and Edmond arrive impeccably dressed. They wear tight denim jeans and complementary flannel shirts, and both have precisely sculpted hairstyles.

"Good risen!" says Edmond energetically. "Lovely day for an expedition, eh?!"

"Would you *really* call your task an '*expedition*'?" remarks Glenda sarcastically, sticking her tongue out at Edmond.

"Oh, give over, darling," says Hector, dropping his wrist on Edmond's shoulder. "Finding a decrepit old gay man lost in the city is far more fabulous than trudging up a great dirty mountain for some water!"

The comparison tickles Glenda, and in her mirth, she spits her marble out, and it smashes with a hiss on the floor.

It turns out Hector and Edmond are only planning to join the group for the morning. They will begin their journey to London this afternoon. But before they go, they want to hear Gareth and Hassan's memories of Commander Newman. Hector and Edmond were close friends with Albert the last time he was in the Meadow. They had even been groomsmen for his wedding. They are keen to hear how he might have changed in the intervening forty years.

"So tragic," says Hector, crossing his legs and lowering his eyes. "Albert and Sebastian were the perfect couple. Each so brave and so determined. They were both on the first Cwtch Mission, you know? The Mission that was sabotaged."

"Sabotaged?" asks Gareth.

"Someone in the expedition was a traitor," continues Edmond, leaning in so everyone could hear. "Everyone but Albert perished before they even reached the Mountain. We found Albert in Merseyside after the tragedy. He was despondent and angry and in such pain. But he couldn't be talked around from completing his Mission. Trust me, we tried! He went off to Pont Fawr on his own. That was the last time we saw him."

The tale of Albert Newman enthrals Gareth. It is incredible to hear about the old man's life the last time he was in the Meadow. Albert had held his cards close to his chest at the workhouse and for good reason.

After a good hour of conversation and introductions, Milton and Naliah get the expedition members down to business, planning the journey ahead. Their expedition will comprise two main stages. First, getting to the Source and collecting the pure water. Then, second, finding an Opening from Earth through which they can travel.

They are not going to dwell too much on the second stage. No one is known to have successfully even achieved the first, except Commander Newman. They aren't going to get carried away with their chances just yet. After all, Openings are frequent in the cities – especially in London. If they do somehow achieve the first stage, they will head to London and wait there to attempt their incredible step between the realms.

Milton tells the group how they plan to achieve the first stage. "We will be travelling exclusively by night along the Distillery train lines that bisect the Meadow to the northwest," he says, tracing his finger along an old road map of the British Isles. "We will need to avoid detection until we get to Merseyside." Milton prods a point on the map where the Irish Sea meets the English coastline.

"What's special about Merseyside, brother?" asks Hassan.

"The Merseysiders are famously anti-Distillery," says Glenda.

"Sadly, they're not exactly welcoming of Well Wishers, either," says Milton grimly. "But they will not hunt any fugitives of the Distillery or allow the Distillery onto their lands to hunt for them. So, this will allow us time and space to take stock and prepare for a final phase of stage one – travelling through the Distillery strongholds of Wales all the way to the Mountain and the Source."

Milton goes through the details of his plan to commandeer a fishing vessel in Merseyside to sail around Wrexham and the Vale of Clwyd, areas known for their brutal treatment of fugitives, to make landfall on the North Wales coast and the edge of the mountain range after a day at sea. At this point, they will journey on foot into the mountains in heavily guarded Distillery territory.

"Assuming all goes well, we will find our way to the Source Mountain within a week of leaving here in Lin," Milton concludes, folding up the map. "After that, we just need to navigate the Mountain and try to collect water tumbling off the Perihelion Cliffs..." He chuckles to himself, ironically.

The expedition will need to find an exact location on the cliffs where they can collect the pure Source water. This isn't as simple as hiking, seeking, and evading the Distillery (not that this would be simple in itself). The exact trajectory of the falling water is not mapped, and the cliffs are known to be treacherous and deadly. Then, when they find pure water, there is the challenge of collecting it. Source water is a highly dense substance, the densest known in the Meadow. Just a teaspoon weighs more than a kilogram, and they will each need to collect a cup-full. Collecting and carrying the pure water will be a test of strength and stamina. This is all compounded by the enhanced danger of atmospheric water around the Mountain. Water in the form of *mist.*

"Two days in the mountains on my last expedition, we became surrounded by the deep, dense mist," Milton says, his eyes glazing over as he recollects the trauma. "It put immense strain on our minds. Navigating in low visibility was one thing. But breathing was worse. Breathing in the mist is like constantly sipping on a glass of groundwater. Simeon and Douglas – two good men from my team –lost their minds. And a soul that loses its mind in the mist drifts away..." Milton looks up at the sky and sighs.

"How did you survive?" Glenda asks.

Milton looks back at them. "I don't know..." he starts and pauses. A flicker of something like nervousness passes over him. "My mind was in a haze, but something compelled me to keep living," he says, his voice cracking. Nailah reaches her arm across her husband's back and squeezes his broad frame.

"Without knowing what I was doing, I found a precious marble lost at the bottom of my bag. A marble that contained a memory so essential to remembering who I am that it reconnected my mind and soul when I dissected it. I had just enough energy then to flee the mist."

"What this means," says Nailah, taking up the reins from her husband and looking around at the group, "is we should each spend some time over the next week implanting our most treasured and precious memories into marbles. Those memories that connect our minds and our souls. If we always carry these marbles with us, they could save our lives."

Gareth looks at Milton, his rugged exterior fractured for the first time, and feels the locket around his neck holding the Inseparable Stone from the Tide and Time Tavern. He starts to wonder whether it could end up saving his life. But then he decides this is far too hypothetical to worry about now.

"Be warned," Milton says, looking up and brushing off his emotions. "Any distractions in your mind – things that turn your attention away from the expedition's goal – will make you more susceptible to the mist. For the sake of yourself and the expedition, you must come forward if you ever have any concerns you are getting distracted or if you suspect anyone else is."

Milton looks around at them all, but Gareth feels certain he lingers on him the longest. "I don't expect anyone to come forward now. But make sure you do it before we enter the mountains. Before it is too late."

Gareth shifts nervously in his chair. His mind flits from Kasiya to Cerys and back again. He knows he is distracted already, and he knows he doesn't feel ready to leave the Meadow. But he hopes this feeling will go away. He won't out himself to Milton. Not yet.

* * *

Aside from coming to terms with the journey's dangers, the expedition must develop some survival skills for what lies ahead. They must thrive in a wild existence – fending off predators and protecting their bodies from illness and injury. They must also learn to travel without leaving a trace, master starlight navigation, and develop solid backstories for any encounters with the Distillery. They have their work cut out.

There are some skills already in the group. Unsurprisingly, Glenda is skilled in fending off wild animals; Circus Security didn't just protect the circus from the Pond Life. She is also an expert in night navigation at sea – it turns out she was a crew member on the sinking ship that brought her into the Meadow.

The biggest surprise, though, is little Billy McGregor. He reveals a detailed knowledge of wilderness medicine and its practical application. When he and his family entered the Meadow, they came through an opening on a mountain road in the Scottish Highlands. Billy and his sister had travelled with their drifting parents for months and, in that time, learnt – by trial and error – how to treat animal bites and stings and how to adequately heal burns and lacerations right up until the Distillery found them. Billy's skills could be essential for the journey ahead.

"Is this all of us?" asks Milton, counting the expedition members as they convene outside the Princess Victoria, ready to head into the forest to learn basic bushcraft with him and Nailah.

"I think so," says Ashley, wagging her finger around the group, counting them. "Yes, there's eight of us." They had already said their goodbyes to Hector and Edmond a few hours previous.

"No, not quite," says Hassan. "Milton, you said last night that we still have space for last-minute volunteers. I spoke to Rosalyn this morning. She has agreed to join us. I told her to meet us here." A smug and eager grin stretches across his face.

"Yay!" says Ashley, girlishly.

"Ah, not so fast," grumbles Milton. "I don't think you have the latest information, Hassan."

"What?" he says sharply. His grin tumbling off his face as quickly as it formed.

"Well," Milton continues. "A lady like Rosalyn – a Flicker – has never joined a Cwtch Mission before."

"Well, actually," Nailah enters the conversation, a look of consternation filling her face. "*No* woman, irrespective of their background, has been selected for a Cwtch Mission before." She casts an accusatory eye towards Milton.

"OK, OK," Milton concedes dismissively. "But either way, I also got wind of Rosalyn's intentions this morning. I've already consulted Veronica Lacewitt, Head of the Sisterhood of the Flickers. Veronica has confirmed what I suspected. Flickers, who have no memories from Earth, cannot conjure any hope of returning there. The only route available to these women is to 'go on', even if they get the Source water. Therefore, for Roslyn's sake, Veronica advises that she stays in the Meadow with the Sisterhood. This guarantees her the most pleasant and fulfilling life possible. I have just spoken with Rosalyn, and she agrees." Milton glances at Hassan. "Sorry."

"That's bullshit!" Hassan blurts out. He kicks the dusty ground petulantly, sending stones hurtling in all directions.

"It's OK, Hassan," says Glenda, gently putting her hand on Hassan's shoulder.

"Don't touch me," says Hassan grumpily, wriggling free. "Let me go and talk to Rosalyn myself. I'll talk her around. This can't be the only way."

"Hassan," says Milton. "Think of what's right for Rosalyn, not just you."

"What are you implying, brother?" Hassan asks, casting a threatening glare at Milton, daring him to go further.

"She's an attractive woman, and you're not a subtle man," says Milton, plainly, not intimidated by Hassan. "I can see why you want her with us."

Hassan mutters something bitterly under his breath but turns his gaze, throws up his hood, and strides away down the track. "So are we going to this forest or what?!" he calls back.

The hour or so walk to the forest after Hassan's childish outburst is tense. Hassan walks a few dozen metres ahead of the expedition, muttering to himself and chucking loose foliage from the track over hedges and at trees. Gareth tries to chat with him, but Hassan isn't interested in any mature reconciliation. He is happy to dwell in his petulance, at least for the time being.

As the walk to the forest meanders down a long dusty track, the group get spread out, falling into little pairings. Gareth finds himself an opportunity to speak with Milton alone. Cerys and Kasiya are on his mind, and he needs some reassurance that he isn't going to damage the chances of the expedition. He doesn't dare bring up what had happened between him and Kasiya, though, so he just mentions Cerys.

"I know Cerys came into the Meadow conscious," he explains to Milton. "She was taken to the Palace with Rosalyn. I don't know where she is now, but the fact that she could be here in the Meadow, somewhere…well, I don't think I could return to Earth without knowing…"

"Have you spoken to Rosalyn?" Milton asks.

"I daren't," Gareth responds. "I don't want to be insensitive and bring up her trauma, you know?"

Milton frowns. "You're the opposite of Hassan…"

"What do you mean?"

"Sometimes you need to put your own needs first."

Gareth doesn't know how to respond to this. He heard the same thing from Cerys all the time.

"Listen, kid," Milton continues. "There a long way before we reach the Mountains and the mist. There's no sense in you worrying about this as a distraction right now. And I think I can pull some strings and see if we can get news of Cerys' current whereabouts."

"You can?" Gareth asks.

"I'll send word to members of the Sisterhood and the City Circus working in London. We can determine if Cerys has been spotted or picked up after leaving the Palace. There's a good chance she'll have been seen so long as she left the Palace conscious – even if she's now a Flicker."

Gareth smiles at Milton. "Thanks," he says. "I'd appreciate that."

"No worries, kid. Just try and put her out of your mind for now." He pats Gareth on the back. "At least you're not distracted by a girl like Hassan."

\* \* \*

Gathering together in the forest, Nailah teaches the expedition about the common plants and fungi they can safely use for their medicinal qualities in the Meadow. Gareth does his best to concentrate, but his thoughts are on Kasiya. He knows he needs to talk to her and soon. He looks across at her, standing next to her mother. She looks tired and distracted like she hasn't slept in days. Any of the energy and vitality that had been teased out of her on the journey from London has evaporated. She isn't saying a word to anyone and clings to her mother's shadow. Gareth tries to catch Kasiya's eye. Not like before. He merely wants to try and console her without words. But she never looks his way.

Nailah gathers the group around some fallen logs covered in moss and weeds. She lifts a log to uncover a cluster of small brown mushrooms. "Psilocybin mushrooms," she says. "More commonly called 'magic mushrooms'. Not for adolescent experimentation, I'm afraid. Their effects in the Meadow are not the same as Earth, I hear." She winks at Glenda.

"The compound inside these mushrooms can help the mind to stay clear. Chewing on these will be essential when we're in the mist. They won't completely numb the effects, but they at least make it possible to keep a clear mind in a light fog. Wherever we find these on the journey, we should gather them."

Nailah plucks the mushrooms from the ground and drops them into a cloth sack she has slung over her shoulder. Then she beckons the group to a large clearing bathed in sunlight.

"Most of the plants we can forage in the Meadow are familiar to Earth," she says. "The main difference is recognising the signs that they are about to be ready to pick. With the changing weather and unpredictable seasons, the plants have all developed to become hardier than they were on Earth. They grow tougher stems and waxy flowers. A plant might look dormant, but it is moments from ripening. Many of the plants fruit and flower within a day. *'Make hay when the sun shines'*. Our favourite phrase in the Meadow. Apt once again."

Nailah points to a patch of nondescript green weeds waving in the gentle breeze. "Except for Billy, does anyone know what we have here?"

Gareth inspects the weeds. They look like any old weed to him. Hard to see how they differ from the other weeds in the clearing.

"Dandelions?" Ashley suggests when no one else comes forward.

"No…" says Nailah, smiling. "Oh, too late. It looks like the plants are about to give the game away. Billy, over to you."

"Opium poppies!" says Billy, smiling. All around them, in a matter of seconds, thousands of red poppies spring up from the weeds. The bright sunlight reflects off the flowers and washes a warm glow over them all. It is a fantastic spectacle.

"One of the most important plants we can forage for our expedition," says Nailah. "Injury is likely to hit one, if not all, of us at some point on the journey. Pain relief is going to be essential. The circus has gathered some pain relief medicines from the vehicles and items left behind after previous arrivals into the Meadow, which we will take on our journey. We also have stockpiled some special marbles containing sensations that mimic anaesthetics. But the opiates from poppies are free, abundant, and potent. The trick is catching them just as the seed pods appear and before they flower."

Suddenly the scarlet floor around them darkens and becomes brown. A hissing sound, like falling rain, follows. The seed pods of the poppies have dried all at the same time and are rattling against one another.

"Already, the seed pods are useless unless you want a rattle for a baby," says Nailah. "They will only be right to harvest for about a minute. The main lesson for you all is to forage them if you notice ripening poppy pods at any point on the journey. Don't wait to need it or until your stocks are low. Interrupt your journey when you see them and collect what you can."

After Nailah's session on identifying medicinal plants, Milton takes over teaching, enlightening the group on how to find and forage these plants. Specifically how to forage for magic mushrooms. This is the main reason for being in the forest this afternoon.

"Fungi," says Milton, "Are one of the most common sources for sensations, outside of marbles, for travellers in the Meadow. The regularly changing weather means that forest floors are always cool and damp. Perfect for spores to form fungus all the time. Sadly, like on Earth, not all fungi are safe."

Milton shows them the shapes, the colours, and the smells that indicate the suitable fungus to forage. Then he sends them out in pairs to have a go themselves.

Gareth manages to pair up with Kasiya. She doesn't volunteer to be with Gareth, but she can't find a good reason to refuse when he directly asks her. It will be the first bit of alone time he has been able to manufacture since arriving in Lin.

Together Gareth and Kasiya traipse through the forest in silence, gazing at the floor and disturbing tree debris in an attempt to uncover sprouting fungus. Once the other pairs have dispersed, the only sounds are of their feet thumping the damp ground and their clothes scraping past overhanging foliage.

Gareth plans to wait for the right moment to mention the monastery, but Kasiya beats him to it. "It should never have happened," she starts, without context or invitation. "I don't know what I was thinking at the monastery. I'm sorry, Gareth, you're a nice guy, but I'm just not sure it's what I need. What I want, I mean." She isn't asking Gareth his opinion. These are statements of fact without a clear inroad.

"I don't understand," says Gareth. He is taken aback, trying to process Kasiya's words. He wants to be understanding, but he really doesn't understand. Only yesterday evening, Ashley implied that Kasiya was into him. Why would she be pushing him away? "Have I done something wrong?"

Kasiya keeps her eyes firmly on the ground. "No," she mumbles. "You've not done anything wrong. It's me. Someone like me isn't right for someone like you. And besides, my father has always told me of the dangers of forming new relationships in the Meadow."

Gareth feels a sting of irritation that Kasiya has brought up her father. He had feared that Milton had something to do with her change of heart. Kasiya is healthier and happier when her father isn't around. When her father isn't 'protecting her'. Evidently, the shadow of being the High Councillor's daughter is looming again. "Your father doesn't need to know about us," offers Gareth, more hopeful than realistic.

Kasiya briefly looks at Gareth, then quickly averts her eyes again. "No," she says. "We barely know each other. You don't know me. And I'm glad you don't. Someone like you is better off without someone like me."

Gareth grabs her hand. She lets him, but her hand is limp. "Let me get to know you," he tries. "You don't know. Maybe I can be right for you."

She pulls her hand away. "I'm sorry," she says. Her tone has an air of absolute finality, and Gareth doesn't protest.

Those are the last words either of them says to each other in the woods. Walking around in silence for hours is torture for Gareth. They are so distracted that they trample many fungi without even noticing them. An indication, if Gareth needs any, of just how dangerous a distracted mind can be on the expedition, where supplies will be scarce and where the mist will exacerbate a clouded mind.

As dusk draws in, Gareth and Kasiya reconvene with the rest of the expedition at the forest's edge. They present their meagre haul. In contrast, Billy and Hassan have a basket full of magic mushrooms. Milton declares the two men to be the greatest asset of the expedition so far. Billy is delighted, and even Hassan manages a grin.

After a day of being grumpy about Rosalyn not joining the expedition, Gareth expects Hassan's mood to be improved that evening, given the great success of his foraging and assuming they will soon be reunited with Rosalyn and some other familiar faces from the circus. And Gareth needs Hassan in a good mood. His afternoon with Kasiya has wholly drained him. However, it turns out Rosalyn's decision to stay with the Sisterhood means that she is engaged all evening, getting to know her sisters and preparing for their move away from Lin. This makes Hassan more unbearable than before.

Fortunately, aside from Hassan and Kasiya, the others in the expeditionary group start to bond. A day in the sun and a bucket of locally made marbles does wonders for them. Glenda Burgess, it turns out, is a barrel of laughs. With a few marbles sucked, she becomes the heart and soul of the evening.

In an attempt to include Hassan, Glenda tries goading the young man into competitions of strength. Arm wrestles and the like. Usually, Hassan would have jumped at this. Not today. Unperturbed, Glenda entertains them with challenges like; how many marbles you can fit in your mouth. Gareth tries. It is very confusing having all the sensations at the same time.

After Glenda's time in the spotlight, Kathleen brings out her recorded memories from the Meadow. A book, much like Kim-Joy's at the Tide and Time Tavern. She recounts tales of the circus and performances through the ages until the early hours. Everyone stays up late just to enjoy her fantastic storytelling.

* * *

For the next few days, Nailah and Milton teach the expedition about the weather and how to deal with it, including how to construct emergency shelters in the Meadow. Finding and building shelters efficiently will be an essential skill for the journey, especially in the rapidly changing weather. Once they start their hike into the mountains, they won't have the carriages to take refuge in.

Although exhausting, Gareth enjoys this part of the preparations. He has a hilarious encounter with Ashley and Billy one afternoon in a dried-up estuary. The sunny weather rapidly changes into a severe storm, and the three of them try erecting an emergency tarpaulin, neglecting that they are in a tidal zone. They are soon caught out by rising sea waters that wash away their shelter and force the three to splash to safety, giggling all the way. The rest of the group watch the whole debacle unfold and can't help but laugh from their safe positions past the high tide line on the beach.

The next evening the group are joined by the Sisterhood and Rosalyn. Rosalyn is in great spirits. She seems to be coming out of her shell in her time with the Sisterhood. Hassan's mood, which has remained miserable for a few days, still doesn't change to delight. Like a petulant teenager, he blames Rosalyn for not agreeing to join the expedition. And he becomes jealous when he hears of the security detail that will escort the Sisterhood to their new home outside of Lin – a group of Glenda Burgess' Circus Security team, most of whom are strong and athletic men.

In a strop, Hassan excuses himself from socialising unusually early, even before the marbles start, and stomps off to his room. Out of kindness, Gareth follows after him, hoping to try and talk things through.

He knocks on Hassan's door.

"What?" Hassan says glumly from the other side.

"Can we talk?" Gareth asks.

"Why?" comes the blunt reply. The door remains firmly shut.

"I'm worried about you," Gareth concedes. "You have been in a foul mood since we got to Lin. We can't go on the expedition like this. Can you tell me what's wrong?"

"Yeah, like you don't know," Hassan responds aggressively.

Hassan's tone raises Gareth's temperature. "I can tell it's about Rosalyn," he says and waits for confirmation from Hassan. It doesn't come. "I know you're annoyed she's not coming on the expedition. But you must know it's for the best, right? It's what she wants."

"What she wants?!" says Hassan accusatively, swinging open the door so quickly that Gareth almost stumbles into him. "She has been manipulated. She told me she wanted to come!"

"But you heard Milton," says Gareth. "Rosalyn might not be able to leave the Meadow with us, even if the expedition is successful. It would be a huge risk for her to come."

"Yeah, that's what Milton says. And, of course, that's what *you* say!"

"What do you mean?" says Gareth.

"Well, you're alright, aren't you? You've got Kasiya with you! I saw you two at the monastery. Bet you've already slept with her, haven't you?!"

Gareth is taken by surprise. His face flushes red. "I don't know what you're talking about," he lies.

"Yeah, you're just happily sabotaging me, getting Rosalyn chucked off the trip. While you've still got what you need."

Gareth is confused. "I don't understand," he says. "Rosalyn not being on our trip has nothing to do with me."

"No?!" says Hassan in an accusatory tone. "No? I've seen you. Whenever Milton talks about the dangers of being 'distracted' on the expedition, you run over to talk to him. You've been talking to him about me. About my thing for Rosalyn and how I won't be focused on the expedition because I'm too distracted by her. And you have a hang-up because you don't like how I am with women. I told you about the lady I tried to sleep with when we arrived in the Meadow. I saw how you looked at me when I told you. It's my business, you know. It's not yours!"

"I never said anything about you or Rosalyn to Milton," Gareth responds.

"Rubbish!" says Hassan. "Just coincidence about your little meetings, is it?! Always sticking your nose in and telling him how I would be a problem on the journey. Convincing him and the others that I can't focus with a woman like Rosalyn around. Well, how about you take a look at yourself in the mirror?! You are clearly distracted by Kasiya!" Hassan slams the door in Gareth's face.

"Look!" shouts Gareth, his irritation rocketing. "You want to know why I have been speaking to Milton. I have been speaking to him because I am worried about my sister, Cerys. Do you remember her? Remember that things are going on in this place beyond you?!" He bashes the door in frustration.

"Cerys came through into the Meadow with us. She got taken to the Palace, and I haven't seen or heard from her since. I can't face returning to Earth without knowing where or how she is. That's why I have been speaking to Milton. I am worried about my distraction, not yours! I'm worried I won't have my mind fully on the expedition because I want to see my sister again. So, screw you! It's nothing to do with you. Be in a mood for all I care!"

Gareth kicks the door. He never usually lets his emotions show like this; he always holds them in. The moment he kicks the door, he feels embarrassment flood his body. He is fuming. He runs down the corridor without looking back to see or hear if Hassan responds.

Gareth wanders out to the fields at the edge of the hotel grounds. He sits on a log in the dark field and takes a few long deep breaths. Slowly his temperature and breathing calm to a more normal rate. He starts feeling embarrassed and ashamed, as he always does after losing his temper.

The stars are out, drifting northwards. Gareth stares at them. He thinks of his mum, and he thinks of Cerys. And, probably because of the familiarity of his rage, for the first time since arriving in the Meadow, he thinks of his dad. The man he never knew, whose death and absence have unfairly loomed over him his entire life. He imagines his dad as one of the slower stars up in the sky above him now, waiting for the star of his mum to catch up. The stars that had sparkled before now glare.

*Late in the afternoon on 2nd May 1845 the main event of Cooke's Royal Circus in Great Yarmouth was in full swing; a clown, named Arthur Nelson, was sailing up the river Bure in a bathtub being pulled by four geese. Several thousand local people had turned out to enjoy the spectacle. The crowds found the best vantage points around, and on, Great Yarmouth Suspension Bridge. Amidst the excitement of the crowd, the weight that was on the bridge suddenly made the southern suspension chains fail. In a moment the south side of the bridge deck collapsed, falling all the way into the river below and tipping hundreds of people into the fast-flowing water. In the collapse, many children, who formed much of the bridge's crowd, were trapped against railings, and taken under the water as the portion of the bridge plunged into the river. In all seventy-nine people lost their lives in the disaster, of whom fifty-nine were children.*

# Chapter Twelve

◆

# Preparations Destabilised

The final preparations for the expedition are nearly done. With survival training complete, the expedition spends some time, in pairs, talking of their fondest memories from Earth, creating a stockpile of memory-infused marbles. Marbles last sucked during conversations about the people they loved and of the specific sensations they miss: sounds, smells, and sights. Holding a bank of these memories, each of the expeditionary group will have resources they can release should the expedition take its toll. Gareth records a handful of memories from times with Cerys, but he finds it hard to identify specific sensations he misses. He is still struggling to reach out with much fondness for his former life.

The expedition agrees on a cover story for why they are travelling through the Meadow, just in case any Pond Life stops them. They will say they are scrap merchants journeying around the Meadow, collecting artefacts from Openings and repurposing them for Meadow life. There are plenty of interesting trinkets around the Princess Victoria that they can gather to start them off. They also have access to three former merchant caravans for the journey. These can be kitted out with the things they will need but also be made to look like active merchant vehicles.

The next job is to select the animals to pull the caravans. Ashley and Billy are sent to choose three pairs of sturdy shire horses from the fields. The rest of the group go to the charred wreckage of the stables – another victim of the Distillery raid – to see what useful riding equipment they can salvage.

Gareth and Hassan have settled their differences now. Gareth's uncharacteristic explosion of emotion jolted Hassan out of his slump, and the two men are on good terms again. In contrast, Gareth's gulf with Kasiya has widened. He can never think what to say to her anymore. The spark that he had felt towards her before Lin has well and truly gone out. In fact, the whole expeditionary group have become so accustomed to Kasiya's silence that her presence is almost taken for granted. The fact that Gareth doesn't feel any impulses towards her anymore also solves the lingering anxiety he felt that he should discuss their entanglement with Milton. This is the usual way Gareth addresses difficult conversations, not having them at all.

The stable yard is littered with debris. Charred harness lines and old saddles are trampled into the mud. Twine from hay bales is tangled around broken timber frames. The entrance to the stables is caved in, a collapsed mess of fire damage. The broken and black ribbed timber stains their boots as they clamber through. Although heavily damaged, the rear end of the stable building holds the majority of its structure intact. Here, saddles and harnesses are piled up, covered in ash. Many of them could still be useful for the expedition.

Halfway into the stable, where the fire damage is worst, boxes bearing the logo of another circus, Cooke's Royal Circus, are piled up against a stable door. The boxes are charred and disintegrated. They had been full of old horseshoes. The iron hoops are now a crooked and wonky pile of metal against the charred door.

On Milton's instruction, Gareth and Hassan start to un-pile the horseshoes. They are looking for useful bridles in the less damaged boxes towards the floor. Milton always allocates the physical tasks to the men in the group, much to the frustration of Glenda, who is evidently stronger than either man. Nailah comments on Milton's casual sexism, not for the first time, but it lands on deaf, or rather, stubborn ears.

As they pull away the horseshoes, Hassan stops Gareth. "What's that?" he says.

"What's what?" replies Gareth.

"Be quiet."

The two men listen. There is a faint tapping noise coming from behind the charred doors. "There's something in there," says Gareth.

"Hey Milton," shouts Hassan. "I think there's still a horse trapped in this stable."

"There can't be," says Milton, wandering over. "All the horses were accounted for after the fire." He steps up to the door and listens. "Quick. Help me get the rest of these boxes out of the way," he says urgently.

They fling the metal hoops aside frantically between them, sensing Milton's haste. Milton tries the stable door. It is locked. He picks up a horseshoe and starts striking the brittle charred lock. It breaks off, and he thrusts open the doors.

Standing in the stable doorway, wearing damp and charred riding gear, is a young woman. Her body is emaciated and grubby. Ash from the fire chars her face, and her hands are badly burned. The young woman has an unfocused stare. She tries to step out of the stable when the doors open, but her legs get caught in a pile of reins. She stumbles and trips, falling onto her face before anyone can catch her.

"This is Rosie McGregor," says Nailah solemnly. "Billy's sister. The third victim of the assault from the Ferrymen. Nobody saw Rosie go 'on' that night. We had assumed she had left unnoticed."

This is the closest Gareth has been to a Drifter. It is disconcerting to see someone, for all intents and purposes, alive but wholly unresponsive and unaware of all around them. It is also jarring how Nailah speaks about the young woman in her presence, as though she isn't there at all.

"Glenda, Kasiya, can you go to the hotel and inform Kathleen about Rosie immediately, please?" says Nailah. "Hassan, I need you to hold Rosie here with me and Milton. Gareth, I need you to go and get Billy from the fields." No one asks any questions. They do as Nailah asks.

Hassan tries asking Rosie to stay where she is to stop the young women from leaving the stable. Milton scoffs ironically. "Drifters can't hear," he says. "They have to be stopped by force."

As Gareth leaves the stables, he glances back to see Nailah, Milton, and Hassan taking it in turns to grasp Rosie's arms and shoulders and reorientate her for every few steps she takes. The unconscious woman stumbles but doesn't resist.

Gareth has no idea how he will talk to Billy about Rosie. But before he can dwell on it, Billy and Ashley wander into the stable yard leading six shire horses by their reins.

"Aren't they beautiful?" Ashley calls out, seeing Gareth approaching them. "Billy has a real knack for riding," she smiles, then senses something is wrong. "What's the matter?" she asks.

Gareth tries to look Billy in the eye, but he can't. So, he speaks to a space between the two of them. "We found something…" he says. "We found someone… in the stables. Billy, I'm so sorry…"

"Rosie?" says Billy, looking at Gareth. "You found Rosie?!"

"I'm sorry," says Gareth.

Letting go of the horses, Billy hurtles towards the stable building. Gareth lunges forwards and grasps hold of the loose reins. The horses don't bolt, but they are unsettled. "You found Rosie?" Ashley asks Gareth, fighting with her own horse's reins. "Is she OK?"

"She's a Drifter," says Gareth. "We found her locked in the stable."

"Those brutes," she says.

Inside the stable, Nailah grabs and embraces Billy as he comes running in, calming him before he can approach his sister. The young man's tears drip onto her ash-covered clothes. When Billy eventually grasps Rosie's hands, he looks into her vacant unfocused eyes and lets out a silent, desperate wail, and his knees give way.

With help from Milton, Nailah drags the young man to his feet and leads him away from his unconscious sister. They embrace him tightly while he continues to sob. "She's gone, Billy," says Nailah. "She's going to a better place. She is not suffering anymore."

Still holding the young man, Milton looks up and mouths to Hassan. "Let her go."

The unconscious form of Rosie McGregor drifts past them all and out of the stable.

"What can we do for her?" Gareth whispers to Ashley.

A tear rolls down Ashley's face. "There's nothing we can do," she replies. "Rosie will find her way to the Source. She'll probably be picked up en route. There is nothing we can do for a Drifter. The next chapter of her story has already begun."

Gareth watches the unconscious girl wander past the tied-up shire horses and disappear out of sight. The group stand silently, except for Billy's sobs. Then Hassan calls out. "She's left a marble." In his hand, he holds aloft a shining green sphere.

\* \* \*

The mood is solemn in the marble dissection room as evening descends on the Princess Victoria. All the expedition members, save for Billy, are there. A handful of lamps flicker in the failing light.

"People do not leave memory beads for no reason," says Nailah. "We are honouring Rosie's memory by bearing witness to her marble… despite any trauma we might feel in doing so."

Like last time, Milton walks amongst the group, offering them the subtly luminescent marble mist. Gareth leans into Milton's palms and inhales.

As the mist settles around Gareth, the stable appears on a warm summer evening. In the distance, music from the trapeze tent is just audible. Rosie McGregor is scraping the muck off an old horseshoe in the stable opposite another woman, a fellow stable hand.

"Where's Billy tonight?" the woman asks Rosie. "Did he get tickets to see the Trapeze?"

"Yes, he did," responds Rosie, her voice more lilting than Gareth had expected. "I'm so glad. He loves watching the trapeze, and he never usually gets to go. Not with all the mucking out that has to be done."

A horse whinnies in the stable. Rosie gets up to check on it.

"It's OK, Shadow," she says to the horse, stroking his mane. "It's just a show. Billy will be back later to give you a brush." The horse rubs its nose against Rosie's shoulder and takes a mouthful of hay out of her hand.

"It's gone quiet out there," says Rosie, sitting back in the stable. "Strangely quiet."

"They haven't finished already, have they?"

"They can't have," says Rosie.

Both women walk into the yard and look towards the Princess Victoria beyond the trees. There is a distant roar, the sound of many voices in unison, before the sound of cracks, bangs, and smashes. They exchange concerned looks. "Let me go and investigate. Rosie, you stay here and keep the horses safe."

"Look out for Billy," Rosie calls back. "And be careful."

The woman jogs away, leaving Rosie alone.

Rosie grabs a handful of hay and sets off to settle the horses. Looking back out into the yard, she can see, above the trees, some smoke rising. She looks worried.

Suddenly two young men burst into the yard. "Billy!" shouts Rosie. There he is, Billy McGregor, running with another young stable hand.

"It's the Distillery," calls Billy, panting. "They are attacking the circus. We need to get the horses to safety. Out in the fields will be best."

The three of them frantically seek out harnesses and hurriedly attach them to the horses. Billy throws a harness over Shadow. "I'm sorry, boy," he says, patting the horse's flank. "It'll only be for a moment."

They have just started to lead the horses out into the stable yard when, "Oi, you!" calls out a man brandishing a flaming torch. He is standing in the gateway at the edge of the yard.

Billy looks back to Rosie, who is still in the stable, out of sight. "Rosie, hide!" he instructs his sister. Before she can ask why, Billy leaps on Shadow, still holding the other horses' reins and canters towards the man in the gateway. The stable hand with him does likewise.

The man with the flaming torch looks like he considers standing his ground before realising that would be insane. As he dives for cover, the two men and six horses thunder past, heading away from the stable yard towards the fields.

Rosie peers out from the stable. She still hasn't been seen by the man in the yard. Not yet. She ducks back inside. The two horses still with her are restless. She tries to calm them.

Peering through a gap in the doorway, she watches two more men brandishing flaming torches climb over the stable fence. The horses are spooked by the flames and bolt – galloping out of the stable and past the thugs.

Rosie holds her breath. The three men advance towards the stable. She retreats quietly into a stall and gently closes the door behind her. Crouching there, she hears the men enter the stable.

"Ah, they're not going to be in here," says one man, trampling over damp hay and pulling clean saddles onto the floor as he looks into the stable stalls. "They all fled when they saw us. You saw it. The horses fled as well."

"We need to be sure that no one is in here," says another man, his stature indicating a hierarchy over the other two.

"Why do you think the three fugitives would be out here in the stables? They didn't know we were coming," the smaller man responds.

"It wasn't just three. There was a fourth," the superior replies. "A woman is suspected to have been travelling with the three men. We're here to capture her as well, remember. Sanger's circus are famed for bringing women like her here."

"Still," says the other man. "Why would she be hiding in the stables?"

Rosie shifts in her hiding place to try and peer through a gap in the stable doors and see the men's faces.

"Stop!" one of the men orders. "I heard something. If you're in here," he shouts, "make yourself known." Rosie stays completely still.

"Oh, come on. She's not in here. You're hearing things. Let's torch the place. If she's in here, she'll burn anyway."

The superior holds his hand up to silence his accomplice. "The Princes will want to know if we've got her."

He starts working his way around the stable stalls, kicking open each door and checking it. In a few moments, he is outside Rosie's stall. He kicks the door and tries to open it. The latch is bolted on the inside. He plants another heavy kick against the door.

"This has been bolted from the inside. Now I don't know many horses that can operate a latch, do you?" he says sarcastically.

The man pummels the door with his fist. "I know you're in there," he says loudly and clearly. "Come on out. I won't hurt you…much!"

Rosie, on the other side of the doorway, is breathing heavily. She doesn't say a word.

"Look, I know you're in there. If you don't come out, we'll burn you alive in here." Rosie still doesn't respond.

"Show her we mean business," says the man.

One of the other men leans in and forces his flaming torch into the hay around the bottom of the door. Flames lick under the door and light some scattered debris inside the stall. There isn't enough debris to start a fire, but enough material to create a cloud of smoke in the room. Rosie coughs.

"There's no point pretending anymore," says the man, hearing her cough. "Come on out and let me see you."

"Go away," shouts Rosie defiantly. "I don't know why you are here. There's nothing here for you. Just go away."

"Nothing here for us?! Why would you say that?" he exclaims. After a pause, he announces, "We know who you are, Rosalyn Lockyer! A Foundering whore with no prospects. A spent resource from the Palace of the Distillery. Well, the Distillery need to speak with you again. We know how you got to the Meadow with those three men from your train on Earth. The men are now the most wanted fugitives in this realm. So don't pretend you don't know what we want from you. You either come with us, or we send you 'on'."

"I don't know what you are talking about," Rosie shouts back. "My name is Rosie McGregor. I'm a stable hand here in Lin. I've never heard of this, Rosalyn. Or these three men."

"If you aren't Rosalyn, then maybe you will show your face. Prove you're not the woman we're looking for."

"I'm not her," says Rosie, pleading.

"Prove it!" the man shouts back. Rosie inches to the stable door. Then she changes her mind. "Come on. Prove it!" the man shouts again.

Rosie stands still, gently sucking the marble in her mouth. She looks at her wrists. Gareth notices they are scarred, but not like his Satan's Scalds. Rosie's scars are self-inflicted. She has been tormented and abused by men from the Distillery before. She grabs her wrists and defiantly steps away from the door.

"Fine! If you are not going to play our games," says the man, and he picks up a box of Cooke's Royal Circus horseshoes, shoving it up against the door. "Come on, lads; she doesn't want to play."

The three men pile box after box in front of the door before plunging their fiery rods into the hay hanging from the stable door. Flames lick up the doorway, filling the ceiling with acrid smoke. Rosie knows she has to try and get out. She undoes the bolt and rattles the door. The man has padlocked it on the outside. "Let me out!" she screams. "Let me out, you evil men!"

"Ah, now she wants out," grins one of the men. "There's a fire in the way, love!" He laughs.

"Let me out!" she screams.

The man wanders towards the door and sniggers to the other two men as he undoes his trousers and starts urinating on the fire. "Sorry, love," he shouts. "I haven't got enough piss in me to put this fire out!" The other two men laugh. The man spits at the doorway before the three of them wander nonchalantly out of the stable building.

The next five minutes are horrific. Witnessing a memory, you can't close your eyes or your ears. Gareth watches as the young woman screams for help and bashes at the door frantically.

Eventually, as black smoke fills the stable, she succumbs to the fumes.

\* \* \*

There is silence in the small room as they re-emerge from the memory. No one says a word. Gareth bends over and stares at the ground.

The last to emerge are Hassan, Nailah, and Milton. Shocked but alert, Hassan looks around the room for some suggestion on how to react. Nailah falls forwards and puts her head in her hands. Milton leans back in his chair and lets out a sigh.

"Those thugs are imbeciles," he announces, his hands bracing the back of his head. "But for goodness sake, the girl should have opened the stable door, right? She could have saved herself or at least put up a fight. Better that than die cowering in fear."

"Oh, show some dignity!" Nailah snaps at her husband. "Are you incapable of seeing the woman's bravery? She refused to do what those men wanted. She knew she was in mortal danger, but she stood firm." Nailah's face is a raging red. Gareth hasn't seen this side of her before. "Fighting isn't always the bravest thing to do, you know? One day you might realise that!"

There is a tense silence in the room following Nailah's condemnation of Milton. Emotions are running extremely high. Milton doesn't respond to his wife. Not verbally, anyway. Instead, he looks back at her, unblinking. Either he deems a retort inappropriate in the company or doesn't respect Nailah's words enough to respond. No one else dares say anything or even raise their heads.

Nailah breaks the silence. "Rosalyn is in danger!" she announces, standing up. "She must not be allowed to leave Lin tonight. Glenda: the Colney Hatch Sisterhood are packing their carriages as we speak. Go and find Veronica and Rosalyn. Tell them I will meet them in the lobby straight away… It looks like we are going to have an additional member on our expedition."

Glenda and Nailah hurry out of the room. The rest of the group sits in shock. Ashley has her head in her hands and sniffs, wiping away tears. Kasiya is sitting upright, staring forwards, not blinking. Hassan, in contrast, looks like a weight has been lifted from his mind. Fighting hard to show respect, he looks at Gareth eagerly. Gareth offers him a conciliatory nod.

*On 12th August 1875, the Ellen Southard, an American merchant ship, set sail for Liverpool from Canada. She carried a load of softwood that she hoped to trade in England. The captain's wife and fifteen crew members were on board. Approaching the English mainland six weeks after departure, she was hit by the most violent storm to sweep the region in over three decades. On the night of the 26th September 1875, the Ellen Southard met her fate. As the storm grew, the crew tried to drop anchor to ride out the storm, but the anchors did not hold. They sought help from a local tugboat and lifeboat, but even they couldn't do enough. By midnight, when the storm was at its peak, the Ellen Southard was de-masted and grounded. The waves crashed destructively over the ship's hull, and she broke into pieces on the sandbank. The crew were unable to signal for assistance because they did not carry any flares. So, to try and save themselves, they lashed their bodies to the fractured hull and hoped they wouldn't be swept away by the hungry sea. Nine of the crew didn't survive the night.*

# Chapter Thirteen

♦

# The Expedition Begins

The Colney Hatch Sisterhood of the Flickers leaves Lin without Rosalyn Lockyer. Along with most other circus folks, they depart, seeking safer settlements around the Meadow. Those that remain in Lin are unable or unwilling to leave, ready for a confrontation with the Distillery, and prepared to meet their fate. This group of people, around fifty in number, accompany Kathleen Montague around the grounds of the Princess Victoria hiding precious artefacts owned by the circus. It is hoped that the exodus from Lin is temporary and that someday the ancient treasures will be rediscovered. The 'remainers', as they refer to themselves, also collect potent groundwater, which they keep in flasks on their person at all times. They will be willing to send themselves 'on' when the time comes. Better than being sent 'on' at the hands of the Distillery.

The stinging tension between Nailah and Milton doesn't let up. Their clash after seeing Rosie McGregor's marble threads a bitter note into their relationship, and it quickly becomes entangled with the rest of the expeditionary group. Much to Gareth's disappointment, Milton tries to get him and Hassan on his side, using any moment he has alone with the two men to obtain the validation that he hasn't done anything wrong. He wants them to back him up that Nailah is simply 'over-reacting' and that just because he thought if Rosie had been a guy, she'd have fared better against the Distillery thugs, this doesn't make him sexist.

Hassan rather naturally sides with Milton without encouragement. Gareth, however, absolutely does not. The problem is that he struggles to find the strength to say this. Instead, he internalises his thoughts, feels sick every time Milton tries to get his opinion on the matter, and desperately tries to suggest to Nailah that he is actually on her side without Milton knowing. He doubts Nailah ever realises this.

Despite their marital spat, Nailah and Milton agree on some essential things to keep the expedition on track. For one, it is decided that there is no value in hanging around the Princess Victoria for much longer. They will set off as soon as they can. They just have one more essential thing left to do: disguise the fugitives– Gareth and Hassan, and now, Rosalyn. The three of them are on the Distillery's radar, and there is a good chance they will come face-to-face with Distillery personnel at some point on the journey to the Source.

Sat out in the garden, the three fugitives are given the 'prisoner' treatment. Their heads are shaved (including Rosalyn's long silvery-blonde locks), their clothes are replaced with ill-fitting and unflattering overalls (the drab garb of tradespeople in the city, according to Nailah), and any identifying idiosyncrasies are altered. Hassan's beard is removed. Rosalyn's make-up is washed clean – not to be applied again. And Gareth's naturally neutral vibe is tweaked with large-gauge piercings of his ear lobes and the insertion of black circular ear plugs.

"From now on, when we meet people on the route," Nailah says to Gareth. "You will be known as Tyler Bennington. You came into the Meadow five years ago, crashing your car after a night smoking pot with your friends."

In a similar vein, Rosalyn and Hassan are given new names and roughly sketched backstories. Rosalyn is to be Skye Savic. She arrived in the Meadow last year after a crush at a gig on Earth. And Hassan is to be Carlo Chiesa. A second-generation Italian migrant from wealthy parents. He arrived in the Meadow ten years ago from a boating accident.

"You might want to drop your accent a touch, Carlo," says Nailah, grinning.

"What are you saying, sista?" says Hassan, his black country accent hitting even deeper, flatter notes than usual. "A brother like me can't have come from money?" He smirks sarcastically back at Nailah.

With their transformations complete, the fugitives are barely recognisable. Gareth rather likes his new look. It gives him more of an edge. An edge he never shows but always feels. Or, at least, he wishes he feels. In contrast, Hassan hates what he sees.

"Without my beard, I look like a prick!" he grumbles, catching his reflection and frowning. "Seriously, I ent never gunna pull now!" He rubs his chin, inspecting the contours of his jawline. Feeling disappointed by what he sees, he chucks a marble into his mouth. It has become a customary habit for Hassan to have one on the go at all times.

"How many marbles is that today?" asks Glenda disapprovingly.

"None of your business," Hassan responds, dropping the marble from his mouth – it isn't potent enough – and selecting a different one from the rattling pouch in his hand. He chucks it into his mouth and grins defiantly.

"It *is* my business, actually," says Glenda, her voice deepening. "It's all our business. If you're constantly on a marble run, hazed in the fog of their sensations, you're hardly going to be able to concentrate when we're in the mist on the Mountain, are you?"

Hassan shrugs. "We're not even on the expedition yet. Chill out!"

"Glenda's right, Hassan," says Ashley, weighing in. "Marbles are really addictive. If you indulge too much now, stopping later'll be much harder."

"Listen, alright, I can handle myself," says Hassan defensively. "Just get off my back, will you?!" Without looking, he plucks another marble from his pouch and tilts his head.

The darkest, blackest marble Gareth has ever seen is pinched between Hassan's thumb and forefinger. So black that it is almost sucking the light from the surroundings. Hassan hasn't even noticed that this is the marble he selected.

The moment the black marble drops onto Hassan's tongue, a firework of sensation explodes through his mind. His eyes shoot open, and his pupils dilate. The fibres in his nerves twitch and fizz, making his whole body wriggle and writhe frantically.

Without hesitation, Glenda launches herself at Hassan, knocking him to the ground. Her tall frame sprawls on top of the young man, and he tries to fight her off, but she is more determined than he expects. She forcefully thrusts her gangly arms at his face, and her long bony fingers claw into his mouth.

In the scuffle, Glenda's smock rucks up, exposing the pale flesh of her legs. Gareth is surprised by how muscular and masculine they appear. Unconcerned by her exposure, Glenda scoops the black marble from Hassan's jaws just in time.

Before Glenda can throw the marble away, it bursts in her hand with a pop and a fizz, throwing out a fine mist. This mist condenses into a handful of cloud floating just in front of Hassan's face. Glenda blows out forcefully and wafts the cloud away from him.

Awkwardly and clumsily, the lanky woman clambers to her feet and rearranges her smock.

"You're a foolhardy idiot, Hassan," says Glenda. "I don't care who you are or where you are… you *never* put a marble in your mouth without checking it first. You were seconds from that marble bursting in your mouth and sending you on."

Hassan stays on the floor and stares at Glenda. Gareth tries to offer him a hand, but he ignores it. He stares at Glenda, looking like he is lost for words, but he isn't.

"You've got big fucking hands and powerful legs for a woman!" he exclaims rudely and ungratefully, clearly emasculated by his rescue. "Tell me next time you're going to try and ride me?!"

Glenda stops still and looks down at him. There's fury mixed with shame wallowing in her eyes.

"I think what you mean to say is '*Thank you, Glenda*,'" interjects Ashley, smiling kindly at her friend.

Glenda smiles back at Ashley gratefully, then returns to Hassan. She stares triumphantly down at him and nobly offers her hand to help him up.

Hassan is obstinate and rude. He ignores Glenda's hand and gets himself up. "Fuck this," he mutters. "I need some space."

And he wanders off towards his room in the Princess Victoria without a word or glance towards anyone.

"Are you OK?" Nailah asks Glenda in the calm that follows. "You saved that ungrateful boy's life."

Glenda smiles back. "I'm fine dear. Just glad I got it out in time. He has no idea how close that was."

"Honestly, Glenda… you're amazing," says Ashley, sidling up and squeezing a hug tightly around her friend's waist.

Glenda is more than a foot taller than Ashley. She stoops down to reciprocate the affection. "Well, I wasn't going to give him a Redeemer's Kiss!" she exclaims, smiling– Nailah and Ashley chuckle.

"What's a Redeemer's Kiss?" asks Gareth.

"The one and only way to save someone surrounded by a cloud of Thermocline Mist," explains Ashley. "The type emitted by a bursting marble…" She looks across at Nailah for confirmation. Nailah nods.

"What's that? You kiss someone, and it saves them from the mist?" asks Gareth.

"When a cloud of Thermocline Mist enters the stream of a soul's consciousness," responds Nailah, "it finds its way into every bond between the mind, body, and soul of its victim. The mist is drawn in through their mouth and into their body, making their back arch and rolling their eyes into the back of their head. You might have seen this if you've ever seen someone become a Drifter?"

Gareth nods.

"Well," Nailah continues, "if a different, conscious soul were to redirect the flow of the mist back out through the victim's mouth, then the victim could be saved... Saved with a kiss."

"That's great," says Gareth, feeling upbeat at this revelation. "The way I've heard Thermocline Mist being spoken about, I always thought it was guaranteed to be fatal."

"Oh, but it is," says Nailah, looking anxiously at Glenda, who bows her head. "Sorry, Glenda," she says.

"No, it's OK," the tall lady responds. "I can take over from here… a Redeemer's Kiss can save the life of the person kissed, but the destiny of the mist is already established… Like a surge of water racing down a river, attempts to redirect the flow will not halt the inevitable flood. While one soul is redeemed, another must fall. The redeemer is condemned…"

"Is that for real?" asks Gareth, immediately deflated. "The person who kisses someone as they inhale the mist can save them…but at the expense of themselves? Like a self-sacrificing rescue." He looks at Ashley, who nods gently. "Wow…just imagine that. Have you ever seen it happen?"

Opposite Gareth, Ashley and Nailah close in on Glenda and hold her hands. "Yes," says Glenda. Her voice is deep and sincere. "I have seen it happen… The woman I loved with all of my aching heart. Geraldine…she performed a Redeemer's Kiss almost ten years ago…She saved my life at the cost of her own."

* * *

In the late evening, a warm breeze blows through the grounds of the Princess Victoria. The whole expedition sits together outside on the roof terrace, trying to enjoy their last social in Lin. Hassan is back with them, but he hasn't done anything to ingratiate himself since his ungratefully close call with the bursting marble. In fact, he has ignored everyone's warnings and has kept on sucking marbles all afternoon.

Pushing his way around the long table, Hassan, inebriated, makes Glenda stand up so he can squeeze past. As he does so, he loses his balance and brushes his backside against the tall lady's crotch.

"Ooh, momma, I know you've got big hands, but what's tha' in your pocket?!" he says, thrusting his hips away and sniggering.

"I think you've had rather too many marbles…and your 'jokes' are getting a bit old and predictable," says Glenda, tired of Hassan's puerile ignorance.

"Ooh, it might…be getting' old," says Hassan, slurring his words and ignoring Glenda's tone. "But I'm sure it still works…

that little secret lurking under your smock, Glenda." He makes a vulgar motion with his clenched fist.

Hassan's pathetic behaviour is met with stony silence. Then Kasiya jumps up from her chair, knocking it over, and marches away. Nailah follows her.

"What's her problem?!" says Hassan, trying to play the victim.

"You!" says Glenda plainly. "You're becoming everyone's problem!"

"Oh, lighten up," says Hassan. "It's just a joke."

"Well, you're not funny," says Glenda, as bluntly as she can.

There is an awkward silence that follows. Hassan looks around for someone to stand up for him. Milton will not do it; that would be too divisive in the circumstances. Even Rosalyn avoids his gaze. This irks him the most.

"Ah, screw this!" says Hassan. He chucks yet another marble into his mouth and storms off.

There is silence around the table for a moment. An inaudible exasperation passed around like a hot potato. "I'll go and talk to him," says Gareth getting up. He doesn't want to, but for some reason, he feels, of everyone in the group, he has a responsibility to. And he hates the tension.

On his way to Hassan's room, he passes Nailah and Kasiya sitting on the stairs. Kasiya's eyes are red with tears. When she sees Gareth, she looks away. Nailah offers him a consolatory smile, which he returns, apologetically.

Hassan is pacing up and down the corridor when Gareth gets there. He looks ten times more threatening with his shaved head. He is boiling with rage. "You come to dig the knife in? Come to tell me how crap I am? Just because I'm not as careful with my words as you and the others?"

"No," says Gareth. "That's not why I'm here. I came to see if you're OK."

"I'm fine," says Hassan. "Just sick of being told what to do. Sick of being told what I should and shouldn't say. I was just having a joke, and everyone got up on their high horse and has a go at me. Just like Nailah did to Milton the other day."

He paces to the window at the end of the corridor and leans on the sill, looking queasy. "You know what, I'll just go and find my own way to the Source. Or I might just make a go of it in the Meadow. I don't need any of this."

Gareth approaches Hassan carefully. He is going to try appeasement, not verification or confrontation. "I think everyone's just a bit anxious at the moment," he says. "Seeing Rosie McGregor's memory bead opened all our eyes to the dangers we face from the Distillery. I think the reality is just hitting home, especially for those who have been in the circus for a while. Their homes for many years, this hotel, and the town of Lin will no longer exist for them soon. There's a lot of uncertainty ahead. I know I'm feeling it."

Gareth looks at Hassan. His words land gently.

"Yeah, well…," says Hassan. "That's fair enough. I'm just sick of having to be careful all the time. Not do this. Not do that. Everyone's just so bloody sensitive." Gareth doesn't respond. Hassan lets out a long, loud breath. "Look, I'm not apologising to anyone," he says. "I've not done anything wrong."

Gareth holds his opinion on this. It is necessary to keep the ceasefire intact. "I think everyone needs a bit of rest and comfort tonight," he says instead. "It's going to be cramped, unsettled, and even more uncertain on the journey from tomorrow."

"Yeah, you're right," says Hassan, rocking unsteadily on his feet. "Look, I'm sorry, brother. I didn't mean to get you on the back foot. You don't need to take my side. I just don't like being treated like an idiot by Glenda or any of the others."

Gareth judges he has said enough. "OK," he says. "I'm going to go down and see what the others are doing."

Hassan nods but opts to stay where he is, away from the group for a while.

Back outside on the decking, the atmosphere has settled back down. Most of the group is deep in conversation, discussing navigation routes, safe passages, and various other things about the trip. Gareth pulls up the only empty chair next to Milton. Milton is sat quietly, deep in contemplation and smoking his pipe. He isn't Gareth's first choice of company around the table, but he is his only option.

After sitting in an awkward silence for a moment, Milton turns to Gareth. "You've got a noble soul, kid," he says rather directly.

"Erm, thanks," says Gareth.

"You didn't need to go and check on Hassan," says Milton. "But you did. A noble person looks out for others, even when they are not the most popular."

Gareth looks away bashfully. He senses that Milton is trying to get him as an ally again. Milton breathes in and slowly lets out a long plume of smoke. "Are you looking after yourself, though?" he asks Gareth quizzically.

"What do you mean?" Gareth responds.

"You remind me of someone I once knew," says Milton. "The kindest person you could imagine. There was never a bad word anyone could say about her. Sadly, she never saw the world that way. She doubted herself terribly, and she couldn't believe she was ever good enough. She was always better at looking after others than herself."

In Milton's eyes, Gareth sees his own reflection. "She sounds like my mum," he says. Milton looks back at him, studying his face intently. He doesn't say a word.

"Who was she?" Gareth asks.

"My mother."

"Will she be there when we get back to Earth?"

Milton looks up at the stars. "No," he says sorrowfully. "No one will be waiting for me when I return." He closes his eyes and lies back in his chair. Gareth nervously observes Milton's face. The scar on his top lip twitches nervously. Gareth has never seen a vulnerable side to Milton like this before.

\* \* \*

The day comes to leave the Princess Victoria. A wild wind blows off the sea as the sun drops towards the horizon. The wind had started howling the previous night, and it hadn't let up all day. Gareth had lain awake most of last night. The noise had woken him, but his mind had swirled on its own. The journey, danger, and chance of returning to Earth were all terrifying and uncertain.

By the time the sun touches the horizon, the expedition is ready. The three merchant caravans look magnificent. Kathleen Montague and some of those staying at the circus had redecorated and repurposed them over the last few days.

Ashley, Billy, and Rosalyn have prepared the shire horses. The six animals are expertly groomed, looking majestic, with shiny harnesses and bridles sparkling in the lamplight. Gareth recognises one of the horses from Rosie McGregor's marble memory. Shadow, the grey shire horse, is harnessed to the caravan that Billy is to travel in.

Inside each caravan, a cosy refuge of colourful blankets and textiles is draped over soft furnishings. There's also a little wood stove and a nifty storage chest full of marbles and medicines. Against the walls, wooden benches double as beds. Gareth's clothes and a book given to him by Kathleen Montague lie on his bench.

Knowing that Gareth had studied Philosophy and Politics at university before he had come to the Meadow, Kathleen had rooted out an old leather-bound copy of Franz Kafka's *The Trial* held in the circus library. Kathleen told him that, even if he doesn't read it on the expedition, he should take it back to Earth to read it there.

On the front of each caravan is a rider's platform, large enough for three people. From here, the caravan is steered. Milton sits holding the reins on the front caravan's platform. He has a scarf tied around his neck and a rabbit hair trilby on his head. A lantern illuminates him but swings wildly in the breeze.

Glenda Burgess holds the reins to Gareth's caravan. Inside, he and Billy stare out the window where Kathleen and the remaining circus folk are congregated to wave the group off. Gareth hates saying goodbye. It feels like he has to do it too frequently in the Meadow.

The caravans rattle and rock in the wind as they leave Lin. They head east first along the main road in Lin before following the coastal paths north. This is not the direction anyone in the Distillery would expect the fleeing fugitives to go if they are heading to the Source.

As they follow the coastline in the shadows of dusk, their shire horses struggle and strain into the wind. Out at sea, Gareth watches the flickering lights of fishing trawlers smashing into steep waves. He hopes they have some of Cyril Speight's special marbles to cope with the sea sickness.

After travelling north until the daylight has gone, the expedition turns inland into an undulating landscape of dense forest. The forest is dark, and the ride bumpy, but they keep travelling without rest until they reach its western edge in the early hours– a point where they can see right down into a vast open plain to the west.

Cutting across the plain are the Distillery's train lines heading toward the Source. The plan is to monitor the train lines from here, getting a sense of the schedule of return train journeys. They will be using the train lines to navigate west, and they will need to know when the railways will be clear– the times when it will be safe to travel without risk of being seen.

"There is only one period of the night when the Distillery's trains pass along the lines," says Nailah. "They are grouped into armed convoys. The Distillery doesn't trust the capability of the police in Water Board territories, you see, and for good reason… Raiding parties are common in these parts."

"Raiding parties?" asks Gareth.

"Groups of mercenaries looking to steal Founderers from the trains. They trade them as cheap labour to work in the cities."

"That's horrible," says Rosalyn.

"How do the Distillery stop them?" asks Hassan.

"They flank a single convoy of trains each night with soldiers who are ready, even eager, to deploy Thermocline Mist," says Milton, pulling out a pair of binoculars and training them on the distant rails. "The tactic has been hugely successful for years…"

"It means that after the sun goes down, there will only be a single, large convoy travelling to the Source. And there is a general rule of thumb; if the Distillery trains pass at a certain time one night, they won't repeat this timing the following night."

"So, if we observe the timings of the trains each night, we will know the best time to travel the next?" says Hassan.

"Exactly," says Nailah, giving Hassan a rare smile.

**\* \* \***

Gareth wraps a blanket around himself and looks out across the plain. Stars shine brightly, drifting through the night sky and illuminating the landscape below. He and Ashley have been nominated to keep watch for the trains tonight. It is a deadly silent and still night.

"Camping under the stars reminds me of weekends with my brother Dennis," says Ashley. "We used to love getting out of the city on little adventures together." She lets out a sigh and runs her fingers through the damp grass. "Oh, I miss Earth," she says.

"How have you managed to keep your memories of Earth so vivid?" Gareth asks her. "You must have been in the Meadow for decades now."

"Seventy years," she confirms. "Time flies by in the Meadow. If you try to hold on to memories, they are fairly easy to keep. But if you don't, they are so easy to lose. The circus was a great place to make new memories, but I always remembered where I came from."

"How did you end up in the circus?" he asks, hoping it isn't too personal a question.

"It's a long story," she says. "I wouldn't want to bore you."

"I've got plenty of time," says Gareth, grinning in the dark.

Ashley looks away for a moment. "OK," she starts. "If you insist…"

"When I finished my stint in the workhouse, the city I arrived in was a chaotic place. The Distillery was struggling to control the influx of arrivals from the Blitz, and the weather was changing every hour. They tried to enrol most of us workhouse graduates into the colleges, but there wasn't space. So, we were thrown into cramped, temporary hostels in the slums, with little or no support for adjusting to our new life."

"Because of this, we never got a formal introduction to the Meadow. We were just told we were bad people, living in shame, with the sole purpose of atoning for our guilt. Many people I knew lived like this and turned to marbles to make themselves feel better. The problem was that while marble production at the time was accelerating, the quality and stability of the marbles themselves were low. Many people in my accommodation got addicted, and many marbles burst. It was a depressing place to be."

"I tried to look after the addicts I knew. I found myself travelling the streets with them, trying to keep them away from too many marbles, or at least away from the darkest marbles. I felt supporting them was part of my atonement. I had led a privileged life on Earth, and I assumed living in squalor with addicts was my way of paying back."

"I existed in the shadows and learnt the city and its streets like the back of my hand. My home became a myriad of alleys and silent groves. And soon, I discovered dozens of other young women just like me. Women who were wandering the streets alone. But these women had suffered differently…they had been abused at the Palace... Seeing their desperate plight, I wanted to help in any way I could."

"I spent years living on the streets, helping the Flickers and the marble addicts, finding them shelter, and keeping them away from unstable marbles. And in that time, I crossed paths with the Distillery police, who became familiar with what I was doing. In their eyes, I was helping to keep the streets free of Founderers. I was doing their job for them."

"The police told me that they wanted to support my mission. They said they could support the Founderers by moving them to safe lands outside the city. In this way, I was duped into escorting the women and marble addicts to the train stations."

"For years, I thought I was doing a good thing. I even wore a purple armband given to me by the Distillery in recognition of my work. Little was I to know that they were not sending the

Founderers to a better life but were sending them with the Drifters to the Source to get these 'undesirables' out of the Meadow. I am so ashamed of this period of my life, Gareth. It was only when I came across the City Circus did I realise my errors, and my life changed course."

"What happened?" asks Gareth.

"One evening, I spotted a group of rebels raiding a train I had just loaded with Founderers. They bundled the captive passengers out of the carriages and into their wagons. I chased the wagon down and caught up with them in the suburbs. They were rebels from a group called the City Circus. I confronted them, saying I would report them to the Distillery for kidnapping, but they persuaded me to see something first…another train full of Founderers waiting in sidings nearby. Inside that train, I saw what the Distillery were really like. I saw the guards abusing Founderers. I was horrified."

"The circus folk told me why the Flickers were semi-conscious. They told me about the Palace and took me to see the despicable building, the prison, where so many women are taken. I didn't need much persuading to reject the Distillery after that. I joined the City Circus and became part of their rescue teams, raiding the same trains I used to load with Founderers."

"All the time with the City Circus, I learnt more about the wider circus network. I started to make connections with the other city rebels. This is where I met Kim-Joy. The folk who run the taverns in London don't all belong to the circus, but most are sympathetic to the plight of the Founderers. Then, maybe ten or twenty years ago, I was given a chance to lead a City Circus group out of London to Lin. This was where I found my true calling."

"To be a circus performer?" says Gareth, guessing.

"No…Animal companion. I always had pets on Earth. I love animals. So, when I had the chance to work with the mammals, the elephants, and the circus's lions, I was so happy. This was when I became a fully-fledged member of Sanger's circus." Ashley looks at Gareth, relieved to have told her story.

"Did you ever meet Commander Newman? Before he went back to Earth?" Gareth asks.

"No," says Ashley. "I never met him. I heard of the Cwtch Missions, mostly in updates at Circus Councils. But the expeditions back then were very secretive. Even amongst the circus folk, some thought they shouldn't happen – they were considered too dangerous. We just got cryptic updates at monthly Councils. I vaguely remember an update about his Mission being sabotaged, but I can't recall the details…it was decades ago."

"What do you think the chances are for our expedition?" Gareth asks.

"Ha!" Ashley chuckles. "That's a big question…Honestly?… I don't see us having any more chance than the Missions back then… But then, well …things also feel different now. I mean, we know it's possible and…well…," she grins cheekily at Gareth in the starlight. "… There are women on the expedition this time!"

Gareth smiles back at Ashley and gazes at her wild green eyes. Her integrity makes her shine in the darkness. He senses he might have gazed too long and looks away quickly. Glancing back, she is still looking at him. His face burns red, but this isn't perceptible in the dark. Ashley looks at him quizzically.

A distant rumbling and rattling down in the plain draw Gareth's attention. There they are – the trains to the Source.

Leading the convoy, two packs of dogs pull wheeled Distillery sleds along the rails. Packs of sturdy horses pull each of the snaking trains behind. Half of the carriages in the trains are illuminated by lanterns. These front carriages are full of people, Founderers, Gareth presumes. The rear carriages are dark. These are the tightly packed carriages of Drifters. There are about half a dozen trains, and it takes them the best part of an hour to move through the landscape. Once they are gone, Gareth and Ashley are free to turn in. Gareth is exhausted.

* * *

Gareth is woken by the rhythmic tapping of loose strapping, caught in the breeze, and the warm morning sun beaming onto the caravan. He heaves himself up. The caravan is empty. Everyone else is already up. He steps out into the sunlight and looks across the plain. A clear and breezy day is emerging. The train line is empty again, now just a dark line shooting out as far as the eye can see.

Sat on benches pulled out from one of the other caravans, the rest of the expedition are sat around absorbing the view and sucking on warm cinnamon marbles. Gareth sits himself down and gratefully accepts a marble from Glenda.

"Over there," says Milton, pointing to the hills on the distant horizon. "Those are the Pennines. If we do well, we should get there sometime early tomorrow morning."

"Yes, hopefully," says Nailah, taking over. "But today, we will take it easy. We need to continue observing the railways, check the kit, and do some foraging in the forest."

Milton smiles back at Nailah in agreement.

Around mid-morning, while they are processing the poppy pods they have abundantly foraged, Gareth notices a dark patch of isolated cloud forming over the plain.

"Look," he says, pointing it out. "It looks like the weather is about to change." As he says this, a white light erupts around the cloud and shoots down to the ground.

From the white flash, a battered metallic white mini-bus appears and skids to a stop on the grass. The blinding white light lingers behind the vehicle briefly, then fades away. As it fades, a storm cloud billows out from its shadow. Quickly the entire landscape is consumed by its darkness, and the first specks of rain fall on the plain.

"You've just witnessed an Opening," says Milton.

Gareth watches the minibus. A side door opens, and half a dozen people step out. Surprisingly none of them looks around or stops to take in the scene. In single file, they start walking west, parallel to the train line.

"They are all Drifters," says Nailah.

"Should we go and see if there are any conscious arrivals?" says Glenda.

"Too dangerous," says Milton. "The Water Board will have lookouts in the plain. We can't be caught on a retrieval."

Nailah nods in agreement.

Soon after Milton's words, a brass horn sounds far away. Two individuals on horseback are spotted galloping across the plain, west to east, throwing up flocks of startled birds and plumes of seeds as they hurtle through the long grass and the rain.

Both riders wear bright red bandannas around their necks—an indication of their Water Board allegiance. The first rider peels off to intercept the Drifters. He holds a lasso and captures the first unconscious arrival as he slows his horse before riding around the group, encircling them with rope. In no time, the six Drifters are loosely bundled together and held firm by the rider.

The second rider gallops alone towards the minibus. As he approaches, he pulls out a truncheon. He dismounts and wanders around the vehicle, peering in before stepping inside, his truncheon raised. A moment later, he emerges empty-handed.

"There can't have been any conscious arrivals," says Nailah.

The rider leaps back onto his horse and gallops to rejoin his partner.

"What will they do with the arrivals?" asks Hassan.

"Most likely, they'll take them to the nearest train station," says Nailah. "The Water Boards don't have much use for Drifters. They use Founderers for labour in the cities, but they will happily give over Drifters for the Distillery to transport them onto the Source. The Water Boards don't want too many Drifters wandering through their lands. They trample poppy fields and interrupt transport routes."

"As expected, the Water Boards are watching the land during the day. Waiting for arrivals," says Milton. "They would intercept us very quickly in the light of day. It would be wise not to advertise our presence unless we have to. The more we're seen, the more we're scrutinised."

"Will we investigate if there are any supplies left in the minibus?" says Glenda.

"Definitely," says Nailah. "As soon as the sun has set."

*Late at night on 19th September 1906, the Atlantic No.276 sleeper and mail train from London thundered through Grantham station on its way to Edinburgh. The night was clear with a few scattered showers. As it passed through the station, staff recognised that it was travelling much too fast to negotiate the bends in the track after the station. To the horror of the onlookers, the No.276 had an explosive derailment. Parts of the train's locomotive destroyed the parapet of a nearby bridge, while the remainder of the engine, and the carriages, were slung sideways across the tracks and down an embankment where they burst into flames. In all more than a dozen souls were lost in the tragedy.*

# Chapter Fourteen

♦

# Into the Long Grass

The night is particularly dark without the light of the stars, and the storm continues to blow. The journey west along the track will start imminently, but Nailah and Milton agree there is time, first, to investigate the minibus in the plain. Gareth, Hassan, and Glenda volunteer to go.

The vehicle is ominous, as it has been all afternoon, standing silently in the dark and wet plain. The rain rattles noisily off its dented roof. Inside, it looks like the arrivals must have been on some stag do or 'lads' weekend away. There is aftershave, empty beer cans, and hair gel all over the floor. These won't be useful to the expedition. But there is a package which will– a bag of painkillers, vital medicines for the journey.

"I'll take this as well," says Glenda, leaning in and pulling a torch from the glove compartment. "I won't use it any time soon. Once the batteries run out, that will be it…Best save it for emergencies."

Gareth feels eerie inside the minibus. It has been on Earth so recently. It almost feels like you can touch where it came from. He hasn't felt this close to home since he arrived in the Meadow. It is as if some air is still in the vehicle that has come straight from Earth. He wonders what disaster befell the group that brought them through the Opening. Looking at the dashboard, he sees a series of scratches. They look recent and desperate.

\* \* \*

Stormy winds and heavy rain rock the carriages as they finally leave the forest. The night is young, and there has been no sign of the Distillery trains yet. But, despite the risk, they are all keen to get some miles under their belts. They will have to vigilantly monitor the tracks for the tell-tale signs of approaching lights as they travel.

In the current weather, only the three riders steering the horses are outside, holding the reins and watching the tracks. Milton, the front rider, will watch for oncoming trains and the rear rider, Ashley, for any approaching ones. They are going to take turns steering through the night. Facing the torrential downpour, the first three riders have drawn the short straw.

As soon as the three carriages drop into the open plain, they take up their route, following the paths running alongside the rails. Paths compacted by the Distillery's horses and dogs. Navigation is simple. Follow the train lines and keep moving.

After an hour or so splashing through the countryside, the caravans come up on the town of Grantham. A large settlement on the bend of a river is known to have welcomed the circus folk in the past. It is a regular stop for travelling merchants, so their presence won't raise any suspicions. Nonetheless, they don't plan to stop – not with the Distillery trains still absent – and the three fugitives are kept inside: no unnecessary risks.

Peering out of the curtains as they rattle through the town, Gareth spots a bustling pub brimming with life. The Atlantic 276 looks much like the Tide and Time Tavern. He can see revellers laughing heartily inside in a mist of marbles and music. Those joyous memories from the Tide and Time feel a world away right now. He clutches the locket dangling around his neck and thinks of Kim-Joy.

Gareth's turn to steer comes during the early hours of the morning. They have covered dozens of miles by now, and mercifully, the rain has abated, although there is a cool nip in the air. Grantham has long since disappeared behind them, and the landscape has become sparse and exposed. The occasional copse of trees is all that interrupts the long expansive views. If all goes well, the intention is to push on to the safety of the Pennine Hills tonight without stopping.

In the Pennines is a place called Crofter's Hope. The settlement of a community of hoarders, whose isolation from the

Distillery and the Water Boards, means that the expedition will have a safe and uncompromised location to rest.

"I stayed at Crofter's Hope last time," says Milton, leaning across the platform he sits on with Gareth and Hassan. "They are mercenaries. Hoarding all sorts. They live in caves hidden in the hills, selling their wares in exchange for medicine and marbles. It's the perfect place for us to lie low."

"And they won't say anything about fugitives staying there?" Gareth asks.

"They don't integrate with other people much – and it tells!" Milton sniggers. "Even if you used your real names, they'd unlikely even know you were wanted men. They are a funny bunch. It takes a certain type of person to choose to live underground. Their main contact with the outside world is via their Arrival Archives."

"What's that?" asks Hassan.

"A hoard of historical records from the Meadow. They are open to the public to trace their family histories. Most people in the Meadow will have heard of Crofter's Hope at some point. Many have paid a visit at some time or other. I think it's only you two, Rosalyn, and Billy, who haven't been there before."

There is a challenge to getting to Crofter's Hope. Especially as they need to be there before sunrise. The Pennine Hills are located beyond the river Derwent. A wide meandering river that bisects the landscape from north to south. They should reach the river in about an hour. But it isn't possible to travel through the waters themselves. They are too deep and fast flowing. The only route they can take is across the railway bridge at Belper.

Bridges like the Belper Crossing tend to lie at the border between one Water Board and the next. Border guards patrol the entrances and exit to all railway bridges requiring a tariff from any vehicle or train that passes them. Tariffs are usually paid in either marbles, valuable artefacts, or, in some cases, even Founderers are traded at these points. Not wanting to draw too much attention to themselves, Nailah suggests that the expedition be staggered into three separate bridge-crossing parties. Arriving at the bridge at different times, they will rendezvous at Crofter's Hope sometime just before sunrise.

Agreeing enough time has passed since the penultimate caravan left for Belper Crossing, Glenda, Gareth, and Rosalyn – the last caravan party to approach the bridge – pack up and set off towards the river. As far as they can see, the other carriages have all gotten away without incident.

Gareth sits alongside Glenda at the reins while Rosalyn watches at the rear. About a mile from the bridge, the structure becomes visible, silhouetted over the vast river reflecting the stars above. At each end of the bridge, gatehouses are illuminated by burning lamps, and Gareth can make out the figures of guards at each. They are standing around, smoking pipes, and sucking marbles. It is quite a pleasant night to be guarding a bridge in the starlight, he thinks.

Just then, there is a call from Rosalyn.

"The trains are coming! The trains are coming!" she hollers down.

Glenda pulls sharply back on the reins.

"Are you sure?" she calls back to Rosalyn.

"Absolutely!"

"Quick, we have to get away from the rails," ushers Glenda, steering the horses perpendicular to the tracks and into the long grass.

The ground is soft and marshy, and the horses struggle in the bog. But it is a blessing in disguise. The wheels sink quickly into the marsh, meaning the tall reeds reach higher than the caravan. Going is slow, but in a few minutes, they are a hundred metres from the rails and completely hidden.

Glenda brings the horses to a stop and rushes forward with a salt lick for the animals. "That'll keep them quiet," she whispers. "I'll stay with the caravan. You two should wander away and hide. Just in case any of the convoy comes snooping."

Gareth and Rosalyn tumble into the undergrowth together. But as the first Distillery sled trundles by, they realise they have inadvertently crept to a position only fifty metres from the tracks. They hold their breath.

The noise of the straining dogs and the rattle of harnesses is followed by the creaking of a sled in which three Distillery figures are talking loudly to each other. In the light of their lanterns, Gareth can see they are heavily armed with canisters of Thermocline Mist, truncheons, and short blades. They have full body armour and a purple armband indicating their allegiance. They are more like soldiers than train guards.

Two sets of these military sleds trundle by before the first train appears. Thankfully the dogs and the men are unaware of those hiding in the reeds nearby. Six huge horses strain as they pull the train, their heavy clomping feet shaking the ground. Armed Distillery riders, lit by lanterns, sit atop the first carriage, holding a knot of reins.

The first train carriages are lit inside. Gareth can see the passengers. They look much like Rosalyn had done when he first met her outside the Tide and Time Tavern. Not unconscious but heavily drugged. They loll from side to side inside the carriage. Most of the passengers are young women. With them are a handful of Distillery guards. These guards aren't in armour or combat gear. They are stripped down to their vests and are clearly drunk on potent marbles, pushing and shoving the semi-conscious women between them, roaring with laughter and bravado. To Gareth's horror, he notices one of the guards thrusting his body against a female Founderer bent over against one of the chairs. He looks away, repulsed.

"Those despicable brutes!" hisses Rosalyn, leaping up from where she is, incensed by what she sees.

"Rosalyn! No!" Gareth gasps. He grabs her arm before she can expose their position. "We can't be seen."

"Can't you see what they are doing?!" exclaims Rosalyn, pleading with Gareth.

"Yes, of course, I can," Gareth says desperately, holding Rosalyn's arm. "But please. We must not give ourselves away here. We mustn't get caught."

Rosalyn looks at Gareth. There is pain and rage etched across her face. She struggles against his grip for a moment, then falls into his arms and starts to cry. Gareth holds onto her tightly.

In the dark, the two of them stand in a tight embrace. Gareth can feel the warmth of Rosalyn's tears soaking into his sleeve. The rattle and clunking of the train carriages continue behind him.

Through sobs and sniffs, Rosalyn looks up at Gareth. "You remind me of her, you know."

"Of who?" Gareth asks.

"Your sister," she replies.

Rosalyn's voice reverberates through Gareth's chest, and her breath is warm. Gareth feels the blood drain from his head, and he holds tightly to Rosalyn to keep his balance. He has long wanted to speak to Rosalyn about Cerys, but he has been reluctant to bring up her memories of the Palace.

"You remember Cerys?" he asks.

"Yes, I was with her at the Palace," says Rosalyn, still crying. "I'm sorry I never told you. I wanted to."

Gareth holds on to her. "Can you tell me now?" he asks cautiously. "Please?"

Rosalyn wriggles free from Gareth's embrace and steps back in the starlight, looking straight at him. She wipes her eyes. "I haven't told anybody about my time at the Palace," she says. "I can't remember everything."

Rosalyn stares at Gareth in the stillness of the night, and Gareth looks back at her. "The farthest back I can remember is some point early on from my time at the Palace. Cerys was there with me," she pauses. "At that time, we were being treated well. We were well rested and given the freedom of the Palace grounds. We even had horses to ride and beautiful gardens to explore. Cerys and I loved riding the horses together.

"But there were also the interrogations from the priests. Awful, humiliating, and degrading experiences, though I cannot really remember the details now. And then there was the fact that we were under the obsessive gaze of the princes who lived in the Palace and watched us with their salivating grins everywhere we went.

"At some point, I can't remember when exactly – maybe a month in – we started to be invited to the dances. Opulent and lavish affairs every night where we were plied with crimson marbles and escorted up to the dance hall of the Palace. There were hundreds of us women and girls at the dances. Everyone in those halls was giddy and over-fed on marbles, and the atmosphere was chaotic. The princes were there too – middle-aged, overweight, and over-eager. Cerys always refused their advances. I respect her now. But back then, when she would return from each dance bruised and tearful, I thought she was foolish to push the men away.

"Over time, the princes' advances became too much for me too. Their hands violated me first, hidden from view, under tables or against walls. Then they didn't seem to care if anyone saw. Their entire body and mind became an arsenal of weapons to violate me. I started to resist. A cold shoulder at first or a polite refusal. But this wasn't enough. I tried pushing them away. When that didn't work, I scratched and hit. Soon, like Cerys, they punished me.

"When Cerys and I didn't stop fighting, we and all the other women who resisted were taken away from the dances altogether and sent to the confessionaries – sanitary wards to cure us women who fought back. The matrons ran the confessionaries. They told us that the shame of our pasts was so deep that we needed special cleansing.

"We were strapped down to hospital beds in the wards, and priests were invited in. These hooded men with long ornate purple robes were there to 'exorcise' our demons. The priests shouted, spat in our faces, and groped our bodies while the matrons forced us to suck on potent marbles. The exorcisms felt like an excuse for the priests to violate us further in the name of ridding us of sin. But we couldn't resist any more. The straps holding us down held our bodies, and the marbles held our minds. And soon enough, we became addicts – marble addicts.

"Once we were addicted and compliant, the princes were invited to approach us again. They came down to the confessionaries and shared the drugged women between them. And each night, we were taken up to their chambers where we were made to dance and consume more and more marbles with the princes.

"Eventually, the nights themselves became a blur, and I couldn't distinguish one night from the next or even night from day. I lost sight of Cerys over these weeks, maybe even months, of fog. Then I started waking in the mornings, and my body ached. I noticed bruises on my arms and legs and hot red streaks of scalded skin on my back and chest, but I couldn't remember where they had come from. I would tell myself that I must have had a clumsy fall when in a marble fog or that I must have scratched myself when wandering in the gardens. I don't know if I ever believed that, however. I started to worry that I had some illness or disease that was wasting away my body in the Meadow. Maybe it was the marbles. Too many of them, I wondered. Was that a thing?

"Then I discovered the terrible truth about having too many marbles in the Palace. The more marbles you had, the less potent they became. Like any addict, I longed for the sensations the marbles gave me, but they could no longer satisfy me. And worse, they could no longer cloud my vision.

"Like all women from the confessionaries eventually found out, I began to witness through my own eyes exactly what was being done to my body at night to give me the bruises and scars. And I couldn't stop what the princes did to me or the other girls. It was like being a passive observer of your shared nightmare. The potency of the marbles might have lost their grip on our minds, but not our bodies. And so, we were trapped in our minds, with the horrors of the princes flashing in front of our eyes.

"It was around then I saw Cerys again, but I don't think she noticed me. Those of us in the confessionaries who had become addicted to marbles first, it seemed, were also the first to become aware of our nightmare. There were still those, like Cerys, who had that stare of someone stuck in a marble fog. The marbles still potently controlling her mind. She would have been unaware of our living hell. Probably waking up every morning, like I had done, wondering why she felt so appalling.

"However, as the princes became aware the marbles were losing their potency in me, they stopped letting me ever wake up. They forced marbles into me just as the sensations of the last one wore off. And this was when all my memories started to fade. Living perpetually in a passive nightmare, I forgot who I was. I lost track of where I had come from or even where I was. All I knew was *what* I was. What I was to the princes. With only this present nightmare, I let my mind shut down. I just wanted it to end.

"But then occasionally, I would see Cerys and be reminded there was a time before the nightmare. I felt I could glimpse past what was happening to our bodies and sense something more. Something just worth fighting for. There was something familiar in her. A sense that our souls had bonded. I felt this feeling when I first saw you in the caravan out of London. And this prevented me from letting go of myself completely."

Rosalyn looks right into Gareth's eyes for a moment, and he holds her gaze sincerely.

"The Palace smothered the spark in my soul. Even though I never let go completely, the princes let go of me. They could tell my mind had shut out my past, and I was merely a passive observer of the present. To them, I was a spent resource. To them, with no past, I was ready to start my new life in the Meadow. Like all who pass through the Distillery initiations, I had now 'graduated' in their warped belief.

"As the very essence of my soul flickered, I found myself alone, lost, and without a sense of who I was on the streets in the Paddock. I couldn't remember anything except for my experiences at the Palace. I didn't know what had happened to the other women. And I just wanted to forget. But like so many women in the Palaces, I will *never* forget."

Rosalyn peers through the long grass, her eyes following the windows of the carriages as they pass by. "I'm sorry, Gareth…I don't know what happened next to Cerys. I wish I could tell you more…and less." She looks across at Gareth, her eyes glistening.

"It's OK," he says. "Thank you…"

Rosalyn smiles back politely. "I can't live in the Meadow anymore," she says.

"I know," says Gareth. "That's why we are on this journey, right? That's why we have to succeed...we must get back."

"I won't be going back," says Rosalyn.

"You won't?"

"I can't," says Rosalyn. "...I don't want to."

"Why not?"

"I have no memory of the place we call Earth," she says. "It is as though the place is just a story. To me, it doesn't seem at all real..."

"But...?" Gareth can't think of anything to say.

"I've spoken to Nailah, and she agrees. There is no way back for me. Well Wishers believe in returning through a love of the Earth. Through a love of the people on Earth and the hope of seeing them again. I don't have that love. I don't have that hope."

"Don't worry, I'm not afraid," she says, noticing Gareth's sorrowful expression. "I'm almost excited. I feel a longing to 'go on'– a longing to go to the Source. I think I can almost sense the draw a Drifter feels. A blissful momentum in my soul, that I am ready for the next place."

Rosalyn teeters towards Gareth. He embraces her in a warm, brotherly way and holds her tight as more trains pass them by. But both of them avoid looking into the carriages anymore. Rosalyn closes her eyes. Gareth looks up to the stars and thinks of Cerys. He hopes that if her soul passes him right now, she is up there amongst the stars and not on the trains that trundle past.

"Gareth? Rosalyn?" Glenda's voice cuts through the marsh. "That's the last train. Help me get the horses and the caravan out of this bog."

Glenda is uneasy about the time. It is getting extremely close to sunrise. There is a real risk that they won't make it to Crofter's Hope in time if they don't move soon. If this is the case, they will have to camp in the open.

Gareth and Rosalyn don't talk to Glenda about what they just witnessed inside the train carriages or about Rosalyn's time at the Palace. Instead, as they haul the horses out of the marsh, they allow Glenda to quiz them on the details of their false identities. Identities, she reminds them, they will be adopting as they approach the bridge.

Gareth and Rosalyn have rehearsed their fake identities for this kind of scenario numerous times since leaving Lin. Their names are Tyler Bennington and Skye Savic. Tyler is twenty-four years old. He has been in the Meadow for a year, graduating from the Glasgow Workhouse, and is keenly interested in travel and trade. Skye is thirty years old, has been in the Meadow for five years, and had been at Holyrood Palace in Edinburgh before working as a jewellery maker, then joining the travelling merchants a year ago.

Glenda, although keeping her name, will also embellish her past. She will claim to have been in the Meadow for just a few decades, arriving during the Great Influx around the Second World War. She will say she had been a merchant on Earth and has continued her trade in the Meadow. The group, they will say, are on their annual pilgrimage to sell their artefacts in Merseyside, where a trade fair congregates with merchants from all around the Meadow, even those from overseas.

\* \* \*

The river Derwent is still and calm as they make their way to the gatehouse. The border guards on this side of the river spot them approaching. The half dozen guards light their lanterns and send a scout rider to intercept. This is expected. The scout wants to check the nature of their travel and receive their toll offer, which he will take back to the other guards for approval.

The scout rider could quite easily have been one of the riders they witnessed intercepting the minibus yesterday. His loose black combat gear and red bandana indicate his status as an officer of the Water Board. As he approaches, Gareth and Rosalyn go inside the caravan to prepare some items to barter for their toll.

They have plenty of marbles to offer, but it is possible that as a merchant caravan, the rider might be more interested in the rare items that they can offer instead. Glenda suggests some decorative personal things; jewellery or watches. The kind of thing that cannot be easily created in the Meadow and will serve as something he can trade on further or use to adorn himself and increase his status.

Rosalyn opens a chest of artefacts from the cupboard and picks out two silver chains with gemstone pendants. Gareth selects half a dozen marbles which he expects might appeal to what, he assumes, is a thuggish border guard. Bright red marbles and cobalt blue marbles. The types of marbles that usually give the sensations of virile energy and competitive edginess. He places the marbles into a cloth pouch and pockets them.

Glenda keeps the caravan moving as the rider comes alongside. "Good risen," she says.

"Good risen," the man replies. "You hoping to head across the bridge tonight?"

"That's right. Plenty of trade to be done up in Merseyside this time of year."

"That where you're heading, is it?"

"Oh yes," Glenda replies. "Big merchants fair in a week. Annual do."

"What's your trade?"

"We're Arrivals merchants. Plenty of stuff from the last few decades. Really nice stuff if you're interested?"

"Not my thing," says the rider. "Unless you've picked up any weapons?"

"Oh no, we don't carry weapons. Too dangerous."

"So, what are you offering for the toll?"

"Well, if you're not an artefacts man, one of my kids can probably get you some marbles?" Glenda taps on the caravan hatch. "Tyler, my love. Can you grab a bag of marbles for the border guard?"

"Sure," Gareth responds, trying to sound relaxed. He opens the hatch and holds out the bag of marbles to Glenda.

"Out you come, don't be shy," says the guard.

"Sorry, sir," Gareth responds and clambers out to sit next to Glenda.

The border guard looks intently at Gareth. Checking him out, looking at his piercings and shaved head. "Got anyone else in there?"

"Just our kid, Skye. She's sleeping," says Glenda. "Three of us have been travelling together this last year. Good little team we are."

The rider looks back at Glenda. "Just the three of you, then?"

"Good to keep the caravan light," she responds with a smile. "You looking for someone?"

"Oh, not me in particular. There's word going around you see that the Distillery has got some high-reward fugitives on the run. Wouldn't mind bagging me that bounty," he says.

"Oh," says Glenda. "Well, if they travel this way, you're in a good place to catch them. Everyone has to cross *this* bridge, right?"

"That's right," agrees the scout. "Though I'd probably have to share the bounty with the other guards in that case!"

"No doubt," says Glenda. "Anyway, will this do you for now?" She throws him the bag of marbles.

The rider peers into the pouch. "Good quality marbles these. Yeah, I think six is a fair price. I'll check it with the others, but I can't see there being any trouble. Just keep left when you get to the bridge, and be careful as you travel over. We've just had the Distillery trains go past. You know what they're like for kicking up rubble and debris."

"Thanks," says Glenda. "Good risen."

"Good risen," says the rider, and he kicks his heels into his horse's flanks before speeding back towards the gatehouse.

There is no trouble at all getting onto the bridge. Six marbles had been a sufficient tariff. As the caravan passes over the bridge, they enter the jurisdiction of the Peak Water Board and are immediately greeted by another guard. This guard brings his horse alongside the caravan while they are still on the bridge. He isn't looking for a tariff or to inspect their caravan – evidently, the two Water Boards trust one another enough not to double-check. Instead, he just wants to have a nosey at the passing merchants.

"Who else you got in there then?" the guard asks without the politeness of a greeting. He is riding a jet-black horse and wears his yellow bandanna of the Peak Water Board tightly around his forehead.

"Good risen," says Glenda, greeting the rider rather sardonically. "Just my two kids in the back."

"Let's see them then," the guard instructs.

"Please?" Glenda replies instinctively. Manners cost nothing. But the guard just narrows his eyes and doesn't respond. "OK," says Glenda. "Tyler, Skye, can you pop your heads out, please? There's a polite young man out here who wants to take a look at you both."

Gareth and Rosalyn, sitting inside the caravan listening, tentatively step out of the hatch and onto the caravan's platform. Gareth glances at the young guard on his horse. The rider's hair matches his animal – slick, black, and neatly groomed. About fifty metres up ahead, he can see the Peak Water Board checkpoint at the end of the bridge, where the guard's colleagues are sitting around smoking pipes and laughing. Laughing in that full-bodied way that men do when they herd together.

The guard on his horse whistles like an eager peacock as he catches sight of Rosalyn. "Oh, hello!" he announces. "Who do we have here? Fancy a ride on my stallion, darling? There's room for two." The guard shuffles on his saddle and caresses the leather before him.

Rosalyn looks back at the man with disgust. "Not likely," she responds curtly.

"Oh, come on," says the guard, pulling his horse beside the caravan. So close that he can almost reach out and grab her. "I don't bite… unless you want me to?" he grins with lustful menace.

"Get lost," says Rosalyn, moving behind Gareth and out of the man's reach.

The guard leans forward, trying to regain sight of his prey, but Gareth is in the way. "Is your sister always this cold?" he asks Gareth rhetorically. "Tell her it's just a bit of fun, won't you?"

Usually, confronted with the intimidating arrogance of such a man, Gareth would have shifted uneasily and acted with reluctant compliance. However, by the pure chance of circumstance, an opportunity arises at that moment for him to be different. In his quest to ogle Rosalyn, the vulgar guard has leant himself precariously on the latched gate of the caravan's platform. Gareth takes his chance.

"You want fun?" Gareth levels at the guard. Without waiting for a response, he kicks the latch. The gate swings open under the weight of the guard's torso, and the man tumbles clumsily off his horse. Gareth catches a glance at the shock written across his face before he hits the ground and is smothered by the dust kicked up by the caravan.

Gareth's timing couldn't have been better. The man's colleagues, who are sat around the checkpoint, have a clear view of his fall, which, from their position, looks simply like he had slipped off his horse while bothering some passing merchants. The men roar with laughter, revelling in his misfortune and not once suspecting foul play. A few of them even wave jovially at the caravan as they pass.

Glenda and Rosalyn beam with joyful smiles at Gareth. "That'll teach him!" says Glenda, patting Gareth on the back. "I didn't know you had that side to you, Gareth. I like it!"

Gareth feels his cheeks redden. He didn't know he had that side, either. "Let's not linger, though," says Glenda. "Men like that don't usually deal with humiliation very well." She gees the horses urgently and gets the caravan moving quickly away from the bridge.

It is a full fifteen minutes later before Glenda feels they have travelled far enough to settle the horses back to a comfortable pace. Only then does Gareth realise just how light it is getting. "How long till sunrise?" he asks Glenda.

"Not long enough," she says. "We're going to need to find somewhere to make camp."

Glenda consults her map. They don't need lanterns; such is the brightness of the early hour. She points to where they are, then prods another point on the map. "That's where we are trying to get to," she says, indicating a small settlement where contours converge at the start of the Pennines. "We are going to need somewhere to take cover today. I know the grounds around here.

It's all short dry grasses, and we'd stand out too much without any cover."

"What about there?" Gareth says, pointing to a small green blob on the map next to an oval of blue (he assumes this is a lake). There is a black cross bisecting the two, and "2007" is written in small font next to the cross.

"Good spot," says Glenda. "That'll be perfect."

"What does the cross mean?" asks Gareth.

"That's a site where we know there's been an Opening in the past. There might even be some remnants from the arrival there. We might be able to pick up some useful things."

* * *

The sun's orange glow is just peaking over the horizon as they reach the copse of trees next to the lake. Willows with cascading sorrowful-looking branches and a curtain of leaves are perfect for their camp, out of sight. Weary from the long night, they agree to do lookout shifts while the other two get a few hours rest. Gareth draws the short straw, the first shift. He finds the darkest coffee-coloured marble and pops it in his mouth to keep him awake.

It is quiet amongst the willows. The branches muffle sound from outside and do an excellent job blocking out most of the sun. A few shafts of light penetrate the canopy, shooting dramatic lines of brightness onto the mossy ground. The trees only stretch fifty or so metres in each direction, with the lake at the northern edge, and Gareth realises he can wander all around without losing sight of the caravan.

He goes to see if anything is left behind from the arrival back in 2007, but there is nothing there, just old fallen trees, rotten logs, moss, and a few rocks. Then his eyes are drawn to some peculiar angles in a pile of rocks by the lake – right angles and parallel edges which are quite unnatural.

The rocks are covered in thick green moss. Careful not to slip into the water, Gareth scrapes off a layer of moss to explore further. It isn't a rock at all. Rusty brown metal comes away in his hands. He pulls a bit more to reveal plastic light covers and wires.

The more he pulls away, the more the car emerges. This must be the vehicle that arrived in the Meadow in 2007.

Left for more than a decade, the car is barely identifiable. Covered in moss, nature has adopted it. As the old vehicle starts to resemble its original form, Gareth can peer inside, where the plastic interior is much less affected by natural decay. The seats, some submerged in lake water, are damp and rotten and are covered in fungus. But the dashboard and steering wheel are all still easily recognisable amidst the cobwebs. None of the side windows have survived, so Gareth leans through the foliage to see if he can find anything useful for the expedition. Brushing away the leaves and debris, nothing seems to be left in the vehicle at all.

Gareth grasps the lever of the glove compartment and opens it. It evidently hasn't been opened since the vehicle arrived. A pile of letters, a vehicle manual, an old, very basic mobile phone, and a purse are all unaffected by decay. Carefully reaching in, he grabs the contents and pulls them out. Intrigued, he carries them back to the caravan and sits on a warm, illuminated patch of the rider's platform to inspect them.

Looking inside the delicate purse, he finds bank cards, membership cards, coins, and three photographs. One shows a beloved pet dog gazing eagerly out of the image. One is a picture of a young couple – a black-and-white photo from some graduation. The young woman in it is propping herself up against a stair bannister, standing next to a short, stocky man who looks very pleased with himself. They both look blissfully happy. The man appears again in the third picture. Older, but with the same blissful smile.

Looking closer at the man, Gareth realises there is something familiar about him. He stares at the picture. Why is his face so familiar? And why does it unnerve him?

Gareth tries the old mobile phone. Incredibly it turns on. Its pixelated, monochrome screen bursts into life with a bright green backlight. While he waits for the home screen to load, he opens some of the documents recovered from the car. Scanning through what appears to be an innocuous insurance agreement, he finds that the owner of the vehicle was Mrs Rose Drinkwater. This discovery stops him in his tracks. Gareth knows the name Rose Drinkwater. Suddenly, the pieces of the puzzle all come together in his mind. His gut wrenches, and he has to hold his chest to calm his breathing.

In 2007, a lady called Rose Drinkwater drowned, trapped in her car after a work weekend away. Her death had led to the imprisonment of the driver. A man who either trapped her or failed to rescue her. A colleague of Mrs Rose Drinkwater. A man called Colin Edwards, Gareth's dad. The man in the photographs is Rose's husband, Clifford Drinkwater. The man whose testimony, accusations, and opinion pieces in local newspapers had put Gareth's dad in the stocks. Clifford Drinkwater had made claims, baseless according to Gareth's mum, that Colin Edwards was a reckless adulterer who had a fiery temper and had previously threatened Rose that he'd kill her if she didn't agree to his advances. Gareth never knew his dad, but his mum had always told him that this wasn't the man she knew.

Staring at the picture again, Gareth feels sick. He has just been rifling through the very car that sealed his dad's fate. He remembers the mobile phone. He nervously picks it up and presses a key. The screen illuminates once more. Clicking through the menu pages, he navigates to the messages. Scrolling down, he sees his father's name multiple times. He must have been in frequent contact with Rose. Cautiously, Gareth selects one of the messages and opens it.

*'hey rose. fancy going for a pint after work? my treat!'*

It is a short and relatively inconsequential message. But this is the closest Gareth has ever got to his father's voice. He reads it over and over. It doesn't say much at all. Nonetheless, in these few short words, it seems that Colin Edwards might have been a generous and sociable man. This ever so slightly lightens the burden that Gareth carries in his subconscious and has done for years. But then he scrolls up to another message from his dad to Rose.

*'hey babe. trish has the kids at grans. same again tonight? xx'*

If the first message had lightened Gareth's soul, this one pulls it back down again. The message seems a little inappropriate, a little clandestine, but not conclusive. Gareth cringes at his dad's use of the name 'babe'. But he can't hold back now; he needs to read the next message.

*'Babe, why arent you responding?! i said i was sorry. i thought it was wat u wanted. let me make it up to you. trish and cliff will never know. xXx'*

There isn't so much wriggle room here. Still, his dad's message doesn't go into details, but it is pretty evident something untoward is going on with Rose Drinkwater. It isn't a great leap to assume that Colin Edwards has been cheating on his wife with Rose. This is the man whose status had been elevated by Gareth's mum and whose shadow had loomed over Gareth his whole life. He always felt the shadow might be a pretty dark one, given what had ultimately happened. But now its darkness feels more real than it ever has before. Stepping out of this shadow and into the bright glare of reality, Gareth feels faint. He looks back at the message on the screen, but it has gone. He tries the buttons on the phone, but it won't reappear. The battery is dead.

Gareth doesn't even notice Glenda get out of the caravan a moment later and greet him. It isn't until she puts her long bony hand on his lap does he look up.

"Are you OK?" she asks Gareth.

"Sorry?" he says.

"You're white as a sheet. What's wrong?"

"The vehicle," says Gareth. "This place is where a woman drowned in her car. The woman that my dad was accused of killing. That's the vehicle over there…"

"Slow down," says Glenda. "What are you talking about?"

"I found the vehicle," says Gareth. "The vehicle from the Opening marked on the map. It's the vehicle a lady called Rose Drinkwater drowned in when I was just a toddler."

"Are you sure?"

"Yes," says Gareth, holding up the pictures, the phone, and the documents. "It's all here." Gareth is now shaking. Glenda puts her arms around him.

A thought suddenly occurs to Gareth, and he pulls away. "Does this mean she's here in the Meadow?! This is where she arrived. Could she be here?!"

Glenda looks at Gareth. "Did you see any markings on the car?"

"What?"

"When the Distillery or Water Board find a place of Opening, they mark it to indicate the nature of the arrivals. Did you not see it a few days ago, scribed into the dashboard of the minibus? Six slash zero."

"I did; now you mention it. I thought they were already there from Earth," says Gareth. "What does it mean?"

"It's a way they indicate the number of conscious and unconscious arrivals. The first number is the number of Drifters. The second is the number of conscious."

Gareth leaps down from the caravan and runs back to the vehicle in a haze of anticipation. He splashes in the water, scrabbles through the damp, mouldy seats, and wipes the cobwebs and debris off the dashboard.

*0/1.*

Rose Drinkwater had arrived in the Meadow, conscious.

*In the early hours of Monday 10th May 1938, there was an unexpected explosion of gas at the coal face of the Black Shale Markham Colliery, Derbyshire. The heavy thumping sound of the explosion echoed through the mine tunnels, immediately followed by a rush of air and a blue-ish cloud of dust. The explosion itself caused fatal injuries to many of the miners in an instant. Many others were overcome by the rushing wave of carbon monoxide. In all seventy-nine men lost their lives in the pit on that tragic morning.*

# Chapter Fifteen

◆

# Crofter's Hope

As the dirt track steepens up the hillside, Glenda gees the horses struggling under the caravan's strain. The sun is starting to rise, silhouetting the hillside behind them, and illuminating the upper reaches of the hill in front. It has been a short night ride from the Willow copse without incident. Gareth hasn't slept much. He has been looking over and over at the photographs and documents belonging to Rose Drinkwater, wondering if Crofter's Hope might give him some indication of her whereabouts.

As part of their Arrival Archives, the people of Crofter's Hope collect information on the disasters that have killed people on Earth. They store and archive these records in their vast libraries underground.

"I'm sure they will have some record of Rose Drinkwater," says Glenda. "At the very least, I reckon they will know which Palace she had been sent to."

Gareth hasn't mentioned the phone messages to Glenda. They are etched permanently on his mind. He has pocketed the lifeless old mobile without her knowledge. Gareth is haunted by the phone and its inaccessible contents, but he is equally afraid of losing it too. "*babe*".

Mid-way up the hillside, a handful of stone buildings appear amongst the rocky outcrops and the course dry grass. Evenly cut timber piles litter the ground outside one of the cottages. Crofter's Hope is much smaller than Gareth envisaged. Indeed, Gareth struggles to see any evidence that Crofter's Hope is inhabited at all. Maybe the settlement has been abandoned since Milton had last been there.

Just then, the door to one of the cottages swings open. A little pale man in dungarees comes out and raises his hand in greeting.

"Good risen," hollers Glenda.

"'G'risen," the man calls back, nodding his head. "We've been expecting you. I take it you're with Mr Milton and the merchants of Pimlico?"

"That's right," says Glenda. "A bit delayed."

"Name's Derek," says the man. "Follow me; I'll show you where you can leave the horses."

Inside one of the old barns stands the gypsy caravans of Milton and the others. Their horses are contentedly eating from a trough.

"I think some of your friends are awake," says Derek. "Breakfast marbles will be being served inside." The small man smiles cheerfully at them, revealing several missing teeth. Between the gaps is an unusual tooth– a bright blue one made of sapphire. Gareth has seen a tooth like this before, but he can't put his finger on where.

"Do we owe you anything for our stay?" Glenda asks him.

"Oh no," Derek replies. "Mr Milton has covered the costs."

Derek leads them back to the cottage where he first appeared. The little stone building has a very pretty exterior. Vines grow up its walls, and flowers fill raised beds. But inside the cottage is quite a contrast. The dark hallway is bare. The walls are chipped and dirty. The floor is mucky with grit, and it is damp. A stone staircase stands to one side, just about. It is crumbling and doesn't look like anyone has ventured up it for decades. Save for a few stray boots and a rack of coats; there is nothing else in the hallway. Nothing except some scratched writing on the wall; "Markham 1938", "Thornhill 1893" and "Swaithe Main, 1875".

Derek reaches under the stairs and pulls out a lantern. Striking a match against the wall, he lights it and beckons them to follow. Glenda pauses.

"After you, Tyler. After you, Skye," she says, ushering Gareth and Rosalyn past her. This is a subtle but necessary reminder to the two of them of the identities they continue to assume.

Stepping through a dark doorway at the end of the hallway, they descend some wet stone steps. Gareth presumes they are going to some cellar. The stone walls are cold, and drips of water land on their heads. When the tunnelling staircase continues, Gareth realises they aren't going to a cellar at all; they are heading deep into the hillside. The stone cottage is a disguise for a cave entrance.

"Stay close," calls Derek from the front. "It's going to get a bit tight." Derek's candlelight flickers off the walls, revealing the swirling layers of rock carved out to make the tunnel. Derek wasn't joking. The tunnel gets so tiny that Gareth has to crouch, almost on his hands and knees.

"Nearly there," Derek calls again, and his voice echoes back down the tunnel.

"Who carved all this?" Glenda asks, stooping much further and more uncomfortably than the others.

"That'd by my ancestors," says Derek. "The first settlers of Crofter's Hope. They were miners from Earth. They suspected these mountains might hold mineral wealth, and they were right."

Derek leads them around a sharp bend into another narrow passage. They shuffle sideways, rubbing against the cold, damp stone before, all of a sudden, they step out into the light and find themselves standing high up on a platform above a vast cavern illuminated by thousands of candles and flaming torches.

The cavern looks like a library or museum. Aisles and chambers are carved into the rock, and a maze of passages leads to different collections and displays. There are dozens of people milling around the cavern, but the books and artefacts that fill the aisles dampen the noise to a distant hum. Gareth takes a moment to comprehend his unique bird's-eye perspective of the immense underground space. Then he notices, sat in an atrium far below them and deep in conversation, are Milton and Nailah. Both wave when they notice them up on the platform.

Derek gestures towards a narrow staircase carved into the rock wall that leads down to the atrium. The precarious vertigo-inducing staircase is protected simply by a rope bannister. Gareth feels his stomach drop, seeing the route they must navigate.

With barely a goodbye, Derek leaves them on the ledge and makes his way back up to the cottage. Glenda, Gareth, and Rosalyn tentatively wander to the platform's edge again. It isn't as bad as they feared; the steps are stable and carved deep into the rock.

"Good risen," says Nailah, beaming when they reach the cavern floor. "We were starting to worry that we would have to travel without you three."

"We got caught behind the Distillery trains," says Glenda.

"I thought that might be the case," says Milton.

"It's good to see you," says Nailah.

"Where are the others?" asks Rosalyn.

"They had a big night of cards," says Milton. "I'm sure they'll all be down soon. Well, maybe not Hassan; I mean Carlo. I think he went bigger than the rest last night!"

"Cards?" asks Gareth.

"Crofter's Hope is famously big on gambling," says Nailah, frowning at her husband.

"I thought they were recluses here?"

"Even recluses can enjoy a good flutter!" grins Milton. "Every night, the biggest cavern is transformed into a gambling hall. The community happily play amongst themselves... but if there are visitors, well... visitors are enthusiastically encouraged to bet big and bet often. There's also plenty of marbles... it can be quite a laugh!"

"Only if you exercise some self-control," says Nailah, again rather stern and pointedly at Milton.

"You should be saying that to Hassan!" Milton jabs back.

"I thought he would be the most susceptible to *cavern fever*," says Glenda, frowning.

"Yeah, his marble consumption is getting a bit too out of hand," says Milton. "Someone's going to have to intervene soon... for his own good." Somewhat unfairly, Milton turns his gaze to Gareth. As though somehow the responsibility for Hassan lies with him. Gareth avoids his gaze.

Soon the rest of the expedition joins them, except Hassan, of course. In no time at all, the reunited expedition members are chatting enthusiastically, catching up on what they have missed.

"Wow, what are the chances of finding the exact car?" says Ashley to Gareth. "We must go and look through the Arrival Archives right away. Rose Drinkwater might live somewhere nearby!"

Gareth is so grateful to Ashley for identifying the opportunity to search the archives. He was reluctant to bring it up too soon, feeling his interests should take lower priority than the expedition's needs. He feels the heavy, lifeless phone in his pocket. "Do you know where the archives are?" he asks her.

"Yes, I've been there before," she replies. "We're not due to leave today, are we, Nailah?"

"Not unless something drastic happens," says Nailah. "Feel free to go exploring."

\* \* \*

The archives are in another cave system, down the valley from Crofter's Hope. It is a pleasant few-hour hike, traversing the hillside. As they walk, Ashley tells Gareth about her last visit to the archives many years ago when she was looking into the fate of her brother Dennis. They had no record at that time, which didn't mean much. Dennis could still be on Earth, or he could have died and bypassed the Meadow altogether. She plans to have another look today, anyway.

Walking and chatting, Gareth loves listening to Ashley's enthusiastic recollections of circus life in the Meadow while she confidently negotiates the rocks and rough ground. She has a way about her that makes him relax and smile. And he seems to have a similar effect on her.

Arriving at the entrance to the cave archives, it is much more in line with how Gareth had previously envisaged access to the home of a cave-dwelling people. The grand archway in the rock is carved with precision and exquisite decoration. *Crofter's Hope Arrival Archives* is chiselled in vast letters above the arch, and flaming torches lead visitors into the ominous darkness below it.

Wandering into the cave, Gareth and Ashley enter a small chamber where the air is cold and dank. The space is lit by half a dozen small fires in grates scattered around its edges. In the centre sits a fortified dark ebony desk occupied by a tired-looking security guard. In the firelight, it is possible to make out the great bags under his eyes and cold sallow skin. He nods his bald head in recognition at Ashley and Gareth before smiling to reveal great gaps in his teeth. Between the gaps is a bright blue tooth made of sapphire. Gareth suddenly remembers where he had seen such a tooth before: during the administrative entry requirements when he first arrived in the Meadow. He wonders if this process was linked to Crofter's Hope somehow.

"Good risen," says the man. "Personal archive, or something else?"

"A personal record for me," responds Ashley. "And an archival deposit for him."

"Deposit?" says the guard, intrigued.

Gareth pulls out the photographs and documents from his pocket. "I found these on a wreckage recently. If I can, I'd like to see the original record of the arrival and leave these documents for anyone else interested in the arrival."

"Right…" the guard responds, inspecting the documents. "And who is the record of?"

"A lady called Rose Drinkwater."

"Rose Drinkwater, you say?" The guard looks over his glasses to inspect Gareth. "Interesting… What's your name, young man?"

"Tyler Bennington," says Gareth. "Is there a problem?" He tries to sound confused.

"Nothing for you to worry about, Mr…Bennington. Unless, of course, you are not really Mr Bennington." The guard stands up from his desk and leans towards Gareth, who tries to maintain a look of confusion while he feels fear rising. "Tell me, Mr Bennington, how and when did you arrive in the Meadow?"

Gareth pauses. His fake arrival story won't stand up to scrutiny at the Arrival Archives. What should he say?

"Tyler arrived with me," says Ashley. "The Number 88 bus in Balham, London. We crashed into a bomb crater on 14 October 1940. I was the driver. Tyler was a passenger on my upper decks."

"And your name is?" asks the guard.

"Ashley Arnold."

"Well, before I can take you to Mrs Rose Drinkwater's record, Mr Bennington, I will escort you to Miss Arnold's record first. To check what she says is true."

"No problem," says Ashley. Gareth looks at her desperately. He is surprised to see how confident she seems. "I wanted to see the records around my arrival anyway."

The guard looks suspiciously at Gareth and Ashley, then holds out his hand. "Nine marbles, please."

Access to the archives isn't free. A stable income for the people of Crofter's Hope comes from recent arrivals visiting the archive to see if they can trace the histories of family and friends in the Meadow. It isn't an activity encouraged by the Distillery or the Water Boards, though, who feel that life on Earth should be forgotten in the Meadow. But this doesn't stop the trade from thriving. There is a standard rate of three marbles per record.

"Nine?" says Ashley. "We only want to see two records."

"I will have to check a third record for Mr Bennington."

"But that's the same record as mine…" she starts, then recognises the guard isn't interested.

Gareth counts out the marbles and hands them over. He is still looking for something from Ashley to indicate how they will play it when they found no record of Tyler Bennington's arrival. She doesn't give anything away.

Getting to the arrival records is quite a feat. It involves either a long ascent up a rope ladder through a narrow fissure in the rock or a descent down a rope ladder through one. The guard paces the chamber floor, muttering. "*1940… London, bombing…* Ah, yes!"

He reaches down and slips his fingers under a notch in the rock. Only it isn't rock. Gareth suddenly realises that the floor, and the ceiling in the low cave, are tiled with hundreds of circular wooden hatches. The guard heaves the hatch to reveal a dark round hole, like a well. Lighting a lantern for each of them, he reaches into the hole and grasps an iron handle just below the surface. He beckons Ashley and Gareth to enter the pit.

"Keep one hand and one foot on the rope ladder at all times," he instructs. "You don't want to fall in there. Attach the lantern to your belt or shoelace. You will need both your hands, trust me."

Gareth peers into the hole. It is so deep that he can't see the bottom. "You two first," the guard instructs. "Keep working your way down the ladder until I tell you to stop."

Gareth clambers in first, and then Ashley follows. The hole is only wide enough for maybe two people alongside one another, although this wouldn't be possible on a single rope ladder. The ladder, therefore, sways in the hole as they descend. Gareth finds his feet and bare hands bashing against the rock walls repeatedly.

In the lamp light, Gareth can see that the rock walls are pock-marked with fist-sized holes. The rock has a porous honeycomb-like structure. In each of these holes is a wooden tube with a rope handle and a label with a date and a short description.

One label reads *Alderney Street, October 16, 1940. Airborne bombing. 23 Arrivals.* Another reads *Broadcasting House, Portland Place, October 15, 1940. Airborne bombing. 7 Arrivals.* In fact, almost all of the wooden tubes indicate some airborne bombing or wartime disaster from 1940 in London. These archives must represent that chaotic time when Ashley arrived.

"Here we are," comes the guard's voice above them. "*Balham Tube Station and Number 88 Bus. October 14, 1940. Airborne bombing. 68 Arrivals.* That's you, right?"

Gareth looks up. Beyond Ashley, he can make out the guard swinging on the rope ladder a few metres above them. He has removed the wooden tube from the rock and unfastened the lid. A long parchment is contained inside.

"Arnold, Ashley. Yes, you're on there," he calls down. "Arrived conscious. Graduate of Southwark Workhouse. Curious but believable. OK… Ashby, Sylvia... Bates, Kieran…"

The guard struggles to read the list in the flickering light. Gareth holds his breath. What is Ashley planning? Surely the game is up. Is she hoping to come up with an excuse or make up a story about why Tyler Bennington isn't on the list? He tries to think of something vaguely believable he might be able to say.

"Ah ha!" blurts the guard. "Bennington, Tyler. Arrived conscious. Graduate of Southwark Workhouse. Poor health on exit. Limited life expectancy… Well, Mr Bennington, it looks like you outlived expectations! Good for you. OK. I'm satisfied."

Gareth can't believe it. Ashley must have known. He has so many questions. "So, what did you want to know about your record Miss Arnold?" asks the guard.

"My brother. Dennis Arnold. Or my parents, Ebony, and Benedict Arnold," says Ashley. "Last time I came, there was no record that they had passed through the Meadow. Is that still the case?"

There is silence while the guard pulls his lantern to the parchment again. The three of them swing gently on the rope ladder in the flickering dark. It is freezing in the hole. Gareth dares not look down into the blackness below his feet.

"Hmm. No, nothing on those three entering the Meadow," says the guard. "There's an Eve Arnold, arrived 1972. Car crash. One of three Drifters to arrive that day. Daughter of Mr Dennis Arnold, if that's any interest?"

"Dennis had a daughter!" exclaims Ashley. "He must have survived the war! Oh, that's the best news possible. Thank you!"

"Don't thank me," says the guard bashfully. "I'm just reading the records." He is confused why someone would be so pleased to know their brother had a daughter, now deceased. If anything, surely this is a tragic revelation. But Gareth knows what this means. If Ashley can return to Earth, back through to when she arrived, she will know that her brother is destined to return from the war and have a daughter. Even if tragedy awaits Eve Arnold.

The guard pushes the wooden record back into the rock and instructs Gareth and Ashley back up to the surface.

"So, we're looking for the arrival of Mrs Rose Drinkwater next? 2007. Car crash. Near Middleton," he says to himself, wandering around the chamber, looking towards the ceiling. He reaches for a hatch and swings it open, causing a shower of dust and pebbles to fall on his head.

This time, the guard leads the way into the hole, followed by Gareth and Ashley. It is much harder work clambering up the ladder, and they seem to have a long way to go. The first wooden tubes start back at disasters from the 1990s. There are hundreds to get past before they approach the early 2000s.

"Here we go," says the guard stopping above Gareth a few arduous minutes' climb later. "*New Road, Middleton. 2007. Car Crash. 1 Conscious Arrival.*"

Gareth watches from below as the guard heaves the wooden tube out of its hole and prizes off the lid. "Yes…Yes, this is right," says the guard. "*Mrs Rose Drinkwater. Arrived in 2007, conscious and alone. Picked up by the Distillery and educated at Whitby Hall, Palace of the Distillery in Ellesmere Port.*"

The guard reaches down with the open wooden tube. "Here you go, Mr Bennington. Place your deposit in here." Gareth grabs the tube and pushes the role of documents into it. As he does so, the guard speaks up again, reading from the parchment. "This is interesting. It says more about Mrs Drinkwater…It has her current occupation. Says she is a jeweller specialising in Pennine copper here at Crofter's Hope… She's one of our own!"

"She's here, in Crofter's Hope?" exclaims Gareth.

"Oh yes," says the guard. "I don't know her, mind you. There are hundreds of jewellers in the mines. They are very isolated folk. Not usually ones for socialising. There's usually a reason someone chooses to live in the dark."

Gareth isn't listening. He knows what he will be doing as soon as he can. If he can find Rose Drinkwater, she might be able to tell him all about his dad.

\* \* \*

Gareth is giddy and excitable on the trek back across the hillside. There is so much explaining for Ashley to do and so much for him to speculate.

"Why was there a Tyler Bennington in your arrival record?! That wasn't a lucky coincidence."

A wide grin fills Ashley's face. "When she was working on your fake identities, Nailah asked a few of us to share details of a fellow arrival that we knew of in the Meadow who had gone 'on'... These details were to form your identities, so that should the Distillery, or another interested party, interrogate the records, they wouldn't draw a blank."

"Smart," says Gareth.

"I think that is why Nailah allowed me to come to the archives with you today," says Ashley. "She must have suspected your identity would be checked. Although, we were still rather lucky. The Tyler Bennington I knew was only a young boy. Twelve years old when he arrived in the Meadow. The guard evidently didn't interrogate those details that carefully."

"So, do you think Nailah and Milton will let me meet with Rose Drinkwater?" asks Gareth.

"Oh, they've got to!" says Ashley. "I mean... you can't miss a chance like that. Do you think she'll remember your dad?!"

"I've no idea," admits Gareth. "I mean, assuming she's not a Flicker, surely she'll remember her final moments on Earth, and I know he was there..." A grainy newspaper image of the car being pulled from the lake flashes in Gareth's mind, and he shivers.

"I wonder how she ended up as a jeweller in Crofter's Hope?" says Ashley, adjusting the focus for the sake of Gareth's stress levels. She smiles kindly at him.

Gareth and Ashley spend the next half hour speculating about the life and journey of Rose Drinkwater. Their theories get wilder and sillier as they wander happily together through the valley, from imagining Rose Drinkwater as a hooded witch-like woman who has ended up in the mines after being exiled from her community to being a motherly cuddly-type who made copper tat to fill middle-class homes and loved the smell of lavender.

Impersonating a witch version of Rose Drinkwater, Ashley isn't looking where she is going when she trips on a rock, tumbling sideways into a shallow stream that wriggles down the hillside. Gareth wheezes with laughter as Ashley somehow keeps in character and curses at the rock while still lying in the stream.

He reaches down to heave Ashley out of the water but slips as he does so and falls into the stream next to her. Ashley roars with laughter this time, but Gareth screams with pain. He has caught his hand on a rock as he tries to avoid colliding with Ashley. Bright scarlet blood spills from his palm into the water.

"Oh my god," says Ashley, realising what has happened. "Are you OK?"

"I think so," says Gareth through clenched teeth. He holds his wounded hand in a tight fist to stem the blood. "I think I need a bandage."

Ashley looks around for anything they might be able to use. There is nothing remotely cloth-like on this patch of the hillside, unsurprisingly. Thinking quickly, she unzips her hoodie and grasps the hem of her T-shirt.

"Don't get any ideas," she says and grins at Gareth as she lifts her T-shirt over her head, exposing herself for a frantic moment. She throws the T-shirt onto the ground and quickly puts her hoodie back on over her bare torso. She rips the T-shirt to create a long thin strip of cotton which she hands to Gareth.

"Thanks," he says, a slight pinkness obvious in his cheeks. But he can't tie the bandage with only one good hand. Ashley leans in to help him. Gareth holds his hand still as she tightly winds the frayed strip of material around his hand, the crown of her head lingering inches from his nose. Looking down, Gareth accidentally glimpses past the partially open zip of Ashley's hoodie at her bare chest. He looks away quickly, but his heart starts to race.

"Done," she says, holding his wrist proudly and looking at him. "We'll get you some poppy seed anaesthetic when we're back with the others."

Gareth looks at Ashley. Blood is still pumping around his body. They both pause for a second. Then Gareth lets the rush of blood take over. She might have moved towards him too, but Gareth can't be sure. It all happens so quickly. He jolts his head towards hers with frantic and uncontrolled energy and kisses her. She kisses him back. And for a long and fabulous moment, with his eyes closed, Gareth feels like every firework in the universe is joyfully exploding all around him.

Ashley pulls away. "Oh my god," she says. "What are we doing?!" Gareth looks at her, returning to the present moment with a thud. He stutters. He doesn't know what to say. He doesn't know what possessed him to kiss her. He knows immediately that this makes everything too complicated.

Why did he do it? He knows it can't be undone. He wishes it could. But then, it was also so amazing. The edges of his soul are still tingling. Then Ashley leans in and kisses him again. Gareth loses all sense of sense. For a second incredible moment, it feels like his heart is a kaleidoscope of sensations like he is sucking a million marbles or dipping his soul in a cool mountain stream. Everything everywhere becomes inconsequential. All that matters is now. This.

Ashley pulls away again. "No," she says, more sternly and more to herself this time. "No, we can't."

Gareth looks at her. He has no idea what to say. He has no clue what he wants to say. Her eyes avert his gaze, and she starts a jumbled outburst. "We must have clear minds. I need to return. I have to get back to Dennis. What were we thinking? Oh, God. This can't have happened. Oh, I'm so stupid." She lets out a quiet anxious moan and rubs her face vigorously. A similar non-vocalised monologue tumbles through Gareth's mind.

"This was a mistake," Ashley says, turning to Gareth. "We must never talk of this to anyone ever. OK?"

Gareth feels obliged to agree. And anyway, his mind is not functioning enough to form coherent thoughts. "OK," he says.

"Come on, let's get back to the others," says Ashley, trying not to look at him or act flustered. She marches off ahead of Gareth. "Let's focus on finding Rose Drinkwater."

*The Combs Pit was part of the Thornhill Colliery in Yorkshire. On 4th July 1893, paraffin lamps were burning brightly, lighting the porches and various key points in the tunnels aiding the work of the one hundred and forty-six men who were down the mine, including fifty-seven boys. Just after midday, during the men's dinner hour, miners who were above ground heard an unusual sound from inside the mine, then they saw smoke and flame burst out of the pit's mouth. An explosion down below had caused a devastating disaster. This and the subsequent choking afterdamp, fatally harmed almost all who were working below the surface. In all one hundred and thirty-nine souls were lost on that tragic day.*

# Chapter Sixteen

◆

# A Familiar Face

Clumsily smoking a pipe of anaesthetic poppies, his hand throbbing painfully, Gareth tells the group about Rose Drinkwater. His haste to go and find her deep in the mines has already been chastened by Milton.

"If the Distillery has any sense," he had said, "they will have studied the histories of their prize fugitives and have spies keeping watch. Someone with such a close tie to your family will be being monitored. Your best bet will be to find Mrs Drinkwater when she is alone. Maybe in her private chamber after finishing a day's work in the mine."

Milton agrees to go with Gareth to the miner's chambers just before they leave Crofter's Hope tomorrow. That way, they are ready to make a quick getaway if there are any issues. In the meantime, he encourages Gareth to concentrate on healing his hand and enjoying the remaining time in the caves. Easier said than done. No one knows about Gareth and Ashley. She is acting as though nothing ever happened, but Gareth can't. Something has started that he doesn't want to lose, and he can't take his mind off her.

The gambling cavern at Crofter's Hope is like a vast underground casino. It is only early evening when the expedition head there, not that anyone can tell the time in the caves, but already every inch of the cavern, including rock ledges and platforms, has card tables and revellers crowded around. Some of the tables have high-stakes games going on. The players sit around, closely eyeing their cards, while groups of interested parties stand tightly packed behind them. Occasionally a cheer goes up, and metal tokens go flying.

Floating around the ceiling, a luminescent cloud billows as the gamblers consume pouches full of marbles. There is a frequent hiss of discarded marbles, sending more mist into the air. To add to the vibe, a band plays on a small stage at the far end of the cave. Locals to Crofter's Hope, the band play a mix of drums, strings, and an old upright piano.

The expedition chooses two card tables at the edge of the gambling den. A croupier welcomes them and deals a deck of cards, two each. Blackjack. The game is no different in the Meadow. Gareth enjoys that the cards are decks recovered from Meadow arrivals – mostly free promotional packs mixed from various causes and events on Earth. One of the cards in Gareth's first hand is from a limited-edition pack commemorating the 2012 London Olympics. Gareth remembers watching the games with his mum and Cerys all those years ago.

Next to Gareth, Hassan's luck is in. Starting with only ten tokens – the currency in the casino – he amasses over one thousand. He starts enthusiastically flinging spare tokens to anyone who pleads for some, even people he has never met. As always, Hassan consumes rather too many marbles. He is all over Rosalyn, much to her disquiet. Occasionally he makes a comment or a suggestive move so obvious that Rosalyn looks straight at Gareth, almost pleading that he says something. Gareth knows someone will have to talk to Hassan about his marble habits soon, and it'll probably fall on him. But right now, it doesn't seem to be the right time. Instead, Gareth tries to distract Hassan whenever Rosalyn gives him the eyes– distracting him with a gambling challenge to goad his attention back to the cards.

Across from Gareth, Ashley sits at the other table. He keeps trying to catch her eye, but she never looks over. It is torture. She seems to have been able to compartmentalise and dismiss their kiss. He feels so pathetic for craving her attention but can't stop it.

Completely escaping Gareth's attention is the number of marbles that Kasiya is consuming opposite him. While everyone else at the table is gambling and popping in the occasional marble, Kasiya is slowly working her way through marble after marble without gambling at all. And the more marbles she has, the more she starts to emerge from the passive state she has been in for the last few weeks. The first Gareth notices is when he glances at her after he has just won with an unusually low hand.

Kasiya is staring right at him. Her eyes are glazed over, but there is no mistaking the signals she is giving. She holds his gaze and moistens her lips, parting them slightly as though aroused and giving him a knowing grin. Gareth tries to pretend he hasn't seen anything and looks away.

A short while later, it is much harder to ignore. The configuration of the tables changes. Ashley and Rosalyn join their table, and Kasiya manages to find her way around the table, placing herself at Gareth's side. Then, while everyone else is distracted by Hassan dropping all his tokens on the floor, Kasiya reaches under the table and draws her hand up Gareth's inner thigh.

Gareth freezes. He doesn't know what to do. He cannot pretend that he hasn't felt her hand. He shuffles in his chair to buy a few seconds, pretending to aid Hassan, who scrambles around the floor below them, picking up tokens. But Kasiya's hand remains resting on his lap. He turns to look at her. She is looking right at him with an eagerness he has never seen before.

Kasiya leans in. "Let's get out of here," she whispers. "We can go to my room. Let's finish what we started…"

Gareth needs to say no, but for some reason, he stutters. And before he says anything, Kasiya loses her balance and falls off her stool. She clatters awkwardly and painfully onto a considerable scattering of marbles that litter the floor. Only now, Gareth realises just how many marbles she has been consuming.

"Oh my God, Kasiya! Are you OK?" Witnessing Kasiya's fall, Ashley shoots around the table.

Kasiya lies flat on her back. She looks up at them, or generally in their direction, and laughs uncontrollably.

"I think she's had a lot of marbles," says Gareth.

"Oh, Kasiya," says Ashley sympathetically. "I think we need to get you up to bed."

Gareth helps Ashley lift Kasiya onto her unsteady feet. Kasiya leans against Ashley with her eyes closed. "Ashley," says Gareth, "I need to speak with you."

"Now is not the time, Gareth!" exclaims Ashley. And with that, she half walks, half carries, Kasiya away. Ashley has no clue what has just happened between Kasiya and Gareth. Gareth stands, watching the two women as they leave, feeling unhealthily entangled with them both.

Completely distracted, Gareth sits back down at the card table. As wrong as he knows it is, he allows himself to drift into a fantasy of what would have happened if he had entertained Kasiya's invitation. The forbidden fantasy excites him a little bit. That was why he had stuttered. Realising he has this urge, he feels an immense and consuming guilt in the pit of his stomach. Then an image of Ashley flashes into his mind. Her bare chest glimpsed on the hillside and the kiss. He feels even more condemned by these thoughts. Both fantasies are forbidden, shattered by the faces of both women rejecting him.

Gareth leans back on his stool to clear his head and takes in the atmosphere. The marble mist has now descended to such a level in the cave that anyone standing up has their vision partially obscured. Looking at the gamblers around his table, Gareth realises someone is missing.

"Where's Hassan?" he asks Glenda.

"You mean Carlo?" says Glenda, winking at him. "I think he's gone up to the chambers. He'd had too many marbles anyway and was frustrated with not getting the attention he wanted." She nods towards Rosalyn, who is chatting animatedly with Nailah.

"I should go and check on him," says Gareth.

"I'll come with you," says Billy, looking like he's had his fair share of marbles too. "I need to get to bed!"

\* \* \*

The cluster of men's bed chambers is located around a warm communal space. A lit log burner is in one corner, throwing warmth and an orange glow over the rugs and sofas. There is no need to search for Hassan in his room. There he is, lying back on one of the sofas, his eyes closed.

"Hassan. Are you OK?" asks Gareth as he approaches. Hassan doesn't move.

"Hassan?" says Gareth, concern rising in his voice. "Hassan…?! He's unconscious!"

Billy rushes over. It is true. Hassan is unconscious. His arms hang limply off the side of the chair. His head is rocked back. Gareth tries a gentle shake with no response. He tries peeling back Hassan's eyelids. His eyes are rolled back into his head. He is still breathing, but he is motionless.

"What's wrong with him? We need help!" says Gareth, panicking.

"Hold on," says Billy. "Look…" and he gestures towards the table next to Hassan.

A pouch of Hassan's most precious marbles lies open on the table. There was space for a dozen marbles in the pouch, but now there are only two. A set of tweezers and a marble cracker lie next to it. Hassan has been breaking into his memories, roughly dissecting the marbles, but he hasn't done a very thorough job. An unstable mist lingers in a growing cloud over the table. Too much of this cloud and Hassan will go 'on'.

"Crap, he's going to overdose," says Billy. "We need to get rid of this cloud."

"How?" asks Gareth.

"The open marbles," says Billy. "They are creating the mist. Throw them into the log burner. That'd get rid of the mist."

Gareth holds his breath and pushes his hands and face into the mist on the table. He gathers the fizzing marbles. They are surprisingly warm. He has never touched an open marble before. The fizzing is making them vibrate slightly.

He scampers over to the fire, where Billy has the door open, and starts throwing the marbles carefully into the furnace, one at a time. They sparkle and fizz as they burn up. Holding the last marble, Gareth feels a tickle in his nose. Before he has time to prepare himself, he sneezes and breathes in. Inadvertently, a small sharp burst of marble mist shoots up his nostril. Immediately the world around Gareth blurs, and he falls backwards into Hassan's memory.

\* \* \*

Snow is falling on a cold winter evening. The street lamps are on, their lights sparkling off the floating crystals down the cluttered terraced street. Two figures shuffle their way up to the front door of a mid-terrace. The only house without Christmas lights sparkling in the window.

Hassan wears a thick duffle coat with the hood pulled up and a woolly hat resting snugly on his head. A woman is clinging to his arm, equally dressed for the cold. Her face is mostly covered by her headscarf, but the depth of her eye makeup and the over-application of blusher is apparent.

"We aren't staying long, are we?" asks the woman.

"I wasn't planning on it," says Hassan. "But one day you'll have to get used to my family…they'll be relations soon." He grins at the woman.

"Don't remind me," she replies.

Hassan knocks on the door, releasing loose paint chips onto the mossy mat. They stand for a moment, but there's no response. Rather than knock again, Hassan tries the handle. It's open, so he steps in.

"Mum? Dad?" he calls into a bright hallway illuminated by a harsh yellow light. He stops still. A baby's cry cuts through from the front room, where the door is open, but no light is on. "For fuck sake!" Hassan shouts as he dashes into the room, flicking on the light. The woman follows him.

Inside the front room, lying on a bare mattress, is a wriggling baby, crying its eyes out. The little one's nappy is full and uncomfortable, with sore streaks of reddened skin clear on her bare legs and tummy. The woman plunges down to pick up her daughter, swaddling her in a blanket.

"It's OK, Tia," the woman says, rocking the baby gently from side to side. "Mummy's here."

Hassan approaches his daughter and girlfriend, reaching out to offer a comforting pat. The woman spins their daughter away from him and shoots him a glare. "You promised me," she levels at Hassan.

"Yasmin, I'm sorry. My mum said they'd be fine with her," Hassan offers. "I swear, I thought they would…"

"You better hope they've got a good excuse," says Yasmin, still holding her baby tight with her back to Hassan.

"I'll go get them," says Hassan, looking nervous.

He wanders back into the hallway and starts climbing the stairs, past pictures of him and his brothers from school. From one of the bedrooms, an angry voice shouts out. Hassan rubs his beard anxiously as he strides onto the landing.

"Stupid mindless bitch!" an older man's voice thunders from the bedroom at the end of the hall. "It's a Mercedes Benz. You should treat it better… better than you treat anything! A 'little scratch', you say?!? You've fucking desecrated my most precious thing… you stupid… fucking… woman!"

Hassan crashes into the bedroom as his father strikes his mother. She is cowering by the wardrobe, tears streaking down her red and puffy face. Hassan leaps at his dad, knocking him to the floor while his mum screams.

"What the fuck are you doing?!?" shouts Hassan's dad, startled and sprawled underneath his son.

Hassan has a furious rage in his eyes. "I've told you before," he shouts. "Don't you ever lay a finger on my mum again!" He lands a heavy fist into his dad's jaw, knocking him out cold.

"Hassan!" screams his mum. "No!"

Hassan holds back on the second punch. The older man underneath him lets out a blubbering snort. "He's just knocked out," says Hassan. "Come on, mum… I'm taking you out of here…"

Amidst sobs and a half-hearted struggle, Hassan shuffles onto the landing with his mum in a tight embrace. Her husband's unconscious snores are still audible behind them.

Standing in the hallway at the bottom of the stairs is Yasmin. Tia is cleaned up and no longer crying. She clutches tightly to her daughter. Yasmin looks up at Hassan and his mother, who look back.

"Enough is enough, Hassan," screams Yasmin. "Your daughter deserves better… I deserve better!" She turns to leave.

"Yaz… wait!" Hassan calls back. "Please, one more chance…" he shouts as he tumbles down the stairs after his girlfriend and daughter.

"No!" shouts Yasmin, "We're done..."

Hassan slips on some dirty clothes cluttering the stairs. His legs fold under him, and his head collides with the bannister before he comes to rest in a crumpled heap at the bottom of the stairs.

Yasmin looks pitifully down at Hassan before stepping outside into the snow, slamming the door behind her. A deep wound on Hassan's head starts to weep dark crimson blood, and he closes his eyes. As the memory fades, the sobs of Hassan's mum at the top of the stairs are all Gareth can hear.

* * *

Before Gareth's eyes adjust back into the chamber, his shoulders are grasped, and he is thrown heavily against the wall.

"What the hell do you think you are doing?!" Hassan shouts in his face. "They are private memories. You have no right to look at them!"

He grasps Gareth again. Gareth's eyes come into focus, and he can see the fury in Hassan.

"I can explain," says Gareth.

"There's no explanation!" says Hassan, slamming Gareth against the wall again. "Just like to pry, don't you? Just like to…like to know everything! You had no right to look!"

"He didn't mean to," Billy's voice cuts in.

"Yeah, you keep saying that, Billy. It's nonsense."

"It's true," says Gareth, "I didn't mean to…"

"How can you accidentally breathe in someone's memory?" says Hassan, staring at Gareth.

"We found you here unconscious," says Gareth. "The marbles were all over the table. We were worried about you."

"That gives you no right to look into my memories! You don't hear me prying into your life, do you?! How would you like it if I told everyone I saw Kasiya touching you at the tables tonight? Eh?"

"What's that?" says Billy.

"Screw you!" shouts Gareth at Hassan, his face flushing a deep scarlet. "You have no idea what you saw!"

"Touché!" shouts Hassan, grabbing Gareth and flinging him to the floor.

"Woah!" says Billy, trying to grab hold of Hassan.

"Stay out of this!" Hassan says to Billy, shrugging him off. He steps over Gareth, kneels and grabs the scruff of Gareth's shirt. "Which memory did you see?" Hassan pulls Gareth right up close to his face, breathing heavily.

"Woah, what the hell is going on here?!" Milton's voice booms into the chamber. In a moment, he grasps Hassan and pulls him off Gareth. "What are you two doing?!" he says.

"This prying prick snuck into one of my marble memories," says Hassan, spitting with rage.

"What?" says Milton.

"It was an accident," shouts Billy from behind Milton.

"Hold up," says Milton. "What are you talking about?"

"Look, I came up here. I needed some alone time. I dissected some of my marble memories, just as you showed us earlier."

"You are supposed to be saving those key memories, not consuming them," says Milton. "Dissecting marbles in public like this is reckless. Anyone could have come in and seen your memories."

"That still doesn't excuse Gareth's actions!" shouts Hassan.

"That's not how it happened," says Gareth, looking at Milton. "I was worried. We came up, and he was unconscious. There was loads of mist coming out of some opened marbles on the table, right by his head. I thought, if we didn't dispose of the marbles, he could have gone 'on'. I tried putting the marbles in the fire, but I accidentally breathed in some mist."

"Is that what happened?" says Milton looking at Billy.

"Yes," says Billy. "That's exactly what happened. I've been trying to tell Hassan."

"You had no right to interfere," says Hassan.

"Look," says Milton, staring straight at Hassan. "Gareth and Billy may well have just saved your life. You never do more than one marble dissection at a time. I told you that. This was a stupid and dangerous thing you did. You're lucky they came when they did!"

"Now, I think the best you can do is go back down and join the others, clear your head a bit, but don't gamble anymore." He turns to Gareth, "I need a word with you."

Gareth catches Hassan's eye; there is a vindictive malice dwelling there. Gareth holds his breath, preparing for Hassan to blurt out about Milton's daughter. Mercifully Hassan holds his tongue.

"I'm sorry," says Gareth, looking at Hassan, "I promise, I was just trying to help."

"You're always trying to help, aren't you?" he responds curtly and wanders away to join the others. Billy looks at Milton and Gareth, then follows after Hassan.

"How many marbles do you think he dissected?" Milton asks.

"About half a dozen," says Gareth. "They were all fizzing on the table when we arrived."

"He is one lucky man," says Milton. "Usually, any more than three memories opened simultaneously will send someone on. Maybe he hadn't inhaled them all yet. What did you see in the memory?" he asks.

"It was just a memory of his daughter, back on Earth," says Gareth, unwilling to divulge further. He is keen, at least, to do something to protect Hassan's privacy.

"You must try and keep Hassan's memory stored in your mind now," says Milton. "I'm worried that by the time we get to the Source, Hassan might not have any marbles left to use. You might be his only hope of remembering things when he needs to."

Gareth looks up at Milton. "I'll try," he says.

"Have you still got all of your core memories intact?" says Milton.

Gareth feels the locket around his neck and the pouch that is permanently on his belt. "Yes."

Milton smiles at Gareth, then heaves himself out of his chair. "You know, you *are* allowed to fight back sometimes?" he says.

"What do you mean?" Gareth asks, taken aback by the sudden and unexpected criticism.

"When I came up here earlier, I found you on the floor with Hassan holding you by the scruff of the neck. You weren't resisting one bit. Had I not intervened, I am inclined to think you'd have let Hassan beat you senseless. You've got to learn to stand up for yourself sometime. At least put up a fight."

Gareth looks at the floor. He is well accustomed to these indirect accusations of cowardice. Cerys had always laid into him on Earth for rolling over too quickly and never standing up for himself. He doesn't know how to respond. It isn't like he chooses to react like he does. At the moment when Hassan grabbed him on the floor, he hadn't decided not to fight back. He just hadn't decided anything. As usual in that situation, his mind had simply frozen. It freezes again now in the presence of Milton Drake's looming shadow.

"I'm just trying to help you, kid," says Milton condescendingly. "I know you grew up without a dad. I figure there's a few lessons about being a man you might have missed."

This last statement irks Gareth immensely. If Milton is even remotely receptive to Gareth's body language, he'd realise that his words have just lost him a load of Gareth's respect. Why do men like Milton always assume that growing up without a dad somehow brings into question his manliness rather than expose the fragility of their own? Does he genuinely have no appreciation that a 'man' could be, and always is so many different things? His version of a 'man' is sterile, bland, and stubbornly aggressive. But he can't see it. Most irritatingly for Gareth, though, he also knows Milton has a point. He would benefit from having the confidence to stand up for himself once in a while. Not necessarily to fight, per se, but in that moment where he usually freezes to have the presence of mind to choose his response. He just wishes he knew how.

"Listen. Well done tonight," says Milton, patting Gareth on the back and signalling an end to their chat. "I think Hassan owes you one."

\* \* \*

The atmosphere is tense as the expedition prepares to leave Crofter's Hope. Hassan isn't talking to anyone, and Glenda and Billy aren't talking to him – apparently, he picked a fight with some locals after the incident with Gareth last night, which they had to break up. Added to this, Kasiya is only talking to her mum, and Ashley is still avoiding any alone time with Gareth. The only person in good spirits seems to be Milton. He is busy plotting the two-night trek that awaits them – the trek to the lands of the Mersey Water Board. They plan to leave tonight, after sundown, and after Milton and Gareth have gone and found Rose Drinkwater for a chat.

Despite Ashley's best efforts, Gareth manages to steal a moment alone with her while she is re-stocking the marbles in the caravans. "I need to talk about Kasiya," he says.

Ashley is blind-sided. "OK?" she says tentatively.

"She tried it on with me last night," he says nervously.

"What?" Ashley replies, stopping in her tracks. "What happened?"

"When she'd had loads of marbles, well, she started hitting on me. Then she invited me up to her room."

"You're *sure* she was hitting on you?"

"Absolutely."

"What did you say?"

"I… I said, no," Gareth lies. "That was when she fell off her stool."

"Oh god," says Ashley, burying her head in her hands. "She told me she was over you… days and days ago, before we left Lin even. I believed her. I would never have let anything happen between us otherwise." She gives a quiet anxious moan and rubs her face vigorously, just like she had done at the stream after they kissed.

"I'm so sorry," says Gareth. "I wish I could go back and change what happened by the stream."

"Do you?" she asks, looking up at him.

He pauses, looking at her and then looking down. "No," he admits quietly, "No, I don't wish that. Sorry."

A moment of quiet washes between them. "I cannot hurt Kasiya," says Ashley. "She has enough hurt in her soul already. We have to try and forget what happened between us, OK?"

Gareth knows she is correct, but the fact she said 'we' and not 'you' gives him a glimmer of hope. She can't forget the kiss either.

* * *

The evening can't arrive quickly enough for Gareth. When it does, he sets off with Milton down into the cave network, seeking Rose Drinkwater.

Following the directions to the copper mines, Gareth and Milton struggle through narrow passageways, sometimes shuffling with their backs against the walls, other times crawling through tiny openings. The corridors are lit, although the frequency of lanterns reduces the further into the hill they get. Sometimes it feels like they have to pass through complete darkness before finding the next flickering iron lantern. Squeezing past one of these lanterns, Gareth reads the name Thornhill Colliery engraved on its base.

Eventually, when they feel they must be near the heart of the hill, the passageway opens to reveal a wide-spacious chamber. A shaft is in the centre, plunging deep into the ground below. The chamber is large, so there is plenty of space to walk around the edge of the shaft. They can smell the hot embers of the smelting furnaces, far below, extracting the precious metal from the stone.

Echoing up the shaft are the sounds of chiselling and hammering by miners far below. Looking into the shaft, Gareth is reminded of the furnace he spent months at the workhouse. Above them is an opening to the surface, where smoke from the furnaces ultimately exits the hillside. Around the edges of the chamber, signs indicate various workshops associated with the

mines. There is a metal tokens workshop – for the gambling den –
a tools and hardware workshop, a rare minerals workshop, and
several jewellery workshops. Milton and Gareth approach the
copper workshop.

Inside the long, low-ceilinged cave, copper artefacts hang
from the walls and ceiling, sparkling in the candlelight. There are
ornate necklaces, bracelets, and copper figurines depicting all sorts
of religious scenes and fables. A dozen workbenches stand
regimented down the cave, but no one is there. Work has ceased
for the day. A passageway leads out to the jewellers' residences.

Gareth and Milton walk through quietly, ignoring the sign
above the residences that reads '*Private. Visits by appointment only.
Please respect the silence of our community*'. They wander through the
tunnel into a communal space. In meagre light, a few individuals
hunch alone at tables, sucking marbles in silence. Hanging from
the ceiling, wooden chimes echo melodically.

The private chambers are further down a corridor off the
communal space. A roughly cut corridor that snakes for a hundred
metres or so. Old candles flicker in their holders, hanging next to
copper numerals, indicating the doorway of a single residence.
Below each number, scratched into the rock, is the inhabitant's
name. Many names have been scored off. Old residents must have
gone 'on' and their rooms reallocated.

A door just ahead creaks open, and a frail older man pokes
his head out. He wears a nightgown with a matching nightcap and
peers into the dimly lit corridor.

"Can I help you?" The man asks, sounding more put out
than polite.

"We're looking for Rose Drinkwater…" says Milton, just
above a whisper.

"Ah," says the man, inspecting Milton and Gareth. "End
chamber. Number 23."

Rather than return to his room, the man bows his head to
Milton and scurries in his nightclothes down the corridor towards
where Milton and Gareth came from.

Milton nudges Gareth forwards, deeper into the dark
corridor. They count the rooms beside the candles until they reach

number 23. There, scratched very clearly in the wall, is *Mrs Rose Drinkwater*. It looks like it has been scribed into the rock quite recently.

Milton knocks confidently on the door. Gareth holds his breath. There is no reply. He strikes again and calls out. "Mrs Drinkwater? Are you in there?"

There is the sound of shuffling furniture, but it soon goes quiet again.

"Mrs Drinkwater? Can we come in?"

It stays quiet this time. Milton looks at Gareth and tries the handle. It opens.

A bare and poorly maintained chamber stands in front of them. A bed lies in one corner, moth ridden and damp. Shelves and a desk are dusty, with minimal personal items. A bin on the floor overflows with discarded marbles. A couple of candles burn in their holders, barely lighting the room. In the far corner, turned away from the door, a lady sits in an armchair with her back to them.

"Mrs Drinkwater?" asks Milton.

"Yes…?" says the lady, not turning.

"Sorry to bother you, Miss. My name is Milton. My friend and I are visitors to Crofter's Hope…"

"We don't like visitors down in the mines," says Rose, keeping her back to them and, in doing so, holding their gaze.

"My apologies," says Milton. "We do not mean to invade your solitude. But, if you permit us five minutes of your time, my friend here is keen to meet you… He thinks he may know you from a lifetime ago…"

Cautiously Rose turns around. She appears youthful, maybe creeping into her early thirties. She has a voluminous crop of short blonde hair, doubtlessly ageing her as an arrival from the early 2000s. Gareth immediately recognises Rose Drinkwater from the newspaper photograph etched into his memory. The overwhelming familiarity makes his legs wobble. Only Milton's sturdy presence keeps him upright.

Rose stares at the two men but doesn't utter a word. She has a ghostly stare. Cold and distant. Milton puts his hand on

Gareth's shoulder, squeezing it gently. "Go on, kid," he says, nudging Gareth towards the armchair opposite Rose Drinkwater.

Holding Rose's gaze, Gareth quietly lowers himself into the armchair. Candlelight dances around the room, but it is a silent disco. Deathly silent.

"I know who you are…" says Rose. Her voice is soft and delicate. "I wondered if I would ever see you, or any of your family here in the Meadow…it has been fifteen long and lonely years…"

Gareth stares back, stunned. His thoughts are chaotic, his emotions stifled by the moment. He can't speak. He can barely blink.

"You remind me of him," says Rose, inspecting Gareth, the delicacy in her voice becoming calculated, her eyes narrowing. "But he would never sit so hunched and awkward."

"I'm sorry," says Gareth, mustering the functioning of his voice and lowering his eyes. "I mean, I don't know what happened with you and my dad or how, but… I'm sorry…"

Rose doesn't take a breath. "How can you be sorry if you don't even know what happened?" she accuses.

Beads of sweat trickle down Gareth's back. His face flushes red, and he can feel a nervous resonance in his breath. He doesn't know how to respond, so he reacts instinctively. "I'm sorry," he mumbles again.

Rose breathes out, exasperated. "I'll make a bargain with you," she begins. "You tell me what happened to your father after I died. And I will tell you what happened between us before… Then, you can tell me if you're *really* sorry for what happened." She looks at Gareth, who nods sincerely.

"Now… I know your father must have died," she starts. "I've seen his record in the archives…" Gareth sits up, moving to respond, but Rose shuts him down. "He has already gone 'on', so you're not going to find him here," she says, reading Gareth's mind. "Tell me what happened to him on Earth…"

Milton steps up to Gareth's chair. "You don't need to do this, kid," he says to Gareth. "Not if it's too painful…"

"It's OK," says Gareth. "It happened when I was very young… and I owe it to myself to know."

Gareth turns back to Rose. The room starts to come into focus. Either his body has exhausted its supply of nervous energy, or he is mustering some self-control.

"It all happened before I was old enough to remember," he starts. "But from what I have pieced together, I know there was a car crash where a vehicle ended up in a lake. My dad survived, but the passenger died."

"*I* died," says Rose sharply.

"Sorry," Gareth lowers his eyes, "You died…And after the tragedy, my dad was arrested and tried for manslaughter…"

"And?" asks Rose impatiently.

"He was found… guilty," says Gareth solemnly. "He was given a life sentence…"

"Good," says Rose, her jaw noticeably relaxing. "Sorry to have to say this to his son, but, well… he got what he deserved."

Gareth sinks into the armchair. This is what he feared but also expected. It doesn't make it any easier to digest. "He deserved it?" he asks tentatively.

Rose raises her palm to halt Gareth's question. "Our bargain," she says. "First, tell me how he died."

Gareth takes a moment before he responds. He feels the weight of the Interrogation Stone in his marble pouch, and he rubs the scars on his wrists. "He took his own life."

Rose's jaw drops. The touch of malice in her eyes shifts to guilt. She is lost for words. Milton steps across and puts a sturdy hand on Gareth's shoulder, squeezing it gently.

"It was less than a year into his sentence," says Gareth, looking across at Rose. A memory floods into his mind. A police officer standing at the front door, his mum collapsed on the floor sobbing, and a realisation that the shadow which loomed over him had just got darker.

"It wasn't just his own life that was taken away," says Gareth, almost to himself. He feels a boiling frustration inside him that he had forgotten he held. "My mum's spirit was broken. My family's hope extinguished. And the young me started life without a father."

"I'm sorry," says Rose. It is her turn to soften and apologise unnecessarily. "I take back what I said before…you don't remind me of him. Only in looks…"

Gareth looks back at Rose, and their eyes make a truce. "Can you tell me what happened now?" he asks.

"Yes," says Rose. "I'll be as quick as I can."

"It's OK," Milton cuts in. "We've got all the time you need." He smiles at Gareth.

Rose glances at Milton but doesn't respond. Her lip twitches nervously. She turns back to Gareth, leans forwards and starts to talk with an unexpected urgency.

"In the year before the crash, I developed a friendship with your father. We were work colleagues. I should have recognised the signs that he wanted more, but I was naïve, and he was exciting." Rose glances nervously towards the door. Milton and Gareth turn, but there is nothing there.

"Your dad started finding reasons to see me outside of work, suggesting your mum was fine with it. But I suspect she never knew. Then, he started telling me how unhappy he was in his marriage. I felt awkward, but he was determined to draw me into his private life.

"Before I had really accepted what was happening, he started making uninvited advances. I resisted…but this didn't stop him." Rose's eyes again flick to the door, and she blinks as though close to tears. This time Gareth can hear footsteps in the corridor outside.

"Who's coming?" asks Milton.

Rose ignores him and continues urgently, looking pained and distraught. "Your dad was used to getting what he wanted, Gareth. I think he stopped seeing me as a friend in those last few weeks and started to see me as prey. The more I resisted, the more he hunted.

"I decided to tell him that we had to end our friendship. I got a new job. I had to get away…I was scared… But I had no idea he would respond how he did. He was *never* going to let his prey get away."

There is a sudden harsh knock at the door. Rose grasps Gareth's hands. "I'm so sorry," she says, her voice cracking and a tear falling down her cheek. "I thought you were going to be just like him…I would never have agreed to this otherwise."

There is a strong and aggressive knock again.

"Agreed to what?!" Gareth asks, feeling a wash of fear soak over him.

"Too late," shouts Milton, grasping Gareth by the scruff of his jacket and hauling him up next to him. There's no time. The door bursts open, and two men charge into the room brandishing canisters of Thermocline Mist. Gareth and Milton freeze.

One of the men strides straight up to Gareth. He is tall and determined. He has slick black hair, a pointed nose, and small sharp eyes. He wears a decorated black uniform emblazoned with the purple armband of the Distillery. Gareth instantly recognises him. A memory scratched permanently into his mind and his wrists. His interrogating minister from the workhouse. The man who had pried for months into his private and darkest memories, peeling back the layers of his internal guilt and shame.

"It *is* you," says the officer with a grin. He reaches forwards, still pointing his canister at Gareth's mouth, and runs his free hand over Gareth's shaved head. "You've done a good job trying to hide yourself. The problem is that haircuts and piercings are superficial. They don't quite cut it when you've seen into someone's soul. When you've seen them broken in the furnaces, you can recognise the pain in their eyes, Mr Edwards!"

The second Distillery officer, holding a canister up to Milton's mouth, leans across to look. "You're right; that's him, Dad. We've got him!"

Gareth recognises the younger officer too. James Chadwick. The intolerable graduate from the banquet in Dante's College just after he had graduated from the workhouse. James has the same pointed nose as his dad– the same small dark eyes.

"I knew you'd come looking if I presented some link to your dad," says the older officer. "One of the benefits of being an Arrivals minister, we get to know our subjects very intimately. I altered all the records associated with your dad's crime months ago.

Since then, I've relied on a few informants here at Crofter's Hope to tell me if anyone has been snooping around the records. Then, voila, I get word that a young man and his friend were poking around Rose Drinkwater's archive."

Gareth and Milton stay very still. The Thermocline canisters are held just below their mouths. The officer's fingers resting on the triggers. One wrong move and a spray from these canisters will send them on.

"How do you plan to get us out of here then?" asks Milton coolly. "Crofter's Hope isn't known for their sympathy with Pond Life like you. The people here won't take kindly if they know you've been operating in their caves."

"Don't you worry," says the officer, smirking. "The community might not like us, but individuals are easy to buy out." He glances down at Rose, who has stayed in her chair, scared and silent.

"I'm so sorry," she sobs.

"Silence, woman!" shouts James.

"We have a whole team standing by," the officer continues. "They have been disguised as visitors here for months, ready to extract you. We just need to wait down here a minute while they mobilise…"

Suddenly Gareth thrusts himself forward. "Run!" he shouts to Milton. He has decided, much to his own astonishment, that he isn't going to freeze up and cower today. He is fighting back.

The element of surprise works. The officer and his son fall backwards, stumbling over a table and landing at the feet of Rose. As he falls, James Chadwick accidentally deploys his canister. The mist sprays all over his father's face.

Gareth and Milton are already running towards the door as the young man screams, "No!"

Gareth glances back to see a cloud of mist surrounding the older officer on the floor and Rose seemingly wrestling James to the ground next to him. He doesn't see the older officer inhale the mist, nor understand if Rose is aiding his escape or trying to protect James from the fog. Either way, the cry from James Chadwick moments later confirms his father's fate. Gareth and Milton don't look back again. They run.

They run down the corridor and through the copper workshop, clattering and crashing past jewels and benches, sending copper everywhere. They know, right at this moment, somewhere high up in the cave network, the Distillery backup team are on their way. They have to get to the surface as quickly as they can.

They run past the mine shaft and up to the gambling den, past the deserted card tables and through a narrow set of tunnels to the central atrium.

There's a commotion. Black-clad Distillery officers, maybe a dozen of them, are running between the aisles of artefacts on the other side of the cavern.

"I hope you're good at climbing!" shouts Milton, pushing Gareth towards the rock face beside him.

Looking up, Gareth can see, fifteen metres or so above them, the platform he had arrived on a few days earlier. Milton starts climbing. Gareth follows.

When Gareth is about five metres off the ground, he hears a shout from the Distillery officers. "Up there! Quick, they are getting away!"

The officers thunder over. Items start pelting the rock face. Shoes, books, plates. All sorts of things clatter around them. Evidently, the officers are content to knock the two men off the wall. A few things strike Gareth's legs, sending sharp pains through his body, but he keeps going.

Milton scrambles over onto the platform first. He reaches down and helps pull Gareth up the final stretch. On the platform, they can see a handful of Distillery officers below, still throwing anything they can up at them. A few other officers have peeled off and are climbing the steep staircase towards them.

Milton reaches into his pocket and pulls out a foot-long plastic tube with a metal ring dangling from the bottom. "I wondered if this would be useful!" he grins to Gareth.

Pushing Gareth towards the exit, Milton pulls the metal ring. The shipping flare erupts, sending thick billowing red smoke in all directions. Milton bundles into the passageway with Gareth.

The two men rush through the narrow corridor and crawl through the small gaps.

Very soon, sweating and out of breath, they find themselves in the Crofter's Hope entrance cottage hallway. Standing in his dungarees and confused, there is Derek, the Crofter's Hope guard. "Everything alright?" he asks.

"Fine, thanks," pants Milton, dropping the expended flare. "Just on our way out. Thanks for the stay! Good risen!"

"You need to work on your fitness," says Derek chuckling and unaware. "Good risen!"

Outside, the sun is setting, a bright orange slither of light descending behind the hill. Milton and Gareth dash across the courtyard and burst into the barn to find the rest of the expedition chatting cheerfully.

"We've been discovered!" shouts Milton. "We have to leave now!"

There isn't time to answer any questions. Milton jumps onto the platform of the front caravan next to Ashley and grabs the reins. Gareth jumps up onto the platform of the middle caravan next to Glenda. In a moment, all the horses are pulling the caravans out of Crofter's Hope.

Looking back at the cottage, Gareth sees some red mist from Milton's flare emerging from the doorway. A confused Derek is trying to waft it away with his newspaper.

"Full speed west!" shouts Milton. "Follow the stars! No stopping until I stop!"

The front caravan picks up the pace. Glenda gees her horses to keep up, and Gareth hears Nailah do the same behind them. Crofter's Hope quickly disappears as they thunder down the rough, steep track and into the dark valley below.

*Warrington Sailing Club, located on the river Mersey, hosted an annual boat race for local sailors. The course for this race on Saturday 6th April 1912 went from Cooper's Yard, near Widnes, to Bank Quay near Warrington. Entering the event were eight eager crews aboard eight finely tuned racing boats. As the start to the race approached the winds were growing and the waters becoming increasingly choppy. By the time the starting signal was given, gale force winds ripped down the channel, and the water was a riot of waves. Early in the race one of the racing boats got into difficulty. With too much sail up, its boom snapped, and the rigging fell into the angry waters. Soon the weight of the water-logged rigging pulled the boat itself over onto its side and filled the hull with water. It didn't take long for the vessel to disappear under the waves, taking its crew of two souls to the bottom of the river with it.*

# Chapter Seventeen

◆

# Fidler's Ferry

The lands of the Mersey Water Board are known to be staunchly anti-Distillery. They will not entertain any Distillery riders entering their grounds. If the expedition can reach Merseyside without being caught, they will be safe. But it is a risky journey. They had initially planned two gentle night rides, but with the Distillery onto them, it will be a ferocious sprint through night and day. They have to travel faster than news of their exposure at Crofter's Hope and assume the Distillery officers hiding at Crofter's Hope will be hot on their tails.

The nearest checkpoint in the lands of the Mersey Water Board is a place on the banks of the river Mersey called Fidler's Ferry. Presuming they manage to enter through here, they will be safe. They will even resume their true identities. The Mersey Water Board doesn't share information on fugitives with the Distillery; such is the extent of their distrust. The fugitives will still need to keep the nature of the expedition secret, though. Like all Water Boards, the Mersey Water Board still hunt the 'Evil Thirst'.

The ride through the night is treacherous. Travelling at full speed without the luxury of lamps for fear of being spotted, the caravans hurtle blindly through unseen rough terrain. Numerous times the caravans clatter into unexpected streams and down scree slopes without any warning. The structures creak and strain under stress. The members of the expedition, on high alert for interceptors, look out for lamp lights closing in and listen for the whinnying of horses. Straining their eyes into the darkness around them, they try to simultaneously navigate, keep the lead caravan in sight, avoid obstacles, and spot approaching danger. It drains their energy.

The weather is against them as well. A cold, blustery wind batters the caravans without letting up. They are soon shivering and exhausted, but they must keep going. Then, in an apparently cruel twist of fate, a distant rumble is followed by cold and heavy snowfall. Great white flakes tumble in dizzying waves, settling instantly. Soon the valley is blanketed, and the sound and their senses are dampened. The horses slip and slide, and the caravans skid and veer off course.

Gareth senses their progress slow significantly. "Can we not go any faster?" he says. "We'll be caught at this speed." He looks at Glenda and Rosalyn, wrapped in scarves and ponchos, next to him.

To Gareth's surprise, Glenda looks back at him with a smile. "We might have slowed, but this snow is a blessing," she says, glancing over her shoulder. "This snowstorm is travelling away behind us. It will slow them as much as us, but it will also hide our tracks and the scents of our horses. Until the snow melts, they won't be able to pick up our trail. All the progress we make now is gain."

Gareth looks ahead at the front caravan, sliding and trudging slowly through the snow. It is hard to believe this is gain.

"Hopefully, the snow will peter out as we head further west," says Glenda. "If we can reach the end of the snowstorm before we exit the forest, then we might have a clear run through the plains to Fidler's Ferry. This is our best chance of reaching the Mersey lands without being intercepted."

"Have you ever been to the Mersey lands?" Rosalyn asks Glenda.

"No," says Glenda. "The entry requirements have always put me off."

"Why?" asks Gareth. "What do they ask for?"

"Entry into Merseyside is only granted if you either hand over the most precious marble you have – your Interrogation Stone – or you volunteer to endure a whole new interrogation at the hands of the Mersey police," says Glenda. "Obviously, the former is less traumatic. But the contents of your Interrogation Stone are only held in one other place, your soul. If you are ever required to prove who you are, a court summons say, and you don't have your Interrogation Stone, the contents will have to be extracted from your soul again. Either way, your most intimate secrets and deepest memories will be shared with the Mersey Water Board, and they will be able to use them as leverage against you, so long as you reside in the Meadow."

Glenda shuffles in her seat and produces a small cobalt and crimson-swirled marble from a pouch on her waist. "Do you still have your Interrogation Stones?" she asks Gareth and Rosalyn.

Gareth feels into the leather pouch that has been tightly fastened to his belt since they had left London. He has added half a dozen new precious marbles to this pouch since they set off on the expedition, and it now bulges on his belt line. In the pouch is the marble he has held onto from the workhouse. A small red marble with a single bright yellow spot in the middle – his Interrogation Stone. He plucks it out of the pouch and shows Glenda and Rosalyn.

"I've had this with me ever since my first day in the Meadow," he says, rolling it between his thumb and forefinger, feeling the mental burden associated with it. "I would hate for anyone to dissect it and see what memories it contains."

"How about you, Rosalyn?" asks Glenda.

The young woman looks at Glenda, her eyes wide. "I wasn't given any marbles when I left the Palace," she says. A silence echoes between them. "Does this mean that I will be interrogated at the checkpoint?"

Glenda looks sympathetically back at Rosalyn. "I'm so sorry," she says.

* * *

Exactly as Glenda predicted, the snow lightens the further west they travel. The horses speed to a trot, and the caravans trundle through the shallow snow on the track. All around them, the fir trees sparkle in the frequent bursts of morning sunlight. Before they know it, they come to the edge of the forest.

Stretching out, as far as the eye can see, a vast plain is punctuated with old oak trees and small rural settlements. A low-lying autumn mist drifts amongst the settlements, dissipating in the warmth of the now dazzling sun.

Gathering the expedition around her, Nailah points to a tower just visible on the horizon. "That's the Fidler's Ferry border checkpoint," she says before pointing to a long straight road stretching out into the plain, "and that is our route to get there."

"If we are lucky, we will be able to canter the whole length of the road and arrive at Fidler's Ferry by lunchtime…If we are lucky." Nailah peers into the shadows of the forest behind them nervously. "There is safety, warmth, and a pub just past the checkpoint at Fidler's Ferry. *This* is our extra motivation to get there!" she smiles.

Gareth looks out into the distance towards Merseyside. If the pub at Fidler's Ferry is half as good as the Tide and Time Tavern, he can't wait to get there. He glances over at Rosalyn. She looks sick and apprehensive.

With the luggage straps secured down extra tight and everything packed into cupboards or protected by blankets, the expedition takes up their allocated seats on the platforms. Glenda ties a makeshift belt to hold her, Gareth, and Rosalyn into their seats on the middle caravan. It is going to be a very bumpy and uncomfortable ride. The last thing they would need is for one of the group to tumble out. The delay alone could be catastrophic.

Making one last check of the caravans, Milton is the last to take up his position at the reins of the front caravan. He gives a thumbs up to Glenda, who responds in sort, but she looks troubled.

"What's wrong?" Gareth asks her.

"Oh, nothing," she says. "It's just that I've known Milton for years. I've not seen him look this worried before."

"Oh great!" says Gareth. He can feel the marble pouch on his hip digging into his thigh, and he struggles to shift it to a better position. The sooner this ride is over, the better.

Bursting out of the forest, the six shire horses pulling the three gypsy caravans thunder between a canter and a gallop. Their hooves spew up the thin dusting of snow into great white clouds behind them. The three riders at the reins, Milton, Glenda, and

Nailah, gee their horses with loud hollers and the occasional crack of their whips.

The caravans rattle and creak. The odd thud or crash indicates that something inside hasn't been secured tightly enough. Hopefully, it isn't too important. Gareth holds on to the platform tightly. His knuckles are pale with tension, and his eyes are keenly focused on the road ahead. Talking isn't possible at this speed. Occasionally, he catches Rosalyn's eye and tries to smile reassuringly at her. She looks scared, but she holds on tight.

At one point, a large farmhouse passes by their right-hand side. Gareth sees a man and a woman threshing the bushels of some dried plants at the entrance to a large barn. It looks like tiring work. In the barn, a combine harvester lies dormant and rusty. Gareth wonders if this is the vehicle that brought them into the Meadow. The man and woman look up, shielding their eyes from the sun, and watch the caravans speed by. They wear yellow armbands of the Peak Water Board but aren't remotely concerned by the expedition.

After a couple of hours hurtling through the landscape, the snow-covered forest has almost completely disappeared from view behind them. The bright sun has made the ground dry and dusty, and Gareth notices streaks of congealed dust on the brows of Rosalyn and Glenda. They will all be quite a sight when they get to Fidler's Ferry.

A distant sound cuts through the air, a flat brass note sustained for a few seconds. Gareth looks at Glenda, who looks back. They both listen for the sound to repeat, and it does. It comes from behind them.

"Climb up on top," Glenda calls to Gareth over the noise of the caravans, gesticulating to the canopy above them. "See if you can see how far away they are."

"Who is it?" Gareth asks.

"The Distillery riders have noticed us!"

At the edge of the distant forest far behind them, Gareth can just make out a dozen riders on horseback emerging into the daylight. Their horses and their uniforms are as black as night. The front rider sounds his warning horn once more before the riders set off at a gallop. Their speed over the ground is frightening.

"Have they left the forest?" Glenda asks Gareth.

"Yes," he replies. "Will we make it in time?"

"Hold the reins," she instructs him.

Glenda scrabbles around her feet and pulls out the old map they had used before Crofter's Hope. She struggles to fold it onto her lap while the caravan bumps up and down, swinging from side to side. Glenda traces her forefinger around the features on the map until she settles on a point that she can triangulate. They are just outside of a place called Lime.

Gareth watched as Glenda does the calculations in her head. He holds his breath. "We should just about make it!" she shouts, smiling. She pulls sharply on the reins, accelerating the horses to a full gallop. The other caravans follow suit. They are going faster than they have ever gone before.

\* \* \*

The checkpoint at Fidler's Ferry comes into view. Alongside them, deciduous trees line the banks of the river Mersey. Looming high above the treetops, a grey stone tower bulges into the sky, heavily occupied by border guards. A huge striped blue and yellow flag flies languidly from the top of the tower, the flag of the Mersey Water Board. A high border fence decorated with loops of sharp razor wire stretches into the distance.

The approach road to the border is chequered with mounds of sandbags protecting dozens more armed guards. The piles force the approaching traffic to slow down and meander towards a dark iron gateway. The gateway is decorated with more blue and yellow flags, which welcome visitors to Merseyside.

Without stopping to process the cacophony of instructional signs, Milton leads the expedition straight through an opening emblazoned with the words *Asylum Processing* and into a wide-open yard.

"The cost to enter Merseyside is one Interrogation Stone," says a square-jawed border guard who strides over to greet the expedition. "A fifth of an ounce of your soul and your asylum is granted." He pauses, inspecting them. He gestures towards the door of a dirty windowless concrete building. "For those unable or unwilling to hand over their Interrogation Stone, that's your door. The price is a fifth of an ounce one way or another."

Not waiting for any questions, the border guard nods his head. "Good risen," he says and wanders back through the iron gates, which creak closed behind him, trapping the expedition in the yard.

A familiar bugle call echoes from beyond the gate, back where they had come from. There is a commotion at the lookout tower, followed by a volley of Water Board horns. The Mersey horns carry in harmony back against the single bugle.

Through a megaphone, an officer in the tower sets out conditions for the approaching Distillery riders. "Enemies of Merseyside, keep your distance! The Distillery have no jurisdiction here. We are armed, and we will not hesitate."

Gareth can't see what is happening on the other side of the gate, but quickly the commotion in the tower settles down, and no more is heard. The Distillery riders must have given in.

"That was close then!" says Glenda, looking at Gareth with a cheeky smile.

No sooner has one concern disappeared, another emerges. There is a crash in Nailah's caravan, which grabs their attention. Someone is turning everything over inside. Gareth and Glenda jump down and wander over to see what is happening.

"It'll be here somewhere," they hear Nailah call out. They step into the caravan and find Kasiya collapsed on the floor, looking distraught. Tears are running down her face. "My Interrogation Stone," she cries. "It's gone!"

\* \* \*

Gareth feels utterly helpless as he watches Kasiya and Rosalyn wander towards the interrogation building. Two huge men with faces shrouded under cloth hoods are waiting for them. They grab the two women and thrust them through a doorway without a pause or introduction and slam it shut.

"Come on," says Milton to the rest of the group. "Our door is this way."

Handover of the Interrogation Stone is a lengthier process than Gareth expects. He is taken to a booth where an administrative clerk from the Mersey Water Board takes his basic details: name, approximate length of the stay in the Meadow, arrival location, and place of initial interrogation. Then she asks for his Interrogation Stone.

The clerk processing Gareth's arrival is a large middle-aged woman with podgy fingers, greying hair and a wide neck adorned with jewellery. Gareth reluctantly passes his Interrogation Stone to her. It feels cumbersome in his hand.

In the lady's grasp, the marble's bright crimson colour shimmers, and Gareth sees his own distorted reflection. He feels exposed, relinquishing control of the marble.

The lady places the marble on the scales– precisely one fifth of an ounce. Pulling out a sharp sewing needle, she inspects the marble's shape and colours before piercing it carefully, just a few millimetres below its surface. A tiny drip of the marble's colour oozes out of the pin prick. The lady licks her finger and dabs it on the surface of the glass sphere. Gareth notices how the colours get more vibrant at the touch of her finger. She places her finger into her mouth and closes her eyes.

The lady is perfectly still for a short moment; then she comes round. "The lustful sins of a young man…" she says, looking at Gareth, inspecting him. "Not the wholesome image you present, Mr Edwards," and a smile stretches the lines across her face, as though this is why she loves doing her job. She starts writing things down on her file and then licks her finger again.

Each time the lady comes round from a lick of her finger, she writes feverishly into her file. She mutters a few words or phrases, hinting to Gareth that she has just seen another shameful recollection from his first workhouse interrogation.

"OK, Mr Edwards," she says after half a dozen licks of her finger when the pinprick has resealed itself. "Welcome to

Merseyside." She places his Interrogation Stone into a locked drawer with the file she just completed.

Gareth wanders back into the yard, feeling sick and exposed. The bright sunshine feels like it beats down on his head oppressively. Milton, Nailah, and Billy are already there. Within a few minutes, Ashley, Hassan, and Glenda also emerge. All look sheepish and violated by the experience. With the seven of them back on the convoy, Milton leads them through an open archway and into Merseyside.

"What about Kasiya and Rosalyn?" Gareth asks Glenda.

"Their interrogation will take more time," she says. "We'll stay at the local tavern and collect them in the morning."

* * *

The Ferry Inn is located on the banks of the river Mersey, a short ride from the border. It is a small public house made of grey stone and covered in thick ivy. Outside, some old benches look out over the river, and great wooden barrels are piled high against the walls, full of discarded marbles. Nearby, a wooden racing yacht decays amongst the brambles. An etched mark indicates it was an arrival vessel, zero dash two.

Down from the pub, a handful of small sailing boats are tied to the bank. Their owners, no doubt regulars inside the pub, are sorting the rigging. A few of them doff their caps when they spot the expedition.

The seven members of the expedition wander into the pub. They are hungry and exhausted. In contrast to the bright sky outside, the Ferry Inn is dark and dingy inside. Curtains are open, but the small windows and the ivy outside keep the daylight out. An orange glow pulses from an open fire that crackles in the hearth.

Two men stand behind the bar. They watch the expedition enter with curiosity. Both men in their forties are dressed in loose-fitting white shirts and waistcoats. One wears a flat cap.

"How can we help you?" asks the man in the flat cap.

"Good risen," says Nailah politely. "We are new to Merseyside. A few of our group have overnight processing at the checkpoint. We're looking for somewhere to stay for the night."

"You've come to the right place," says the man, smiling. "Plenty of room here for you all."

"And will you be wanting marbles?" the other man says.

"Absolutely," says Nailah. "Do you forge your own?"

The man raises his eyebrows flirtatiously. "Have you heard of *Sailor's Mist*?"

"Have we ever!" says Hassan, his eyes bright and eager. "Best marbles in the Meadow!"

"Oh aye," says the man confidently as he wanders out.

The other man removes his cap. "Name's Charles Doyle," he says. "Landlord here at the Ferry Inn. My colleague Gerald and I, we've been here nearly a century now. We don't get many visitors these days. Where do you all hail from?"

"All over," says Nailah. "We're heading into the city tomorrow to sell some of our wares. We want to get a boat at the port and do a bit of seafaring."

"Sounds good," says Charles. "You aligned to any Water Board?"

"Oh no," says Nailah. "We keep ourselves out of politics."

"Wise," says Charles. "That's why we run a pub."

Charles climbs out from behind the bar and ushers the group to a lounge where half a dozen tables are clustered around lit stoves. "Help yourselves to the coffee marbles," he says. "I'll bring your *Sailor's Mist* as soon as it's been sterilised."

"Have you got anyone else staying at the moment?" asks Milton, catching Charles before he leaves the room.

"Just the one group. Four chaps from London. Keep themselves to themselves. Been here a few nights, but we don't hardly see them. I think they're bounty hunters or something like that."

The floorboards creak upstairs. "Speak of the devil," says Charles, leaving the room. "They might be coming down for marbles …they usually do. Be nice to them!"

With Charles gone, Gareth looks nervously at Milton. "Should we hide?" he asks urgently.

Milton puts his finger to his lips. The expedition listens quietly to the sound of men descending the stairs and wandering to the bar in the next room.

"The usual, I assume?" they hear Charles say. There is no audible response. "Right you are then, sir. A pot of *Sailor's Mist* coming up."

"You have guests?" One of the unseen men asks. He has a thick home-counties accent. Gareth glances over at Hassan. He recognises that voice.

"Seven of them. Just arrived," says Charles. "Yeah, they're just through there…"

"Careful, MP," calls out another of the unseen men.

The door into the lounge cautiously creaks open, and a tall, skinny man steps in.

"Professor Pelling?!" exclaims Hassan.

A bright, beaming smile fills the man's face as he recognises Gareth and Hassan.

"My notorious friends," he says in his thick accent. "It has been a long time since I saw you two. How the devil are you?"

Hassan strides up to the Professor and extends his hand. "We're good, brother!" he says. "Really good. Lots has happened since we last saw ya, though! What are you doing here?!"

"Let the man sit down first!" says Milton, standing up and patting Hassan on the back.

Professor Pelling catches Milton's eye. "High Councillor Drake," he says. "A pleasure!" He puts his hand in front of his face and bows. Gareth recognises the prominent scar on the back of the Professor's hand and the tan line on his bare wedding ring finger. Milton reciprocates the gesture.

"Are you a Well Wisher too, Professor?!" asks Gareth.

The Professor grins at Gareth knowingly. "There's a lot to catch up on…" he says.

\* \* \*

It transpires that bumping into Professor Pelling at the Ferry Inn is not a completely unlikely coincidence. When the expedition left Lin, Nailah had sent word to her friendly contacts at Virgil College requesting the latest research coming out of the Professor's department, the Department of Openings. This research would be essential in equipping them with the latest knowledge of when and where an Opening was most likely to occur.

Nailah informed her contacts of the expedition's route and hoped they would find a way of leaving a package of documents somewhere safe. She never expected an actual audience with Professor Pelling.

"I have some students working here in Merseyside," says the Professor, getting comfortable and dropping a coffee marble into his mouth. "They're at EBJ… Ernest Brown Junior University. I thought they'd be best placed to present our work, and I couldn't miss a chance to see my fugitive friends." He grins at Gareth and Hassan.

"And are you a Well Wisher then…in London? Right under the Distillery noses?!" asks Milton, impressed.

Professor Pelling smiles awkwardly. "Well, I wouldn't exactly label myself a Well Wisher… I'd rather just say I'm open-minded and well-read…"

"Meaning?" asks Milton.

"A few of us academics are sympathetic to your cause… though naturally, we don't advertise this." He leans back and tucks his long greying hair behind his ears. "Hiding in plain sight of the Distillery, we take huge risks…sometimes daily. Mind you…my risks are nothing compared to the risks taken by you lot hanging around with these two!" He cheerfully nods towards Gareth and Hassan.

"You know, your faces are everywhere in the city these days," he says. "I've never known the Distillery to single people out like this. Wanted Posters are littering every street, and *The Forecast is* running daily opinion pieces peddling fear about you. They say you are the worst Satanists to come through to the Meadow in centuries!"

"These two?! Ha!" Milton guffaws at this jealously.

"Yes. And with that attention comes notoriety," says the Professor. "The fact you've evaded capture for so long has given you a cult status. Right now, there is an underground movement in London, calling themselves 'The Thirsty'. They idolise you. Your names are graffitied in alleys, on post boxes and on other street furniture around the city. You have given people in the city a sense that the Distillery's power is fragile."

"You're welcome," says Hassan cheekily, his ego engorged by the Professor's update. He basks in the idea of notoriety, chucking a marble into his mouth with nonchalance.

"Do you know the *real* reason the Distillery fear these men?" Milton asks the Professor, casting a condescending eye towards Hassan.

"That I do," smiles Professor Pelling. He turns back to the door. "Hector! Edmond!" he shouts.

"Coming, darling!" they hear Hector's voice call out from the bar.

A moment later, the two men, finely dressed as always, sashay into the lounge. Immediately their joy at seeing the expedition is radiant. Edmond even has to wipe a tear from his eye.

"Well, bravo you!" exclaims Hector, looking at everyone. "You've done ruddy well to get here…I had *no idea* just how hunted these two boys were!" He casts an astonished look towards Gareth and Hassan.

"Gosh, yes!" says Edmond, leaning on Hector's shoulder. "Your faces are, like, *everywhere!* Seriously. And so are the girls! Rosalyn, darling, they have a fabulous picture of you on the wanted poster… really smoky and gorgeous." Edmond looks around for Rosalyn. "Where is she?"

"She never received an Interrogation Stone," says Nailah solemnly. "She had to remain at the checkpoint for a new interrogation. Her and my daughter Kasiya."

"Oh, poor girls," says Hector, bowing his head. "My Well Wishings, darling," he says to Nailah.

"Thank you," she responds.

"And you know the other girl they're hunting, right?" asks Edmond, regaining his composure.

"What girl?" asks Milton.

"I haven't said yet," Professor Pelling cuts in, looking nervously back at Edmond, then across to Gareth. Edmond throws his hand theatrically over his mouth.

"Who is it?" asks Gareth.

"Your sister, Gareth," says the Professor. "They're hunting Cerys."

"They're hunting Cerys?!" exclaims Gareth. "What?! Why?!"

The Professor reaches out and grasps Gareth's hand reassuringly. "She's alive," he says, smiling. "…Well, she's in the Meadow at least… and she's out of the Palace."

"That's great, Gareth!" says Ashley.

"It's not all good news, I'm afraid," says the Professor. "Cerys was cast out from the Palace sometime just before the Distillery identified all arrivals from your train as key targets. She lived on the streets and stayed safe long enough to be found by the Colney Hatch Sisterhood. They didn't know who she was or how much danger she faced, but they took her in."

"When I heard about you being on this expedition and saw the wanted posters for Cerys, I connected two and two and reached out to the Sisterhood. They managed to locate Cerys, living in one of their houses just north of the Lethe. My contact couldn't give me any details on Cerys' condition or if she has any memory of her life before the Palace. But they promised me they will send word to move Cerys to the safest location known in the city; to the Tide and Time Tavern."

The Professor looks at Gareth, trying to read his emotion. "It is likely Cerys' memory is, at best, very faded. But I'm sure Kim-Joy will be working with her right now to rebuild her memory of you and her life before the Meadow."

Gareth grasps the silver locket around his neck, his lasting connection to the Tide and Time Tavern. He isn't sure how he feels. Is it possible to feel elated, sick, and afraid all at the same time? Yes, he realises. It is.

"Um, is it just me, or is there another pressing question?" asks Glenda. "Hector, Edmond… you had a mission of your own…why are you in Merseyside?"

Both men beam at the group. "We found him! We found Commander Newman!"

* * *

"Albert is very weak," says Hector, leading the group up the stairs. "He was barely conscious when we found him. He said he was trying to make his way to Lin… on foot! Without access to marbles or other sensations, his mind and body were almost wasted away. I think we found him just in time. Anyway… he is in a better state now. We've been plying him with *Sailor's Mist* for a few days. Seriously, those marbles are incredible!"

They stop outside one of the upstairs rooms. Hector waves his hand to usher a bit of space so he can open the door. In the anticipation, even the stoic authority of Milton and steadfastness of Nailah are momentarily absent. Both are at the front of the crowd, encroaching on Hector, desperate to lay eyes on the hero of Well Wishing.

"He'll be thrilled to see you all," says Hector. "But just go easy… he's very weak."

Hector pulls open the door. "Albert," he calls in. "We've got guests!"

Stepping into the dim, dusty room, they can see in the corner on a bed covered in blankets, Commander Albert Newman, the old man from the train.

Albert sits up awkwardly as the group pile in. He looks frail and uncomfortable. A wound above his left eye leaves his eye socket sunken and bruised. He has messy, unkempt hair and beard, and his face is extremely gaunt. But he looks determined.

"Commander Newman!" exclaims Milton, rushing towards the bed while trying to bow and do the Well-Wishing greeting simultaneously. His movements are clumsy and comical.

"Mr Drake!" says Albert, chortling at Milton's entrance. "I understand it is High Councillor now!?"

"It is," says Milton, a proud smile stretching the scar on his top lip.

Albert glances around at everyone else entering the room, and his face lights up. He even has to wipe a tear from his eye. "Oh golly," he says. "What a wonderful surprise!"

Introductions and reunions with Albert are joyous and enthusiastic. Despite the old man's condition, so many friendly faces energise him, making him stronger and more like the man from the workhouse that Gareth remembers. Most touching is when Albert asks Nailah about Kasiya. It seems Albert had been very fond of Kasiya when he was last in the Meadow, acting as an uncle to her while Milton was away, climbing the ranks of the Well-Wishing hierarchy.

"And you two," says Albert, turning to Gareth and Hassan. "What a delight to see you both. Sorry that I never said goodbye before… I left in a bit of a rush! But I must say… you have made some excellent life choices since I last saw you!"

"I don't think we had a choice, brother!" says Hassan, smirking.

"I'm sorry I didn't tell you about my past," says Albert. "It didn't feel fair or right to say anything in the workhouse. Did you ever suspect me?"

Gareth grins. "Not in the workhouse," he says. "But when I heard about the Distillery interest in our train, I did start to suspect you had something to do with it!"

"Smart lad," says Albert, beaming at Gareth before a realisation strikes him and his smile fades. "I'm sorry to hear that you haven't been reunited with your sister yet," he says sorrowfully. "The Professor told me she is with Kim-Joy at the Tide and Time now… I assure you there's no better place for her in the Meadow."

Albert grabs Gareth's sweaty palm, offering him a reassuring smile. "You'll see her again, I'm sure of it."

Gareth looks back at Albert and feels a wash of comfort in the old man's sincere wrinkled face and the warmth of his hand. He smiles back.

"And I suppose you'd like to hear about what happened to me in the lead-up to that train ride?" Albert asks Gareth.

"He's not the only one," says Milton, vocalising an eagerness in everyone present.

The expedition crowd around Albert in his bed, leaning in as the old man gets comfortable.

"About forty years ago," Albert starts, "I regained consciousness on Earth, lying on a riverbank where a paramedic had just revived me. I felt like I had just woken up from the most incredible dream. A dream that felt like it had lasted for decades. But a dream that had ended."

"It was strange. My whole time in the Meadow was cast into doubt in the blink of an eye. My mind opting to recategorise my memories as mere figments of imagination. And the reality was, my heart had only stopped for a millisecond on Earth... Decades of life, disavowed in a literal heartbeat."

"But the dreams haunted my life in the years that followed. A constant whisper in my ear telling me not to forget. Sadly, like all dreams, time was its mortal coil. For the first few years, I looked everywhere for evidence of the Meadow but found nothing. I looked for proof that I had been away for decades, but there was none. And then, as the dream faded, I looked for the people in my dream, but they were nowhere to be found."

"In a final desperate attempt to hold onto my dream, I tried communicating back to people in the Meadow. I stuck images of the Encircled Drop on every vehicle I travelled in, hoping one might get through someday. I left written words of Well Wishing in places where I thought people might have tragic accidents. I even befriended people who worked in dangerous professions, hoping to pass a message through them. But I never knew if my attempts got through." Albert looks up at Milton and smiles.

"I lived a good life on Earth but never forgot my dream. The details faded, but the dream never disappeared. I reached my ninetieth birthday alone, and my longing for the dream became too much. I booked an appointment with a doctor in Zurich who could give me a way out. A doctor who would end my life early for me. And I took a train. But *that* train crashed and brought me back. Back to the Meadow."

A single tear rolls down Albert's face as he looks at the crowd around his bed. Nailah reaches across and holds the old man's hand, squeezing it. Gareth looks up and notices Ashley opposite him. Her eyes are glistening, and she looks overwhelmed. He smiles at her, and she smiles back, chuckling inadvertently.

"My kind and committed friends," announces Milton, stepping back from Albert's bed and turning the attention onto himself. "Commander Newman bears living witness to the truth that we hold dear. Our souls can and *will* traverse the realms. Now, more than ever, I know our expedition will be a success. What an honour...and what great encouragement to meet Albert today. Thank you, Commander." He nods reverently to Albert.

"I wish we could stay longer," Milton continues. "But tomorrow, we must journey on. The next and most dangerous part of our Mission awaits. Tomorrow, we head to the docks, and from there...the mountains."

Albert tentatively raises his hand, diverting attention from Milton's rallying call. "A bowl of Sailor's Mist and a good sleep should have me back to full strength in the morning," he says. "I'd like to ask, High Councillor if you're willing... well, my experience might count for something... and I like to ask if... well... can I join your expedition?"

Milton almost stumbles with joy. His stoicism evaporating once again. "Yes, Commander! Yes!"

* * *

A cold autumnal breeze blows off the sea and up the river Mersey. Hector and Edmond have just said their goodbyes, leaving Albert Newman in Glenda's care. Both men were offered the chance to join the expedition too, but they declined. Coming from times on Earth separated by over a century, they have no intention of returning and losing their connection with one another. Given that Albert is insistent on joining the expedition, they plan to journey together back to London and attempt to establish links between the City Circus and the underground uprising of *The Thirsty*.

Gareth sits on the grass amongst the sailing vessels on the bank outside the Ferry Inn, thinking about Cerys. A tugboat splutters past, heading out to sea. The trawlermen are all in their cabin, and the ghostly vessel's wake gently washes against the shore. Images of Cerys at the Palace and on the streets of London won't leave Gareth's mind, no matter how much he tries. He sighs. This, the impending danger, and the re-emergence of Albert Newman are all proving a bit too tough on his mind. And he knows there are still the most challenging parts of his time in the Meadow to come.

"Mind if I join you?" Ashley's voice comes from behind, startling him. "Sorry," she says. "I thought you might like some company?"

Gareth smiles at her. "Thanks."

"You are thinking about Cerys?"

"Yeah," says Gareth. "I wish I could return to the Tide and Time Tavern. I've been such a useless brother. I should have been there for her. I should be there for her now."

"That's tough," Ashley replies, wisely choosing to neither side with nor against what Gareth says. She sits beside him, and they watch the tugboat disappear into the distance for a few calm and peaceful minutes.

Nonchalantly, Ashley reaches across and grasps Gareth's hand for comfort. He turns to look at her. "I'm sorry," she says and pulls her hand away.

"No," says Gareth. "Please don't be sorry."

He looks at Ashley in profile. She purposefully avoids his gaze and distracts her hands by brushing a cobweb off her shoe. Gareth wonders how Cerys might get along with Ashley if they were ever to meet. For a start, Cerys couldn't tease him for meeting Ashley online. He re-lives the kiss with Ashley again in his mind. He has re-lived that moment so many times since it happened. He knows he is supposed to be trying to forget. But he can't. He doesn't want to.

"Will *we* ever be possible?" Gareth asks Ashley tentatively.

Ashley doesn't say anything.

The river washes up against the bank below them. Back and forth. Back and forth. After plenty long enough, Gareth exhales. "I've got to get to bed, I think. Today has been too intense."

Ashley grabs Gareth's hand and looks into his eyes. She doesn't say anything, but it seems like she wants to. Gareth looks back. "I know," he says.

Gareth wanders back to the room he is sharing with Hassan. On the way, he passes Milton in the stable yard. Milton is searching in the caravans frantically and doesn't notice Gareth. Gareth presumes he is looking for Kasiya's missing marbles. They are something that she will definitely want to have a closer hold of when she returns in the morning.

Gareth wanders past Albert's room, hearing him chatting passionately with Glenda, and clambers straight into his bed in the room next door, exhausted. He doesn't even notice if Hassan is in the room. He is asleep in seconds.

As he sleeps, a dark menacing dream fills his mind. He sees Cerys, Ashley, and Kasiya. The three women are tied up in some dark and damp cellar. They are beaten and gagged, with tears running down their faces. And Gareth is there too, standing in the room looking at them. He is trying to save them, but guards are coming. He doesn't have time to save them all. He has to choose just one of them. Or, if he doesn't choose, they will all be dead.

He looks at each of the three women, and they all look back. He makes up his mind. He starts to untie Cerys' hands.

The gag falls from her mouth. "Who are you?!" Cerys shouts. "Get off me. What are you doing to me?!"

"It's me, Gareth," he exclaims. She spits at his face, and he recoils. There is no familiarity in her eyes.

If not Cerys, then who? Cerys screams as Gareth runs over to Ashley and pulls down her gag, attempting to untie her hands.

"No!" shouts Ashley. "Not me. Leave me. Save Kasiya."

"But I want you," he says.

"No," she shouts back. "Not me." She struggles and wriggles to stop Gareth from untying her.

"OK," responds Gareth. "OK." He runs over to Kasiya. He pulls down her gag and starts to untie her hands. Too late.

"No!" shouts Kasiya.

Three guards wearing gas masks enter the room, canisters held aloft. They don't stop, and they don't hesitate. The room fills with spray.

Gareth wakes. He is sweating profusely. His sheets and pillow are damp and uncomfortable. His heart is pounding in his chest, and he feels wide awake. His eyes quickly adjust to the dark shadows of the dormitory. He takes a moment to calm his breathing, and the dreadful image of the three women starts to crack and dissolve away. Eventually, Gareth is able to reason; they are all safe and well. He shuffles out of his cold, damp bed to go and find a towel.

The landing is silent, and all the lights are out. It must be the middle of the night. Each floorboard creaks under Gareth's feet as he wanders to the bathroom. He pushes open the bathroom door, not noticing the candlelight flickering through the cracks. He sees Hassan's feet at the stall and quickly shuts the door. "Sorry!" he whispers. He pushes open the next bathroom door and finds what he needs. Scrambling around in the cupboard, he pulls out a soft towel and shuffles back to his room.

He feels so much better when he clambers back into bed on his towel. A dry bed makes a world of difference. He is just drifting back off to sleep when Hassan returns to the room.

Hassan places a candle down beside his bed and sits bent over, looking sick and worried. Gareth pretends to be asleep but watches through squinted eyes as Hassan runs his hands through his hair before rubbing his face vigorously and reaching over his bedside table. Hassan grasps a few items, which he plunges into his bag, making sure they are pushed right down to the bottom. He blows out the candle and lets out a long sigh as he lies back on his bed.

In the dark, it doesn't take long for both men to fall asleep.

\* \* \*

"When are they going to get back?" Hassan asks impatiently, sitting around the bar the next morning. Rosalyn and Kasiya are due to return from the checkpoint soon. Milton and Nailah had left at sunrise to go and collect them. "They've been gone ages!"

Uncharacteristically, Hassan is showing concern for the well-being of others this morning. He has just collected a bowl of warm morning marbles to share amongst the group but hasn't brought any just for himself. He barely acknowledges the thanks he gets for his generosity and sits down, looking distracted.

To everyone's delight, Albert Newman has joined them at the bar. As he had hoped, the *Sailor's Mist* and the good night's sleep did wonders for his exhausted body. He is in high spirits and very willing to regale everyone with the fractured memories he can muster from his last time in the Meadow and the successful Cwtch Mission.

Almost as though Hassan's impatience is a cue, the sounds of hooves rattle in through the open window. A moment later, the old front door creaks open.

"Rosalyn!" Ashley calls out.

The young woman stands in the doorway. Tears are streaming down her face, and she shakes with panic. Glenda is the first to her feet. She embraces Rosalyn and pulls her in tight. "It's OK," she says. "It's OK."

"It's not OK," Rosalyn sobs. "Kasiya!" she half sniffs, half cries.

Before she can say anything else, the door swings open again. Milton stumbles in, stunned and exhausted. Held tightly in his arms is Nailah. She is sobbing and shaking like Rosalyn. Tears stream down her reddened face, and her breathing is shallow and rapid.

Milton struggles to keep Nailah upright. Professor Pelling and Albert Newman shoot up to help.

"She's gone!" wails Nailah. "My darling daughter is gone!"

*It was November 1940. Throughout the cold dark nights of winter, the Luftwaffe had carried out bombing raids across the British Isles. Liverpool was one of the cities devastated by these lethal attacks. On the night of 29th November eight hours of relentless bombing rained down over Merseyside. One of the targets of the bombers was Edge Hill railway station, a key supply line for goods in the city. Nearby the station around three hundred people, mostly factory workers and local residents, were sheltering from the bombs in the basement of Ernest Brown Junior Instructional College. One of the bombs intended for the railway station missed its target and made direct impact with the college building. The explosion collapsed the building down into its basement and burst gas pipes. The ignited gas started a devastating fire in the wreckage. Despite the best efforts of firefighters and local volunteers, one hundred and sixty-six people lost their lives in the disaster.*

# Chapter Eighteen

◆

# The Wind from their Sails

The day they learn of Kasiya's passing is a blur. The expedition agrees to stay at the Ferry Inn for a while, giving Milton and Nailah time to begin processing the loss of their daughter and a chance to consider if they want to stay with the expedition in light of the tragedy. Milton is adamant that they should only delay by a day. Nailah doesn't voice an opinion.

Everyone feels a heart-wrenching sorrow for Nailah and Milton's loss and a sickening dread at the dilemma they are now facing. The dilemma of whether they still want to return to Earth or if they would actually rather go on to be with their daughter. For the first time, Gareth feels like these two great forces in their group, Milton Drake and Nailah Hussain-Drake, are pulling in different directions.

Gareth doesn't know what to do with himself. He feels numb and dizzy, simultaneously chastening himself for the selfishness of his pain and a bitter regret that he never resolved things with Kasiya. His nightmare from the night before keeps re-visiting him. He tries to busy himself, helping Glenda prepare the survival equipment for the next part of the journey, but concentrating is so hard.

Ashley, one of Kasiya's closest friends in the Meadow, is floored by her loss. With Rosalyn, she sits on the riverbank all morning, silently absorbing the peaceful lapping of the river against the shore. Every time Gareth steps out from the Ferry Inn for fresh air, the two women are in an almost identical embrace, not saying a word.

Milton handles his grief very differently. His very essence is infiltrated with anger, and his muscles twitch with rage. While Gareth and Glenda separate the survival equipment from the unessential items in the carriages, Milton obsessively turns over every item. Gareth presumes he is looking for Kasiya's lost marbles. As though, somehow, finding them would help him to process his grief. But he dare not ask Milton if this is what he's doing. Milton's blind rage ensures that everyone keeps their distance.

Around midday, Gareth wanders to the riverbank to join Ashley and Rosalyn and spend some reflective time with them. As he approaches, he recognises that the two women are deep in conversation. He swivels back towards the pub, but Ashley has heard him approaching and beckons him over.

"Sorry," says Gareth. "I didn't want to interrupt."

"No, it's OK," says Ashley, her voice quiet, her eyes red and puffy.

"I was about to tell Ashley what I saw last night," says Rosalyn, just as quietly.

"Oh, right," says Gareth, shuffling onto the dry grassy bank beside them, not knowing what to say.

"I knew something was wrong even before Kasiya went to the interrogation chamber," she says. "She seemed really panicky when we were in the holding cell. She was breathing frantically, and she had this awful twitch." Rosalyn looks resolutely sad, re-telling what she remembers. "I tried to reassure her that things would be OK, but she was still in a state when they came to collect her."

"She was only in the interrogation about ten minutes when I heard shouting from the chamber – angry and threatening shouts from forceful male voices. Extra guards were called in. Half a dozen of them ran past the holding cell. They were wearing gas masks…"

"They had already sprayed her?" asks Ashley, horrified.

"Maybe," says Rosalyn. "There was shouting and commotion for a long while. But eventually, the noise all died down, and those of us in the holding cells were instructed to stay away from our cell doors while they brought the 'casualty', as they said referred to her, back through…"

"I managed to catch a glimpse of Kasiya… Clear as day, she was now a Drifter. She had that typical unfocused stare and loose unconscious posture. But she didn't look like she had suffered physically at all…thank god. She just looked serene and calm… I had never seen Kasiya like that before."

Rosalyn wipes her eyes and looks across at Ashley and Gareth. "I wish I could have helped her."

Ashley reaches across and grasps Rosalyn's hand but doesn't say anything.

"I don't understand why they would spray her," says Gareth angrily. "Kasiya would never have posed any kind of threat to them."

"Well, that's just it," says Rosalyn. "*They* didn't spray her… Apparently, she grabbed the interrogator's spray and turned it on herself!"

"Oh, god!" exclaims Ashley, slapping her hand across her mouth.

"No," says Gareth dismissively. "No. I can't believe that." He doesn't want to believe it.

"It's true," says Rosalyn, looking at them both. "Milton verified the guard's account from her dissected Interrogation Stone this morning."

Gareth looks out at the river, feeling dizzy. "Shit," he says. "Shit."

* * *

Although for most of the time that Kasiya had been on the expedition, she had been silent and absent, her literal absence is felt much more keenly amongst the group. Losing one of the expedition brings home the very real consequences of their journey and draws into sharp focus the endpoint they are rapidly approaching. The space vacated by Kasiya is filled with nervousness and a keen sense of uncertainty.

Nailah's grief remains acute and debilitating. She asks to take some time away from the expedition to be alone with her thoughts. Professor Pelling agrees to take Nailah to the university, where she can spend a day in the botanical gardens alone. Contrasting his wife, Milton buries his grief with a determined rational momentum. As promised, he leads the rest of the group from the Ferry Inn the next day into Mersey City to prepare for the next, most dangerous part of their journey.

The first task in Merseyside is to head to the docks to obtain a boat. A substantial boat: a ten-berth seaworthy vessel that can take the expedition and all of their survival equipment to the coast of North Wales and the edge of the mountain range containing the Source. With limited use of currency in the Meadow – its production being minimally developed – barter and auction are the most common form of exchange. The expedition enters the docks, therefore, intending to use the six shire horses, the three merchant caravans, and the assortment of trinkets from the circus as their bartering material.

Mersey City is much like London. The buildings that have been constructed, and those that have come through Openings, are a mismatch of style and substance. In amongst the dense urban fabric, nature thrives. Giant Oaks and other trees and shrubs fill the streets while crawling plants cling to walls and street furniture.

Mersey dock itself is noisy and busy. Flocks of seabirds fly overhead, squawking disruptively, scavenging wherever they can. Hundreds of people from all eras are gathered around, carrying slips of paper and catalogues, wandering amongst the auction houses and display yard. In the dock itself, shipping vessels of different sizes, ages, and quality are on display. The boats are tightly packed in the confined murky water, lashed to the floating pontoons. Hulls squeak and creak with the undulation of the sea swell.

Each auction item has a lot number, and each lot has an owner to barter with. Glenda and Albert stay with the caravans once they have established a lot in the concrete loading bay. Albert is much stronger than he was a few days ago, but he is still not ready to spend a whole day on his feet. Milton removes all the jewels and valuable items from the caravans while Ashley and Billy walk the shire horses at another lot. The horses and jewels will be extra bartering power to try and get their chosen boat at a reasonable price.

The route to auction has already been prepared for the expedition by Professor Pelling – another task he was assigned before the group arrived at Merseyside. There are plenty of punters at the auction already aware that they would be coming with horses and carriages for sale. Likewise, Professor Pelling has short-listed the ships that are up for auction.

Before the tragedy of Kasiya's passing, Nailah had picked out a boat called the *Eliza Fernley,* a nineteenth-century ten-berth sail-powered lifeboat that would suit the expedition perfectly. They hope that the boat's owner, Viceroy Jones, an elected councillor of the Mersey Water Board, will be amenable to the group's offer. Councillor Jones, it seems, is the dominant boat trader in the area. Dozens of boats in the dock are his to sell.

The bartering starts as quite a private affair. Milton approaches Councillor Jones alone on the pontoon alongside the *Eliza Fernley* while the rest of the expedition stay out of the way and check out the fascinating array of items up for auction. All except Hassan, that is.

Since Kasiya's passing, Hassan has taken his marble consumption to the next level, sucking them from the moment he wakes until he goes to sleep. Everyone knows this can only lead to trouble, but there is a general acceptance of one another's coping strategies in the immediate aftermath of grief. Even if it does seem somewhat self-destructive. So, while the others wander the dockyard and Milton barters with Councillor Jones, Hassan cowers alone in a shady alleyway, rattling marble after marble around his jaws.

Councillor Jones is a large overweight man with a flushed red face – a combination of being well-fed and getting lots of sun at sea. Once the initial niceties of their opening negotiation are complete, Milton invites Councillor Jones to inspect the caravans. All but Billy and Ashley (who stay with the horses) and Hassan (who remains with his marbles) join in to assist in the bartering.

Councillor Jones has a brisk and straight tone. He is clearly an expert at auctions. He wanders around the caravans silently, shaking the axles and inspecting the craftsmanship. Instead of talking with Milton, whom he perceives has the most knowledge, he picks on the group members he thinks might give away some of the faults, helping him to lower the price of the barter.

"Tell me…" he says to Rosalyn, closer to her than is comfortable. "You've ridden in these caravans, have you?"

"Oh yes," Rosalyn responds confidently.

"And they are… a bit *uncomfortable,* I presume?"

"Oh no! They are *very* comfortable," she says.

"And I imagine you've done a *lot* of miles in them?"

"Wrong again," says Rosalyn. "Just the occasional day trip here and there. We've never had any trouble with them."

"No?" he says, disappointed. "But you've travelled in some *harsh* weather… snowstorms, heavy rain?"

"Not really," Rosalyn lies. "We tend to save them for nice trips into the country. As soon as the weather turns foul, we tend to stay in shelter. The caravans are so lovely and warm inside; we just stay inside until the weather improves again."

On their way to the docks this morning, Milton had prepped the expedition on how to barter. Yes, it might be lying, but he told them that everyone who trades at the auctions lies, and everyone knows what they are trying to achieve. In reality, you buy what you see.

After asking lots of questions, Councillor Jones does a rehearsed, worried ponder. Lingering for an awkward silence to the inexperienced auctioneers. "I'm not sure," he says. "Not sure it is worth it for me…"

"No," he says, striking an air of finality. "No, it's *not* going to be worth it for me."

"No problem," says Milton. "Thanks for your interest." Milton is bluffing. They *need* his interest.

The bluff works.

"Well," says Councillor Jones. "It's a shame you don't have more to offer. I mean, the caravans will be hard for me to shift on their own."

This is Glenda's cue. "Well, we do have six healthy shire horses that could go into the bargain, I suppose. Lovely animals. They happily pull the three caravans."

"Interesting," says Councillor Jones. "And might I inspect the horses?"

"Of course," says Glenda, smiling. "Rosalyn. Will you accompany Councillor Jones and me to show him the horses?"

Rosalyn smiles agreeably, and the three of them wander off together.

"It's all going to plan," mutters Milton. "I'm sure he'll push for more. But we've still got the jewels. I think we're going to win this one."

* * *

Councillor Jones returns with Glenda and Rosalyn a short while later. Glenda sports a big beaming smile.

"You've got yourself a deal," says Councillor Jones. "Finest set of well-looked-after shire horses I've seen in Merseyside. Those and the caravans will do me nicely. I'm sure the *Eliza Fernley* will suit your needs too. I'll run the paperwork through with the auction houses. You can meet me first thing in the morning, and we'll do the exchange."

"We were hoping to do the deal *tonight*," says Milton, looking at Councillor Jones.

Milton's eagerness plays right into the councillor's hands, and he smiles. "Ooh... that'll be difficult," he says, playing the game. "Lots to sort out... *Lots* of paperwork."

"I understand," says Milton. "But we really would like to get our voyage underway."

"Probably going to be a bit hard for me..." says Councillor Jones.

"Well, if there's anything you can do," says Milton. "We've got a few items to sweeten the deal... if you're interested?"

This is Milton's masterstroke. He pulls forward the small chest of jewels he had saved for the bartering. With his heavily jewelled neck, the councillor looks into the chest. Fantastic and rare glittering gems sparkle in his eyes. They are huge status items.

The councillor turns back to the others greedily. "I think I'll be able to sort something for you all tonight," he says. "I don't know what time it'll be, mind. Where can I find you?"

"We'll be at the university," says Milton, "Department of Openings. The jewels are yours if you can find us there before midnight."

"Pleasure doing business with you," says the councillor, and he shakes Milton's hand. Glenda holds out her hand too, but the chauvinist councillor ignores her.

\* \* \*

It is already late in the evening when they arrive at Ernest Brown Junior University. Professor Pelling and Nailah are waiting for them. The botanical gardens have done Nailah a world of good. She looks solemn, but the steel has returned to her eyes. This is quite a contrast to Hassan, whom they have basically carried to the university. He has stopped having more marbles in the last hour or so, but the effects of a day 'marble-running' (that's what back-to-back marble sucking is known as) will take a while to wear off.

Professor Pelling introduces the expedition to some fellow academics who work on Openings with him. Then he leads them to a round observatory on the top floor of the campus.

A detailed map table fills the middle of the room. It is intricately marked with pins and dots. Pointing up at the roof is a great telescope trained on the sky.

"This," says Professor Pelling, pointing to the table, "is the most detailed map we have of the British Isles in the Meadow."

The group look down at the cartographic table in front of them. The broad outline of the British Isles is very familiar, but the settlements and their connections aren't. The big cities can be easily pinpointed, and Gareth traces his eyes due west from Birmingham, trying to pick out the town he grew up in. The rest of the expedition do likewise.

"The red dots," says Professor Pelling, pointing to the hundreds of red marks on the map, "are all the known Openings to have come into the Meadow. The green pins are those Openings from which we have collected first-hand reports."

Gareth inspects the green pins. They are mainly located around the cities, with the occasional pin out in the countryside. He focuses on London, around the area of Euston station. There are dozens of red dots in this area alone. He presumes one of these red dots would be related to his arrival.

"Now, the green pins," says Professor Pelling. "These have provided most use to our department. The red pins have given us a sense of events on Earth and their impact on the Meadow – numbers of arrivals, types of transportation, types of disaster. But for the *green* pins, we have much richer data. We have things like weather, arrival materials, arrival live matter, plants and animals that have arrived. These are much more helpful details for predicting the future of Openings in the Meadow."

The Professor unfurls a large parchment. On it is a detailed line graph. "Here, you can see a shift in the events from Earth and the likelihood of arrivals. From interviews with recent arrivals, we have deduced that many things on Earth today – technology, climate, and even large events from the annual social calendar – are having a greater and greater impact on sending people into the Meadow. More people are suffering the effects of modern society's risks. By combining our knowledge of the artefacts coming into the Meadow, we believe we are starting to be able to predict the disasters that are happening on Earth."

Professor Pelling unrolls another chart. This time a map of the British Isles with some social events, traffic details, and weather marked on it. It is dated 'today', but on Earth. The very thought that this is the weather on Earth right now, the place where his home is, his friends are, and possibly where his mum is, fills Gareth with hope and excitement. He feels like he really is within touching distance of Earth.

"Our projections aren't perfect," says the Professor, lowering his voice. "But with every new arrival, we are improving our predictions. It is *this* information that you must use. Our information is your best chance at predicting an Opening and getting through."

The Professor blows out a few candles illuminating the room, plunging them into darkness. Pulling a lever, he opens a hatch in the observatory roof, revealing the night sky, and removes a lens cap from the telescope. "There are so many areas of our research into Openings that we do not fully understand," he begins. "One of the more intriguing lines of research, if I may, is when we turn to the heavens."

"You will no doubt have heard that we believe the stars here are the souls of people who have perished on Earth, making their way through to the Beyond. This idea has been held in the Meadow, across all beliefs, as far back as we know. But that has been it; just a theory, just a belief. But now, with this telescope, we have been able to look more closely at the stars. And what we have seen is fascinating. When we watch the stars, we see they have a degree of agency. They move at different speeds across the night sky. And not constant speeds, either. We have followed individual stars that have sped through the night sky until they have met up with other stars and have formed new constellations."

"We have also observed a correlation between arrivals in the Meadow and new constellations appearing in the night sky. All of this points towards our belief that these stars represent the souls of people from Earth. This joining of constellations and the hovering of stars over the Source Mountain indicates some connection between the stars and the souls here in the Meadow."

"But as I say, this is a whole new area of research, one in which we are only making tentative first steps. Nonetheless, it is fascinating. It is also beautiful to observe." He adjusts the lens of the telescope, and it projects a shaft of light onto the wall of the observatory. The image that it presents shows the night sky. The stars aren't just points of light but malleable shifting orbs moving amongst one another, creating new connections, and tumbling through the sky together. It is a dance of light. The expedition sits, mesmerised.

Suddenly there is a knock at the door. Professor Pelling quickly shuts off the telescope, covers the documents, and re-lights the candles.

A young man, probably a student, opens the door. "Sorry, Professor," he says. "Is there a Mr Milton Drake with you?"

"That's me," says Milton.

"Two gentlemen from Councillor Viceroy Jones' office have just arrived for you, sir. They say that the *Eliza Fernley* is ready for your collection. They will escort you to the docks right away."

"Excellent," says Milton. "Tell the gentlemen we will be down in just a moment."

"Well, Professor," starts Nailah. "Thank you *so* much. There is a lot for us to take on board. Will we be able to take some of the maps with us? If we *are* successful at the Source, we will want the best chance to find an Opening as soon as we can."

"Absolutely," says Professor Pelling. "As you know, Openings are much more frequent in London. If you are successful, and I hope you are by golly, go to London and find me at the Tide and Time Tavern. I'll help you reach an Opening myself."

Gareth looks at Nailah, keen that she accepts the offer. If they could get to the Tide and Time Tavern, he would get to see Cerys.

"That sounds like a grand idea," says Nailah.

After a few cheerful words, Professor Pelling bids a final farewell to the group. He shakes Gareth and Hassan's hands and smiles at them (Hassan only manages a drunken grimace of acknowledgement) before warmly embracing Milton and Nailah.

"Godspeed," says Professor Pelling. "May the Daughter of God be with you." He places his palm on his forehead, as do Milton, Nailah, Albert, Ashley, and Glenda. They bow. Gareth joins in tentatively. He isn't sure if it is appropriate to join in, but he wants to show where he is at. Ashley notices and smiles at him.

* * *

The two men from Councillor Jones' office are muscly, placid men. There is no small talk or chit-chat. They are just doing a job: collecting and escorting the expedition to the *Eliza Fernley*. Both men have heavily scarred arms. The depth and extent of their Satan's Scalds indicate that they spent a significant period of their lives at the Distillery workhouses. Given their passive compliance, Gareth suspects that these two men were a few of the barely conscious who made it through the workhouses after years of toil and trial.

It is a clear, dark, and quiet night as they enter the dockyard. The iron gates creak, and the bustling auction spaces from earlier are now silent. There is almost nobody about. Many bartered items have been collected, and large concrete spaces are empty in the yard. Nonetheless, there are still a few scattered items awaiting collection. In contrast, the dock is almost as full as it had been during the day. The boat trade is not thriving.

The *Eliza Fernley* has been moved and is now moored against the main pontoon, its lights on inside. With their belongings slung into large sacks over their shoulders, the expedition shuffles carefully down the slippery walkway. Milton and Nailah carry the chest of jewels between them.

The pontoon creaks and rocks, and although it is a still night, the seawater wash splashes up against the side. They each turn their heads away to avoid inhaling any of the potent and dangerous seawater.

"Good risen?" Milton calls out as they reach the *Eliza Fernley*.

There is some thumping inside the boat and a clinking of marbles. A moment later, with a lantern held high, a pale, balding middle-aged man steps out onto the aft deck.

"Good risen. Mr Drake, I presume?" he says, dropping a marble from his mouth into a large pouch at his waist. Milton nods, squinting to take in the man's features. "The name's Aidan Elfman," he says. "I'm head of client transfers for Councillor Jones."

"Thank you for getting the boat ready so quickly," Milton says.

"You're welcome," says Aidan. "My master is a man of his word."

"Come on in then," he continues, unfastening a rope from one of the stanchions. "Ignore the staff; they are nearly done. I'll show you around the *Eliza*. Get you familiar with her form. She's a lovely old girl. Leave your bags for now. The staff will load them on for you."

The old lifeboat is spacious and clean inside, but nothing to write home about. Two female Founderers are in the galley scrubbing the floors. Aidan Elfman ignores them as he explains about the equipment onboard. He opens a few cupboard doors next to where the women are cleaning. One of the doors crashes into the face of one of the women.

"Steady on!" shouts Glenda. "You just hit that poor woman in the face?"

"She's a Founderer," says Aidan. "A semi-conscious slave. Doesn't matter if she gets a knock here and there."

"Well, I'd appreciate it if you didn't hit her," demands Glenda.

Aidan mutters something under his breath but backs down and tries to change the subject. He shows them some navigation equipment in the small room off the galley before wandering down the corridor to the sleeping quarters.

Another Founderer is in the hallway tidying up. He doesn't hear Aidan coming and bashes a bucket of cleaning products into Aidan's shins as he turns around.

"You worthless, good for nothing!" shouts Aidan, pushing the young man to the floor.

Albert helps the young man to his feet. "I think we can see the rest of the boat *ourselves*," Albert says, dismissing Aidan.

"If you wish," he scorns. "You know you don't need to pander to these worthless semis?" He says this with his face close to Albert's as he squeezes past him in the corridor. "They're only useful for *one* thing, you know. They work like dogs, so you should treat them like dogs."

Aidan grabs the young Founderer by the scruff of the neck and drags him after him. The young man trips over his bucket.

"Stop treating him like that!" shouts Ashley.

Aidan stops again, cutting a frustrated figure. "Look here," he exclaims. "He is *my* property. Unless you want to buy him off me? Useless piece of crap this one anyway. He's a dirty nonce. I caught him the other night with another man. Filthy waste of space."

Albert snaps. In a split-second, he lunges at Aidan and grasps the skinny man's weak neckline, shoving him up against the wall. Albert's move shocks everyone, but incredibly Nailah and Glenda immediately come to his aid. Between them, they have heard and seen all they need to hear and see and want to teach the man a lesson.

In a show of defiant force, Nailah, Glenda, and Albert wrestle Aidan Elfman into the galley, where they tie him to a chair. Meanwhile, Milton ushers the Founderers onto the deck, where they join Hassan. Despite the boat being moored, Hassan had claimed he felt 'seasick' and had stayed above deck during the brief tour.

"What the hell is this about?!" Aidan screams at them. "The trade was fair. You agreed to a price, and that's what you pay. You didn't buy the slaves; they belong to Councillor Jones. I treat them how Councillor Jones tells me to treat them. They're his property, and I'm his staff. I'm just doing what I am told."

"And you've been told to abuse these poor people?" asks Nailah.

"Yes," says Aidan. "Councillor Jones has told me, you give them an inch, they take a mile. He wants a professional workforce."

"And what about you? What do you think?"

"It doesn't matter what I think," he says, snivelling. "I'm doing a job. Councillor Jones pays me well, so I do what he tells me."

"Are you not troubled by the way you treat them? Do you not realise that you could easily have been a Founderer yourself?" asks Albert.

Aidan looks at his forearms tied to the table. The Satan's Scald marks still etched sharply into his wrists. Gareth feels his scars tingle. "That's not the point," says Aidan. "I don't get paid to think. I get paid for doing my job, and my job is making sure that the Founderers do theirs. It's a machine, and I'm just a cog."

"Just a cog?" exclaims Nailah. "Pathetic. You still have your own responsibility."

"What Councillor Jones orders is nothing unusual," claims Aidan. "Everyone in the Meadow, Water Board or Distillery, knows that the Founderers are only worth their work. They don't bring anything else to the table. It's not unusual to treat them like this. What's your problem?"

"Just because the Water Board or the Distillery say something doesn't make it right," says Glenda. "Don't you feel shame for the way you treat the Founderers? Can't you see the hurt you are causing?"

This time Aidan doesn't respond straight away. "Are you questioning the understanding of the Water Boards and the Distillery?" he says. "What are you?! Are you part of the Evil Thirst?!"

"I question *anything* if it doesn't seem just. If it is cruel," says Albert.

"You *are* part of the Thirst, aren't you?! I bloody knew it!" An evil menace comes over Aidan's face. "Just you wait. Councillor Jones will find out about you. He won't let one of his boats fly under the flag of the Thirsty. I know… I've helped him scuttle ships before."

Albert steps forward and slaps Aidan hard around the face. "This is why we've tied you up," says Albert. "I doubt you'll even recognise me?"

Aidan recoils from the strike, opens his eyes, and inspects Albert.

"Well, I recognise you," says Albert before Aidan says anything. "Forty years ago, you and I bought a ship together. Forty years ago, we set sail with our expedition from *this* port. And forty years ago, you scuttled our ship, fleeing like a coward, aboard a life raft. You *murdered* my husband!"

Aidan looks at Albert again. "But…I…you?…It can't be," he says. "The *Ellen Southard*? Are you talking about the *Ellen*

*Southard?*" Albert smiles a wry smile. "But all of you on that ship perished…"

"I didn't," smirks Albert.

Aidan looks at Albert again. The truth strikes him down. Not only is he looking at someone he thought had died. That very someone had *aged*. Nobody aged in the Meadow. "How?!" he says, "How are you…older?!"

"It's only in the Meadow that you don't age," says Albert. "I am Albert Newman. Leader of the first Cwtch Mission to the Source, your expedition leader, a true adherent to Well Wishing. You killed our team. You killed my husband. But you had no idea who you were dealing with that day. Nor this!"

"The group you see in front of you. The group who have just purchased the *Eliza Fernley* will also travel back to Earth. And there is *nothing* you can do this time to stop us. You have facilitated this. You are an accessory to this miracle!"

Aidan is dumbstruck. "The way you have treated me and the Well-Wishing community, you deserve the harshest judgement. But those are crimes of the past. The way you treat the Founderers are your crimes of the present. The brutality with which you disrespect their lives is shameful. *I* will not be your judge today. But your workers. We will let *them* decide your fate."

Aidan suddenly looks desperate. It only now occurs to him how powerless he is. "OK, OK," he stammers. "I'm sorry. What I did, I only did it because I was told to. The Distillery threatened my life. I didn't want to sink our ship. It was just my job. I was just following orders. That's all I have ever done. Do you have to understand me? It's not my fault."

"Everybody has a choice," Nailah comes in. "You have chosen to absolve yourself of the responsibility *to choose*. You may not have wanted to kill, but you have killed. You may not have wanted to wound, but you have wounded."

"Please," says Aidan, pathetically. "I can change. It's not my fault."

"I'm afraid," says Albert. "It is not us that you need to convince anymore."

They drag Aidan onto the deck where the Founderers stand with Milton and Hassan. Aidan's hands are still tied. Albert leads him by the rope to his staff. The young boy who had been struck earlier is handed the rope.

"This man has no control over you anymore," Albert says. "You no longer work for Councillor Jones or Aidan Elfman. On the pontoon, you will find a chest full of jewels. They are worth enough for each of you to leave Merseyside and make a new life outside the city. You have been treated appallingly by this man and his master. So, we leave this man's fate in your hands."

Bemused at first, very quickly, the workers rally around Aidan. The two muscular men who had collected the expedition from the university stride up to him. They grasp him by the shoulders, and his eyes fill with terror.

"You killed our Ma. You killed our Pa," says one of the men. "May the Lord have mercy on you." The other man crouches down over the side of the pontoon and pulls up a bucket full of cold seawater.

"I think, old master," says the man, "we'd like to take you for a drink." And with that, Aidan Elfman is marched away up the pontoon, fear burning through his eyes.

"OK," says Nailah, turning to the expedition. "Councillor Jones will be after us soon. Let's make haste. Ready the boat. We set sail tonight!"

*On the evening of 9th December 1886, a three-masted sailing ship, the* Mexico, *bound for Ecuador from Liverpool, went aground in gale force winds. Hearing distress signals from the stricken vessel, a Southport lifeboat, the* Eliza Fernley, *was launched to her rescue. However, disaster struck the rescue craft. The rough seas capsized the* Eliza Fernley *and consumed her in the storm. Fourteen of the sixteen lifeboat crew perished in the tragedy.*

# Chapter Nineteen

◆

# Pain on the High Seas

The *Eliza Fernley* leaves the harbour in the dead of night, unprepared for her voyage. The fate of the expedition lies in the hands of six Founderers. If they don't send Aidan Elfman 'on', he will undoubtedly raise the alarm, and they will have a whole fleet of the Water Board after them.

With no fuel in the Meadow, the headway of every sea-faring vessel depends on its crew's strength of arm and the weather's kindness. The former is not a resource that the expedition holds in abundance. However, not for the first time, they find Mother Nature on their side. A breeze blows offshore tonight, helping them out of the harbour. It even rises to a steady, consistent wind as they enter the open sea.

Within half an hour, the dock's lights and noises are distant enough to feel unthreatening. Instead, the vastness of the dark, swelling sea becomes their preoccupation. The waves slosh against the side of the vessel, and the hull of the *Eliza Fernley* creaks. High above them, the mast strains and the sails swell, flapping with sharp snaps and whips, helping them to make good headway into the Irish Sea.

"My apologies," says Nailah, stifling a yawn and breaking a silence that has settled across the deck an hour or so later. "I'm going to have to turn in. I'm shattered. Glenda, are you OK up here?"

"Oh aye," smiles Glenda, a fresh Sailor's Mist marble rattling around her teeth.

"I'll stay up too," announces Milton, the starlight casting a brooding shadow off his furrowed brow. "The rest of you should follow Nailah and get some rest."

Gareth doesn't need asking twice. He is exhausted from the last few days' trauma, excitement, and chaos.

As he follows Nailah below deck, he overhears Glenda detailing the navigation plan to Milton. They will be heading out into the Irish Sea as far as they can tonight and getting far enough from the land so that they won't attract the attention of any Distillery boats. They will then spend the day at sea before turning back to make landfall at some point tomorrow night.

As is now customary, Gareth is sharing a room with Hassan. Hassan, though, is still up on deck. He sits alone on the bow, finishing the last few marbles he pocketed from the Ferry Inn. Gareth finds himself in the cabin, trying to sleep before Hassan even turns in.

When Hassan eventually comes into the room, he looks absolutely spent of energy. Despite this, he goes straight to his bag and rifles through, checking for something before he even acknowledges Gareth. He finds what he is looking for, tightly rolls his bag back up, and pushes it under the hammock.

"What a day," he says to Gareth, holding a lit lantern aloft and ignoring that Gareth might be asleep. "There's no letting up, is there? You ready for what's next?"

Gareth isn't asleep. He is too restless. He rubs his eyes. "I'm nervous," he says. "You?"

"Nah, I'm not nervous. But don't you worry," says Hassan. "I've got your back."

Hassan sits on his hammock and looks at Gareth. His face flickers in the lamplight.

"You alright?" Gareth asks him, feeling he should say something.

"Oh, er, yeah…" says Hassan, as though he has suddenly been brought back to the present. "I'm fine."

Gareth has picked up on this today. Although Hassan is being generally more agreeable, he seems distracted, and it isn't just the marbles.

"You sure?" asks Gareth. "You can tell me if something is wrong."

Hassan looks as though he is about to say something, then catches himself. "No," he says, laying down in his hammock and extinguishing the lantern. "Everything is fine."

The gentle rocking and the repetitive creaking of the hull are ideal circumstances to fall asleep, but Gareth is tense and uneasy. He lies on his side with his eyes open. Under his covers, he holds Rose Drinkwater's phone tight against his chest and revisits the short conversation with her at Crofter's Hope. The dull rectangular lump feels like his own ball and chain. *"babe"*.

After lying in silence in the cabin for the best part of an hour, Gareth hears Hassan get up from his bunk and light the lantern again. He must be struggling to settle down too. Gareth doesn't have the energy or the desire to talk with him, so he pretends to be asleep. Lying on his side, he just listens and observes Hassan's shadow as it flickers on the wall beside him.

Hassan is being very curious. Gareth watches as his shadow sits up on his hammock and is very still for a few minutes. Hassan waves his hand as though trying to see if Gareth is awake. Intrigued, Gareth doesn't respond.

Hassan starts shuffling around under his bunk. Gareth hears his sack of belongings being pulled out from under the hammock before he carefully and quietly rifles through it. He shuffles around for a few minutes more, then Gareth hears the recognisable clinking of marbles, and a moment later, Hassan gets back into his bunk.

The hammock creaks under his body. A familiar sound of a marble being dissected comes next– the crack followed by the hiss. Gareth waits a few moments before he dares to look at Hassan in the lamplight.

Hassan is lying unconscious on his bed, deep inside a marble memory. Gareth knows better than to get too close this time. He carefully pulls himself out of his hammock and wanders over to Hassan. The young man looks troubled and in pain. The memory he is viewing is obviously causing him a great deal of discomfort.

Hassan utters a quiet but genuine moan, and Gareth can see his breathing and pulse racing. Cautious of being caught by Hassan, waking from one of his memories, Gareth returns to his hammock. He rolls over and faces the wall. It must have been a long memory that Hassan is revisiting because, by the time he resurfaces, Gareth is fast asleep.

* * *

When he wakes the next morning, Gareth looks at Hassan's hammock. He is already up and out of the cabin, and his marble pouch is gone. The rest of his belongings are strewn across the floor.

Gareth peers out of the port hole. It is barely sunrise. He can't have been asleep for long but feels wide awake. He pulls on his most comfortable clothes and wanders up on deck.

The wind that had carried the boat out into the Irish Sea last night has blown itself out. The boat rocks side to side over the calm sea. The sky has a scattering of clouds, and a pink, red, and orange hue clothes the atmosphere.

"Good risen early riser," says Nailah, standing at the helm.

"Good risen," says Gareth, rubbing the sleep out of his eyes and adjusting to the bright morning light. "Is Hassan up here?"

"He is," says Nailah. "He's been up for quite a while." Gareth gazes towards the bow where Hassan has sat again, looking troubled.

"And Milton and Glenda?" asks Gareth.

"Oh, once the wind died, I relieved them of their duties," replies Nailah. "I think they are both sleeping below deck now." Gareth nods. "Why don't you take a few coffee marbles up for Hassan?" she suggests. "He looks like he could do with one. And so do you!"

Unconvinced that more marbles are what Hassan needs right now, Gareth goes down to the galley and pulls out two dark espresso marbles from the drawer before making his way up and along the port deck, joining Hassan on the bow.

"Couldn't sleep?" he asks Hassan.

Hassan turns slowly to look at Gareth. He is paler than Gareth has ever seen him. "You OK?" Gareth asks. "Seasick?"

Hassan opens his mouth, then closes it again as though choking on his thoughts. Gareth waits a moment to see if Hassan will speak. Hassan turns and stares out to sea again.

The boat's bow dips slightly into the calm water, and a small splash of spray shoots up towards the two men. Gareth instinctively turns his head away from the potent seawater. Hassan doesn't. It doesn't look like he cares.

"Seriously, Hassan, what's wrong?" asks Gareth. "Talk to me."

Hassan continues looking out to sea. "I did something terrible," he says, not turning to look at Gareth. "And I've discovered something even worse."

Hassan is being very cryptic. Gareth reaches out and puts his hand on Hassan's shoulder. "You need to talk," he says.

Hassan looks at Gareth. It is the first time their eyes have properly met, and Hassan is entirely vulnerable. Gareth takes charge.

"Tell me what you've done," he says to Hassan.

"Not here," says Hassan, looking nervously down the deck towards Nailah.

* * *

Gareth gently closes the door to the dark anchor room. They are below deck in the bow, where none of the walls are shared with the sleeping quarters. They won't be overheard. Hassan lights a candle which he places on the floor between them.

"I found something, brother," he begins. "Something personal. Something unforgivable." He puts his head in his hands.

Gareth reaches across and puts his hand on Hassan's shoulder. It feels strange doing so. "It's OK," he says.

"It was the first night we stayed at the Ferry Inn," says Hassan, "...when everyone was in a good mood after finding out about Albert. We had shared a few decent marbles, and I was gearing up for a big night...a proper blowout...especially after the stress of Crofter's Hope… And then everyone turned in early. They even closed the bar... I was gutted."

"I went for a hunt around to see if I could find any potent marbles lying about to enjoy on my own. I was determined to have a good night, even if no one else was. I suspected Milton might be the kind of bloke with that sort of stash. And I was spot on… tucked under his seat in the lead caravan was a pouch of very intriguing marbles…"

"You remember that glow from the Inseparable Stone we saw with Kim-Joy?" Hassan asks.

Gareth nods, fingering the locket hanging around his neck.

"Well, this pouch had marbles that did the exact opposite. Not all of them, but a handful seemed to *suck* the light from the surroundings. They were darker than anything I'd ever seen, and they drew me in... They must be potent, I thought. I was about to suck one there and then, but I stopped myself: what if Milton found me and saw me with his secret stash? He already hates me. I was sure he'd chuck me off the expedition. So, I hid the marbles in my own pouch and waited to try them later when I was sure everyone was asleep."

Hassan looks up at Gareth nervously in the flickering candlelight.

"It was the middle of the night before I was sure I was in the clear. I sat at the empty bar and stared at the strange dark marbles. And I realised I *couldn't* suck them… I was too intrigued about the memories that made them so dark." He rubs his chin. "I wish that thought had never crossed my mind, brother."

Hassan shuffles irritably. "Do you remember how they inspected our Interrogation Stones at the checkpoint?" he asks Gareth, not waiting for a response. "Well, I found a needle in a drawer behind the bar and took the marbles with me to the bathroom to inspect them… I didn't want to get caught prying. Shut in the cubicle, I carefully pierced the marble and let a tiny drop of the dark sticky resin ooze onto my finger… I licked it."

Hassan loses himself in his recollection. He stares into the darkness beyond the candlelight.

"What did you see?" Gareth asks impatiently.

Hassan takes a moment, choosing his words carefully. "I saw a fragment of *Kasiya's* memory."

"I don't understand?"

"The marbles belonged to Kasiya," says Hassan.

Gareth doesn't catch up immediately. He looks at Hassan bewildered. "Oh god!" he exclaims, eventually. "Milton had Kasiya's lost marbles?!"

Hassan nods sadly. "And from what I saw in that memory fragment, and from a full memory I dissected last night, I think I know why Milton stole them…and…and…" his voice cracks. "And I think I know why Kasiya took her life."

* * *

Gareth and Hassan step onto the rear deck together. Nailah is still at the helm. Rosalyn, Albert, Ashley, and Billy are on deck with her. Milton and Glenda are still asleep below.

"Good risen," says Albert.

"Good risen," Gareth responds quietly.

"What's up with you two," asks Ashley, sensing their trepidation.

Gareth looks at Hassan, who looks at the ground. Everyone else stares at them.

"What is it?" asks Nailah.

Hassan stutters, so Gareth takes over. "Hassan has discovered something terrible," he says. He turns again to Hassan, hoping that he might just come in and help him out, but he doesn't. He simply stares at the ground.

"What is it?" Ashley asks impatiently.

Gareth clears his throat. "Hassan has stumbled on some evidence that… that some men in the Well Wishing hierarchy… have…" He takes a breath, unsure if he can formulate his words delicately enough. "Have taken advantage of vulnerable followers…"

Gareth again looks to Hassan to help him out. He feels very uncomfortable talking about this on his behalf. But Hassan keeps his eyes firmly on the ground.

"Taken advantage?" asks Glenda.

Gareth can't bring himself to elaborate. He looks across at Rosalyn, remembering what she has gone through at the Palace, and lowers his eyes.

"These sound like grave allegations," says Albert.

"I know…," says Gareth.

"And, *highly* unlikely to be true," comes in Nailah defensively. "You do know Milton is part of the spiritual hierarchy, don't you?! I think he would realise if anything like that was happening."

"Well, that's the thing…" says Gareth tentatively. "It seems he does…"

"What?!" exclaims Nailah, daggers in her eyes. "What are you accusing my husband of?!"

The full force of Nailah is too much for Gareth. He cowers away from her as she swells with rage. "Hassan, this is for you to say, not me," says Gareth, relinquishing the responsibility to its rightful owner.

All eyes turn to Hassan. He looks up, fear sweating out of his pores. He locks eyes with Nailah bravely.

"I am accusing your husband of being complicit in exploiting your daughter," he says firmly, without blinking.

Blind-sided, Nailah's defensive rage is knocked out. She stumbles and lets go of the helm. Albert catches her arm.

"How can you say that?" Nailah manages to blurt out at Hassan. "What evidence do you have?"

Hassan is scared but musters his courage to look back at Nailah. "I have *seen* it," he says.

Nailah lets out a noise, something between a yelp and a gasp. She pulls her hand in front of her mouth like she is going to be sick.

"What have you seen?" asks Albert calmly, one arm around Nailah.

Hassan looks at Gareth for reassurance. From his pocket, he produces the leather marble pouch.

"Kasiya's marbles!" exclaims Rosalyn. "Where did you find them?"

Hassan lowers his eyes. "I have a bit of a marble addiction," he concedes. "I wish I could turn it off, but I can't... My eyes are always on the lookout for potent marbles lying around... And I found this pouch..."

"You stole them?!" Ashley shouts, leaping up and slapping Hassan hard in the face. "How could you?! You made her go to the interrogation. You...you..." She can't get her words out. Hassan doesn't react.

"No, Ashley," Gareth comes in. "Hassan didn't *steal* Kasiya's marbles. He *found* them at the Ferry Inn."

Ashley looks at Gareth, confused. Hassan rubs his sore, slapped cheek.

"I have no good excuse for sneaking around pinching other people's marbles," says Hassan, calmly and resigned. "I didn't realise I had found Kasiya's missing marbles. I thought they were a secret stash belonging to Milton. They *had* been hidden by him after all." He looks directly at Nailah. "I am so sorry."

Nailah, hunched over, inspects Hassan. She doesn't look angry anymore. She seems as desperately sad as she had done the day they learnt of Kasiya's passing.

"You're accusing my husband because of what you have seen in one of her marbles, right?" Nailah asks Hassan calmly. He nods. "And do you have more of her marbles?"

Hassan opens the pouch and shows the remaining dark and mysterious marbles. His hands are shaking.

"*Trauma Stones!*" exclaims Albert, picking one of the marbles and turning it in his fingers. Like Hassan described, the light around it seems to be sucked inwards. "Poor girl."

"Before I, or any of us, act," says Nailah. "I need proof. I need the facts so that my judgement is clear and just. Nonetheless, Billy and Ashley, please can you go below deck and lock my husband's door? Rosalyn, please go and wake Glenda quietly. She needs to see this too. Hassan, I assume these Trauma Stones resemble the marble you have already witnessed?"

Hassan nods.

\* \* \*

It would be a strange sight for anyone looking down from the heavens at the *Eliza Fernley*. The large wooden fishing boat, with its sails furled and its deck clean and tidy, drifts on the calm, wide Irish Sea with eight of its nine crew lying unconscious around the helm. It looks like some cult suicide at sea. The quiet and calm are a stark contrast to the memory these eight people are witnessing.

The world in the marble memory is dark, its edges blurry. Milton Drake cracks a whip against the sturdy buttocks of a dirty grey horse. The animal pulls the two-berth carriage he rides with his daughter, Kasiya. They are hurtling through dense conifers while a storm rages overhead.

Pine needles, small branches, and bullets of rain smash against the two riders. Milton angrily shouts at the horse to keep galloping. He looks furious and determined. The state of his clothes indicates that they have been riding through the storm for many hours.

Next to her father, Kasiya lies in sodden blankets. She is strapped to the platform like Glenda had strapped Gareth and Rosalyn on the dash from Crofter's Hope. She looks dazed.

Kasiya's mouth droops, and a marble falls out, smashing with a hiss as it impacts the ground under the carriage. The memory clears momentarily, with Milton coming into sharp focus. He plunges his hand into a deep sack by his feet, pulling out another marble and forcing it into Kasiya's mouth. The young woman, who had momentarily looked more alert, falls back into a sleepy daze, and the edges around the memory take on a blur again.

Staring into the dense forest, Milton tugs on the reins to slow the horse down. He checks where they are on a crumbling wet map and then whips the horse back into a frenzy, driving them further into the forest.

A short, chaotic, and bumpy ride later – which Gareth discovers can actually make you nauseous even when visiting as a memory – a familiar location comes into view.

Milton brings the carriage to a clattering halt. He ties the horse to the gateway and hauls Kasiya over his shoulder, trudging arduously into the cloisters. The clumsily built old stone monastery looms in front of them.

"Good risen!" Milton hollers through the rain and the wind. There is no monastic chanting around them this time. "Good risen?" he shouts again earnestly.

Gareth looks around the cloisters. High above him, the bells from the tower toll twice, just like they had when they had been there before. He looks by the river to where the wash-up is situated. It brings back a haunting memory. That moment he had stolen with Kasiya is now drowned in deep and painful regret.

Milton hauls Kasiya over to the base of the tower, where an old and unfamiliar monk opens the door. "Mr Drake," he says in a wiry, frail voice.

Milton struggles to raise his hand over his forehead in the salute of the Well Wishers. He bows his head.

"*May the seas warm and the clouds form…*" begins the monk.

"*…and may the rain fall, filling the rivers of Love,*" Milton completes.

"Is this her?" the monk asks. "Your offspring. Your Isaac. Your babe to the slaughter."

Milton doesn't pander to the metaphors. "This is my daughter," he says. "Presented in service to the great leaders of Well Wishing."

"Excellent, Mr Drake. Excellent," responds the monk. "As God tested Abraham, you have been tested. You have shown yourself worthy to become High Councillor of Well-Wishing. The Lord expects his servants to be willing to sacrifice anything for him. Even our own flesh and blood."

Milton steps into the doorway and lays Kasiya on a dark wooden bench. "I am the Lord's humble servant," he says, not looking at his daughter.

"Then, Mr Drake, I will send word of your elevation to the position of High Councillor. You have fulfilled all of our requests."

"And the expeditions?" says Milton. "Will I now be granted leadership of my own?"

"Oh, yes, yes. Of course," says the monk. "I'm surprised you still want to go ahead with these expeditions of yours. You've got more here than you'd ever have back on Earth, you know? And besides, do you *really* think we can return?!"

"My faith is not as cynical as yours," says Milton.

The old monk chuckles and looks at Kasiya. "You're deluding yourself, Mr Drake," he says. "But that's your prerogative… Now go, make yourself at home over the way. And send over His Wellness. I don't believe our priest has met your daughter before."

Before Milton has even left the tower, the monk strikes Kasiya with his palm, waking her. Milton doesn't come to her aid. The old monk is savage in his impatience. He pulls off the wet robe covering Kasiya and inspects her before leaning in and stroking her damp hair. Still, Milton does nothing.

The old monk's depravity for the semi-conscious young woman makes Gareth sick and angry. He can't witness any more. He knows enough. He's seen enough. He tries to get out of the room through the door that Milton stands in, but as Kasiya's memory doesn't stretch that far, he is locked inside the four stone walls with her.

Gareth screams at Milton with venom and rage as the shameless coward leaves the tower, but no sound comes out of his mouth. Gareth tries to close his eyes, but they won't close. He tries covering his ears, but he can't. Witnessing a memory is *witnessing* a memory. All he can do is look away. Indeed, Kasiya looks away the whole time. But the sounds alone are traumatising.

Gareth feels himself plunging into the deepest despair when the priest – the same man he recognises from when he was last in the monastery – bursts in a moment later.

* * *

Glenda reaches across and holds Nailah's hand while she remains unconscious, witnessing the end of her daughter's traumatic memory. Nailah is the last of the group to come around. The others have returned but say nothing. Rosalyn looks to the floor. Ashley and Billy sob. Albert and Hassan look out to sea. No one looks one another in the eye, for in each other's eyes is too much pain.

Nailah's shock when she eventually emerges quickly turns to rage. She stands up, knocking a coil of rope onto the floor. Albert and Glenda leap to their feet beside her. "Let me do what I need to do," she says to them.

"Let us help you do it," says Albert.

Gareth stares into the hatch as Nailah, Glenda, and Albert crash below deck. He hears the lock rattle on Milton's cabin and a startled moan from the man himself. There is a muted thump as Nailah lays her first blow on him.

There aren't many audible words in the minutes that follow. The fury of Nailah's sharp screams slices into their ears. Milton's gruff shouts and grunts become less and less recognisable. The slaps crack, and the kicks thud, providing an irregular beat to the melody of Nailah's rage.

A short while later, Milton Drake is dragged up on deck, in full and shameful view of the entire expedition. His hands and feet are tied; his mouth gagged. He is heavily bruised with a deep cut above his left eye. His breathing is shallow and laboured. Having just witnessed Kasiya's memory, the man's very presence is sickening.

Nailah instructs Glenda and Albert to hold Milton on deck. She goes back down into the galley and returns with a mug and an inflatable life raft. Throwing the raft overboard, she watches it inflate and float away slowly. Then she shoves Milton down onto the step that splashes in the water at the stern. She pulls out a knife and cuts loose Milton's hands and feet, thrusting the mug into his grasp. She leaves the gag in place.

"You despicable, disgusting being!" Nailah spits at Milton. "Never will your soul wound mine again. I forbid it. This mug is for you; if you have any courage or decency, you will drink from the ocean. If not, you can pray for forgiveness and hope your raft doesn't sink." She points to the inflatable raft floating away from them.

"You make me sick!" she exclaims, thrusting both hands into Milton's chest, making him fall backwards.

Milton's back arches as he falls, but with his mouth gagged, he falls silently. He plunges with an almighty splash into the deep cold ocean.

At first, Gareth thinks Milton has sunk. Then his body comes to the surface, his arms and legs flailing. There is shock in his eyes. Nailah spits into the sea beside Milton and turns away, wandering across the deck and into the cabin.

"Make sure he doesn't swim back," Glenda says to the others as she follows after Nailah.

Gareth watches in disbelief as Milton Drake, mug in hand, struggles in the water, fully clothed, towards the raft that is rapidly drifting away. He never looks back at the boat. He doesn't even try and remove his gag. He just swims. The disgraced man has accepted his fate.

The last they see of Milton before he disappears over the horizon, he reaches the raft and hauls himself like a wounded sea lion onto the vessel. But Mother Nature has already sealed his fate. A gentle breeze grows to a rasping blow, and the hungry sea swells.

The *Eliza Fernley* unfurls her sails, and the next phase of the journey begins, south by southeast towards the coast of North Wales. They will not see the life raft or Milton Drake again.

*On the morning of 20th August 1868, a complicated shunting operation on the train lines near Abergele, North Wales, didn't go to plan. A goods train was derailed in the process and was left blocking the main line to Holyhead – a key coastal port linking the British Isles to Ireland. Trying to rectify the situation, rail crews outside Abergele attended the derailment. But in doing so, they inadvertently left a brake-van with six heavily loaded wagons, full of paraffin, uncoupled on the rails. Approaching Abergele later that morning was an Irish Mail train from London. This large train was pulled by the powerful Prince of Wales engine, and in addition to its mail carts, it had eight passenger carriages. Tragically, the uncoupled paraffin wagons left outside Abergele weren't on a flat section of track and, after an accidental shunt by crews working on the derailment, they started hurtling out of control towards the town. Just after midday the wagons collided with the Irish Mail train travelling the other way, exploding into an immense and deadly fireball just outside Abergele. In all, thirty-three souls aboard the train were lost in the disaster.*

# Chapter Twenty

◆

# Sea Fret and Platforms

Keeping the *Eliza Fernley* upright and on course in the blowing gale and driving rain is a fight. Glenda and Albert are below deck with Nailah, re-evaluating their situation. The rest are battling valiantly against the elements, steering the boat through the steep breaking waves.

Around mid-afternoon, Albert pokes his head up on deck. He holds a steaming bowl of marbles. In the chaotic weather, the vapours whip away frantically, and the older man struggles to stand. He offers the marbles to the crew. "Sailor's Mist," he calls out. "This is just the weather they were brewed for!"

"How's Nailah doing?" Ashley shouts back, leaning close to Albert's ear and grabbing a marble.

"She's made of strong stuff," says Albert, smiling reassuringly.

"Are we still heading for the coast tonight?" shouts Gareth from the helm. He looks apprehensively at the next cresting wave breaking across the bow.

"Not sure," he shouts back. "We're still figuring out the best plan of action. For now, set a course due west! Let's head into wind and stall any progress for a while."

\* \* \*

By late afternoon, the wind graciously dies down. The sea is still a bit choppy, but it is much easier to maintain a westward heading. The *Eliza Fernley* rocks back and forth untroubled. With no need for a helm, Albert invites the deck crew down into the galley for a status update.

Nailah sits in the same seat where they had tied up Aidan Elfman at Mersey Docks. Her right hand is bandaged, her knuckles bleeding through the cloth, and her eyes are bloodshot. She smiles bravely at the others as they join her around the galley table.

"We will continue as planned," she tells them precisely and clearly. "As soon as the wind is favourable and the sky is dark, we will seek landfall in North Wales. There is no sense in any delay."

She takes a deep breath and looks around at them. "However, I will not be taking the step with you back to Earth anymore…"

Ashley gasps. Billy throws his hand in front of his mouth in disbelief. Nailah raises a hand to calm them. "There is nothing on Earth for me anymore. A dark stain has been etched on my family. My path has been altered outside of my control."

Somewhere below, the hull creaks and the boat moans into the depths of the sea.

No one knows what to say, so Nailah continues. "I will keep leading our expedition… for now, at least. But don't worry. More than ever, I am determined to get you to the Source and ensure your safe passage home. The integrity of Well Wishing depends on it. But *that* dark stain needs to be cleaned. And *that* is my calling now."

"I will stay in the Meadow after you leave, and I will expose the filth who have tried to defile Well Wishing. Those men my husband associated with and anyone who has turned a blind eye. They should all be afraid. Because I will be after them, and I have nothing to fear and nothing to lose."

Nailah's fierce conclusion leaves a resonating silence. Glenda stands up and embraces her. Albert follows suit. One by one, the rest of the expedition join the huddle, even Hassan. No one says a word.

In the silence, the *Eliza Fernley* slaps gently against the rolling sea, and in the sky above, they hear a distant rumbling sound. A flash of light indicates the emergence of an Opening far away. A change in the weather is fast approaching.

"Let's take a moment to clear our minds," says Albert. "If you need to, take a marble or two. For when the weather gets here, we head for the coast."

\* \* \*

Gareth sits on the boat's stern, looking out to sea, watching the weather coming in. Ashley sits beside him, doing the same. Their feet dip into the water together. It is the first moment they have shared alone since Fidler's Ferry.

"The Meadow is beautiful, isn't it?" muses Ashley.

Gareth looks at her, the colours of the evening sky illuminating her face. "It is," he says.

"Why does such pain always cut through beauty?" Ashley asks, thinking of Kasiya and Milton.

Gareth looks down at the water rushing around their feet and ponders for a moment. He points his toes like arrowheads and punctures the surface. "I wonder if we would be better seeing beauty, not as a state fragile to being slashed, cut, or broken," he says. "But instead, more like flowing water?"

Gareth reaches into his pocket and feels the old lifeless mobile phone from Rose Drinkwater's car. He turns it over in his hands, feeling its weight and the burden on his soul.

"When water is punctured," he says. "It flows around. It can't be broken. Maybe pain can't cut through beauty, either. It just punctuates its flow."

Ashley reaches across and grasps Gareth's hand, interlocking her fingers with his. Gareth feels the goosebumps on Ashley's skin as he strokes her forearm. He wishes this moment could last forever. But watching the cold waves grow to a crescendo, he knows the time is coming for the next part of the journey.

\* \* \*

The first sighting of the land is eerie. Dark mountainous shadows appear off the starboard bow, growing into a looming dark mass. Those not crewing the helm or on lookout are below deck and packing bags, stowing marbles, and strapping essential survival gear wherever there is space. The expedition is ready to make landfall.

It isn't long before the *Eliza Fernley* gently touches down on sand and seaweed. The beach they have found is tucked away behind a bulging rocky land mass, sheltered from the wind and deathly still.

Water laps up against the crew's bare ankles as they disembark, holding their bags and equipment above their heads. Last off the boat is Nailah. Heart aching, she makes one last trip down into the cabin she shared with Milton.

Re-emerging a minute later, she steers the *Eliza Fernley* back out to sea, fastening the rudder for an offshore course and opening the portholes to encourage the vessel to take on water. Finally, she clambers down the stern and lowers herself into the sea.

Altogether, they watch as the uncrewed boat drifts away.

"*This is it,*" thinks Gareth. "*There's no turning back now.*" They are deep in Distillery territory. There is no sympathy for their plight here.

Glenda and Nailah consult the map. They have a few hours' walk ahead of them in the darkness, in which they must cover as much ground as they can before reaching the first band of hills in the Mynydd mountain range – the location of the Mountain of the Source.

The lands on the approach to the mountains are sparsely populated. In the darkness, Gareth feels the remoteness watching him. The hushing of ferns and a distant whistle of wind is all that the desolate grounds offer.

In no time, the ground begins to creep upwards, and the sky lightens before dawn. Soon it is a rocky scramble between Heather and Hawthorn. Then, as the grand vista of the lands they have crossed come into view, Nailah brings them to a stop in a large boulder field. The vantage over the valley below gives the expedition ample warning of any approaching danger.

Glenda unpacks some of the magic mushrooms they have collected on the journey before Crofter's Hope. A very slight fog is drifting up the valley, and chewing the mushrooms should lessen its effects.

"We won't stop long," Nailah says. "We want to be at Pont Fawr by dusk."

"Pont Fawr?" asks Gareth, concerned. "Isn't that where the train lines go?"

"It is," says Nailah.

"Don't we want to be avoiding people?" asks Hassan.

"We do," says Nailah. "But as we approach the mountains, our safest cover will be the chaos of the arriving trains. The entire perimeter of the Source Mountain, and the lands in its shadow, are heavily patrolled by the Distillery. The trains and the station are our best hope of breaking through the border."

Nailah unfolds the large map. An item inherited from Professor Pelling. Gareth notices it is an Ordnance Survey map. One that must have been collected from an arrival into the Meadow. The names on the map have been pencilled over with what Gareth presumes are equivalent names of the places in the Meadow.

Right in the centre of the map, concentric brown contours close in on one another to a trig point. The top of the Mountain. Gareth can see the name that had been there on Earth, Mynydd Aaru. He knows this name all too well, and memories of home flash through his mind.

Nailah traces her finger from the edge of the map to where spidery black lines converge on a point northeast of Mynydd Aaru. "Pont Fawr," she says. "The confluence of the train lines."

Gareth looks closely at the lines– dozens of them, arriving from all parts of the Meadow. Nailah traces a dashed red line from Pont Fawr around the Mountain, creating a sizeable imperfect circle. "These are the Distillery's patrol zones," she says. "Previous reconnaissance helped draw these lines. This reconnaissance also told us the Distillery soldiers who patrol the zone are armed. Armed with a whole assortment of lethal weapons collected from arrivals."

"You don't see many guns in the Meadow," Glenda informs them, noticing Gareth and Hassan's confused faces. "Like fuel, we don't have the infrastructure. We can't produce the parts or make the projectiles. Most weapons that come through an Opening tend to have no ammunition. But some might have a single bullet or magazine."

"The Distillery have scoured all the war-time arrivals to amass a collection of these loaded firearms," says Nailah. "The collection is supposedly held along this perimeter to '*protect*' the Source. It is a perilous place... Whatever happens, we must not give the Distillery guards any reason to be alarmed."

Nailah drags her finger to the edge of the map. "This is where we are," she says, indicating a cluster of contours. "We'll follow this ridgeline down to the trees. We'll arrive somewhere to the north of Pont Fawr, hopefully without incident, in a few hours."

"What do you remember of Pont Fawr?" Glenda asks Albert, who is studying the map intensely.

"Not much," he admits. "I vaguely remember trains, mist, and a bridge. Not much more."

"As long as we stay out of sight, we should have time to formulate a plan," Nailah ponders. "But I expect once we reach Pont Fawr, the shallow mist from the mountains will surround us. We must keep our wits. We'll wear face coverings as well as chewing the mushrooms to keep out as much moisture as we can."

"If we can find a way past Pont Fawr station, we should have a clear passage from there, past the Distillery mountain mines, and all the way to the Mountain. We don't believe the mines are guarded. So, hopefully, we'll make good time and distance once we are past the station. Our priority is to get past Pont Fawr."

Nailah folds up the map. Around her, the rest of the group is silent. They know that they are now heading into significant danger.

"This could be our last view of the Meadow, outside the mist," mutters Billy. "I wish I could appreciate it properly without feeling so afraid."

Gareth looks at the young man. He is shivering, and his teeth are chattering. Rosalyn reaches across and holds his hand.

"It's OK," she says. "We'll all be together in the mist, Billy. If you are right, and we don't see the Meadow again, just think, you'll be going somewhere better. Somewhere to be reunited with your family."

Billy looks back at Rosalyn and tries to put on a brave smile. "I'm nervous," he admits.

"There's no point being scared," says Hassan, clumsily adding his opinion. "Grit your teeth and try not to think of the worst outcomes. That's what I do. You just need to be brave, Billy."

"Thanks, Hassan... I think," says Billy, politer than Hassan's comments deserve.

"Billy," says Nailah gently. "Drifters leave this realm because something is drawing them towards it… drawing them 'on'. I believe that going 'on' could be as beautiful as going 'back' if not more. If it helps, I try not to see the mist as a shroud but more as a blanket. Going 'on' or going 'back', we are all together." She shuffles over to Billy. "Let's all have a good hug," she says, smiling and beckoning the group to join them.

In the embrace, Gareth feels Ashley's hand reach across to his. She squeezes his palm lovingly, and he squeezes back. "*Whatever happens,*" he thinks. "*I'm going wherever you go.*"

* * *

If not for the circumstances, it is a pleasant ramble through the hillside to Pont Fawr. The ridge and then the forest are peaceful and quiet. It is as though human hands have never touched the world here. They even forage perfectly ripened poppy seed pods. The first opportunity to bolster their anaesthetic supplies since Gareth used it for his wounded hand at Crofter's Hope.

Billy's skills as a forager, picking out the most potent plants, is a very welcome asset. But it isn't long before they hear the first sounds of the trains, and their attention turns to their immediate danger. The familiar clanking of iron wheels on iron tracks and the shouts of the Distillery guards encouraging their horses to keep pulling the carriages.

The expedition sneaks through the forest, half a kilometre north of the northernmost rail. It is here that Gareth realises just how much the sky is changing and the light is fading.

"The mist is coming," says Glenda. "Time to cover up."

They each pull neckerchiefs over their faces, looking like bandits about to rob a train. Breathing through the cloth, Gareth feels his eyesight sharpen again. It is amazing what even the shallow mist can do.

Trudging further into the forest, silent and alert, the mist dances around them more and more. Then they hear screams. Blood-curdling screams of the Founderers coming off the trains and trying to escape the guards. Gareth feels like he is sneaking across the borders of a nightmare. At times the mist becomes so thick that he can only see a dozen paces in front of him, and in the darkness, he starts to feel cold and afraid.

Nailah's navigation is good. They reach a planned outcrop of rock without mistake. From here, despite the fog, they can see down to the station in the valley below. Even when expected, it is still quite startling to see all the train lines closely parallel, running through the wild and misty valley, and the dark grey station buildings standing in stark inanimate contrast to the living forest.

Dotted around the buildings are dozens of Distillery guards, all wearing tight-fitting gas masks, protecting them from the mist. They look menacing, even from this distance. And standing proud at one of the platforms, whispering in the fog, is a long snaking train, its rear carriages bearing the label of the *Irish Mail*.

The disembarking of passengers has not quite finished. The last of the Founderers are struggling and fighting with the guards, desperately trying to avoid the Thermocline spray. There is a young woman whose dress is ripped. She kicks and scratches but is eventually overcome by four guards and pinned down. A fifth guard leans in and releases his canister.

From the distance of their vantage point, the expedition sees the woman scream before they hear her. In an instant, she goes unconscious and joins the dozens of other drifting souls at the end of the platform, heading beyond the train line to a steep three-arched stone bridge and the mountains beyond.

As the last of the Founderers leaves the platform, the unloading of the Drifters begins. The hundreds of unconscious passengers are so tightly packed into the old mail carriages that when the first doors are opened, half a dozen bodies tumble straight out onto the platform. Their emaciated forms are filthy and wounded.

The Drifters drag their bodies, limping and crawling, any way they can manage, towards the end of the platform. The guards don't have to do anything to get their compliance. For the most part, they stand back, allowing the Drifters to pass. But at the bridge, they aren't left alone. Guards standing here put shackles around the necks of the unconscious and forcefully lead them beyond the bridge and towards the thicker mist and the Mountain.

The activity doesn't stop there either. Distillery officers in sooty black overalls lead another procession of Drifters the other way, back across the bridge. This procession is, likewise, tied together by shackles, but they carry heavy wooden barrels, two to a barrel. Their Distillery chaperones pull them by a rope, keeping them from wandering in their natural direction back towards the mountains.

"What are they doing?" Gareth whispers.

"Not sure," says Glenda. "The Distillery mines are just beyond Pont Fawr. They dig for rare mineral wealth contained inside the Mountain. I think they might be using the Drifters to help load the extracted material onto the city-bound trains."

"We've seen enough for now," interrupts Nailah, gesturing back into the cover of the trees. "Let's not get ourselves spotted. Are you happy with the plan, Billy?" she asks pointedly.

Billy nods.

"Wait, what plan is this?" asks Hassan. "Have I missed something?"

"I'll explain in a second," says Nailah, crouching under a low-hanging branch.

Nailah gathers them around her in the shadow of a giant conifer, out of sight of the station. "To get over the bridge," she announces, "we must get in amongst the Drifters leaving the trains. Save for being a Distillery guard; no one else goes to the Mountain."

"Did you see, when the doors to the Drifters were first opened, the bridge was overwhelmed by numbers? Well, during the rush, the guards on the bridge stood aside, letting them cross unshackled. You could be forgiven for missing it in the chaos we just witnessed. Anyway, they only started shackling once the numbers had settled down again. So…"

"We need to get ourselves in amongst that main group of Drifters," says Gareth, joining the dots.

"Exactly," says Nailah, smiling. "There's a problem, however. We don't exactly look like Drifters. We're too healthy. We will stand out too much amongst the emaciated. Even in the crowds. Which is why we are planning a distraction." She looks across at Billy and smiles knowingly. "I'll let you detail the plan, Billy."

Billy nervously looks around at the rest of them. "We might not look like Drifters," he says. "But we can easily pass off as recently sprayed Founderers – I mean, we look no different to them."

"The plan is, I sneak down to the station, under a parked train and, while the guards spray the Founderers, open the doors to the Drifter's carriages… They'll be faced with both sets of passengers simultaneously, and there will be chaos." Billy grins mischievously and glances at Hassan, almost seeking his approval.

"I like it," says Albert. "They couldn't shackle everyone. And if we can get amongst the crowds on the bridge at this time, we could definitely sneak through unnoticed."

"I know it sounds risky," concedes Nailah. "There will be a lot of canisters and plenty of people. But I think it's our best option…"

"Does Billy have to be the one sneaking down and opening the carriages?" says Rosalyn looking concerned.

"It needs to be someone small and agile," starts Nailah.

"I want to do it," Billy cuts in defensively.

"It's a *brave* task if ever I heard one," says Hassan. "A *man's* task." He pats Billy on the back and gives him a wink.

* * *

Wind whistles around the station. Up in the sky, thunder rumbles and heavy rain falls. Another distant Opening has changed it to a most unpleasant evening. The large horses pulling the latest train into Pont Fawr are sodden and dirty, straining under the weight of their cargo. A few dozen strides away, crouching deep in the thick undergrowth, Nailah and the expedition hold their breath.

Gas-masked Distillery officers from the station house pile onto the platform, bracing themselves against the wind and rain, gathering around the Founderer carriages at the front end of the platform. There is a sharp whistle, and the doors are opened. Shouts and screams follow, but the expedition members with Nailah aren't watching. While the Distillery's attention is drawn, they peer at the space below the train. Billy is somewhere under there, crawling on his belly, heading towards the Drifter carriages.

Suddenly a Distillery guard starts blowing his whistle frantically. "The Drifter carriages are open!" he hollers. Billy must have succeeded.

The other guards, busy discharging canisters on the Founderers, stop and look around. In a moment, the platform is inundated with Drifters. Seeing their opportunity, some of the Founderers who have yet to be sprayed make a run for it. Soon, people are charging everywhere. The shouting and screaming become even more desperate than a normal disembarking as Thermocline Mist erupts everywhere. It is chaos. But the plan has worked even better than the expedition hoped. The guards patrolling the bridge see the commotion and promptly leave their posts to assist.

Ashley spots it first. "The bridge," she shouts. "There's no guards on the bridge!"

"Let's go for it now!" shouts Glenda, jumping to her feet.

"What about Billy?" screams Rosalyn into the rain.

"We'll have to wait for him on the other side," says Nailah. "We can't do anything for him here."

Rosalyn looks back at the commotion on the platform. Billy is somewhere in the bedlam. "I'm staying," she demands. "I'll come across with the main glut, as planned. I want to be available if Billy needs help."

"Fine," shouts Nailah. There isn't time to argue. "But be careful!"

"If you're staying, I'm staying," Hassan announces, swelling with chivalry.

"OK," says Nailah, knowing Hassan won't be talked down. "But no more." She looks sincerely at Rosalyn and Hassan. "Good luck," she says.

Leaving Rosalyn and Hassan in the trees, the others splash along the dirt track, running heads-down towards the bridge. With their face coverings on, they will be exposed should the Distillery see them. But such is the commotion at the station; nobody turns. They hurtle over the steep hump of Pont Fawr bridge without stopping and run into the forest beyond. As they hoped, there is no Distillery presence on this side of the bridge.

"Keep an eye out for Rosalyn and the others," says Nailah, crouching in the undergrowth.

From their new hiding place, they can only see the exit of Pont Fawr Bridge. They can't even hear the chaos from the station anymore. For a while, that's all there is – just an empty, lifeless and quiet bridge, relentlessly hammered by the rain. But then droves of Drifters appear. They are soaked and buffeted by the wind, tripping over one another as they cross the bridge.

"There's Hassan!" shouts Ashley.

The young man is struggling over the bridge. He's carrying something. Someone. Gareth and Ashley spot them at the same time, and both, without thinking, run out from the clearing to help.

It's Rosalyn's limp body in Hassan's arms. Her leg is badly wounded. Gareth looks around to see if Billy is nearby, but the young man is nowhere to be seen. With no time to waste, Gareth and Ashley help Hassan carry Rosalyn into the trees with the others. Rosalyn moans in pain.

Hassan lays Rosalyn down on the wet ground. He looks absolutely exhausted and worried. Glenda barges in and pulls out some bright green marbles. "These will numb the pain," she says, handing them to Rosalyn. "This is the best we can do for now. Suck on them, my dear."

"I tried," Rosalyn cries weakly, placing two green marbles into her mouth. "I tried so hard, but I couldn't help him."

"Billy," says Hassan, breathing heavily. "There were just so many guards, and they were indiscriminate with their canisters. Billy didn't stand a chance."

"He was sprayed?" asks Nailah.

"Yes," cries Rosalyn. "I tried to help him, but they just sprayed them all."

"I thought you were going 'on' too," says Hassan to Rosalyn. "A canister was discharged so close to your head."

"That's when I hurt my leg," says Rosalyn, struggling with the pain. "I got trampled… I think. I don't remember much…" Rosalyn tries to shuffle her body, but her leg twists violently, and she grimaces.

"We'll need to splint it," says Glenda, looking worried, "The pain will linger despite the marbles. We've got the poppy seed pods we can grind up and smoke later, but for now, the marbles are the best we can do."

Hassan reaches out to help Rosalyn get comfortable. His hand shakes uncontrollably. "I'm sorry," he says. "I tried to keep you safe."

Gareth looks back at the bridge. Dozens of Drifters are still making their way over. He tries to pick out Billy, but there are too many people. The Distillery is gaining control of the situation again, and the guards are now going to each passing person and shackling their necks with thick leather collars and large metal rings.

"Let's get further into the forest," says Nailah. "There's nothing we can do for Billy. He's on a new journey now. We need to get well out of Distillery sight. Then we can grind the poppies and consult the map. I've got a few ideas of where we are most likely to find our way to the Source."

The problem with Nailah's plan is that she has assumed, based on the green section on the OS map of the Mountain, that there is a sizeable expansive forest beyond Pont Fawr. It would usually be a reasonable assumption. Most maps from Earth underestimate the green areas in the Meadow. However, within ten minutes, they reach the edge of Pont Fawr forest, far from the scree slopes of the Mountain. Decades of deforestation have cleared the land. Where once ancient oaks and deciduous trees would have dominated the landscape, now the ground is scarred and bare, covered in debris and littered with the machinery of the Distillery mines.

The expedition could be forgiven for not noticing the land, however. For towering out from the mist in front of them is the Mountain of the Source, Mynydd Aaru. The mountain thrusts itself aggressively into the storm above. A great snow-covered shaft of rock reaching into the dark and angry evening sky. Its slopes are sharp, icy, and daunting.

The whole expedition stands momentarily, mouths wide open, at the Mountain's hostile interruption into the landscape. They each feel its presence in their own way. Hassan feels a throbbing sense of grandeur in the Mountain's wake. Rosalyn feels the thrilling draw of its gleaming distant surface. Albert, the familiarity of destiny. Nailah, the tiresome cries of creaking ice that clings to its cliffs. Glenda, the confronting challenge of its role in her journey. And both Gareth and Ashley feel their own universal insignificance, hidden in the shadows of the Mountain's intimidating form. Gareth wonders how anybody, Drifter or not, could possibly ascend its face.

"I remember standing right here before," says Albert. "I remember trudging through that boggy, scarred earth before getting to the Mountain."

Gareth turns his gaze to the foreground, noticing what appears to be livestock pulling heavy machinery for the mines. "Where are all the miners?" he asks. "The animals seem to be doing all the work themselves."

"They're not animals," whispers Ashley.

Gareth looks again. She is right. The *animals* pulling the carts and heavy excavation machinery are people. Shackled by the neck in groups of twos, threes, and fours, they drag the heavy equipment over the land.

"My God!" exclaims Glenda. "They are employing the Drifters to work *down* the mines as well!"

"So it seems," concedes Nailah.

Half a dozen unburdened passengers from the latest train wander unconsciously through the debris in front of them, heading towards the Mountain. A couple of Distillery guards wearing gas masks are in pursuit. One grasps the loose end of the Drifters' shackles and pulls the group towards an empty mine cart a short distance away. Another connects a thick heavy rope to the group's shackles. This line is fed through a pulley and fastened to a wire rail that leads towards a mine tunnel.

Once attached, the Drifters are left to continue their unconscious wandering toward the Source, but now they are pulling the heavy cart along with them, and the wire rail will pull them into the mine, not to the cliffs.

"There must be thousands of Drifters working here," says Gareth, appreciating the vastness of the operation in front of them.

"You're right," says Glenda, frowning. "This is not the dignified end that any Drifter should be granted."

"Let's not linger while there is still daylight," says Nailah. "We can't get to the Mountain with all the Distillery guards around. Let's take shelter and wait for nightfall."

\* \* \*

The storm lets up as evening approaches. What had been heavy, blustery rain and strong winds in the day turns to cold, gentle snow. Gareth watches a delicate snowflake tumble through the forest canopy and settle silently on a branch above him. All sounds amongst the trees, where the expedition lie waiting, are muffled.

Far in the distance, the clanking of the Drifters' shackles sounds like jingling bells. The whole landscape reminds Gareth of Christmas. He loved Christmas. It was a time of year when everyone, no matter their circumstances, tried to smile. He allows himself to dwell on these fond memories for a moment. It had nearly been Christmas when he arrived in the Meadow. If they manage to return, it will nearly be Christmas again. His heart leaps at the thought, and again, the mist dissipates slightly.

Soon the daylight is all but gone. Nailah stands up and trudges away into the shadows to inspect the activity around the mines. "The land is quiet," she whispers, returning moments later. "The Drifters have been tethered. The guards are gone. Now is as good a time as any to make our way to the Mountain."

Gareth stands up and rubs his hands together. His body temperature has dropped significantly in the last few hours. In fact, the whole expedition feels groggy. Like they have just woken from a deep sleep. The cold and the mist are having a significant impact.

Rosalyn moans with pain. The latest anaesthetic marble is wearing off, and even the poppy seed pipe isn't helping any more. The young woman, pale and cold, lolls her eyes and falls to the ground, her poppy pipe hissing in the snow.

"Rosalyn, are you OK?" calls Ashley urgently.

She doesn't respond.

Hassan rushes to Rosalyn's aid, kneeling next to her. "Rosalyn?" he says desperately, embracing her shivering, damp body. She opens her eyes slowly but doesn't say anything.

"Let me look at her leg," says Glenda, shuffling beside Hassan. "Let's see if there is any more we can do."

Glenda cuts the tight denim jeans from Rosalyn's legs up to her knees. The sight of Rosalyn's right leg makes Gareth wretch. She has a compound fracture. A shard of bone from her shin sticks out. Congealed red bloody sinews, ruptured skin, and bruising, surround the entire lower half of her leg. Her black jeans had hidden the blood loss, which now drips in bright contrast to the snow.

Glenda and those looking at Rosalyn's leg are silent for a moment until Glenda says, "Rosalyn, dear, I'm not sure we are going to be able to fix your leg."

Rosalyn looks at her desperately. "What do you mean?" she asks.

Glenda stutters.

"My brave, brave girl," says Nailah, stepping in. "Your injury is too bad. There is no way to heal you. We can take away your pain with more poppies, and we will. But we cannot fix your leg. There is too much damage."

"What does that mean?" Rosalyn asks, fearing the worst.

"Without remedy, I'm afraid your body will fade," says Nailah. She pauses and grasps hold of both of Rosalyn's cold, shaking hands. "I'm sorry, Rosalyn. I think your journey here in the Meadow is ending."

Rosalyn stares at Nailah, trying to process what she is being told. Hassan tries to protest, but Glenda stops him, embracing him tightly.

"Rosalyn, what you have done for this group, for me, for my daughter, has been incredible," Nailah says. "Thank you."

She reaches into her bag and pulls out a canister of Thermocline Mist. "I've been carrying these since we left Lin," she says. "I have enough for one canister each."

"Oh no!" whimpers Ashley, tears falling down her face.

Gareth inspects the canister in Nailah's hand. The cold metal tube is dull and uninteresting. It has a simple discharge mechanism on its neck. Such a dangerous potential. It would be so easy to end the journey there and now.

Nailah hands the canister to Rosalyn. "Controlling our fate is a gift. Use this on yourself when you are ready."

She pulls out a small pot of ground poppy seed pods. "Rub this into your wounds," she says. "And let us give you the dignity to go 'on' in private."

They are all in shock. Rosalyn shivers uncontrollably but takes the pot from Nailah and pours the dusty contents over her exposed shin, relieving her pain. She looks up at them all and offers a brave smile. Her smile triggers a tear to fall down Gareth's cheek.

"Please send my love to Kasiya when you see her in the beyond," says Nailah initiating a group embrace.

"I will," says Rosalyn.

They hold tightly together for a minute while snow falls on their exposed heads. When they break apart, together they help Rosalyn onto her feet.

"Give Cerys a hug from me," Rosalyn says to Gareth. "Tell her that I remember her and that no matter which way she goes, back or forth, someone is waiting for her."

"I will," says Gareth, smiling reassuringly at Rosalyn, wiping the tears from his eyes.

Rosalyn turns at Hassan. The young man's shock is frozen across his face. She leans forward and kisses him on the lips. Hassan tries to say something. His eyes are glazed.

"It's OK," says Rosalyn. "You don't have to be brave." With her words, Hassan lets a tear tumble down his face.

Without looking back, Rosalyn turns and leaves the group, wandering unsteadily through the forest towards the empty dark landscape and the distant Mountain. She holds the canister of Thermocline Mist in her hand. The expedition watches as she disappears into the shadows, unable to move or speak. And, despite the muffling effect of the snow, they all still hear the unmistakable hiss when she compresses the trigger just out of sight.

They wait for a while in the cold, quiet darkness. No one says a word. When they are sure Rosalyn will have gone far enough into the mist, together, in single file, they make their way out of the forest and into the debris field of the Distillery mine.

It is deathly still. High in the sky, the stars shine bright. The dusting of snow is only a few centimetres deep, and the weather has moved on from the mountains. In the clear sky, the dance of the stars heading over the Mountain is beautiful. The mist has mercifully thinned for the time being, and gazing toward the looming Mountain, the expedition can see a good few hour's walk before they will reach its slopes.

Trying to stick to already trodden paths, they pass the first shackled herd of Drifters quite soon. They can't avert their eyes. The Drifters fastened to a mining cart with the brakes applied, pull gently and fruitlessly on their shackles. Their exhausted bodies are still trying to move to the Source. Each of them is shivering uncontrollably. Gareth wonders what might happen if their bodies give up entirely. Maybe they can't.

Glenda notices something up ahead. A sparkling, shimmering mass. The Lake of the Mountain. It is a crucial waypoint on their journey to the Source, but it spells danger. The Distillery colliery buildings are illuminated at the head of the body of water, illuminated by bright burning lanterns. A large stone complex that stands out as an aggressive interruption in the landscape.

Sealed from the outside mist, a large building in the centre accommodates the Distillery guards and mine supervisors. There will be hundreds of them housed inside. It would spell disaster if the expedition were to be seen by the guards, but according to Glenda's map, they need to pass it. Beyond the buildings, maybe a kilometre further, is a copse of trees where they can shelter and plan their ascent of the Mountain.

Reaching the colliery complex after an hour or so, the group's energy flickers and fades. The emotional and physical toll of the day has been heavy. They can glimpse inside the main building as they sneak through the shadows of the rickety old warehouses, brushing against damp mining overalls that hang on clotheslines. The warm and comfortable accommodation looks incredibly appealing. The guards and miners are visible inside with their gas masks off, consuming marbles, evidently in high spirits. The smell of burning wood indicates the cosy open fires that fill the hearths. If only they could enter the warm, mistless house, thinks Gareth, but they can't.

Arriving at the copse beyond the colliery an hour later, the expedition is quick to work. Despite their exhaustion, the imperative to take shelter is strong. They have a bivouac created in no time, big enough for them all to squeeze in. The sides of the shelter are made from the frozen branches found on the floor. And woven between the branches are frosty ferns compacted with damp mud and leaf litter.

The bivouac is carefully constructed in a way they learnt back in Lin. Around the base of the shelter are large gaps, and on the top is a funnelled chimney. This design means a natural circulation occurs, filtering out the mist. They will be able to sleep with clear minds and, in the morning, will be better able to assess their situation. And with this reassurance, they get themselves as comfortable as possible and rest.

*High winds and heavy rain pelted the Snowdonia mountain-range on the evening of 10th January 1952. Attempting to fly through the storm was an Aer Lingus DC-3 called the 'St Kevin'. Three crew members were piloting the flight that night, taking twenty passengers from London to Dublin. As the plane struggled in the turbulent weather, its crew contacted the radio station at Nevin to report they were proceeding normally at their planned altitude of 6,500 feet. Soon after sending this message the aircraft suddenly fell into a fatal dive, losing part of its starboard wing in the process. Moments later the 'St Kevin' crashed into deep boggy ground high in the mountains on Cwm Edno, just south of Snowdon. In all twenty-three people lost their lives, including all three of the aircraft's crew.*

# Chapter Twenty-One

♦

# The Lady of the Mountain

A grunting noise next to Gareth wakes him early. Glenda is snoring loudly. The brightness outside trickles through the imperfect walls of the bivouac. Poking his head out from his sleeping bag, he can see the dormant figures of Ashley, Hassan, and Albert. Nailah is sitting in the doorway, keeping lookout.

In the brittle coldness of the morning, Gareth's breath, and the breath of the others, billow into clouds that filter out of the shelter's chimney. He pulls on a hat and carefully crawls out to Nailah, keen not to wake anyone.

"Good risen," she says, beaming at him. "What a place to wake up."

Gareth looks out, bleary-eyed. A thick heavy mist hovers low over the lake. All around them, the land is covered in a deep layer of bright white snow. It must have fallen heavily all night. Breaks in the clouds send shafts of winter sunlight sparkling through the atmosphere, illuminating the ripples on the lake. The great Mountain lurks beyond, still shrouded in mist. Gareth can just make out its sharp edges and its violent, obstinate rock face.

"Quite daunting, isn't it?" says Nailah, staring in awe at the Mountain. "I've been looking since the sun came up," she raises an old pair of binoculars hung around her neck. "If the stories are true, a cabin is up on the mountain face. A cabin that ancient travellers used to access on their way to the Source. I've not seen anything yet, though."

"What stories?" asks Gareth.

Nailah pulls out a small red leather book. Gareth had seen it once before. It is Milton's forbidden book of folklore. It looks like the kind of *New Testament* that the Gideons leave in hotels on Earth. The book is titled *Gweirglodd Mabinogion: Dwr Folklore of the Meadow*.

"Old folk tales," says Nailah. "There are so many of them, talked of and recounted, in the Meadow. Their origins are unknown. You will likely have heard some of them sung as folk songs in the taverns."

Gareth thinks back, fondly, to the band that played at the Tide and Time Tavern. "They are songs of rebellion. Merely uttering them has been banned by the Distillery for decades."

Nailah turns the red book in her hands reverently, running her finger gently down its spine. "This book is the *most* forbidden text in all the Meadow," she says. "This version is the only written collection of original folk tales to have avoided the Distillery purges. It was entrusted to Milton as a High Councillor. I don't think he deserved to keep it. I've been studying it these last few days, trying to find out all I can about the Mountain."

Nailah hands the book over to Gareth. He takes hold of it as carefully as he can. Embossed into the bright red leather above the title, a golden line drawing depicts the Mountain. It is surprisingly detailed and, looking up, remarkably accurate. He flicks through the tracing-paper-like pages. They are filled with poems and songs, and even some pictures.

"Other than the tale of 'Beatrice's Hut', there is only one passage where I have found mention of the cabin…" says Nailah, indicating for Gareth to return the book. She licks her thumb and forefinger and flicks through the pages to a stained yellowish one near the end. She hands it back. It is a poem of sorts called *Beatrice's Refuge*.

> "*And from her lofty Mountain seat, Beatrice,*
> *Lady of the Mountain, surveyed the Meadow.*
> *The realm of the Daughter of God.*
> *Like Eden on Earth, the realm had been good.*
> *But now, in the shadow of darkness,*
> *The whips of pain were taunting.*
> *The lake below her Mountain home was no longer clear and calm.*

*It was dark and troubled.*
*Beatrice had lost everyone. She had lost everything except her love.*
*She had been there at the cliffs when those she loved had left.*
*And she regretted they never drank with her.*
*T'was why she chose her home on Mountain face.*
*To help those who came after…"*

"Who was Beatrice?" Gareth asks.

"According to legends, she was amongst the first settlers who encountered the Daughter of God in the Meadow," says Nailah. "The story goes that she chose a hermit's existence on the Mountain, living in the mist and protecting the Source. She helped early believers to find the cliffs and drink the pure water. An ancient shepherd's hut is still believed to be up there on the Mountain. Whether she still lives there or not, we have no idea. But in her cabin, supposedly, are details of a safe route across the cliffs to the Source."

"Did Albert visit the cabin on his Cwtch Mission?" asks Gareth.

"I've asked him," says Nailah. "But his recollections from the Mountain leg of his mission are sketchy. I think the mist nearly took his life. It definitely took his memory."

Gareth looks up at the Mountain. Is it possible that a lady lives up there? A lady who has been in the Meadow for millennia?

"What does a shepherd's hut look like?" he asks.

"I have assumed some kind of stone building," says Nailah. "Something, the Lady of the Mountain could have built herself. Something that blends in, hence why she has never been found…"

Gareth looks at the text again. *T'was why she chose her home on Mountain face…*

"It says she *chose* her home in this poem," says Gareth. "Could she have lived somewhere she found? Maybe, a cave?"

Nailah looks at the text again. "You know what," she says with a chuckle and a satisfied grin. "In all these years, I had always heard the tale of Beatrice's hut, the Ty Cwtch, and taken it literally. I had convinced myself that she *must* live in some stone hut on the

Mountain path. But you're right. It doesn't need to be a literal tale. She might have just chosen a cave."

"Do you mind if I look through the binoculars?" Gareth asks.

"Be my guest," says Nailah, passing them over.

Gareth pulls the binoculars up to his eyes. Focusing them is difficult. The mist makes most things seem blurry. He momentarily takes his eyes from the eyepiece to reorientate. A shaft of light illuminates the Mountain as he looks back, and he gazes in wonderment at the angry rock face.

Drawing his gaze upwards, he traces the outline of the Mountain, a sharp razor edge cutting into the sky. He pans across, and something catches his eye. A flicker of sapphire blue. He pans back. There, between two large boulders, is a dark teardrop-shaped cave. Around the opening, the rocks have been cut and arranged to surround the teardrop entrance, an Encircled Drop.

"There, up there!" Gareth exclaims, pointing excitedly, not daring to move the binoculars. "A cave like an Encircled Drop."

"Keep looking at it. Don't move," says Nailah unfolding her map and orientating it. She traces a line from where they are by the lake to the direction that Gareth is pointing, marking the line on the map. This is the trajectory they will have to follow up the Mountain.

"It's fading into the mist," says Gareth desperately.

"Let me have a look," asks Nailah.

Gareth passes the binoculars over and points back to the cave. He can see Nailah's eyes straining.

"No," she says. "No, it's gone. What did you see?"

"A cave," he says. "An opening surrounded by broken rocks scattered around its entrance, looking like an Encircled Drop."

"That's got to be it," says Nailah. "It's the only cave that can be seen from here at the lakeside." She looks back to her map, re-tracing her finger over the location Gareth had pointed to. "Interesting…" she says. "The cave…it lines up exactly with a disused adit for the Distillery mine."

"An adit?" Gareth asks.

"A pilot hole… a tunnel, into the Mountain. The first Distillery miners used them to locate the mineral wealth that runs through the Mountain. They will have dug many like it. They must have drawn a blank in that one, hence why it is abandoned."

"Does that mean it can't be Beatrice's cave?"

"No, not necessarily," says Nailah thoughtfully. "It could be both."

"Good risen," says Albert, shuffling out of the shelter. Their animated conversation has waked him.

"We think we've found it," says Nailah, beaming. "Beatrice's hut… Up there on the Mountain…a cave."

"Ah, yes," says Albert, chuckling nostalgically. "Now you say it, yes… I *do* remember there being a cave."

* * *

With their packs tied tightly, carrying only the essentials (ropes, warm clothing, marbles, and empty bottles for Source water), the group leave the shelter by the lake. There is a great deal of excitement amongst them. The Mountain climb is the final stage. Simply stepping foot on the Mountain is a legendary achievement amongst the Well-Wishing community.

Their energy sets them off at quite a pace, and they soon find themselves wandering high up on the steep slate slopes of the Mountain. Their route to Beatrice's cave goes directly up the face. The equivalent route on Earth is called the *Asphodel Face*. Gareth is no climber himself, but that face has status. It is known to be treacherous, infamously taking climbers' lives every year. This doesn't fill him with confidence.

Nailah stops on a rocky outcrop of deep purple slate ahead of the others. It is becoming quite a scramble over the sliding plates of rock, and progress has inevitably slowed. Gareth is just behind her. He shuffles onto the ledge beside her and looks down into the valley.

A momentary break in the cloud reveals the lake they had left earlier. Bright white snow covers the ground around the edge, and a harsh wind has whipped up. Trees are throwing themselves around violently, and ripples on the water's surface have turned to cresting waves. On the ledge, though, they are protected from the wind, and it is quiet. All they can hear is each other's heavy breathing.

Gareth peers over the ledge to see how the others are getting on. Glenda and Ashley are helping Albert. The older man is struggling with the physical challenge of the climb. He isn't the man he was forty years ago. The two women stand on each side of him, stopping him from sliding on the rocks. Glenda's flushed red face behind her neckerchief shows she is no seasoned mountaineer either. Behind them, Hassan is making his way surprisingly slowly. He looks pensive and sick.

"Is everyone OK?" Nailah calls down.

Ashley raises a thumb. The rest keep their heads down.

It isn't long, though, before everyone has joined them on the ledge. It is a very welcome break for everyone.

"Are you OK, Hassan?" asks Gareth, looking worried. Hassan is crouched down, looking desolate, with his head between his knees. He has some magic mushrooms in his hand but isn't chewing them.

"I don't feel great," he mumbles through his scarf. "I don't feel great at all." He retches a dry retch.

Glenda reaches into her coat and pulls out a bright green anaesthetic marble. "Take this," she says. "It will help."

"Thanks," he replies, lifting his scarf and popping the marble into his mouth.

"We shouldn't wait here long," says Nailah. "The mist is getting thicker. Our mushrooms and face coverings will only help so much. If we can, let's keep going and find the cave."

Hassan drops his mushrooms, and they tumble off the ledge and down into the hidden mountain face below. They return to their feet and, with collective determination, start the slow trudge uphill again.

An icy fog has started to roar above them, swirling around the summit of the Mountain, unknown and unseen, stripping rocks bare of snow and sending ice flakes crashing into each other in a disorientating dance. They are heading straight into it.

* * *

Within an hour, a cold icy wind has whipped up, and visibility is down to just a few metres. The expedition stays in a tight huddle, shifting upwards, hoping to stumble upon the cave. The snow is falling again too. It is fast becoming too treacherous.

Albert trips several times, and now Nailah, Glenda, and Ashley are all required to help him. They are getting exhausted. Behind them, Gareth tries to help Hassan too. Glenda's marble aided a bit, but he can barely stay on his feet now. His face is pale, and his eyes are unfocused. But they have to keep moving. One step at a time. Gareth knows he just has to keep the others in sight.

Hassan moans something, but Gareth can't tell what it is in the wind and snow.

"Say that again," he shouts, leaning his head as close as he can to Hassan's.

"Urghhh."

Gareth can just make out three syllables, nothing more. Hassan moans again.

"I can't hear what you're saying," shouts Gareth.

Hassan raises his arm and points into the mist. "Rosalyn!" he shouts, or something close to that.

Gareth looks to where Hassan is pointing. There is no one there. "Rosalyn! She's there," tries Hassan again before pulling Gareth in that direction.

"She's not there," says Gareth desperately. "She went on yesterday."

Suddenly Hassan erupts with energy, yanking Gareth roughly. Before he can react, he slips into Hassan, and the two men fall onto their backs.

They start sliding uncontrollably very quickly. Gareth grasps hold of Hassan and plunges his hands into the cold snow trying to anchor their movement. His arm is wrenched violently, but it works.

"Hassan! What the hell are you doing?!" he shouts.

"Rosalyn!" moans Hassan again.

"She's not there. She's not there!" shouts Gareth desperately.

In the mist, Gareth can see Hassan looking scared. He is losing his mind.

Gareth remembers what Milton had told him. He might need to use Hassan's memory, the one he had witnessed at Crofter's Hope. He must remind Hassan of who he is and why he should fight.

He leans in. "Hassan," he says, his eyes inches from Hassan's. "Remember your daughter Tia. She needs her father. Remember your mother. She needs her son. You can see them again. Just stay with us now."

It doesn't do much. He tries again, painting a more descriptive picture of his mum at the top of the stairs and his ex leaving out the door with Tia in her arms. Hassan's eyes start to come into focus. "Tia," he says. "I must get back to Tia."

Gareth helps Hassan back onto his feet and turns them around to rejoin the others. But the others are gone.

Gareth's breathing quickens to a panic. He shouts into the swirling snow and fog, then listens. But he can't hear anything. Looking down, he can just about make out the broken snow tracks the others had cut ahead of them. "Come on," he shouts to Hassan. "We need to move quickly. We can't lose them."

But it soon becomes clear; they *have* lost the expedition. In the disorientating dance of the snow, they have become lost and alone. They keep going upwards. What choice do they have? But Gareth's belief that they are following any track fades, as does his hope of finding the expedition.

Gareth knows, but daren't acknowledge, that their chances of getting off the Mountain are falling quickly. To worsen the situation, Hassan is slowing down again, and this time Gareth feels his own mind beginning to fog. He tries to focus on what he can see in front of him. One step in front of the other. But his mind fills with other things. He thinks of Rosalyn's injured leg and the pain of saying goodbye. He thinks of Nailah's angry face as she thrust Milton into the Irish Sea. He thinks of Kasiya's terrified moans at the hands of the evil men. Everything in the Meadow is like a dream.

Just then, a shadowy figure appears in front of Gareth. A man crouched down near a pile of slate. He can feel Hassan still groping his shoulder, so he pulls Hassan with him towards the man. He is familiar. Very familiar. And as they get closer, Gareth knows who he is.

"Dad?" he calls out into the wind. "Dad, it's me! Your son, Gareth!"

Colin Edwards doesn't look up. He is shivering. That is unsurprising, given he is just wearing a loose nightshirt. "Dad. Don't worry; I'm here. I can save you. Just hold on!" But his dad doesn't look up.

Gareth stumbles on a rock, falling with Hassan face-first into the snow. He shakes himself off and tries to drag himself through the snow towards his dad. In the struggle, he feels Hassan grasping at his belt. He tries to ignore him, pulling with all his might towards his dad. There is a crack beside him and a gentle hiss. Before he knows it, Hassan has thrust the mist of one of his marble memories into his face.

In a moment, Gareth is transported back to the Tide and Time Tavern. He is sat there, by the open fireplace, with Hassan, Cyril Speight, and Kim-Joy. They are recounting fond memories from Earth and enjoying the warmth of the tavern. They have just been helping Cyril with his latest shipment of marbles. All is right, and all is happy. It is only a little memory that had been collected for him by Kim-Joy, but when he emerges, Gareth's mind is clear again. Next to him, in the snow, Hassan is bent double. Where he had seen his dad is just a cold pile of slate.

"Thank you," Gareth shouts to Hassan. "Thank you!"

Gareth helps Hassan back to his feet, and with greater resolve to keep going, he basically carries Hassan with him up the Mountain.

"Gareth! Hassan!" A desperate female voice cuts through the wind somewhere in front of them.

"We're here!" shouts Gareth energetically, not knowing whose voice it is. "We're here!" They stumble in the direction of the voice.

"Gareth! Hassan!" The voice shouts again.

Whoever it is, she evidently can't hear Gareth's response in the wind. He strains his eyes, desperate to pick out something. He plunges his feet firmly into the snow and pulls Hassan up behind him. As he does so, the figure appears through the mist. It is Ashley. Her skinny frame is upright, buffeted by the strong wind, her hands to her mouth, shouting. Behind her is the teardrop entrance to the cave. They have made it.

* * *

Beatrice's cave is dark and dingy, as though no one has been there for forty years. Beatrice herself is nowhere to be seen. The derelict cave bears the scars of an attempt to mine the Mountain a century ago and is filled with all manner of mining debris. There are picks, chisels, and wooden beams littering the floor. There is even a dangerous-looking tunnel heading deep into the darkness. The rockfall of multiple collapses blocks it. A cool breeze whistles out from somewhere deep inside.

Beyond the functional mess in the cave, there is a menagerie of inexplicably weird artefacts – animal skins and rough tools, as well as used army ration packs and metal camping tins. There are even what looks like some old rotten seats from inside an aircraft. The seats bear the logo of the airline *Aer Lingus.*

On the cave walls, a myriad of rough primitive paintings depict people, some joyous and some with anguish, standing on the cliffs and bodies plunging into the clouds. There are also notes scratched into the rock. Most are in some old English and hard to decipher. There is one note with a familiar name.

*"My darling Sebastian,*
*You should have been here with me. As we promised, I*
*will go back first. I will find you again.*
*Commander Albert Newman"*

The present-day Albert Newman is in a bad way. The climb to Beatrice's cave and the thick heavy mist have taken their toll. Ashley, Nailah, and Glenda had basically carried him into the cave. He lies there now, motionless, covered in blankets. His eyes are barely open. Glenda carefully tries to coax life back into the older man. She feeds him a concoction of mushrooms and poppy seeds and wafts any vapours gently away from his face.

The other two men aren't faring much better. Gareth and Hassan managed to crawl into the cave with Ashley's help, but now they are utterly exhausted. The hallucinations have stopped, but they can barely utter a word. Gareth finds concentrating incredibly hard. He can just about cope inside the cool breezy air of the cave but can't fathom the idea of going back out into the savage wind and mist.

Nailah lights an old lantern hanging from the cave ceiling. Holding it up in the entrance, she illuminates a stone tablet. Scribed into it is a message to travellers who have braved the Mountain. It has been eroded by the wind and snow over hundreds of years, but you can still make out what it says.

> *"Enter weary soul; here ends the path,*
> *From the elements shelter, in Beatrice's hearth.*
> *If the lady be not home, rejoice.*
> *The next step beyond, it is your choice.*
> *Her map, it leads to waterfall.*
> *Damascus not; it falls for all.*
> *Her tears of love would never ask,*
> *For Isaac's soul, as trying task.*
> *The splash of life, collect with care,*
> *The weighty drops, the void of air.*
> *The way back home, like passing ships,*
> *In believers' hearts, on believers' lips.*
> *Through open door, your soul nourish.*
> *She wishes well, as well you wish.*
> *And for those who find the lady's home,*
> *Do not stay long. Leap off to Mother's throne."*

Nailah reads the poem aloud twice. The others let it digest. Parts make sense, and parts do not.

"What does it mean?" asks Ashley.

"I think it is confirmation," says Nailah. "We must find the waterfall and collect the heavy Source water."

"But how do we find it?" says Glenda. "Is there an *actual* map somewhere?"

"I think there might be," says Nailah.

Gareth watches as Ashley and Glenda rummage around the cave. They turn everything over, but he can't keep up with their movements.

"I don't think Albert has long," says Nailah, looking at the old man. "We'll have to take him down soon if he is to have any chance."

"We can't just go down," says Ashley desperately. "We've come so far. We need to at least attempt to find the Source water."

"Wait!" says Glenda, rocking the rotten aircraft seat onto its side. Beneath it, scratched into a boulder, is a rough outline of the mountain with a carefully scribed route. Their position in the cave is marked. "This is it, the map," says Glenda, "This has got to be the way to the waterfall."

"We have no time to lose!" exclaims Ashley.

"We're going to have to leave this lot here," says Nailah, turning to the men. Gareth is the only conscious one of the three, though only just. "They don't have the strength to go out into the storm. We'll have to collect the Source water for them... Unless…" She looks directly into Gareth's eyes. "Gareth, do you think you can summon any more strength?"

He struggles to fully comprehend what Nailah is asking, but he feels the gaze of the three women and an insecurity at the core of his being ignite the vapours of fuel in his body. He stands up.

"I'm coming," he says, wobbly but determined.

"Good lad," says Glenda, patting him on the back.

"OK, I think it's worth you having this, though," says Nailah, passing Gareth the rest of the concoction of mushrooms and poppy seeds they had given to Albert. "Ignore the taste…just chew it and swallow."

Gareth rocks his head back and pours the lumpy mixture into his mouth. The moment it hits his taste buds, it makes him retch, but he manages to keep the contents in. He scrunches his eyes and chews. As he chews, he feels some of his strength and clarity return, but it is disgusting. He retches again. He places his hand in front of his mouth, closes his eyes, clenches the muscles in his throat, and forces the contents down.

"Well done," says Nailah. "That should stay with you for the next hour or so… we'll have to be quick. Tell us the moment you feel the effects wearing off, OK?"

Gareth nods as his senses return. He catches Ashley's eye. He can't see her face under her scarf, but he can feel the warmth of her smile.

"Let's sort these two out," says Glenda wandering over to Hassan and Albert, a marble cracker in her hand. "Hopefully, the memories we select are good ones!"

The two men lie placid while Glenda rummages around their pockets, looking for their marble pouches. Where Hassan might once have made a disparaging comment or sarcastic remark about Glenda's hands roving around his body, he is now silent and compliant.

Glenda holds aloft a bright blue marble from Hassan's pouch. She cracks it and holds the mist under his nostrils. He inhales gently and, in an instant, falls back into his memory. Then Glenda holds up a dull orange marble from Albert's pouch. As soon as the old man has inhaled the vapour, she turns back to the others.

"OK, we've got to get going…and quick!"

* * *

With the route marked on her map, Nailah strides out in front, carefully pacing the steps and cracking a new marble every fifty strides. The luminescent glow of the marble's mist leaves a marker for them to trace on their way back.

"We'll have about an hour…maximum," Nailah shouts against the wind. "After that, the marbles will dissolve, and we'll be at the mercy of the weather."

A short snowy trudge later, traversing the steep slopes of the mountain, the ground falls away rapidly, and the group find themselves precariously navigating along a cliff edge. Hundreds of feet of nothingness lie below, and a whispering pillow of mist waits to catch their fall. Gareth, his mind still only teetering on the right side of consciousness, holds his breath. He has never been fond of heights.

A hissing fills Gareth's ears. It starts quietly. Barely audible. But soon, it is impossible to ignore. He wonders if Nailah's concoction is wearing off and his mind is getting consumed by chaos. But as the noise rises to a crescendo, he identifies its origin: the roaring of falling water. They are getting close.

The edge they follow turns to a ledge. A sheer rock face rises above them, disappearing into the mist, mirroring the ominous void below. The thundering of the waterfall becomes all-consuming, and the four explorers are forced to communicate through rudimentary hand gestures. But it is not like they need directions anymore. There is only one way forward along the ledge and one way back.

The mist thins noticeably as they approach the waterfall. The weight and force of the water draw the mist down with it, clearing the vicinity. It is a truly remarkable sight. Like a rainbow curtain hanging from the heavens, the water shimmers with life, energy, and colour. Beside it, the mist swirls and dances with joy, and a bright shaft of light from an unseen sun high above warms and illuminates the sturdy ledge sitting directly behind the water – the perfect place to collect their prize.

Nailah removes her face scarf in the clear air and beckons the others to join her behind the waterfall. She cannot hide her elation. Tears stream down her face, and her smile almost reaches her ears.

Turning to Gareth as she steps onto the platform, Ashley mouths, "*We made it!*". And though he can't hear a word she says, he knows. Without the mist and with the relief of reaching the waterfall, his mind feels as clear as ever. He clenches his fists and pumps them into the air in celebration.

Nailah starts to unpack her rucksack. She removes six metal water bottles, vessels she has carried since Lin. They are to hold the precious liquid that each expedition member requires, plus Gareth's sister (hopefully), to make their step across from the Meadow back to Earth – a bottle of pure Source water.

Nailah unscrews the lid off the first bottle and shifts tentatively on her hands and knees towards the edge. Glenda grasps her shoulder and looks for a purchase on the ledge to grip onto. Nailah reaches the bottle out towards the falling wall of water.

The moment the bottle skims the waterfall's edge, Nailah's arm is wrenched downwards, and in that split second, Gareth thinks she has been swept over the edge. But Glenda holds firm, and Nailah, soaked from the spray, retreats, smiling and holding the small but heavy bottle of Source water. Ashley punches the air in celebration. Glenda holds up a finger to indicate "*One down, five to go*".

Once all six bottles are filled, Nailah encourages Ashley and Gareth to get on their hands and knees and join her near the edge. Ashley does so without question. Gareth, more nervously complies, shuffling up behind her slowly.

Nailah prods her finger at Gareth and raises her thumb as if to ask, "*Are you OK?*". Gareth nods tentatively.

Next to Nailah, Glenda points to the waterfall and gestures as if to take a drink. She looks back at Gareth and Ashley questioningly.

Gareth shrugs his shoulders. "I don't understand!" he shouts, fully aware there is no way Glenda can hear him over the deafening roar of the waterfall.

Rather than try to explain, Glenda grasps Nailah's shoulder once more and nods to her. Nailah nods back and leans her body towards the edge, trusting Glenda's grip, reaching out with her bare hand towards the wall of water.

Again, as Nailah's hand hits the water, she is knocked forwards by its sheer weight, but Glenda holds tight. Rather than collecting water this time, Nailah channels a trickle to splash off her hand towards her face. She opens her mouth and lets it funnel in.

The instant the cold and colourful drops of water enter her mouth, Nailah's head rocks back, a blissful smile stretches across her face, and she looks to the sky. Glenda pulls her away from the edge, worried she might fall. As she tumbles into them all, Nailah looks at them giddily, still smiling with radiant beauty. She pulls her palms to her chest and starts to sob joyfully.

Glenda gestures to Ashley and Gareth as if to say, "*Who's next?*". Before Gareth can process the question, Ashley nudges him forward. Glenda plants a firm hand on his shoulder and gives him a reassuring smile and a cheeky wink. "*Good lad,*" she mouths at him.

Feeling he has no choice, Gareth shimmies towards the cliff edge. A cool breeze from the void draws him in, and the defeating thunder of the waterfall deprives him entirely of his ability to hear. He glances back to Ashley, crouching beside Glenda. She smiles at him.

Gareth looks at the waterfall. In the curtain of water, he can see a kaleidoscope of colour. It is as though every sensation in all the marbles of the Meadow have been rolled into this flowing mat of feeling. It is mesmerising and soothing. All except for some dark objects that shoot past, tumbling and flailing, interrupting the patterns of colour. He tries to glimpse one of these objects more clearly but can't. They fall too fast. He reaches out his right hand to skim the water, bracing himself for impact.

*Crack!* The water yanks down Gareth's arm. A wave of droplets cascades over his head. The water is ice cold and heavy, like being struck by enormous hailstones. Composing himself and reassured by Glenda's tight grip on his shoulder, he cups the stream's edge, deflecting a shower of water droplets towards his face. He opens his mouth.

The instant the water hits his throat, everything becomes peaceful and calm. He can suddenly hear the faint sound of a breeze, birds' crowing, and sheep bleating like he is sitting on a mountainside somewhere else, in another world. Then, like a waterfall tumbling through his mind, memories of Earth flood Gareth's head. The memories he has just about held on to throughout his time in the Meadow. Memories of home, of Cerys, of his mum. But memories that are once again entangled with their emotional, physical, and spiritual counterparts. As though a oneness in his soul has been reaffirmed. Bizarrely, he feels a frantic urge at this moment to leap with the water off the cliff edge and into the cocktail of mist and sensations below. He just about resists and falls back onto the ledge, where he starts crying uncontrollably like Nailah.

*  *  *

After Ashley and Glenda experience the brief ecstasy of tasting Source water, Nailah taps an imaginary watch on her wrist; they need to return to Hassan and Albert. Struggling considerably, she lifts two full bottles of Source water into her backpack and braces under its weight. Before she can divvy up the remaining bottles, Glenda leans down and lifts two bottles into her sack. This leaves a single bottle each for Ashley and Gareth.

Gareth drops the cloth sack from his shoulder and bends down to pick up the small, half-litre bottle. He knows it will be heavy, but he isn't prepared for just how weighty the Source water is. The innocuous metal bottle must weigh more than fifteen kilos. As much as a bag of luggage. He stumbles a little as he places it into his sack.

Knowing Gareth's incurable need to be chivalrous, Ashley swoops in and grasps the final bottle. Gareth tries, half-heartedly, to protest, but Ashley ignores him. Deep down, Gareth knows this is for the best. The effects of the mushroom and poppy mix are starting to wear off, and he can feel his fatigue returning. The mist is coming back to cloud his mind, and he is going to struggle to carry just one bottle.

As they set off, Gareth has one last look at the waterfall. The relentless curtain of colour continues to roar uninterrupted into the mist. In a rare moment, his eye catches a clear look at one of the dark objects falling through the water. It's a body. A helpless human form, flailing in the plummeting rainbow. It must be a Drifter. Someone going 'on', taking their final plunge from the cliffs. Could it be Billy? Or Rosalyn? He immediately shuts this thought out of his mind. He can't go there. He's too weak as it is. He turns back and follows the others, not looking back again.

Nailah leads them along the precarious snowy ledge. It is much slower going this way. The extra burden they carry is compounded by the emotional plummet they feel when they enter back into the mist, and the disconnect in their souls returns.

The cliffs rising above them soon subside into a wide, open, and gently sloping snow field. Gareth doesn't recognise anything in the swirling snow. Visibility is down to less than five metres now. He is aware that somewhere, out of sight, is the steep rocky edge and a fall into nothingness. They had traversed along it on their way to the waterfall, but he can't see it now. Up ahead, Nailah tries to keep them moving. She trudges towards the fading translucent glow of the marbles she left behind.

Sensing Gareth lagging, Ashley turns to him, her scarf covering everything but her eyes. She raises a thumb, checking that he is OK.

He raises his hand to confirm, but as he does so, the ground below him gives way. The slab of snow he is standing on cracks and breaks free from its connection with the mountain. Gareth is thrown onto his back and tumbles like a stone.

During his fall, every sense goes into over-drive. There are noises of scraping metal, thudding bones, whistling wind, and breathless grunts. There are flashes of ice, caverns of darkness and interruptions of glaring light. And there is pain – whips of the biting wind, stabs of obstinate rock, and pelts of rushing ice. It seems like it will never end.

Then, with an aggressive yank on his tired body, the sack slung over his shoulder, holding the metal bottle of Source water, plants itself into a groove of rock, and Gareth is brought to a sudden stop. For a moment, ice, rock, and debris rush past him, careening downwards into the fog.

The chaos subsides, and all that remains is the solitary whistling of the wind. Gareth can't work out what parts of him are broken. It seems like every part of him that can't scream is screaming, and the bit that can has forgotten how.

He can't find any purchase for his feet, which scrabble desperately in the confused darkness. Grasping tightly to the life-saving sack slung tightly across his body, he lunges desperately to get some purchase in the snow. Only now does the frightening realisation strike him – his feet can't help him. He is dangling in the cold swirling air, with no way of knowing how far he will fall if the strap of his sack breaks. He dares to look down with the vague hope of seeing a soft snow pillow below him. Instead, he sees only a tumbling fog beckoning him towards it.

"Ashley?" he half pleads, half whimpers. "Ashley, can you hear me...?"

The wind continues to whistle, but nothing sounds remotely like a response. He strains his eyes upwards to where the bottle is wedged in the rock and looks beyond, hoping to glimpse a friendly face. There is nothing of the sort, just mist. Dark condemning mist.

A short while passes, and Gareth just hangs there, helpless and desperate. His body temperature drops quickly, and the mist infiltrates his mind. He feels a great desire to close his eyes and fall asleep. Pictures start to dance around in his mind, like how the snow swirls and dances around his body. Pictures like those on the walls of Beatrice's cave. The falling bodies dropping into the mist.

Then, suddenly, Gareth feels with complete certainty that something very close by is watching him. His eyes shoot up, looking wildly into the air. He is sure he will see something there, but he doesn't. At least he doesn't see anything with his eyes. Instead, the most peculiar sense engulfs him. Something, or rather someone, is above him on the Mountain, but they aren't there in a form he can see. Nor are they in a form he can hear, smell, taste, or touch. But peering into the fog, Gareth knows they are there, edging towards him. In fact, he is certain that it isn't just someone, but it is a woman. Beatrice, the Lady of the Mountain?

Gareth feels the woman's presence join him, hanging from the rock. Bizarrely, he feels confident he has met her before. They have crossed paths somewhere, a world away. Gareth's mind projects a physical form to her presence. A long flowing blue dress, fluid dark, long hair. Her company is silent, but Gareth knows she is talking to him. She wants to know who he is and where he comes from. She cares about him immensely. She wants to know his heart's desires. She wants him to know he is loved. She wants him to know he is safe.

The lady's flowing blue dress sparkles and shimmers in his mind. She smiles at him, and he feels so peaceful. Nothing else matters. He smiles back. She invites him, if he wants, to let go and fall into the mist with her. But then she listens to his heart. And his heart tells her that he isn't finished here. Not yet.

The lady moves Gareth's hands for him. She reaches them into the pouch dangling from his waist and wraps his fingers around the reassuring warmth of the marbles. She helps him to pull one out. In the frantic, chaotic weather, he inspects the tiny stone grasped between his thumb and forefinger – a perfect glass sphere with a purple teardrop trapped inside.

"*Don't suck it,*" he feels her say to him. "*Crack it with your teeth.*"

He does as told and immediately feels a warm translucent mist fizz out from the marble surrounding his face. As he inhales, he finds himself entering one of his fondest memories.

He is sixteen years old. He sits in the entrance waiting area at his secondary school. Cerys is next to him. School finished hours ago, and they are still waiting for their mum to pick them up. Outside, it rains heavily. Forty-five-degree lines of precipitation slash against the windows. This April shower goes on and on.

Gareth has spent the last six months, if not year, inside his own head. Adolescence, uncertain self-worth, and unhelpful infatuations with the opposite sex have kept him from seeing anything outside his immediate hormonal fog.

Mrs Massey, the school receptionist, leans out from her booth. "Gareth, Cerys," she calls out. "That was your mum on the phone. She's been held up at work again. She won't be able to get here to pick you up tonight. She said that the two of you know the walk home…"

It is the third time this week that his mum's work has taken over, and she has failed to pick Gareth and Cerys up from school. It is only a couple of miles walk home, cutting across the fields to their little cottage. It usually isn't a problem, but in today's heavy rain, without any coats, it will not be pleasant.

Gareth looks at Cerys, expecting her to reflect his miserable mood. Instead, she has a big smile on her face.

"It's only a bit of rain!" she grins. "Water never hurt anybody!"

Cerys throws her backpack over her shoulder and stands up. "Come on, Gaz. This'll be a laugh!" Gareth isn't convinced, but he doesn't want to be outdone by his sister. He follows her out of the doorway into the heavy rain. Cerys is right. It is just water.

Half an hour into the walk, they trudge through the sodden fields, wet to the bone. Their school shirts cling to their skinny bodies. Impractical black blazers weigh a ridiculous amount from wicking the rain, and their ordinarily clean shoes are caked in mud. Cerys has even managed to get dirt in her hair. But for some reason, Gareth and Cerys can't stop laughing. Their situation, wandering in a torrential downpour through a field full of confused cows, feels beautifully and pointlessly absurd.

Gareth is usually so concerned about what he looks like. But right now, he doesn't care. For the first time in ages, it doesn't bother him. Nothing really matters. They are just walking home. They are just being silly. They find the biggest puddles they possibly can and splash in them. They are already as wet as they can be anyway. They even taunt cars that drive past to splash them with the biggest puddles. Many drivers oblige, sending tidal waves of cool spring water over them. It is ridiculous, but it is brilliant.

As their tiny home comes into view, Gareth and Cerys chat cheerfully together, enjoying each other's company. Enjoying the terrible rain. Enjoying being alive.

Walking down the long dirt drive, a car pulls up behind them.

"Oh, you two!" their mum exclaims, leaning out her window. "I'm so sorry! I didn't think I'd be back in time to pick you up. You must think I'm a terrible mum?!"

Gareth looks in at his diminutive mother at the wheel of the red Volvo and smiles at her. Cerys smiles too and shakes her hair, flinging rainwater into her mum's face.

"You two," says their mum, "are the best kids a mum could ask for! How about we get you home, get you warm…Let's have pizza tonight!"

\* \* \*

The memory ends, and Gareth's eyes adjust to his precarious position, dangling off a cliff from his shoulder sack high up in the mountains. The lady is gone, but Gareth's mind feels absolutely clear. He feels energised.

Despite the mist, Gareth can make out the shape of the rocks that arrested his fall. He reaches his hands up and grasps them. He hauls his body up with unexpected strength and determination and crawls onto the rocks. He is no longer helpless. He is no longer stuck.

Knowing that hesitation will open him to doubt, Gareth starts to march back up the snowy slope. He feels an urgent sense of certainty that he knows where he is heading. And even when nothing familiar comes into view, he keeps going, crunching one foot in front of the other.

And then, as though the Mountain is complicit in his blind belief, a gap in the mist reveals the teardrop entrance to Beatrice's cave. Gareth's heart pounds joyously, and despite the depth of the powdery snow, he runs towards it.

"Gareth!!" exclaims Ashley, the first to spot him as he tumbles through the entrance. Her face is red and puffy from tears. Inside the candle-lit cave, she looks exhausted, but she still manages to leap up and throw her arms around him.

Gareth gratefully returns the hug, feeling their bodies relaxing together in a comfortable tessellation. "You're alive," she says.

"I'm alive," he responds, squeezing her tight.

"I thought we'd lost you," she whispers, wiping away a tear.

"Me too," he admits. "I'm just glad you're still here. I thought you would have left."

He looks into Ashley's eyes, but her smile starts to fade.

"What is it?" he asks.

Ashley doesn't respond. She buries her face into his chest and squeezes her arms tightly around him.

Gareth peers around the cave. No one looks well. Glenda offers him a resigned smile, acknowledging his return, but she leans lethargically against the wall, her eyes drooping, and she can barely stand.

Albert and Hassan are huddled together in a corner beside the debris of the blocked tunnel. The remains of their cracked marbles lie on the floor, hissing gently. Neither man is well enough to acknowledge Gareth at all. Hassan just moans and rocks.

"Welcome back, Gareth," says Nailah weakly, smiling bravely. She stoops over Albert, looking queasy and unsteady, offering the old man the vapour from another of his marble memories. Albert inhales gently.

"We have a situation," Nailah declares. "Hassan is completely out of marbles. And Albert is down to his last one. They are not going to make it down the Mountain."

"What?" says Gareth, unable to comprehend.

"We've discussed it and…and, well, sadly, we don't have many options," says Nailah. Ashley sobs into Gareth's chest.

"We can either leave Albert and Hassan here with their bottles of water and hope that some coincidence presents an Opening nearby before their minds have left them completely. Or, we can give them a more peaceful end and spray them with Thermocline Mist now…" Nailah lifts two dull canisters from her bag.

"No way!" Gareth exclaims, horrified.

"There are no other options," frowns Nailah solemnly.

"But," Gareth starts, "they can't have come this far only to… only to *fail!*"

"This is not failing," pleads Nailah, looking like she has had to say this before. "Some of you will still have the chance to return."

"No. This can't be," says Gareth, dropping to the floor and running his hands through his hair. He looks at Hassan. He can't believe that, after all they have been through together, Hassan might be about to lose his chance to return to his daughter.

"I'm afraid this is the way it is," says Nailah. "And in my opinion, it is better to spray them here in the cave… Their ends are guaranteed to be dignified that way."

A cold whip of wind whistles up through the dark tunnel in the corner of the cave and ruffles Gareth's hair, making him shiver.

He freezes. "Wait," he says urgently. "Quiet."

"What is it?" asks Ashley.

Gareth puts his finger to his lips and listens. The storm outside pulses, offering moments of quiet in the cave. During one of these moments, they all hear the unmistakable clanging of iron into rock.

"The mine," says Glenda, looking more alert. "We can hear the miners."

"And?" says Ashley, confused.

"If we can hear them," says Gareth, feeling a pulse of euphoria washing through him, "that means the tunnel is not a dead end." He points at the debris-filled hole next to Albert. "It is a mist-free way down the mountain!"

* * *

Shifting the boulders that block the tunnel entrance is heavy work. Any energy that Gareth had gained from his cliff edge marble is quickly used up. Nailah and Glenda battle stoically through their fatigue, hurling rock after rock away from the opening. Ashley scrabbles on her hands and knees, dragging fallen masonry out of the way. When the entrance is eventually clear, a cool, clean air breathes freely from the mine deep below. The clear passageway draws them in.

With his final marble dissection now inhaled, Albert's mind is more or less revived. Physically he is shattered, but he can communicate again and, importantly, stand on his own two feet. Hassan, however, still teeters on the edge of consciousness, unable to stand at all. Nailah makes the briefest suggestion that maybe they should leave Hassan in the cave after all, but this is met with determined rejection from Gareth.

"I'm not leaving him here," Gareth exclaims. "Even if *I* have to carry him down!"

And carry him, they do. Overstating his energy levels, Gareth ends up lifting the bulk of Hassan's weight, holding the young man's torso under his armpits while Glenda and Nailah take his legs.

Ashley leads the way into the tunnel. It is a relatively straightforward path. A slight descent through the cold rock. The further they go, the clearer of debris the path gets, preserved by the inactivity in the pilot shaft for the last hundred years. The tunnel, though, is only just high enough for Gareth to stand upright as he strains under Hassan's weight. Glenda, being at least a foot taller, stoops painfully and keeps thumping her head into the thick supporting beams.

The breeze up the tunnel pulses continually as they go deeper and deeper like the Mountain itself is breathing through them. The movement of the air proves their path will ultimately exit the Mountain, but there's no way of knowing how far that is. And it isn't long before the light from the cave fails to illuminate the path ahead, and they start to wonder when, or even if, they will see the light again.

"Urgh! What's that?!" Ashley exclaims from the front.

"What is it?" asks Nailah, stopping abruptly.

"It's sticky and disgusting! It's all over the walls!" says Ashley.

*Click!* A bright beam of light bursts out from Glenda's hand. She holds the torch she had picked up at the mini-bus arrival weeks ago. The beam reflects off the rock walls. Up ahead, Ashley is looking at her hands, disgusted. A sticky, slimy substance stretches between her fingers and drips viscously to the floor.

"It's everywhere!" says Ashley.

Gareth looks at the rocks. Indeed, blobs of the translucent sticky liquid emanate from countless pores in the rock.

"It's resin," says Nailah, reaching up and touching it. "The type used to make marbles."

Gareth inspects it. She's right. It is the exact same liquid that his sweat had dripped into in the Distillery workhouse. The base product for the colourful resin that he rolled into countless marbles at the kilns. He remembers it being viscous and horribly sticky.

"Well, that's a relief," chuckles Ashley. "I thought I'd put my hand in excrement!"

"Where does it come from?" Gareth asks.

"The rocks," says Glenda. "This is what happens when pure water filters through the ground."

"You mean this is made of Source water?"

"Same origins," says Glenda. "The moment pure water hits the ground, it picks up all the impurities of the Meadow. As it runs through the rock, it loses its colour and becomes viscous and dull. It would dilute again in a river channel or an ocean. But it has forever lost its purity."

A drip of sweat tumbles off Glenda's brow and splashes into a pool of resin on the tunnel floor. Instantly, in the torchlight, it shimmers a mix of bright orange and blue. Just like in the workhouse interrogations.

"This must be what they are mining," says Nailah. "Marble resin is notoriously hard to create from flowing water. It can take weeks to boil down a few litres just to make a teaspoon of resin. Here the Distillery must have access to all the marble resin they need for their workhouses."

Glenda shines her torch down the tunnel. At the edge of the beam of light, the passageway plunges away. A rusty pulley system is connected to a drum barrel and an old rope ladder. That is the way down.

"Well, this is going to be interesting!" says Glenda sarcastically.

They wander cautiously over to the drop. The shaft falls away ominously into the heart of the mountain. The beam from Glenda's torch doesn't even reach all the way down. Gareth's stomach plunges. He braces himself against the sides of the tunnel to reassure himself that he isn't going to fall. From deep in the shaft, a flicker of candlelight trickles up. Somewhere down there, the shaft must eventually end somewhere near the active mine.

Nailah yanks on the pulley and rocks the dusty old barrel. "It seems secure *enough*," she says. "You think we can get Hassan in here?"

Gareth looks at the barrel. It is certainly big enough. But, like all of the mine works to this point, the rusty pulley and the old barrel appear untouched for over a century. He has no idea if they are suitable to hold someone's weight.

"I don't think we have a choice!" says Glenda. "Come on!"

They haul Hassan's limp body awkwardly into the barrel. His head lolls across his arms, and Nailah lifts his eyelids to check that he has not gone unconscious. His pupils are still there, unfocused, but they haven't yet rolled into the back of his head.

"He hasn't got long," says Nailah. "Hopefully, he'll improve the lower down the mountain we get."

Gareth watches Hassan's chest rise and fall. His moans and groans have gone silent.

Glenda steps onto the ladder first, testing that it will hold her weight. It seems much sturdier than the ladders at the Crofter's Hope archives. It doesn't swing around half as much. Confident it will hold her, she makes her way down, smiling at them as she disappears into the darkness. Five minutes pass before she calls back up.

"It's all good!" she shouts. "Don't leave me down here too long... it's creepy!"

"I'm on my way," shouts Albert, his voice croaking as he steps fearlessly onto the ladder.

This leaves Ashley, Gareth, Nailah, and the task of lowering Hassan down the shaft. Gareth steps onto the ladder after Albert and supports the base of the barrel on his shoulder. He glances down into the darkness. The top of Albert's head dissolves into nothingness. This is not the time to let his vertigo take over.

Inch by agonising inch, he and Nailah travel down the shaft with Hassan balanced precariously in the barrel. Ashley keeps a lookout above them, waiting to come down last. Sticky resin rubs on Gareth's clothes in the narrow shaft, but the barrel always fits just about. When he reaches the base of the ladder, he is shattered. Bizarrely his sweat has mixed with the resin from the rock, covering him in a rainbow of colours. In Glenda's torchlight, he looks quite a spectacle, but so does everyone else.

Having descended so far into the Mountain, the mist is all but gone now. Gareth can feel his energy returning, and a clarity fills his mind. With a broad smile, he helps Ashley step off the rope ladder. They are all down the shaft safely, and he is actually starting to believe they might make it off the Mountain.

A few dozen paces away, a mine cart rail disappears down another passageway. A lit candle flickers in a holder above it. This must be the edge of the active mine. A distant clunking sound and the groan of unconscious miners tell them that company is not far away. Nailah bends down to try and coax life into Hassan, but he doesn't respond. His body is still limp and lifeless.

"He's not improving," says Nailah. "I think we're going to lose him."

"Maybe we should wait here a moment?" asks Gareth. "Allow the clearer air to start making a difference?"

"If it were going to help him, it would have done so already," says Glenda. "Sorry… It's just the way it is. The effects of mist are immediate."

"I think he has entered Limbo," Albert comes in, looking worried.

"Limbo?"

"Hassan's mind has passed a point of no return," he explains. The old man stoops and grasps Hassan's lifeless palms, drawing them towards him. "It is just a matter of time before it lets go…"

"What can we do?"

"Even dissecting a marble of his fondest memories couldn't pull him out of Limbo. It would need a much more potent hit of sensations than that."

Albert places Hassan's hands across his chest and covers the young man's eyes as though preparing his body for burial. "I think Hassan's time has come," he says.

Gareth leans in closer. He is desperate to see some sign that Albert is wrong. Some indication that Hassan can be revived. As he bends forward, his locket necklace falls out from under his jumper. The latch must have come loose as he came down the mine shaft because it tumbles off his neck and lands with a *crack* on the floor. Hitting the jagged rock, the locket swings open, releasing the warm glowing marble from inside.

"I never knew you had an Inseparable Stone," says Glenda stopping the rolling object with her foot.

"I've had it a while," says Gareth, stooping to pick it up. "We made it at the Tide and Time Tavern. Me, Kim-Joy, and…" He stops. His eyes dart to Albert. "I made it with Hassan!" he exclaims.

"Well, I never!" smiles Albert. "I mean, there is nothing more potent than the sensations contained in an Inseparable Stone." He looks sincerely at Gareth. "If you're willing to relinquish this precious stone… well, Hassan might have a chance."

"Of course," says Gareth, without hesitating. He holds out the marble and drops it into Albert's outstretched hand.

Albert produces a marble cracker from his pocket and rolls Gareth's marble carefully between his fingers, inspecting its swirling kaleidoscope of colour. Placing the glowing sphere gently into the jaws of the tool, he cracks the marble into his palm and plunges the bright emanating mist down over Hassan's lifeless face. Everyone watches silently as Hassan inhales the light through his nostrils.

The memory infused in the marble – Gareth and Hassan's recollection to Kim-Joy of their fateful train journey – is a pretty long one. Long enough for each expedition member to doubt that the dissection has been potent enough to revive Hassan. Nonetheless, after an agonising wait, Hassan opens his eyes.

"Where am I?" he says weakly.

He looks up at everyone standing around him. They are all smiling, and a collective breath of relief exhales over his head. Albert reaches down and squeezes Hassan's shoulder. "Welcome back," he says.

Hassan catches Gareth's eye. "That was your marble, wasn't it?" Gareth smiles. Hassan gingerly lifts himself up and embraces Gareth. "Thank you, brother."

"OK," says Nailah emphatically, a huge smile creasing every furrow of fatigue on her face. "There's no use staying here in the dark. Let's get off this Mountain!"

* * *

The six tired explorers creep into the Distillery mine. Rather than the expected confrontation with thousands of Drifters pulling carts, they find themselves traversing a peripheral excavation tunnel. Only the occasional cart passes by, and no Distillery guard is in sight.

Just as they had seen on their trek to the Mountain, each mine cart is pulled by Drifters shackled to a wire rail that forces them to follow the tunnel deeper into the mine. Like their bodies, the Drifters' sweat mixes with the falling resin, covering them in sparkling colours. There's a gruesome irony to the joyfulness of the sight and their grotesquely shackled bodies.

The Drifters scrape and scratch their emaciated forms through the tunnel while their carts fill with drips of viscous resin. As the cart fills, the burden slows their progress to a lethargic shuffle. Eventually, and horrifically, the weight of the resin-filled cart overwhelms the Drifters. Their feet start slipping and scrabbling before, inevitably, one Drifter falls. This creates a domino effect on their colleagues. Within a few seconds, all the Drifters fall and the momentum of the cart shifts, dragging them on their backs, back down the rails and out of the Mountain.

"I can see starlight!" exclaims Gareth.

Below them, a few hundred metres further down the tunnel, the mine shaft ends and the light from outside floods in. They have been struggling up and down the Mountain for so long that day has now turned to night.

The expedition, in their excitement to leave, picks up the pace. Their bottles of Source water jangle in their bags as they jog to the exit. Nailah chuckles, and Glenda can't help but punch the air. It feels wonderful to step out into the bright starlight.

Gareth turns to look back at the Mountain. They have conquered it. They made it down. He feels a massive release of tension and smiles to himself.

The starlight gives enough illumination to make out the Mountain's sharp angular peak. Where the mist is thickest near the summit, this is where the waterfall was. Gareth watches as a spark of light emits from the mist and dances its way into the night sky, joining the other stars. A soul, he presumes, going 'on'. That could so easily have been him.

Looking away from the Mountain face, Gareth observes the miners' rails leading down the scree slope. Dozens are hurtling down from tunnels dotted across the Mountain, each heading to the colliery buildings by the lake. Right now, the rail from their tunnel is empty. The guards in the colliery buildings must be transferring the latest cart full of resin into barrels for the trains. Looking at the slow trudge of Drifters on other rails, it is clearly a matter of time before they'll set the Drifters back up on this rail to collect more.

With their path clear for now and the mist so thin as to be almost non-existent, the expedition's collective mind is sharp and untroubled. As they scrabble down the scree, their discussion turns to Pont Fawr. It had been one thing causing a commotion to get over the bridge. It would be another thing altogether to travel back. The bridge is guarded at all times by the Distillery, and they'll need a safe and deceptive way past.

"Why don't we use our Thermocline canisters?" says Hassan, back to his old self. "Play them at their own game?"

"What? And reduce us to their standards?" says Ashley, frowning at the return of Hassan's brash masculinity.

"Let's not rule it out," says Nailah, offering a bit of pragmatism. "But maybe we should save it as a last resort." She smiles reassuringly at Ashley.

The colliery complex looms up in front of the expedition. Lights are on inside the main Distillery building, and again, it seems that the guards are high in spirits and drunk on marbles. In the courtyard, by the resin silos, they can hear guards dealing with Drifters and extracting the resin from their carts. Hanging between two warehouses, a clothesline of guards' overalls dangles languidly in the cold, still air. One of the guards has left his gas mask. It hangs over the line with the overalls.

"I've got it," exclaims Ashley excitedly, crouching in the shadows. "We saw when the guards used the Drifters to bring the resin barrels to the trains, a single Distillery guard led them. If one of us is disguised as a guard, the rest can be Drifters carrying barrels. There's overalls and a gas mask hanging up there. That's all we need."

"What about the shackles?" asks Gareth.

"I think we can do a bit of community service," says Glenda, smiling. "Let's free a crew of Drifters from their resin cart so that they can make their way to the Source. We can use their shackles around our necks."

They all agree to the plan. It sounds good. Or good *enough*. They nominate Albert to play the part of the guard. The old man could never manage to carry a heavy barrel.

Quietly they sneak into an unoccupied barrel store at the edge of the colliery and gather the empty barrels they need. They bury their bottles of Source water inside and cover them with spare clothes to stop them from rattling around. Albert unhooks the gas mask and overalls from the clothesline and puts them on. He looks frightening. There is no way to tell he isn't a genuine Distillery guard.

Then the group approach a crew of Drifters. The first ones they find leaving the resin silo with an empty cart. The five souls are dirty and weak. They don't resist as they are unbuckled. But once free, they wander quickly away, up the Mountain. Glenda wedges a block under their cart to stop it from trundling back into the silo. Gareth finds it enjoyably rebellious to be setting the Drifters free.

*  *  *

Wandering down the track to Pont Fawr, the expedition's timing is highly fortuitous. Early hordes of Drifters are walking up towards them. They must have recently disembarked at the station. A train will be there at Pont Fawr now. Fate, it seems, is starting to shift in their favour.

"Let's get there as quick as we can," says Albert. "If we get stopped, I'll just say the other guards are somewhere behind. I'll say we're the first barrel-load for this train."

"OK," says Nailah. "Make sure you all have your Thermocline ready if we need it." Gareth clutches his canister tightly in his pocket. It feels cold and dangerous.

When the bridge appears, the uncomfortable part of the walk begins. Pretending to be a Drifter means acting that, without applying force, you want to turn around and head to the Source. This means the shackles around their necks must be taught the whole time.

With Albert essentially dragging them, coupled with carrying the heavy barrels, it is torture. Gareth longs to drop his barrel and relieve the pressure on his neck, but he knows he can't. Added to the pain is the challenge of staying alert. Alert enough to pretend to be unconscious but not actually start to lose consciousness. Gareth tries to breathe slowly, turning his head downwind when he breathes in. The five shackled expedition members obviously can't wear any face covering right now, and the light mist has begun to drift in again. Too long here, and they'll be in trouble.

When they eventually get to the steep arch of Pont Fawr bridge, the last of the new Drifters travelling towards the Mountain wander past them. One of the Distillery guards approaches Albert. Gareth's heart is in his mouth. Slung over his shoulder is a hunting rifle. Around his belt is a full clip of Thermocline canisters.

"You're early today?!" says the guard. "We usually have to send someone to chivvy you lot on for this dawn train!"

Albert grunts in a tone of agreement. "They giving you any trouble, this lot?" The Guard prods his rifle barrel into Glenda's backside.

"Not today," says Albert.

"This is a big one," says the Guard looking up at Glenda, "She must have been a handful at the Palace. I wouldn't say no!" He squeezes Glenda's hip and chuckles to himself. Glenda holds character.

"Go on then, over you go!" he says to Albert. "Load it on the front carriage. It's only a little train this one. Specialist one for the Paddock. Came straight out of the Palace. Lots of tasty arrivals, too, if you know what I mean?!"

The guard violates an imaginary female form with his hands. "I wish it was my job to transport that lot. Shame we can't keep some of those Palace girls here for ourselves. Why should the train crew get all the fun? We should get a reward every now and again. Anyway, I've put me transfer in. Hopefully be on the train crew soon. Think I've done my time on this bloody bridge."

Albert doesn't say anything. The guard pats Albert on the shoulder, reading the silence as a cue to stop talking. "Alright, mate, see you around!"

Gareth allows himself one glance at the vile man. The temptation to spray him is great, not just for Gareth. But they resist. And so, Albert leads the expedition back over the Pont Fawr bridge and onto the station.

*During the afternoon of 9th June 1902, a fire broke out in the London offices of the General Electric Company on Queen Victoria Street. The fire quickly spread up through the tall building and a dozen girls, who worked assembling decorative lamps on the top floor, became trapped with their exits blocked by fire and smoke. The situation was desperate by the time the fire services arrived and was made worse by the fact that their biggest rescue ladder did not reach the top floor windows. Tragically many of the girls opted to jump from the windows to try and escape the fire. In all, ten souls were lost in the tragedy.*

# Chapter Twenty-Two

# Familiar Ground

A profoundly uninterested guard sits on the platform at Pont Fawr station. In his solitary chair, he leans back with his gas mask tightly fastened around his face, peering through the visor at his newspaper. Albert, the 'guard', and his slaves wander past.

"Load her up," the real guard says without looking. "Front carriage." He gestures towards the train at the end of the platform.

The train going to the Paddock has just three carriages. The front, with barred windows, is the cargo carriage. It would have been hosting the Drifters on the outbound journey from the Palace. The Palace where Rosalyn and Cerys went. The other carriages are exquisite and comfortably furnished. There is no one inside them right now, but the clothes strewn on the floor, the marble Jacuzzis still bubbling away, and the mist hanging in the air suggest that the journey up from the Paddock had been a rowdy affair.

A couple of shire horses are waiting at the front of the train, ready to drive the carriages back to London. They wear great silver bridles fastened with thick leather straps. Across their backs are draped the purple velvet coats indicating their use as Distillery transport trains. Housing their reins is the seated platform for a single Distillery rider. It is vacant right now.

"We can't stay in here," says Nailah, dropping her heavy barrel onto the floor of the front carriage. "The guard will need to see us leave the station. I think we can sneak onto the tracks just beyond the station and make our way back down without being noticed. We can wait under the carriage right until the last minute when the train is about to depart."

There are no complaints about Nailah's plan. They resume their unconscious act and wander with Albert back up the platform. The guard doesn't even look up from his newspaper.

Once out of sight, they unshackle themselves and clamber through overgrown weeds onto a section of overspill track that peters out from the end of the station.

"Right," whispers Glenda. "Let's get ourselves under that train!"

They sneak carefully back down the tracks, tucking themselves into the walls of the platform edge, out of sight of the guard above. They walk as quietly as they can across the gravel bank until they reach the rear carriage. Here, while the others keep watch, Nailah lowers herself onto her belly and crawls under the chassis of the train and out of sight. One by one, the others follow.

A short while later, huddled under the cargo carriage, they hear talking on the platform. The real Distillery guards have arrived. Half a dozen of them, each with half a dozen shackled slaves. They come and unload their goods into the front carriage, muttering to themselves, frustrated with their labourers and evidently jealous of the train crew. The last guard bumps into the Distillery rider who is taking the train back to London. He can't help but voice his jealousy.

"A right god damn number you lot have got, isn't it?" he says in a harsh common tongue.

"*All* jobs are valuable to the Distillery," returns the rider's privileged and dismissive voice.

"Seems bloody unfair," says the guard. "I wear a gas mask all day and drag these lot around. Most of me days are cold, wet, and miserable. Early starts. Late finishes. I don't suppose your days are like that?!"

"My good man," says the rider. "The roles the Distillery has given us are our just deserts."

"You saying I deserve this?" says the guard threateningly.

"I am not the one who makes the decisions," comes the firm reply.

The guard grunts. "Bloody city lot!"

"I beg your pardon?" says the rider. "I can have you reported, you know."

"And what?" says the guard. "Get me sent 'on'? That's almost better than life as a guard at the mines!"

"Listen here, Mr guard. I'd toe the line if I were you. There's already word that your lot is causing too much trouble. Quality from the mines isn't what it used to be…"

"How's that my fault?" says the guard. "You don't even know the first thing about mining."

The rider is obviously bored with the conversation. "Well, sir, I think you should take this up with one of your seniors. I have a job to do."

"Job?!" scoffs the guard. Exasperated, he kicks the legs of his Drifters and follows them off the station.

"Filthy low life," they hear the Distillery rider mutter under his breath. A moment later, he blows sharply on a whistle and hollers, "All set!"

Another rider, who must have come onto the platform from the station house, calls back, "All looks good, Theodor. Safe journey to the Paddock. Good risen!"

"Good risen!" he replies.

The expedition, hiding under the train, hears the rider clambering onto his platform, readying himself to get them moving.

"OK," Nailah whispers. "Let's do this. And quick! We don't have long!"

A minute later, as they all squeeze off the couplings and tumble into the cargo carriage, the train starts to creak. The horses at the front pull on the reins, and the carriages begin to move. They are on their way out of Pont Fawr station.

* * *

Nailah had been right. She told them, from her time working in the City Circus, she knew the trains back from the Source would receive no attention from the Distillery or the Water Boards, and they didn't. An agreement had been set years ago that the movement of mined minerals would not be interrupted. And so, their train will travel the length of the Meadow in a single day. Further than Gareth has covered in his entire time in the Meadow.

Such is the ignorance of the Distillery rider to his cargo that the expedition can sneak out of the cargo carriage after about an hour and settle into the more comfortable carriages at the rear of the train. They are even able to get some sleep. But they spend most of their time watching the different landscapes of the Meadow pass by and reliving the adventures of the last fortnight.

"It was frightening," says Ashley, recollecting their journey from Beatrice's cave to Albert and Hassan. "Standing there on the ledge amidst the waterfall's roar with nothing but plunging mist all around. There was tons of water coming down from the Source; it was deafening."

"And mesmerising," says Gareth.

"No doubt," agrees Nailah.

"And when we tasted the water…" Ashley smiles at them all. "It was *so*… well…incredible. I have never felt so alive before."

"Me neither!" says Glenda. "I could have stayed there forever, just drinking from the waterfall. Do you know, I had the strangest urge when I drank, though… I just wanted to jump off the ledge."

"Me too!" exclaims Gareth.

"That's why I sat down," says Ashley. "I knew I didn't *want* to jump, but just as strongly, I felt I *needed* to!"

"Meadow water is one thing," says Nailah with a wry smile. "Pure Source water is something else!"

A flash of light fills the carriage, and everyone turns. Outside, half a kilometre away, a bright shaft of white shoots down from the clear blue sky, hitting the ground just in front of a convoy of horse-drawn carriages cantering towards a distant town.

From where the light touches the ground, a blue hatchback, travelling at great speed, skids out of control, almost slamming into the front horse. The horses panic, throwing their riders and cargo in all directions. Through no choice of her own, one rider is hurled into the shaft of light, into the Opening.

"Oh shit!" exclaims Hassan, watching in horror as the woman writhes in the spotlight.

"I can't watch," says Ashley, covering her eyes.

Gareth can't help *but* watch. Illuminated against the landscape, the woman flails her arms and legs violently. She looks to be experiencing an intense trauma. Then, inexplicably, she starts ripping her clothes off, and as her naked form is exposed, she begins tearing at her flesh. Now Gareth can't watch.

"Fuck," says Hassan, still staring out of the window. "Poor sister… Please… Make it stop," he pleads into the sky.

Eventually, the bright light outside fades away, and a warm afternoon sun returns through the windows of the train carriage. There is a deathly silence inside.

"I promise you," says Albert gently, a short while later. "With our minds and bodies refreshed by pure Source water, the step into an Opening will be nothing like that." He looks at the worried faces all around him. "I promise."

The relaxed atmosphere doesn't return to the train carriage. The six expedition members fall into their thoughts, worries, and anxieties about what awaits them in London, and time passes unnoticed. Eventually, the sun's light droops in the evening sky, and the rickety train slows down.

The flat landscape that fills the windows is familiar to Nailah. They are in Oxfordshire, at a point on the tracks where the City Circus had intercepted many Distillery trains in the past. Here the control of Thames Valley Water Board passes over to the Distillery of London. The Distillery presence in the city's outskirts is much thinner than in the centre, and the City Circus has had great success disrupting outbound trains along this stretch of the train line.

Nailah readies the expedition to disembark. They return to the cargo carriage and remove the water bottles that they had stowed in the barrels. Into their shoulder sacks, they place the weighty prize (Gareth carries an extra bottle for Cerys) before loosely covering them with spare clothes, hiding the precious water should anyone pry inside.

Then, as the sky glows a fantastic array of reds and oranges outside, the first signs of the suburban landscape appear. With everyone ready, Nailah carefully opens the rear door of the cargo carriage and steps onto the coupling.

They each lower themselves to track level and drop onto the loose stones, rolling quietly away from the rattling train. Nailah is last off the train. Looking back at her, standing alone on the coupling, Gareth appreciates the magnitude of her determination and strength. She is a very formidable leader. She is so close now to leading them to the successful completion of their journey.

* * *

In their former lives, Nailah and Ashley were accustomed to sneaking through London. Knowing the shady cover of the trees and intricate criss-crossing of old streets means they can get almost anywhere in the city without being seen. It also means they have seen a side of London that no one wants to see. The two women lead the expedition past desperate groups of marble addicts lingering in dark alleys and the Flickers from the Palaces who wander the streets looking for a home.

As the urban fabric gets denser, Gareth also starts to recognise some of the buildings. Then, finally, after a few hours in the shadows, they pass through a thick coniferous covering on an old cobbled street, and Gareth looks up to see, standing in the warm evening sun, the Tide and Time Tavern.

Gareth feels his body and his mind become light. He hadn't really allowed himself to believe he would be back here. It suddenly feels so very real. He might actually get to see Cerys. He might get to go home. And he'll get to see Kim-Joy and feel the comfort and warmth of the tavern again, putting aside the trauma they had gone through since they were last here.

Nailah knocks on the front door.

As with the first time Gareth had been there, a moment of silence is followed by footsteps in the hallway before an eyehole slides open. Realising who has knocked, Kim-Joy throws open the door and leaps onto them all. The old lady is surprisingly springy for someone her age. Shamelessly, Gareth starts to cry. Kim-Joy's hug is a mother's hug, and he feels safe. He isn't the only one with a tear in his eye.

Kim-Joy steps back and smiles at the visitors. "Come on in, all of you. There is so much to catch up on. You must be exhausted."

The group bundle into the bar. Waiting for them in there is Professor Pelling, standing with a man familiar only to Gareth and Hassan. The weathered and bearded trawler-man, Cyril Speight. The Professor beams as he sees the expedition arrive, but his elation soon turns to concern when he realises the significantly smaller number of them. Before Gareth can hear how Nailah chooses to get him up to speed, Kim-Joy puts a hand on his shoulder.

"Gareth and Ashley," she says, almost catching Gareth's thought as it passes through his mind. "I have some guests that you'd like to meet!"

Gareth feels a shortness of breath. *"This is the moment"*, he thinks. He is about to see Cerys. In contrast, Ashley is utterly confused. Who would she be meeting? Kim-Joy grins cheekily at Ashley, sensing her confusion.

The garden at the Tide and Time Tavern looks like it has been severely neglected since Gareth was last there. Many of the trees have been uprooted, and the lush green grass where they had sat recollecting memories with Kim-Joy, is trampled and messy. This doesn't entirely give Gareth the feeling he had hoped for. Nonetheless, he follows Kim-Joy and Ashley down towards the riverbank.

Gareth spots them first, playing on the shallow bank of the river – a young woman, a few years older than Gareth and a tremendous Indian elephant.

Splashing water on Pimlico, Cerys doesn't notice Gareth approaching. Not until he calls her name. She squints in the evening sun, looking back at the riverbank where she spots the three figures. She lifts her hand to shield her eyes.

"Gaz!" she shouts. The three-letter name that no one has used for Gareth during his whole time in the Meadow. It is the greatest single syllable he has ever heard. Those three letters, the everyday slang for his name, mean one crucial fact. Cerys remembers him!

Gareth isn't sure what happens next, but he finds himself waist-deep in the river, his clothes still on, holding Cerys in a tight embrace. On the riverbank, Ashley can't contain her tears. The joy of seeing Gareth reunited with Cerys, the delight at seeing Pimlico again, and her general exhaustion, are all too much. Kim-Joy puts her arm around Ashley.

In front of them, the sun sparkles on the water's surface as Pimlico dips his trunk and squirts water towards them playfully. Gareth and Cerys laugh.

"I told you he was coming," says Kim-Joy, as Gareth and Cerys wade out of the river.

"Cerys," says Gareth, leading her to the bank. "This is my friend Ashley. She has heard so much about you."

Cerys looks at Ashley and smiles. Ashley smiles back, then looks at Gareth. His face flushes red. Cerys notices and grins.

"Come with me, Ashley," says Kim-Joy. "Let's take Pimlico back to his stable. I'm sure he'd like a bit of dinner from an old friend. And these two have a lot to catch up on. Shall we see you back at the bar?"

"Yeah, OK," says Gareth, smiling uncontrollably.

Gareth and Cerys sit down together on the riverbank. Below their feet, the water laps up against the shore. They let the moment wash over them before they begin telling each other everything that has happened since they were separated in the dark chambers of Euston station.

Gareth starts with his lighter and more pleasant memories. He recollects the snowball fights and folk music with Kim-Joy. He reminisces about Sanger's circus and taking secret night rides along the train lines. And he tells of the underground caves in Crofter's Hope, the gambling den, and escaping the Distillery ambush. Cerys looks at him all the while with wide attentive eyes, encouraging him to talk and talk.

To Gareth's delight, Cerys also has her own cheerful stories to tell. Colney Hatch Sisterhood isn't half as bleak in reality as he had imagined. Cerys talks hilariously of a raucous cèilidh with the Sisterhood, where she danced until the early morning hours and ended up incorporating street-dance moves she knew from Earth into a century-old jig. She also tells of a daring midnight raid she had been involved with, involving a Distillery paddle-steamer on the river Lethe. The women of the Sisterhood had freed a dozen semi-conscious women but ended up setting the ship alight and had to swim to safety.

Throughout her tales, Cerys mentions dozens of other women and girls she has befriended. Gareth is delighted to know Cerys has never been alone. And, of course, Cerys speaks with warm delight of Kim-Joy and her last few weeks at the Tide and Time Tavern.

The memories aren't all smiles, of course. However, Gareth and Cerys are keen to keep their reunion as light as possible. After Gareth tells of his time at the workhouse and how he and Hassan managed to leave, Cerys tells, in very vague detail, of her time at the Palace. It aligns perfectly with Rosalyn's account.

Hearing this story again, Gareth feels a suffocating sadness, and he realises that an imprint of Rosalyn's rage has embedded itself within him. Gareth would not have shown this rage were it not for one significant detail he never heard from Rosalyn.

"The most painful discovery I made at the Palace," says Cerys, her eyes avoiding Gareth's, "was the identity of one of the princes. A prince I never met, who left the Meadow decades ago. I saw his picture in the Palace gallery in my final days there. In the days when my mind had almost shut down and I was merely a passive observer of my pain... It was our dad, Gareth. Our dad. He was a Distillery prince here in the Meadow."

"Are you sure?!" Gareth exclaims without a breath. He doesn't really doubt Cerys is telling the truth. It lines up with Rose Drinkwater's account. He simply verbalises an automatic reaction, hoping to deny what he has heard.

"Yes," says Cerys, looking straight at Gareth and trying to read his reaction.

This horrific detail is devastating, and Gareth sits stunned for a moment. His dad, a member of the Distillery? A mindless thug. A supporter of the very people who had hunted him. Had tried to kill him. And worse, a prince in the Palace. A man who readily harmed the vulnerable. Who broke the souls and memories of innocent women. Who tried to break Rosalyn. Who tried to break Cerys.

The imprint of Rosalyn's rage can't stay within him now. Gareth reaches into his pocket and pulls out Rose Drinkwater's old mobile phone. The item he had held secret and safe through so much. He grasps a rock from the floor and, in a wild rage, begins smashing the phone into tiny pieces.

Cerys leaves Gareth to his rage for a moment. Letting the daggers in his eyes give way to tears and his pummelling arms give way to exhaustion. Without the need for explanation, she pulls her brother into a tight and desperate embrace and holds him urgently and lovingly.

**\* \* \***

The atmosphere in the Tide and Time Tavern on their first night in London is a fantastic antidote to pain. The expedition is relaxed and grateful. They have a very interested audience in Kim-Joy and Professor Pelling, and they are desperate to tell their tales. Tales of mist, mountains, and trains.

It turns out Glenda had been a bit of an amateur actor on Earth. Likewise, Albert had dabbled in the performing arts. With their shared talent, the two re-enact the journey up the Mountain to the Source, adding more than a dash of artistic licence.

Later on, as revellers start to fill the pub, the expedition is joined by the local folk band, the *General Electrics*. The same band of young girls Gareth and Hassan had seen the last time they were at the tavern. It transpires that Kim-Joy has also opened the bar tonight to members of the City Poetry Society. Poetry is a cover for secret Well Wishers who live in the city. They had heard about the expedition to the Source and were all thrilled that Kim-Joy has invited them over to meet the expedition themselves and share an evening at the tavern.

While the tavern is full of energy, Gareth sits with Cerys and reminisces about life on Earth. Between them, they discuss the possibility of finding an Opening and returning to Earth.

"Do you think Mum will be there waiting for us?" Cerys asks Gareth excitedly. He really hopes so.

Professor Pelling, who had overheard their conversation, pulls out a map and lays it on the table. It shows some of the recent work that his department has done on Openings in the city. There is an array of 'hotspots', the places where they have found arrivals on the most regular basis. They generally approximate to locations of Emergency Departments of hospitals on Earth, although these are not typically their uses in the Meadow.

As the Professor talks through the likely locations for Openings, the rest of the expedition gathers around to inspect and offer their opinions on where they should try first.

Professor Pelling warns the group that while predictions for Openings are the best they have ever been, actually placing themselves in the vicinity of one before it appears is challenging. Obviously, Albert had achieved it before, but the old man concedes that he had been very fortuitous on his last return. He actually bumped into an ice climber who came through an Opening at the boulder field at the base of the Mountain just as he was wandering around, confused in the mist. According to the Professor, the group's best approach would be to loiter around the hotspots on his map, the ones nearest to the Tide and Time Tavern, and wait for an Opening to appear. There are a couple of hotspots around a kilometre away, west along the river Lethe.

As the night draws on, Gareth steals a moment to sit with Cerys and Ashley. The two women get along fantastically. They both have the same dynamism and love of adventure. They both like to talk and laugh. Gareth ends up just sitting there between the two women, smiling.

Then, out of the blue, Cerys asks Gareth about Rosalyn. He feels his heart drop with a sickening jolt of memory. With all that had gone on, he had completely forgotten how much Cerys had meant to Rosalyn and, likely, how important she must be to Cerys.

"She was with you on the expedition, right?" says Cerys. "Did she remember me?"

"She *was* with us," says Gareth apologetically. "She was such a kind and generous person. She did remember you, yes. She remembered you fondly. Everything she told me about you I clung on to. She told me that you had saved her life."

"She saved me," says Cerys, then she pauses. Solemnly she asks, "How did she go 'on'?"

Gareth looks down. Ashley leans forwards and grasps his hand. He feels a warmth of blood pulse around his body. "Rosalyn went on," Ashley begins, looking at Cerys, "taking a risk to save the rest of us. To give us a chance to get to the Source. She was brave and selfless. She went on peacefully, of her own choosing."

"Thank you," says Cerys. "I'm so glad to hear it was peaceful. She was so hurt and lost when I last saw her. I just hoped she found freedom from pain... From what Professor Pelling has told me, it sounds like you all loved and cared for her. She could not have had a better send-off."

Cerys glances down at the table, where Ashley's hand still lies on her brother's. "I don't mean to pry," she says. "But are you two...well, an item?"

Gareth goes bright red and carefully pulls his hands off the table, suddenly realising how intimate it must have appeared. He looks at Ashley, and she avoids his eyes.

"Sorry," says Cerys when neither responds. "Me and my big mouth. Pretend I didn't say anything."

Gareth can't pretend. Like him, Ashley hadn't denied that something was happening between them. What does that mean?

Gareth doesn't get to find out what Ashley's silence means until much later. As minor celebrities at the Tide and Time Tavern, Gareth and the others are soon busy fielding questions from strangers and receiving their adulation and generous marble offerings. It is a whole other level of exertion. But, sensing the energy-sapping amongst the expedition, Kim-Joy kindly rings 'last orders' early.

Many Well Wishers take the cue and wish the expedition well before filtering into the unwelcoming city. Eventually, just a few inebriated revellers remain, a group of young men whom

Hassan has spent much of the night sharing marbles with. Cerys decides to call it a night too.

"What a day," she says, yawning. "See you in the morning," and she hugs Gareth.

"Can we go outside for a minute?" Ashley asks him.

Cerys winks at Gareth as she disappears up the dark stairs in the pub. "OK," he replies.

Out in the garden, it is quiet and still. Gareth looks at Ashley in the lamplight. She leans against the stone wall of the pub. "What is it?" he asks.

She looks at him for a moment and smiles. "Before the Mountain," she begins, "I knew I liked you. But then, with everything that was going on, with the journey, with Kasiya...well, I just thought they were all signs that we shouldn't let it happen. It was too messy..." She pauses.

"And…" he prompts.

"On the Mountain, when you were lost in the mist, I realised something, and it scared me…" She holds his gaze. "You remember you told me you felt the presence of a lady on the Mountain?" Gareth nods. "Well, she visited me too."

"When I stood alone at the top of the mine shaft watching you and Nailah descend with Hassan, she came and stood next to me. She asked me what I was thinking about. I told her I was scared. Scared because I had realised I needed you. I was scared that, having lost you and found you once on the Mountain; I was destined to lose you again. That if we managed to leave the Mountain successfully, this would set you on a course that would take you away from me. Seventy years away."

"Come again?" says Gareth, confused.

"If our expedition is a success, we will return to the time we left Earth. *Our* times are seventy years apart…" She looks straight into Gareth's eyes. "Standing in the dark as you descended the rope ladder, an evil thought crossed my mind. I thought that if I cut the rope right then, you would surely plunge to an early exit from the Meadow… I could jump after you and join you, forever, at the same time in the next place…"

"The lady reasoned with my fear. She told me that we cannot and should not control the destiny of love. We choose it, and we trust it. If I chose you, and you chose me, then I should trust that we could be together. Whether we are separated by seventy years or not, our souls will find each other if we choose it." Ashley pauses. "I choose you, Gareth."

Gareth stares at Ashley. The spark inside him, the spark that one day will join the constellations in the sky, he feels it connecting with Ashley. And he knows that wherever and whenever they are, a force in the universe will draw these sparks together. They have already chosen that leap from the waterfall together. Two marbles in a marble run, unable to see the twists and turns ahead, but knowing that ultimately, they are going the same way.

"I choose you too," he says.

*Throughout the daylight hours on 12th November 1642, a pitched battle took place in Brentford, West London, between soldiers of a Royalist detachment and those of Parliamentarian regiments. The fighting was brutal, and many men caught in the battle chose to flee by swimming across the river Thames. Many of these men were unsuccessful in their flight, and drowned in the cold, fast flowing river. In all, around fifty Parliamentarian soldiers perished in the battle, or in the river, and around twenty Royalists died.*

# Chapter Twenty-Three

♦

# One Rainy Night

The Tide and Time Tavern is the perfect place to rejuvenate after the trauma of the expedition. For a few days, Gareth and the others can enjoy the peace, the good marbles, and the good cheer provided by Kim-Joy. Kim-Joy, as always, is a fabulous host. If it weren't for where they are ultimately trying to go, Gareth is sure this is the place he would choose to be.

Soon, inevitably, attention turns to the task ahead of them. From previous studies, the Professor explains that an Opening will only be open for enough time for new arrivals and objects to pass through. A maximum of a minute. This means they will need to be close to make their return. Close enough to drink a good swig of Source water and dash through the Opening before it closes.

The first reconnaissance trips don't see any signs of Openings, but they do get a more accurate perspective of the challenge ahead. The Distillery heavily patrols all the hotspots. They have access to the Professor's maps as well. These maps help them to intercept arrivals before they disappear into the city. Their control of the Meadow depends on the immediate indoctrination of arrivals. Gareth remembers how quickly the Distillery got hold of his train when they arrived in the Meadow.

Just over a week after arriving at the Tide and Time Tavern, they approach a crucial milestone in the annual pattern of Openings in the Meadow. A point in time when the hotspots on the Professor's map see the greatest single night of arrivals in the year. It even has a name: *The Night of Open Doors*. It has happened every year since records began.

"I suspect it aligns with some key calendar event on Earth… probably a time when most accidents happen," says the Professor. "Maybe New Year or some big sporting event. We haven't pinpointed exactly what the event is yet."

*The Night of Open Doors* will be their best chance at finding an Opening. It will also be the most dangerous night to be out in the streets. The Distillery will have extra guards on the lookout, ready to intercept the glut of arrivals. They won't necessarily be prepared to stop people trying to journey the other way, but this doesn't mean the guards will let them approach without a fight.

While the rest prepare themselves for the *Night of Open Doors*, Nailah – relieved of leading the expedition now that they are in London – has time to concentrate on her own priorities. The revelations from Kasiya's marbles need to be aired. The evil men have to be exposed, and the sanctity of Well Wishing restored. It is an intimidating task for one person, even one with the presence of Nailah. But in Kim-Joy, she finds a kindred spirit. The two women confide in one another and plot how they can expose the truth without those same men trying to pull down the whole of Well Wishing with them.

* * *

The *Night of Open Doors* arrives. Kim-Joy lays on a grand celebration of marbles, including some very rare ones collected from the centuries she has been in the Meadow. Marbles with their own fascinating history and potent effects on the user. Hassan is delighted.

The expedition plans to be near the hotspots by eleven 'o'clock tonight. Professor Pelling has shown them that this is when the arrival numbers tend to increase, peaking just after midnight. This means there is plenty of time for marbles, chat, and even the occasional song. But as the eleventh-hour approaches, the mood tilts anxiously, and nervousness fills the air.

When the expedition finally steps out of the Tide and Time Tavern into the night, they discover the heavens have opened. Rains come down with a ferocious clatter, and deep puddles pool in the streets. The sound of rain on rooftops echoes through the coniferous trees, and it is bitterly cold, like a harsh winter night. Quite a night to be saying goodbye.

The six departing souls bid an emotional farewell to Kim-Joy, Nailah, and Professor Pelling. Nailah holds each of them in a long, motherly hug, one at a time, thanking them for the time that they have spent together.

"I hope I see you in the beyond, somewhere, somehow," she says, standing at the entrance to the tavern. "When you get to Earth, remember all you can. Leave etchings of the Encircled Drop wherever you can, and try to prepare the people of Earth for this realm…"

Albert puts his hand to his forehead and begins the creed, "*May the seas warm, and the clouds form…*"

All except Cerys join in, "*…and may the rain fall, filling the rivers of Love.*"

Kim-Joy holds a marble above her head. "May God the Mother protect you," she says, throwing the marble hard onto the ground. It fizzes in a mist around their feet. One by one, each of them pulls out their own marble and does likewise.

With the ritual complete, Glenda leads them away from the Tide and Time Tavern through the rain. Under the heavy hessian robe that Gareth wears – the plan is they look like non-descript marble addicts – he feels his belt line. The leather pouch holding his precious bottle of Source water is there, weighing him down, as well as a small cold canister of Thermocline Mist, should it all go wrong.

They trudge through the wet streets without talking, splashing in cold puddles, and ducking under low-hanging branches. It is now a familiar route towards the hotspots west of the city. Already they can see more Distillery personnel patrolling the streets than at any previous time. Gareth feels exceptionally nervous. He's not alone.

Walking down one dark alley, Gareth spots a new splash of graffiti painted on the wall in bright white paint. An Encircled Drop with a single word, '*Believe*'. This spurs him on a touch. Whether or not they succeed tonight, they may have just started something meaningful in the Meadow.

The good feeling is short-lived. As they near the open park, the critical hotspot's location, they discover dozens of Distillery guards patrolling. They are carefully covering every inch of the space. They are ready for the *Night of Open Doors.*

* * *

The park area is about as big as a football pitch. It is carefully landscaped with trees and shrubs. The precise equivalent location on Earth is a hospital. Along the eastern edge, a line of oak trees stands where the most openings occur, the site of the Accident and Emergency Department. At the northern edge, a clock tower looms. As Glenda leads the group into an alley with a clear sight of the oak trees, the bell gongs eleven times.

A handful of marble addicts crouch in the alley opposite them. Their sallow skins are dirty from the rain and muck. They cling to each other for support, with grey and black marbles rattling around the few teeth they still have. Spotting the expedition, the addicts crawl over, hands out, pleading for more marbles.

The surest way to keep the addicts quiet, happy, and safe is to give them new marbles. Marbles that can be safely sucked for months before they burst. The expedition has prepared for this. They hand clean marbles to the desperate addicts who, although consciously distant, smile gratefully and drop the dirty marbles from their mouths, which burst on the slightest impact with the ground, replacing them with the new.

There is a commotion in the branches above. Crows, using a tree as a nest, have taken umbridge with some magpies who have flown in for shelter. They scrabble and squawk noisily, shaking twigs and large droplets down onto the expedition. Alerted by the noise, a pair of Distillery officers turn into the alley.

"Come on, you lot," says one of the officers, his tone authoritative and blunt. "You're not welcome here tonight!"

Both officers hold aloft their canisters of Thermocline Mist. The real marble addicts react slowly, but the expedition doesn't hesitate. They rush out from the alley, splashing into the street and running alongside the park's edge. However, this draws the attention of more officers. Glenda hurries them down another side street, but they are followed.

"Come on; you've been told to get away from here. Away from the park altogether. No more addicts loitering tonight."

They scurry further into another dark street, where Glenda gathers them under the awning of an old, abandoned shop. The storefront is boarded up. Wanted posters are plastered all over it. Wanted posters with rough sketches, not unrecognisable from Gareth, Hassan and Albert: the *Train Fugitives*. Gareth looks with dismay at the depiction of himself.

"We have to get closer to the park," he says urgently. "We can't afford to wait here."

"If we get caught, though," says Glenda. "They'll spray us."

"We could split into smaller groups?" suggests Hassan.

"I don't like it," says Glenda. "We've come this far together."

"There's likely to be more than one Opening tonight, right?" says Cerys. "That's what the Professor told us. Maybe it's not a bad idea to split up, making us a smaller target to the Distillery."

"OK," agrees Glenda, reluctantly. "But we rendezvous at the Tide and Time Tavern if there's any trouble... *any* trouble. Gareth, Cerys, and Ashley, you be one group. Albert and Hassan, stick with me."

Sensing the significance of the moment, Albert pulls the group in close. "No one will believe us when we return to Earth," he says. "They will dismiss what we say as fantasy, confusion, even delusion. They will put it down to miss-firing neurones in your brain. But don't be disheartened. Tell your story in your way. Write it in a book. Paint it in a picture. Tell it to your children. The more people come to the Meadow with an open mind, the more we make this journey possible."

"When we're on Earth, seek each other out. Gareth, Hassan, Cerys, we will all return to a place at the same time. But we may not remember each other as clearly as we do now, especially if we don't travel through the same Opening tonight. Ashley, you will return to a world very different from ours, a world reeling from war. Do what you can to remember and cherish your memory of the Meadow. Wait for us if you can. Glenda, I suspect you will be long gone when we arrive. Please leave messages of your life. I will seek them out, and I will celebrate you."

The six expedition members embrace in the rain.

"Good luck, brother," says Hassan to Gareth.

"And you," says Gareth.

Albert looks at Gareth and holds out his hand. Gareth glances into the old man's elongated and wrinkled face. Not for the first time, it is wrought with determination. Gareth shakes his hand and smiles at Albert. The warmth of the old man's hand is still there.

"OK," says Glenda, a broad and confident smile forming. "Let's do this!" She isn't afraid.

Glenda, Hassan, and Albert wander east of their position. Gareth, Cerys, and Ashley walk west. They soon lose sight of each other. Both groups sneak along, looking for the quietest and darkest streets leading back towards the park.

There is a little alley with overflowing bins, and graffiti scrawled all over the walls that Gareth, Ashley, and Cerys choose. The edge of the park is just visible at the end. They tiptoe through it uninterrupted before Ashley crouches down and pokes her head out at the end.

A group of four officers stand a hundred metres away, sheltering under a shop awning. They are chatting carelessly and not attentive to their surroundings. Ashley relays this information to Gareth and Cerys.

"Is it OK to look out?" asks Gareth.

"Yeah, I think so. As long as we are careful."

On hands and knees, the three of them crawl on the wet cobbles and peek out onto the park and the large oak trees that run along its edge. The trees are quite a contrast to the conifers in the adjacent streets. Their leaves shine bright in the lamplight.

Gareth looks over at the Distillery officers under the awning. A peculiar-looking group of men. They wear dark buff coats and lobster pot helmets, each with a leather bandolier from which hangs what looks like cricket-ball-sized glass globes. The globes shimmer and sparkle in the rain.

Gareth searches for any signs of changing weather in the sky above – a sign of an Opening. But there is nothing yet. Looking across to the other side of the park, he can just make out distant buildings and streets. Somewhere over there, Glenda, Hassan, and Albert are probably crouched down as well, waiting for an Opening.

Suddenly there is a shout. Gareth squints to see what is going on. Half a dozen Distillery officers leave their positions and run over the green. A horn sounds in the distance.

"What's going on?" asks Ashley.

"I can't see," says Gareth.

Through the rain, they hear boisterous cheering from the Distillery officers.

A moment later, Ashley gasps. Horrified, they watch four men in black jackets and soaked tight jeans march into the park. They drag with them the lanky frame of Glenda Burgess and the insolent body of Hassan Dar.

The Ferrymen stop with the two captives just below the line of oak trees, looking triumphant. Behind them, half a dozen Distillery officers follow. Mercifully none of the captors has sprayed their Thermocline Mist yet. Hassan has a deep cut above his right eye and bruising to his cheek. Glenda is hobbling and evidently in pain. There must have been a fight.

"Where's Albert?" Gareth whispers.

"I don't know," Ashley responds.

"What can we do?" asks Cerys.

"I don't know," replies Ashley.

There is another trumpeting sound in the distance. The thugs holding Hassan and Glenda look up uncertainly. One of them shouts out into the darkness.

"We know you're out there! We've been waiting for you devil worshippers. Albert Newman and Gareth Edwards, come out now. Show yourselves, or we will spray your friends while you watch."

"Do they know we're here?" Gareth asks Ashley uncertainly.

"Yes, we do!" says a man behind them.

Gareth turns. To his horror, standing behind them in the dark alley is a man holding aloft a canister of Thermocline Mist. He freezes. Looking into the eyes of the Ferryman, Gareth remembers him. He is one of the thugs who investigated the Tide and Time Tavern when they first stayed. Thankfully the man doesn't recognise Gareth.

"So, who are you three then?" the man rasps. "Clearly up to no good. What are your names?"

Ashley speaks first. Her name doesn't ring a bell to the guard. Knowing this is the time for his false identity, Gareth says he is Tyler Bennington.

"And you?" the Ferryman says, looking at Cerys. She stutters. She needs a fake name, but she can't think quickly enough. She doesn't have a prepared back story like Gareth.

"Right boys, grab 'em!" says the man, sensing something is wrong. There isn't just one thug in the alley. There is a whole group of them hiding in the shadows. Gareth, Cerys, and Ashley don't stand a chance.

Ashley bravely stands in front of the thug who goes to grab Gareth first, but the man needs no invitation for violence. He swipes Ashley hard around the face.

In a moment, the three of them are wrestled to the ground. Their faces are pushed into the wet cobbles, and their hands are tied behind their backs. Lying on the damp floor with rain splashing against his face, Gareth hears the distant trumpet sound again.

"What *is* that?!" says one of the thugs.

"No idea," says another, with his knee up against Gareth's back.

"It'll be those damned rebels. So much disruption from them these days. Scum! They need harsher punishment."

"Too right!"

"Come on, let's drag these three into the park. If Albert Newman and Gareth Edwards know them, it won't be long. They'll do something stupid, and we'll 'ave' 'em."

The thug's ignorance gives Gareth hope. He really doesn't know who they are. Maybe this is why he hasn't sprayed them yet.

Gareth, Ashley, and Cerys are marched into the park and forced down onto their knees beside Hassan and Glenda. Glenda looks to be in severe pain. Hassan is bullish. He grits his teeth and gives Gareth a nod when he sees him approaching.

"They got you too then, brother?" he whispers. "Bastards!"

Gareth can't lean far enough forward to see Glenda. "How's she doing?" he whispers.

"She was beaten real bad, brother. I'm sure her leg is broken," says Hassan. "She's not in a good way... What do we do?"

"I don't know," says Gareth, turning to Ashley and Cerys. They look frightened. "What happened to Albert?" he whispers back to Hassan, careful not to mention the old man's name too loudly.

"Don't know," says Hassan. "He managed to slip away when the thugs appeared."

"No talking!!" shouts a Ferryman furiously, glaring at Hassan and Gareth.

A trumpeting sound echoes over the trees again. This time it is much closer. It is followed by shouting, like a battle cry. The Ferrymen and the Distillery guards don't ignore it this time. All around them, the guards grab their canisters, blades, and truncheons. A whole unit congregates in front of the captives.

Gareth looks helplessly out into the streets. There are dozens of guards blocking their way. He tries desperately to cling to some hope that the expedition isn't doomed. They have come so far. But he can't see any way out.

Suddenly, all hell breaks loose in the streets. The trumpet sounds again echoing all around the park. At once, crowds of people, some on horseback, some simply running, charge towards their location. The people are screaming at the top of their lungs.

At first, Gareth is in shock, assuming the worst. Then he notices that some people charging towards them are flying flags bearing the Encircled Drop. They are Well-Wishers– hundreds of them.

The Distillery guards and Ferrymen are caught entirely by surprise. Before they can react, some of the Well Wishers manage to breach the parkland behind them. The Distillery is significantly outnumbered, for now. Gareth watches in delight as the guards run about in all directions, in disarray, trying to figure out how to quell the uprising.

Four Well-Wishers on horseback whizz past, scattering the thugs guarding the fugitives. Gareth recognises the young girls from the *General Electrics* folk band and Cyril Speight. Cyril throws a defiant fist into the air and smiles at the captives as he tugs on his horse's reins, turning towards another congregation of guards down the road.

"Mist the captives!" an angry voice shouts. Half a dozen Ferrymen emerge from a nearby side street, running determinedly towards Gareth and the others. They hold out their Thermocline canisters.

"*This is it,*" thinks Gareth, writhing on his knees, unable to loosen the binds on his hands.

Not so. There is the loudest trumpeting sound yet, and a great Indian elephant comes charging into the park. The sight of the elephant throws the Ferrymen completely. The tonnes of the great mammal charges towards them, swiping his trunk left and right.

Riding Pimlico are Kim-Joy and Nailah. Nailah wears an ammunition belt full of Thermocline canisters and looks up for the fight. Kim-Joy holds the reins and encourages Pimlico to swipe his dangerous trunk at the Ferrymen. One swing of his trunk makes its mark, smashing into the chest of a thug and sending him flying into the air. The Ferryman lands in a crumpled heap a few metres away. Hassan cheers.

Three or four Well Wishers jump on the dazed Ferryman, tying his hands and feet and kicking his canister across the street. The other thugs fall back. Kim-Joy turns Pimlico towards the oak trees, plodding him over to the six captives on their knees, helplessly watching the drama unfold. Nailah slides down the elephant's trunk with a blade in her teeth. She splashes onto the sodden grass and gets to work quickly, cutting the binds tying their hands. As she does so, they hear whizzing sounds and smashing glass.

"Watch out!" shouts Kim-Joy. "Thermocline bombs!"

Gareth ducks as one of the glass spheres whizzes past his head. The Distillery officers in lobster pot helmets, who were cowering under the shop awning, are now hurling the small glass spheres from their bandoliers.

"Don't breathe it in!" shouts Nailah over the sound of the raging battle. "Stand up, and don't let the bombs hit you!"

A glass sphere smashes into one of the large oak trees next to Gareth. The glass shatters into tiny shards that fall all over him, cutting his hands as he covers his face. Thankfully, the cloud of mist contained inside is too far above him. It fizzles in the rain and dissipates into the tree canopy.

"No!" shouts Ashley.

Gareth swivels. A glass bomb has hit its target. Glenda, already teetering on the edge of consciousness from the pain of her injury, is struck hard in the body. The glass shatters all over her, and a mist erupts around her face. She looks across at Ashley and the others. She offers them a kind but resigned smile in the briefest moment of serenity. Then her back arches, and she inhales the mist. Gareth watches in horror as her eyes roll back in her head and her body goes limp. She has gone.

Before Gareth can even start to process what has happened, more glass spheres fizz past, smashing on the hard cobbled ground and sending mist fizzling up into the branches of the trees.

"We need to find shelter!" shouts Nailah.

"We need to fight!" contradicts Hassan.

"No!" shouts Nailah back at him. "You need to make it through an Opening! These people fight for you to succeed. Don't blow it!"

Nailah leads them, charging into the street, crouching to avoid more Thermocline bombs. As they run across the wet cobbles, Gareth glances back at Glenda. Her long and languid body drifts through the fighting crowds, bumping into Distillery officers and Well-Wishing rebels. Quite a few Drifters, like Glenda, are emerging from the battle. They bash into the conscious as they start on their journey north.

The expedition keeps running until they reach the front door of a large townhouse on the edge of the square. Behind them, Kim-Joy pulls up Pimlico to shield them from view. Out of sight of the Distillery, Nailah tries on the handle of the oak front door. It opens. Hastily she bundles them into a hallway, slamming the door behind them.

Inside the townhouse, the commotion of the street is extinguished. Heavy breathing and drips of rain falling from their robes are the only sounds for an exhausted second. Ashley falls to her knees. She looks completely spent. Gareth crouches down and puts an arm around her. Hassan stays standing. A cut above his eye bleeds heavily, sending a mix of water and blood onto the cream carpet floor, already muddied from their footprints.

"They must have known about us," says Hassan.

"I agree," says Nailah. "Someone, somewhere, has told the Distillery something. But they haven't got you yet!"

"What about Albert?" says Hassan suspiciously. "What happened to him?"

A door off the corridor opens, and out steps Albert Newman with Professor Pelling.

"Albert! Professor!" Gareth cries out.

The old man looks shattered. His thinning hair is plastered and wet across his long forehead. The Professor, likewise, is soaked.

"What? How?" Hassan stutters before he settles with, "What is this place?"

The Professor looks at them sheepishly, rubbing the ring finger on his left hand. "This is my ex-wife's house," he says. "I shouldn't still have a key. We have been lucky; she's out tonight."

"But Albert, how did you get here?"

Nailah cuts in. "None of you would have been saved if it wasn't for Albert!" she starts. "While you were ambushed, he got away and returned to the Tide and Time to raise the alarm. We knew there was a risk that something like this might happen tonight. All the community were ready to fight. One trumpet from Pimlico's trunk mobilised them all. I have to say; I'm impressed by the number of people who came out!" She pauses and gives a proud smile to Albert and the Professor.

"Now listen," she continues. "We don't have long. Kim-Joy will try and lead the Distillery away from the square. We should see an Opening from here if one appears, but we need to be ready to make a run for it."

They wander into the front room. It is neat and ordered with expensive furnishings, all in some nauseating shade of cream. It is quite a contrast to the laissez-faire, messy style of Professor Pelling. Gareth can't imagine him living here with his ex-wife.

Nailah peeks through the curtains. "Kim-Joy has already moved them on a few blocks," she says, relieved. "The attention of the Distillery and Ferrymen is all on her."

The group sink into the chairs and onto the floor. Only now does Gareth start to feel just how cold he is. He shivers uncontrollably. Next to him, Professor Pelling tends to the wound on Hassan's head. He rips a tablecloth strip and ties it around the young man's forehead. Hassan looks like a war veteran.

"OK, let's make sure you're all ready to get across the green," says the Professor. "You won't need your thick robes anymore. You want to be light over the ground. Have your bottles ready and your Thermocline Mist, just in case."

The final remaining expedition members start pulling off their heavy wet robes. As they do so, a bright light flashes outside.

"What was that?" says Gareth, but he thinks he already knows. Nailah throws open the curtain. Up in the sky, a bright beam of white light shines.

"It is time!" she screams.

They don't have a moment to think. Holding hands, the group of five hurtle towards the door.

"I love you all!" Nailah shouts after them.

"God be with you!" shouts Professor Pelling.

In the street, the shaft of light is even brighter. All around them, the noise from the battle still rages. From somewhere out of sight, they hear Pimlico trumpeting in a triumphant roar. Gareth feels Ashley squeeze his hand.

They thunder all together towards the bright light. Suddenly, a yellow ambulance appears from within it and careens down the street, its blue lights flashing chaotically. It skids out of control across the wet cobbles and topples over. It has just come through the Opening. This is their chance.

From where the ambulance emerged, they see the Opening itself. A swirling black hole coming from another realm. They have less than a minute. They pull out their water bottles as dozens of glass spheres come whizzing through the air, trained on their position. Most miss their mark, but one smashes into Hassan's face just as he pulls out his bottle.

"No!" shouts Gareth, trying to grasp Hassan and pull him away from the mist.

It is too late– Hassan's back arches into the sky.

Then something unexpected happens. Albert swigs his Source water and pulls Hassan up against his body. He grasps the young man and plunges his head into the mist, kissing Hassan – a *Redeemer's Kiss.*

The Thermocline Mist that had swirled around Hassan's head starts to stir the other way, and Hassan's arched back straightens again. He pulls away from Albert, stunned but conscious. The same can't be said for the old man.

Gareth watches, horrified, as the mist now surrounds Albert's face. As he inhales the mist up his nose, Albert shouts his last words.

"I'm coming home, Sebastian!" The mist shoots up his nostrils, and his back arches. In a moment, his eyes lose focus, and he is unconscious.

"Come on!" shouts Ashley, pointing to the swirling black hole. It is getting smaller.

Hassan quickly downs his Source water and dives into the Opening. He disappears from view.

Cerys pulls out her Source water. "OK," she says bravely and takes a swig. She doesn't even say goodbye before being sucked into the black hole.

Gareth looks at his bottle. Before he can bring the water to his lips, Ashley pulls him in and kisses him. "I love you!" she cries.

"I love you!" he shouts back.

Ashley forces Gareth's bottle into his mouth before he can offer her to go first. In a moment, his mind is absolutely clear. He loves the Universe. He loves Earth. He loves Ashley. He loves Cerys. He loves his mother. And amidst all this love, the magnetism of the opening pulls him towards it. He has no choice.

Diving into the opening, Gareth looks back at the Meadow, and there he sees Ashley, her back arching, the bottle of water held to her lips. Then everything goes black.

# Chapter Twenty-Four

✦

# Sparks and Fragments

Rain lashes down over the train wreck. Around the tangled remains of two carriages, the engines of dozens of emergency vehicles are left running, unoccupied. Like journalists' flashbulbs, their bright blue and red lights flicker endlessly. Up on nearby roads, overlooking the train lines, nosey commuters ogle at the scene. Dozens of rectangular black bags are laid out at one edge of the wreckage – an orderly line of inanimate bulging shapes. In occasional bursts, sparks from firefighter's cutting equipment twinkle into the air and fizzle out with a hiss in the rain. Paramedics in soaked green overalls and thick black rubber boots pepper the wreckage, trying to revive or condemn the victims they find. A group of firefighters gather around a particularly gruesome mangling of metal and glass. In the midst of them, a single paramedic kneels, cupping the scalp of a young man.

The engines, the angle grinder, and the noise of dozens of people scrabbling over broken wreckage are the first things that Gareth Edwards hears. He feels his neck and arms burn with pain before he even opens his eyes. He coughs as a heavy weight thumps into his chest, and his eyes shoot open.

A young paramedic, with her hands crossed and her arms locked straight, is thrusting compressions into his chest. When she sees his eyes open, a burst of joy and relief flickers in her eyes. "Welcome back," she smiles.

Leaning over Gareth, the paramedic shelters his face from the rain. He looks at her, bewildered. The rain licks across her face, and the coloured lights reflect in her eyes. He blinks over and over, then tries to get up. Pain shoots through his neck and arms.

The paramedic places a gentle hand on his forehead. "Steady," she says. "Take your time."

Gareth coughs. He feels a warm liquid in his mouth. Water? Or blood?

"Where am I?" he asks the paramedic.

"You've been in a terrible accident," she says. "You're just outside Euston station. Don't worry. You're safe now."

Gareth turns his head to take in the world around him. Trapping his right arm is the contorted remains of a train seat. It is sodden with rain and blood. Lying next to his head are two paper cups, full to the brim with rainwater, splashing against his face.

Ignoring the pain in his neck, Gareth wrenches his head around the other way. On this side, paramedics and firefighters are working together, carrying a stretcher. The body is covered in a sparkling silver blanket. The victim's arms are crossed over her chest. Even though he can't see her face, Gareth recognises his sister.

"Cerys," he tries to call out, but his voice is a whisper.

The paramedic puts her hand on his forehead again. "It's OK," she says. "It's OK."

Gareth looks at the paramedic desperately. "We'll get you up as soon as possible," she tells him. "We just need to make sure we lift things carefully."

As she talks, Gareth realises it isn't just the paramedic who stands around him. Firefighters work at his feet and near his head, gently cutting through the tangled metal to free his trapped body.

"Here, sip this," says the paramedic. She holds a plastic bottle of spring water in front of his face. "Just little sips," she says. "Your body is very dehydrated."

Gareth does as instructed, and as the water splashes over his lips and down his throat, he starts to feel more aware and more alive. Monitoring Gareth's heart rate through his pulse, the paramedic smiles as he starts to calm down.

"Hello," she says, as though they are starting the conversation again. "I'm Jenny Hussain-Drake. I'm a paramedic with the London Ambulance Service. What's your name?"

"Gareth," he says.

A firefighter's voice, just above his head, shouts out. "Cutting! Stand clear!"

Jenny Hussain-Drake leans over Gareth, shielding him again as the sharp whine of an angle grinder cutting metal fills his head. Past the paramedic's shadow, Gareth watches the sparks fly up into the sky, like stars all heading in one direction, away from him.

All of a sudden, his arm feels light and free, and the cutting stops. The paramedic sits back up and smiles at him. "Carefully," she says, "see if you can move your arms and legs."

He can move! What a relief.

"OK," she says. "Now, don't get up. We need to assess you properly."

The firefighters, with Jenny Hussain-Drake keeping his head in a neutral position, lift Gareth onto a long rigid orange stretcher. Like Cerys before him, he is passed down a chain of emergency workers. He lolls his head to the side and takes in the sight of the train wreck. There are dozens of black body bags, all in horrible, contorted shapes. Some, unable to be zipped up, are filling with rainwater. Two paramedics are working frantically on the body of another man – a man in a high-visibility jacket.

The young victim, an Asian man in his twenties, isn't moving. The paramedic leans in and forms a seal around the young man's mouth. He breathes a life-saving breath. The victim on the ground re-animates before Gareth's eyes. Then Gareth's stretcher is bumped violently. One of the firefighters holding him has stumbled. He loses sight of the victim in the high-visibility jacket.

Once out of the main wreckage, four firefighters and Jenny Hussain-Drake, rush Gareth down the railway track towards some parked ambulances. They pass another wrecked train carriage lying like a fallen giant on its side. Inside, two paramedics give up hope on another victim. They roughly pull a blue sheet over the man's ballooning belly and rush off for another body bag.

The firefighters carrying Gareth slip again, tripping over another crew's water hose, left lying across the railway line. The hose rears up with its nozzle aperture open. Like an elephant's trunk, it curls over and sprays them all. Forgetting he is supposed to be holding a stretcher, one of the firefighters grasps the hose with both hands. Gareth's feet fall sharply and thump into the ground.

"For goodness' sake!" shouts Jenny. "We have a casualty here!"

"Sorry. Sorry," grunts the firefighter.

In the chaos, a defibrillator tucked next to Gareth's head falls off the stretcher into a puddle. Jenny bends down to pick it up, letting out an exasperated sigh. A silver pendant necklace slips out from the collar of her green overalls. The pendant's sparkle catches Gareth's eye. A delicate teardrop-shaped pearl is encircled with a silver arrow. It looks like something he has seen somewhere before, giving him a warm feeling inside.

When they eventually get to the bank of ambulances, Gareth is soaked through and cold. Jenny passes him a thick multi-coloured blanket from the front of an ambulance as the firefighters, embarrassed by their unprofessionalism, avoid eye contact with him and wander off. Jenny stays with him in the ambulance.

"You've been through quite an ordeal," she says. "Amazingly, your vital organs have been stable the whole time. How do you feel?"

Gareth blinks in the bright LED-lit ambulance. Surprisingly, he feels fine. Cold and wet, but fine. The pain in his arm and neck has gone, and he just feels a sharp scratching sensation on his wrists. He looks at them and sees that shards of glass have cut little scrapes down them. They are reddened with little specks of blood, but that is all. No scars.

"I feel OK," says Gareth. "What about the others? Where's my sister? Where's my mum?"

"Let me do a few last checks," says Jenny. "Then we can find out together."

She goes through a checklist with him, feeling every part of his body for breaks and bruises, taking detailed notes, including a bit of personal history. Gareth does his best to remember who he is and where he has come from, but it is harder than he would imagine.

Wrapping a foil blanket over Gareth, Jenny leads him out of the ambulance to find the other survivors. They pass a haunting water-logged pile of unclaimed belongings. A child's backpack, its contents strewn over the floor. There are a few animal teddies, a book about the circus, and a bag of marbles floating in a muddy puddle. There is also an old leather traveller's suitcase, still tightly strapped closed. It bears a destination tag to Zürich and the name *Mr A. Newman.*

Mr A. Newman. Seeing that name, Gareth feels a fizz inside him which he can't place. Then he spots a train guard's ticket machine and her shoulder bag. Stuffed into the bag are *Horse and Country* magazine and the soggy remnants of today's newspaper. A picture of a great mountain is plastered to the front page, and the headline *Welsh Mountain Tragedy*. Suddenly, what appears as random pieces of information, start to form around an unexpected puzzle in Gareth's head. But before he makes sense of it, he hears a shout.

"Gaz! Over here!"

Sat in the back of an ambulance, with cuts and bruises all over her face and body, and her arm in a sling, is Cerys. As though he hadn't been in the same crash himself, Gareth rushes over to her, splashing across the loose stones at the edge of the tracks. He leaps into the ambulance and throws his arms around his sister. They both start to sob.

"It's OK," Cerys says to Gareth. "We're alive. We made it."

"I can't believe it," he says. "I don't know what to think or say. I feel like I've been in the most incredible dream. And it doesn't make sense."

"That'll be the morphine I gave you," interrupts Jenny Hussain-Drake. "You've had plenty of it."

Gareth smiles at the paramedic but is unconvinced that this explains how he feels. Then he remembers something he urgently needs to ask Cerys. "Have you found Mum yet?"

"Mum?" says Cerys, louder than is necessary.

Gareth looks at her quizzically. How could she have forgotten their mum? Cerys shouts again, this time exclaiming rather than questioning. "Mum!"

Gareth turns. Standing in the rain behind them, her eyes red from tears, is their mum, Patricia Edwards. Frail and unassuming, she is motionless, staring into the ambulance. A thin old lady is next to her, holding a steaming cup of coffee. Gareth and Cerys jump from the ambulance and run over to their mum, embracing her in floods of tears.

After holding tightly long enough to reconnect their spirits, the reality of the day and the situation percolates into Gareth's mind. "Mum, what about the hearing?" he asks her.

"It doesn't matter," she says, pulling away from the embrace. She looks at Gareth and Cerys. "Everything that has happened today has made me realise your dad's hearing never really mattered."

She flings her arms back around her two children. Gareth has the most peculiar sensation in this hug like a fourth person has joined them. Someone who knows all three of them intimately. Knows their hopes and their fears. And while Gareth can't see her with his eyes, he feels the Lady of the Mountain with his soul. She loves them. *"Thank you,"* says his soul. *"Thank you so much."*

Only now does Gareth open his eyes and see properly, for the first time, the thin old woman standing next to his mum. She must be in her nineties, but the youthful sparkle of her green eyes is still there. She smiles at Gareth, and he feels fireworks exploding deep within him. A warmth greater than the hug fills his body.

"Hi," says the old lady. "It has been a while."

# THE RAINS CAME DOWN

By Julian Shaw

# CAN YOU HELP?

Enjoyed this book? You can make a big difference.

Honest reviews of my books help bring them to the attention of other readers. If you've enjoyed this book, I would be grateful if you could spend just five minutes leaving a review (it can be as short as you like) on the book's Amazon page. You can jump right to the page by clicking below:

UK: https://amzn.eu/d/4iFb8mV
US: https://a.co/d/hcyj667

Thank you so much. Your opinions matter so much to me.
And one more thing… If you really enjoyed *The Rains Came Down* and would like to continue the journey, I have a website (https://julianshaw.uk/ ) with a mailing list. Come have a look and join me as we travel deeper into the Meadow and beyond!

Don't lose your marbles,

*Julian*

Printed in Great Britain
by Amazon